Lost
Little
Sister

Michael Prelee

Lost
Little
Sister

Michael
Prelee

North Star Press of St. Cloud Inc.
www.northstarpress.com

North Star Press of St. Cloud Inc.
www.northstarpress.com

Text set in Times New Roman and Source Code Pro

Cover Design and Layout by Elizabeth Dwyer.

Where to Find Michael Prelee:
If you're interested in following along on social media, Michael Prelee can be
found in the following places:
- Website: www.michaelprelee.com
- Twitter: @michaelprelee
- Facebook: https://www.facebook.com/authormichaelprelee/

Previous Works by Michael Prelee:

Milky Way Repo, Book I in the Milky Way Repo Series

Bad Rock Beat Down, Book II in the Milky Way Repo Series

Murder in the Heart of it All

Dedication

This book is dedicated to my sisters: Andrea, Tracy, Randi, and Jen. All of whom are exactly where they belong.

Acknowledgements

Creating a book from nothing more than an idea is a large effort. Tim Abernathy would be the first person to tell you writers don't do it alone because it's just too large a job for one person, and he'd be right. Telling stories, like any worthy endeavor, requires help.

Thanks to Curtis Weinrich and Liz Dwyer at North Star Press for taking a chance on this book and its predecessor, *Murder in the Heart of It All*. Liz also made the awesome, haunting cover for *Lost Little Sister*.

Thanks to editor Anne Nerison for finding all my errors, smoothing out the rough edges, and knowing much more about grammar than I ever will.

Finally, my biggest thank you is reserved for Tina, my partner in crime. She does absolutely everything to keep our lives running smoothly while I'm hunched over the keyboard. Her contributions to this book are as important as my own.

Amber Prentice noticed that whenever it was time to stock the coolers at the Beer & Bait, Linda Jackson always found something else to do. As the hands on the Pabst Blue Ribbon neon clock above the entrance ticked toward the little store's closing time on this Wednesday night, the two clerks were completing the list of things that needed to be done: counting the drawer, sweeping up, fronting the boxes on the shelves so the aisles looked straight, and stocking the glass-door coolers. No matter how they split things up, it was always Amber who ended up freezing her ass off hauling beer, pop, and water from the big walk-in refrigerator in the back of the store to the glass-door coolers.

It was her least favorite job because no matter how often they cleaned back here, the smell of spoiled milk hung in the air. She hated the way the odor stayed with her even after she left the walk-in fridge. She closed the big, insulated door and heard the heavy lock click into place. Then she wheeled the little red dolly they used to move milk cases back into place against the wall beside the walk-in. Despite the heavy air conditioning she had a light sweat going.

They really needed to be out of here on time tonight. Her boyfriend, Jerry, was coming over to her place after work. Having him spend the night in her little lakeside cabin was definitely one of the perks of living on her own. Her mother hadn't wanted her to move out after she graduated last June, but she needed to be out of her parents' house. She was an adult now and wanted to do what she wanted, when she wanted, and not worry about what her folks thought. As far as she was concerned, those days were over. She wiped her hands on a white towel and started back toward the front of the store.

"Okay, the coolers are stocked up," she said, walking through the open doorway that led behind the checkout counter. "Tomorrow night you're doing it. I'm sick of smelling like milk and my back hurt—" She froze mid-word when she saw Linda standing near the cash register with her hands up. Standing on the other side of the counter was a man.

A man with a gun.

This was clearly not some guy on a late-night beer run. He was wide through the shoulders but slim at the hips and didn't have the belly so many guys at the lake had. He wore a camouflage hoodie and beat-up jeans. What freaked Amber out even more than the gun was the black ski mask. A thought flashed through her mind that he must be terribly uncomfortable on this warm August night. His face must be hot and itchy. She pushed the thought away and felt a cold ball of fear form in her stomach.

"Get over here, next to her," he said. His voice was menacing, just a hair above a whisper. She almost didn't understand him. The gun stayed pointed at Linda and the cute high school senior with curly blonde hair stood rock still. Amber saw a single tear roll down her cheek, mute testament to what the poor girl must be feeling. She raised her own hands, and swallowing hard, she spoke.

"You can take the money from the register," she said in a small, jittery voice. "I can open it for you."

"Get over here," he said again.

Amber took three steps to move next to Linda. There was a display of lottery scratch-off tickets under a sheet of glass on the counter. Laying on top of them were two thick black plastic ties, like the ones they used to tie up the power cords for the register and the lottery machine, only these were much wider and longer. They hadn't come from the store.

The man shifted the gun to Amber. "Tie her hands behind her."

Not for the first time, Amber thought about how far away the store was from town. The small city of Hogan, Ohio, was three miles down Route 12, but Lake Trumbull was only a quarter of a mile away, and that's why the store was here. It was for the campers and boaters to pick up whatever they needed for cookouts or a day on the water.

"Tie her hands," he repeated. The gun in his hand was steady as a rock.

They worked two to a shift just in case something like this happened. Ronnie, the owner, thought it was less likely the store would be held up if two clerks were on duty, so why wasn't this guy gone already? Linda could have given him the money as soon as he pulled the gun. She could open the register as easily as Amber.

"I'll give you the money," she said again, that same quaver in her voice. "Just don't hurt us, okay? You can have it all."

He put the gun back on Linda and the little blonde whimpered. She squeezed her eyes shut and turned her head away.

"Tie her hands or I'll kill you both," he said in a guttural whisper. "You'll be dead and I'll walk out into the parking lot."

Amber nodded, and around a thick tongue dry with fear, she whispered, "Okay, no problem. I'll do it."

"Hurry."

She reached out with a shaking hand for the black plastic tie like she was reaching toward a rat snake in a woodpile. Why did he want them tied up? Why wasn't he already gone with the money? Alarm bells rang in her head.

Her eyes flicked over his shoulder and she saw the "Closed, please come again!" sign already hung in the door. If Linda had done it, the door would have been locked so they could finish the closing routine, which meant he had done it. That also meant the front door wasn't locked, because he didn't have the key. If he figured it out, though, and got the key, they'd be stuck in here with him. All alone. No one was likely to come in before they opened at eight in the morning. Was that what he wanted?

Her fingers brushed one of the plastic ties but they were shaking so hard with fear she couldn't grip it. She took a deep breath, forced her trembling hand to steady, and managed to pick it up.

Was she really going to do this? What would he do? Why did he want them tied up? Questions shot through her mind with ferocious speed.

Linda's gaze caught hers and all Amber could see was terror in the seventeen-year-old's blue eyes. She had to be thinking the same thing.

"It will be all right," Amber said, trying to comfort her. "Don't worry."

"Stop fucking around and tie her hands before I shoot you," the man said.

Linda jumped and lowered her hands in front of her. Amber could see them shaking. She gripped one of them and squeezed, trying to give her some small measure of comfort. Then she looped the zip tie around her wrists but he stopped her.

"Behind her back."

Linda whimpered again but she turned and put her arms against the small of her back. Amber slipped the zip tie around her wrists and fed the free end through the locking mechanism. She pulled it and felt two clicks as it ratcheted into place. She tried to leave as much slack as possible.

"Tighter."

Amber pulled it again and a couple more teeth clicked through the fat end.

The man moved closer to the counter and waved her away with the gun. Amber took a couple steps back, toward the doorway that led to the back of the store. The gunman leaned across the counter and grabbed the free end of the cable tie. He yanked on it cruelly, and Linda yelped as the plastic dug into her skin. He aimed the gun at Amber.

"Turn around and put your hands behind you," he said.

Amber did so and saw that she was now looking at the doorway leading into the small stockroom at the back of the store. The counter was still between her and the man holding the gun. If she just took off running right now it was a straight shot to the emergency exit and out into the small lot behind the store where the dumpster sat. Past the lot were woods leading to the lake. She'd run track all four years in high school and had done well. She was willing to bet she could run his big ass into the ground if it came to that, but he had a gun. Could she lose him in the darkness of the stockroom without getting shot?

Amber stared at the back entrance with the red-and-white exit sign mounted over it. The heavy gray door with the silver push bar was no more than five steps away. All she had to do was run, and not think about what the bullet would feel like if he shot her. She rocked back on her heels and flexed her toes, preparing to sprint.

The bell over the front door tinkled and all three of them turned to look at the same time. Linda's mom, Carol, walked into the store, right past the black-and-orange "Closed, please come again!" sign.

Amber saw the chubby, forty-something mom was already dressed for bed, wearing an oversized light blue t-shirt with a cartoon of a snoozing black cat on it and blue cotton pajama pants with fluffy white mice running across her legs. Her hands were empty except for the car keys dangling from her left. She made it three steps up the aisle leading to the counter before she stopped, finally spotting the man in the hoodie. Her eyes widened in fear as she took in the scene.

"Linda?" she said in a small, choked voice. "What's going on here?" Amber saw her swallow hard.

Hoodie Man turned and brought the gun up, pointing it at Carol. He hesitated for a moment, as if he was unsure what he should do. The store was silent as the man with the gun and the mom stared one another down.

The gun barked loudly three times and Carol's face changed to confusion and pain as bullets ripped through her torso. Brilliant red blood erupted through her blue t-shirt, soaking it. The woman collapsed, hands clutching at the shelves as she went. Yellow bags of Lay's potato chips fell to the floor and one bag of Cool Ranch Doritos ruptured under her knee.

Amber had never seen anyone shot before and she and Linda screamed at the same time. The sound echoed across the store. The man turned back toward them and raised the gun.

"Mom!" Linda screamed, her voice full of pain and anguish. "No, Mom!"

Amber bolted into the darkness of the stockroom, running as fast as she could. The expected bullet never came and she hit the release bar on the emergency exit with all the strength she could muster. A loud buzzer went off, splitting the silent night air. The door slammed open so hard it bounced off the metal siding on the back of the building and came back at her. She shouldered it aside and raced across the small lot.

A narrow path leading up into the trees to her left caught her eye but it seemed too obvious. Instead she turned right, toward the blue dumpster, and scrambled up the short embankment leading to the woods. Her foot slipped on the loose soil and thin grass, so she dug in with both hands and pulled herself up.

The tree line beckoned and she reached it just as the emergency door slammed open again. She stopped where she was and crouched behind a wide maple tree. Rough bark scratched her face as she peered around the trunk. Under the orange glow of the mercury lamp she watched as the man stood still, scanning the area. The buzzing alarm sounded until the door slowly slid shut with a click and the night returned to silence.

Her heart slammed in her chest as she tried to control her breathing. The last thing she needed was him hearing her as she gulped air. She tried to shrink behind the tree, willing herself to become as small as possible.

Come on, she thought, *go left*. It was the easiest way to go, where Ronnie had beaten down the grass and brush by going up there to smoke over the years. If you followed it long enough you came out at an access road for a natural gas well.

Hoodie Man stood exposed under the light like he didn't have a care in the world. His feet were planted solidly in the broken blacktop of the lot. He still wore the ski mask and his head swiveled slowly, taking in the area. If the humid night air bothered him, he gave no indication.

Amber felt it, though. Sweat trickled into her eyes and she wiped it away with the back of her hand. Watching him closely, she slowly reached back and patted the rear pocket of her jeans, checking for the familiar outline of her cell phone. If the guy would just leave for a moment she could call for help. If she pulled it out now, though, he might see the screen light up, and help was too far away if that happened.

She looked behind her into the trees and bit her lip. She wasn't as familiar with this section of the woods as she was with the path leading to the gas well. She knew that if she kept traveling in the same direction she had started in, it would eventually lead her to the lake. That's what she would do if he came toward her. Just haul ass through the woods as fast as she could until she found someone's campsite or could call for help.

She tipped her head to the right and stole another peek around the tree. He was gone. The spot where the man had been standing was vacant, the orange light just illuminating the old, cracked blacktop. Fear shot through her like a bolt of lightning, starting in her clenched belly. The hairs on her neck actually stood up and her eyes went wide as she looked around the woods. Panic threatened to overwhelm her. Should she run? Should she stay? Every dark shape among the trees looked like him and her eyes flitted over the shadows, seeing everything and nothing all at the same time. She tasted blood now as she chewed her lower lip.

Where the fuck was he?

Her ears strained to hear something, anything that would let her know if he had gone or was standing next to her. In the darkness of the woods, either could happen. After uncountable minutes she heard a car start up and looked toward the sound. It was coming from near the gas well. She could see the dim glow of headlights in the distance. They moved away until the area was dark again.

Had that been him leaving? Slowly, she stood, and blood flowed back into her cramped lower legs. She stood silently, hugging the tree. It struck her as remarkable how much effort each movement took. How she considered even the smallest gesture and the sound it could generate before making it. Her whole body began shaking with violent tremors, so she gripped the tree once more and fought for control.

After a few agonizing minutes of silence, she decided to act, to get help for herself and Linda, and even Carol, if she could still be helped. She reached into her back pocket and pulled her phone out. She thumbed the fingerprint reader and the screen lit up, seemingly as bright as the sun. She pressed it against her belly, then pulled it away just enough to swipe the control that lowered the brightness. With shaking fingers, she dialed and looked around again.

A voice spoke loudly from the speaker and scared her so much she almost dropped the phone. "Nine-one-one, what's your emergency?"

It took her a minute to find her voice because her mouth was so dry. When she finally did, it was small and tight. She almost choked on the words.

"Please help me."

2

The phone alarm went off at 6:30, an obnoxious selection of electronic chimes guaranteed to rouse Tim Abernathy from even the deepest sleep. The reporter reached out with one hand and his fingers fumbled across the screen before finally shutting the damn thing off.

His other hand stretched out under the sheets and blankets and found the comforting form of his girlfriend, Amy Sashman. It was something he did every morning, checking to make sure the past year and a half hadn't been a dream. She was there, and his hand roamed lower, enjoying her curves.

She snuggled in close, the warmth of her naked body radiating to his. Her hands did a little exploring of their own and they came together with a kiss. They moved slowly in the early morning light, enjoying each other until it became clear that neither would be on time for work if they didn't move things along.

Tim lay in bed, breathing heavily, as she pulled on one of his t-shirts and lit the bedroom with the flick of a switch.

"I don't know how you can have this much energy in the morning," he said. "We only got," he looked at his phone again, "five hours of sleep."

The night before, they'd been at Blossom Music Center, a nearby amphitheater, catching a concert by Five Finger Death Punch. They'd collapsed into bed around one and engaged in some activities that led to them waking up sans clothes. Now Amy was rolling through her morning routine like she'd gotten a full eight hours.

She smiled at him with white teeth and a devilish gleam in her eye. "If you hit the gym with me more often, maybe you'd have some energy. I'm going to grab a shower."

He groaned and watched the lithe blonde disappear around the corner into the bathroom.

It had been about a year and a half since they'd moved in together after catching the Hogan Letter Writer. Bob Ellstrom had terrorized the small town of Hogan for years with a campaign of hate mail, sending anonymous letters to anyone who crossed him or made him angry. He'd been a judgmental prick who'd lost his job and took it out on people living in the small Ohio town. His actions escalated to murder when a break-in by Amy's brother threatened to expose him.

They'd fallen in love while Tim worked on the story as a reporter for the town's small newspaper, the *Hogan Weekly Shopper*. His reporting eventually exposed the letter writer and he'd been there when they found out Ellstrom had murdered her brother. After that, they'd never parted.

They'd chosen to live in his trailer rather than her second-floor apartment on top of a downtown bookstore. As small as it was, the mobile home actually had more room. It wasn't where Tim wanted to live forever, but for now it would do.

Half an hour later they were up and ready to face the day. An air of impatience seemed to envelop Amy and he smiled, realizing that her morning routine was more than her getting cleaned up and dressed for work. It actually transformed her into Business Amy, Bean Counter Extraordinaire. Her whole persona changed to become more serious and responsible. This was when he noticed she got her work voice, changing from light and lilting to clipped tones demanding respect. He'd told her about his nickname for her once with a smile on his face and she'd looked at him like something she wanted to wipe off her shoe. He hadn't brought it up since, but it still occurred to him once in a while.

She poured coffee into a large travel mug from the single-shot Keurig machine sitting next to the stainless steel sink and slipped a Special K cereal bar into her purse. As usual, she was dressed in a conservative jacket-and-skirt ensemble with a white blouse for her job at Whitney Accounting. Today's wardrobe selection was navy blue. Her shoulder-length blonde hair was done up in a bun.

She paused her routine and looked at him. "I might be late tonight."

Tim sat at their small wooden table in blue jeans and an untucked green dress shirt over a black Fall Out Boy t-shirt. His dress code for work was quite a bit more relaxed than hers. "Again?"

In one smooth motion she set her coffee mug on the table, stooped to grab her shoes, and fell into his lap. He steadied her by holding her waist as she slipped on her black heels. "It's for a new account," she said. "Don't worry, these hours shouldn't last long."

"I don't want you to wear yourself out," he said, running a hand over one smooth knee. "And I miss you."

She'd landed the job less than a year after graduating with her accounting degree. Tim wasn't especially fond of the place. They'd attended the company Christmas party last year and everyone there seemed like a bunch of uptight assholes. It had been a boring affair, with a string quartet providing the music and a magician for entertainment. The guy had even pulled a rabbit out of a hat. By comparison, the Christmas party for the *Shopper* had taken place in the backroom of the Lugnut, a bar near the railroad tracks on Main Street near their offices. There had been no magician, just a jukebox and a good time.

She smiled at him, and damned if his heart didn't still skip a beat. "I miss you, too, but don't you have your own work to worry about?"

"I've got enough work for three people," he said, and kissed her. "Have a good day, babe."

He waved as she pulled out of the driveway and the sun came up near the entrance to the West Wind Mobile Home Park. Their day tended to start early because in addition to being a nest of tightasses, Whitney Accounting was a forty-five minute commute for Amy. He started early, too, so their schedules could match up as much as possible.

He slung his bright yellow computer bag—decorated with the logo of the Tyrell Corporation from *Blade Runner*—into the passenger seat of his Wrangler and headed for work.

3

Tim was almost to the office when his cell rang. The display said "CHARLIE" so he thumbed the green button and answered.

"Where are you?" his publisher said. There were no pleasantries this morning, and Charlie was usually the epitome of culture and grace. For him to start a conversation without so much as a hello, Tim knew something must be happening.

"Almost to the office," Tim said. "What's up?"

"Nothing good. Do you know where the Beer & Bait is?"

Tim thought for a moment and drew a blank. Charlie might as well have asked him how many moons orbited Jupiter. "What's the Beer & Bait?"

"It's a convenience store out at Lake Trumbull."

The light clicked on for Tim. Hogan and the surrounding communities were littered with convenience stores. He was pretty sure he and Amy had stopped there for ice during a trip to the lake earlier in the summer. "Yeah, I know where it is. What happened?"

"They were held up last night and there were some deaths. I need you to get over there and get the story. I'll handle the office."

"Do you have any other details?"

"No, so do a good job and get some."

"I'm on it," he said, and hung up the phone. He was on State Route 12, a four-lane highway, but was heading the wrong way to get to the lake. The next exit was at least five miles away. He took a quick scan of the road and saw there was light traffic and no cops in sight. He pulled the steering wheel over and drove into the grassy median, angling the Jeep along the down-facing embankment and then up the other side, throwing dirt as the tires dug in.

Lake Trumbull was in Hogan Township, a few miles outside the City of Hogan. There really wasn't much difference between the two entities or there was all the difference in the world, depending on who you asked. City folks liked living in a place with a main street, schools, and stores nearby. Residents of the township liked living further away from all those things, with larger lots that could be measured in acres and lax zoning laws that let them do pretty much anything they wanted with their property.

The landscape on the side of the road became thicker with trees as it became more rural. The four-lane highway changed to two-lane blacktop with yellow lines as he approached the lake. He passed a billboard advertising jet ski rentals, another announcing boat docking services at a small marina, and a moment later the Beer & Bait came into view on the right. It was already a circus.

He pulled over on the gravel shoulder about a hundred yards from the store's parking lot because it was jammed with police and fire vehicles. The lot was a sea of flashing lights and he saw TV news crews set up behind yellow crime scene tape serving as a perimeter. Tim grabbed his messenger bag from the backseat of the Jeep and threw it over a shoulder as he ran for the lot.

He snapped pictures with his cell phone as he approached. A crowd of lookie-loos was mixed in with the media. Tim could tell the difference because the TV folks were all sporting khakis and polo shirts. The lake tourists wore t-shirts, jean shorts, and ball caps.

In addition to three Hogan police cruisers there were several silver Ohio State Patrol cruisers, a couple unmarked Crown Victoria sedans, and most surprisingly, one of the boxy converted white pickup trucks the Ohio Bureau of Criminal Investigation used. Charlie must have been right about someone being killed. Whatever happened here was more serious than a simple stick-up.

The simplest way to get the lowdown was to ask someone already here. One of the local stations, Channel 26, was setting up to get a shot of the front of the store. A stocky producer sporting a ponytail under his ball cap was adjusting the camera while an attractive brunette named Jean Rodello looked at the notepad in her hand. She was dressed in light tan chinos and a sport shirt embroidered with the station's logo. Tim knew her.

"Jean, you got a second?" he called when he got closer.

She looked up and spotted him. "Oh, hey, Tim, what's up?"

"That's what I'm asking you," he said. "I just got here."

"Almost ready, Jean," the producer said from behind the camera.

"Thanks, Al." She turned to Tim. "I'm going live in a few minutes."

"Was it a robbery?"

She nodded. "That's what they think. There are two dead women inside. It looks like the guy tried to stick up the clerks and one of their mothers walked in, interrupting him. He killed the mom and her daughter but the other girl got out the back."

"Wow," Tim said. "So, they've got a living witness."

"Live in sixty, Jean," Al called from behind the camera.

"Any ID on the victims?"

"No," she said. "They haven't released names yet."

"Can you tell me anything else?"

She shrugged. "Right now, that's all we know."

"Thanks," Tim said and moved out of her shot.

"Hey, Tim?"

He turned back. "Yeah?"

She had a sad look on her face. "I just wanted to say I'm really sorry how things worked out for you at the station. I thought you were doing a pretty good job."

He gave her a small nod. "Thanks, Jean, I appreciate that."

As he moved back, he could hear her go into her live report. She spent a couple minutes going over the small number of facts she'd related to Tim and didn't add anything new. He thought about what she'd said about him working at the station.

After breaking the Hogan Letter Writer story, he had been hired as a weekend anchor for Channel 26 but it hadn't worked out. Reading the news on early weekend mornings had been such a bad fit the station manager said he was more likely to put people back to sleep than get them up and moving. He and the station had parted company after two months. Since then he'd made up his mind that print journalism was where his talent lay.

A group of officers huddled around the front of the store. They were a mix of local and state officers, some in uniform, some in suits. The Hogan officers wore dark blue uniforms with patrol hats. The state troopers sported graphite-gray shirts with black ties, darker pants, and Smokey Bear hats.

A familiar face in the middle of the scrum caught his attention so Tim pulled his cell phone out and fired off a text. A second later, Detective Larry Coogan from the City of Hogan Police Department looked at his phone, scowled, and put it back in the inside pocket of his gray sport jacket. Not to be deterred, Tim popped him with another message. The detective looked again and scanned the crowd. He locked eyes with Tim and held up a finger. Tim was surprised to see it was an index finger. The detective must have been feeling polite this morning.

Come on, Larry, he thought.

Tim looked around at the crowd of reporters and saw that all of the local TV outlets were present, along with the local newspapers from Youngstown and Warren and quite a few from the larger cities of Akron and Cleveland.

After winning the "Excellence in Journalism" award, Charlie had embarked on a plan to grow the *Hogan Weekly Shopper* into something more than just a weekly free paper full of advice columns, dinner announcements, and ads for local businesses. It still contained all that, but now it was larger, covering regional stories as well as the local stuff. The paper published some hard news and had an op-ed column written by either Charlie or Tim.

When Tim started at the paper, he was the sole reporter, and now he was mentoring two others. If Charlie really did want to become bigger, they had to get better at having their ear to the ground. He didn't like showing up last.

"Why are you pestering me, Abernathy?" a voice said from behind him.

He turned to see Detective Coogan standing there, stocky and angry. "This is a crime scene. I could have you locked up in a cruiser just for bothering me."

The senior detective for the City of Hogan, Larry Coogan, was a fireplug of a man. He was on the short side and barrel-chested, with a bit of a belly from sitting in cruisers and behind a desk. His hair was in full retreat on the sides, giving him a widow's peak. Today the plainclothes officer was dressed in a charcoal-gray suit with a white shirt and dark blue tie.

Tim smiled. "It's nice to see you, too, Larry."

The detective held up his hands and moved to slip back under the yellow tape. "I don't have time for this."

Tim grimaced. His relationship with Coogan was complicated. He always felt a little resentment from the detective, as if he was angry that Tim had figured out the identity of the Hogan Letter Writer first. It felt like there was also a grudging respect there, but Coogan rarely showed it.

"One minute, please, Larry, and I'll leave you alone."

"I don't believe that."

Tim thumbed the button on his digital recorder and said, "There are two dead women inside, right? Can you tell me anything about them?"

"We gave a statement to the TV news an hour ago. I don't have anything to add."

"I wasn't here for that and I need a quote."

"Sun's up, Abernathy. You should be working."

"What can you tell me about the clerk who survived?"

The detective looked back to the cluster of officers around the door and sighed. "Okay, but only because I don't want to talk to the staties anymore. When those guys arrive on a crime scene they take over and start acting like I work for them." He took a deep breath. "She survived by escaping out a back door and hid in the woods. The perpetrator pursued her but didn't locate her."

"What's her name?"

Coogan shook his head. "We're not releasing names yet."

"Can you tell me where she is now?"

"At the station. Detective Lewis is talking to her."

That was Darren Lewis, Hogan's other police detective, and a look-alike for Wesley Snipes.

"Did he take the money from the register or anything else?"

Coogan eyed him now, silently studying him. "Why do you ask?"

"It was a robbery, right? What did he get?"

The detective was silent again and looked back over his shoulder at the cluster of officers before answering. "It doesn't appear anything was stolen. The store's owner balanced the register for us and all the revenue for the day is there."

That was surprising, and Tim was fairly certain that information had not been in the morning briefing. Maybe because no one had bothered to ask? Coogan was like that. For all his abrasiveness, he admired someone asking the right question. The man didn't suffer fools, but he recognized effort and had been known to reward it.

"So, if he didn't want the money, what was he here for?"

"It's an active investigation, Abernathy, and I'm right in the middle of it." The detective ducked under the tape and walked back toward the store.

Tim looked around. If the police weren't going to give him anything else, he'd have to find other sources.

He walked back among the crowd, listening as the campers traded rumors. Most were nonsense, the kind of things people made up just so they'd have something to say in the absence of real facts. He passed by a middle-aged couple and heard a guy with an honest-to-God mullet tell the woman with him that he heard it was a gang initiation, that he'd read about it on the internet. She nodded sagely, as if reading about some shit on the web made it automatically true.

His attention was drawn to a guy with a deep, end-of-summer tan wearing a yellow t-shirt with the Lake Trumbull Campground logo on it. The guy was as tall as Tim but a little wider in the shoulders, with dark, wavy hair. He wore sunglasses and sat on the hood of an old blue Chevy pickup that was primer gray along the rocker panels. Tim made his way over.

"Hey," he said to the guy. "Do you work around here?"

The guy dipped his head and looked at Tim over the top of his sunglasses. "Sure do. You need something?"

Tim introduced himself and held out his hand. The guy slipped off the hood of the truck and took it. "Dennis Linchin. I'm a caretaker over at the campgrounds."

"Mind if I ask you a few questions?"

"I guess not, but I don't really know anything. I saw it on the morning news and stopped by on my way to work."

"Did you know the girls working in the store?"

"Amber and Linda? Sure. They work the night shift. I stop in most days for groceries or to play my numbers."

Tim's ears perked up. "Playing one's numbers" was slang for playing the lottery and he knew lottery fiends were notorious for playing at the same place. They often knew everything about their usual spot. "Do you know their last names? Amber and Linda?"

He shook his head. "Nah, I just knew them to say hello, you know? I'd stop in to play, say hi, and grab some beer or a sandwich."

"Do you live at the campground?"

"No, I got a place close by, though, just up the road in the township. It's a little farm my mom left me when she died."

Tim jotted down notes. Just learning the victim's first names was more than he'd gotten from Coogan. "Can you tell me anything about the girls? Were they friendly?"

Dennis ran a hand through his hair. "Oh yeah, they're real nice, you know? Always smiling, never have an unkind word to say about anyone. I've been in there when some drunk asshole showed up wanting to buy more beer and they had to tell them no, or even when someone would come in and play a hundred numbers. Didn't matter what was happening."

"Thanks," Tim said. "Can you tell me anything else?"

Dennis shrugged his shoulders. "Nah, I don't think so. I didn't really know them all that well." He stopped for a moment and looked over at the store. Tim followed his gaze and saw the media mingling with the crowd, getting interviews with the campers. Then the caretaker turned back to him. "The news said one of them was killed. Do you know who?"

Tim shook his head. "Sorry, but the cops haven't released her name yet."

The other man nodded his head and was silent for a moment. "Well, it's a damn shame, I'll tell you that. This is a nice, quiet place."

"I haven't spent a lot of time around here lately," Tim said. That was a bit of a lie, considering he and Amy had been at the lake at least three times that summer, but he wanted an insider's opinion. "What's it like?"

Dennis smiled. "The lake and the campgrounds are great, especially this time of year. Everyone is kind of chill and laid-back. Lots of people come up on the weekends with their kids to water ski or go tubing. It's kind of slow during the week, though, because people work."

"It sounds like you enjoy your job."

"Oh yeah," Dennis said, relaxing and leaning back against his truck. "It's the best job I've ever had. I've always liked being outdoors, so taking care of things up here is perfect for me."

"What do you do?"

"I check up on the campgrounds, make sure people put out fires and clean things up. Maintain the roads and generally just do whatever needs doing. Yeah, for a guy like me, this is a great job."

"Can I quote you on that?" Tim said.

"I guess so," he said.

Tim was already writing the copy in his mind: *The peaceful tranquility of Lake Trumbull, a haven for families, was upset with violence as a store clerk and her mother were murdered . . .*

"If you don't need anything else, I have to get to work," Dennis said.

Tim produced a card and handed it to him. "Thanks. I'd appreciate a call if you think of anything else."

"Will do."

The caretaker got in his truck and drove off toward the lake.

Tim wandered back over toward the crime scene tape and took in the sight. The fire department had left but two ambulances still sat near the front of the store, probably waiting for the bodies to be released by the state crime scene unit. The plainclothes cops, like Coogan, had moved inside the store. Patrol officers in uniforms hung around outside, eyeing the crowd to make sure no one slipped under the tape.

His media brethren were now interviewing members of the crowd, asking them about the store, who worked there, if they'd seen or heard anything unusual. Guys in jean shorts and women in tube tops gave their opinions but the answers weren't any more informative than what he'd gotten from the campground caretaker.

As nice and safe as Hogan seemed, it had a wicked drug problem. The town hadn't been spared the effects of the opioid crisis ravaging the Midwest, so some junkie might consider the isolated store an easy mark. It was probably the kind of place with lots of cash because people bought beer and snacks for cookouts on the lake and played their numbers.

For now, he'd have to wait for Coogan and his posse to exit the building to see if they had any further statements. He tapped his notebook against his leg and started moving toward the crowd to get more background information while he waited. One thing he'd learned was that until you asked questions, you didn't get answers.

4

I t was late in the afternoon when Tim finally made his way to the Main Street offices of the *Hogan Weekly Shopper*. The reddish brick building housing the newspaper's offices had been built early in the last century. Its three-story height made it one of the tallest buildings in Hogan.

The *Shopper*'s publisher, Charlie Ingram, owned the building. The newspaper offices took up the first floor of the building and the second was used for storage. Like most of the property owners along Main Street, Charlie rented out the top floor as apartments to a couple of tenants.

Tim pulled into the narrow driveway beside the building, following it to the small parking lot in the rear. It was almost full but he found a spot.

He threw his messenger bag over his shoulder and headed toward the office. The bag contained his laptop and notebooks, including the notes from the Beer & Bait. He was exhausted from standing around in the hot afternoon sun talking to campers. Most of them had eventually drifted away when it became clear the police were going to take their time investigating the crime scene and that the action was over. At the moment, Tim was hot, thirsty, and eager to get his story written up.

The building's rear entrance was a steel door with a heavy magnetic lock controlled by a keypad. It had been upgraded since the offices were breached by Bob Ellstrom in a last-ditch effort to hide his identity. That confrontation had led to Charlie being shot. The publisher was determined to keep his staff safe and had sprung for the new locks.

There was a large bullpen crammed with half a dozen desks in the middle of the office. Metal filing cabinets lined the back wall and a small folding table held a coffee pot and a box of donuts left over from the morning. A mini fridge hid under the table. Tim helped himself to a bottle of cold water and a stale donut. Then he paused and made a pot of coffee. He thought he might need a little go juice later on.

Charlie's desk was in the center of the room, butted up against Tim's. The two desks were angled so both men could see the front door to the office and the hallway leading to the back door. The arrangement also allowed them to collaborate on stories without shouting across the room.

Tim flopped into his office chair and drained half the water bottle in one gulp. Looking around the office, he saw that he was alone. Charlie was usually here but his desk was empty. He tilted his head to look into the conference room and saw it was vacant as well. The original owners back in the 1920s had probably intended for that space to be a manager's office but the paper needed a conference room where the staff could discuss stories, so Charlie sat out in the bullpen with everyone else and the large office served as their conference room.

Last year, the *Shopper*'s full-time "staff" had consisted of Charlie and Tim. Charlie wanted things to change, though. Hiring Tim to investigate the Hogan Letter Writer was the start of the paper covering actual news stories. Now two kids from the college over in Youngstown with ambitions to be journalists worked there part time. They ran down the stuff Tim used to do, like attending zoning committee meetings. Tim's role was senior reporter, responsible for chasing down bigger stories and mentoring the youngsters.

Tim opened his laptop and started writing up his story. Almost an hour later the front door opened and a chubby black guy with a round face came in and waved to Tim. This was Alonzo Banniker, one of the college kids. He was a head shorter than Tim, with close-cropped hair. He dropped his bag at one of the desks and sat down.

Tim stretched and his spine popped, letting him know he'd been bent over the keyboard too long. He got up and poured coffee into a mug with the *Shopper*'s logo on it.

"How's it going?" Tim asked.

Alonzo shrugged. He wasn't the most expressive guy. He was a senior majoring in political science and really understood how local and state government worked.

"Not too bad," he said. "I've got a county commissioner meeting to cover this evening."

Tim leaned against a metal filing cabinet. "Anything interesting on the agenda?"

"Oh yeah," Alonzo said. "There's a drilling company sniffing around for a place to drill a fracking waste injection well. Protesters will be at the meeting so it's going to be exciting."

Tim smiled. The younger man wasn't being sarcastic. This kind of thing really was exciting for him.

"What's your angle going to be?"

Alonzo pushed his glasses up his nose with one finger. They were forever sliding down. "Well, I've been speaking to the leaders of a local group opposed to wells, so I'll probably follow up with them. Basically, they're tired of this area being seen as the kind of place where drilling companies can just dump their waste."

Tim frowned. "You have to be careful, though. Our job is to report, not give groups a propaganda platform."

"I know," Alonzo said, "but we're talking about a company that wants to inject poisonous chemicals down into the ground where our drinking water comes from. The protesters have a legitimate gripe."

"Of course they do," Tim said. "Remember, though, we have to stay objective in our reporting, even when we're covering garbage people who want to poison the place where we live."

"So, what's the problem?"

"No problem. I just want to make sure your reporting is objective and that it sticks to the facts. Cover all the sides of the story and make sure you get quotes from everyone. I know it's out of vogue, but we can't view everything through a political lens and then write our stories."

Alonzo sighed. "Yeah, I understand what you're saying."

"Hey man, if you want to oppose fracking waste wells, write an op-ed and submit it to Charlie. I think you'll find a sympathetic ear. It's not like the editorial position of this newspaper is going to be, 'Hey, dump your poison here.'"

"Good idea," Alonzo said.

The front door opened and they both looked up. It was Janey, their second junior reporter. She was about five-two, thin, and had light brown hair. The young woman was only a sophomore, but Charlie liked the way she wrote and she had more energy than all of them put together. She buzzed around the area like a bee, covering ground quickly so she could write a lot of stories. The only guidance Tim had to provide her was to slow down and dig in a little farther. Tim thought she sometimes tended to miss details because she wanted to get so much accomplished. When she leveled out, she produced fantastic work.

"Hey, Janey," Tim said. "How's it going today?"

She made her way to the coffee pot and poured herself a mug. "I've got an economics class that sucks, but other than that I'm doing okay."

Tim wasn't really concerned with classes. He'd left all that behind him a few years ago. "What stories do you have in the pipeline?"

"Oh, that," she said, as if cranking out the news was just one more thing they needed to do that day. "City council is considering a hike in water rates. There's a meeting about it this evening. Pretty ordinary stuff."

Tim nodded. This was the stuff they were getting off his plate so he could cover bigger stories in order to fulfill Charlie Ingram's plan for growing the *Hogan Weekly Shopper* into something more substantial.

The back door opened and Tim heard Charlie whistling down the short hall. The publisher was fit for someone in his sixties and well dressed, especially compared to his staff, who preferred jeans and t-shirts. Today he was sporting khakis and a white Paul Frederick dress shirt with a rose-colored tie. Tim knew he bought the shirts monogramed. Charlie looked at them. "Since we're all standing around, I assume we're ready for the staff meeting?"

They crowded into the small conference room and went over their progress and plans. Tim smiled as Charlie did his best impersonation of Ben Bradlee, the legendary editor of the *Washington Post*. He handed out advice, made sure everyone was on the right path, and told Alonzo to go ahead with his op-ed. Tim let the other two reporters go first and then laid out what he knew about the Beer & Bait.

Alonzo and Janey listened as he related the events of his day and handed Charlie a printed draft of his story to review. The publisher gave it the once-over and held it up.

"See, kids? This is how you get things done." They both shot Tim evil looks but Charlie didn't acknowledge them. "If that's everything, let's get out of here. I have a date."

The younger crew bolted for the door so they could get started. Charlie flagged down Tim and sat on the edge of his desk. "Good job on this robbery thing today. It's a damn shame."

"Yeah."

"What do you have planned for the follow-up?"

"I was thinking of interviewing the surviving clerk."

Charlie nodded. "That's good but it may be some time before you can get access, and you still need a name. Check in with your buddy Coogan and see what the cops have learned."

"He's not exactly a friend," Tim said.

Charlie shrugged. "He's a contact. Use him." He held up Tim's story. "I'll look this over and let you know if it needs changes. This is Wednesday and I want in the Saturday edition, so keep your phone handy. You may have to work tonight."

"No problem."

Charlie started turning out lights and switched off the coffee maker. Tim stood and packed his bag. "You look like you have a big night planned. What's going on?"

"Dinner and a play with Mark," Charlie said.

"Really?" Tim teased. "You're still dating your doctor? Is that allowed?"

"Oh, come on," Charlie said. "He operated on me a year and a half ago. He's not my family physician or anything."

Mark Tolliver was the cardiothoracic surgeon who had removed a bullet from Charlie's chest after he'd been shot by the Hogan Letter Writer. The two had been seeing each other for at least the last year.

"I don't know, Charlie. It sounds like a serious ethical breach to me. I'd hate to think Mark was taking advantage of you just because you're grateful for him heroically saving your life."

Charlie barked a short laugh. "I'll be seventy in a few years, Tim. You think I can still be talked into things I don't want to do? Besides, if anyone is taking advantage, it's me of him. Do you know how much a surgeon like Mark makes? I let him pay for everything."

"Wow," Tim said, "I never figured you for the gold digger type."

Charlie swatted him across the back of the head with the printout. They walked out the front door and locked up. An immaculately detailed Mercedes Benz S-class coupe was idling at the curb waiting for them. A tall, trim man with silver hair cut in a style that probably cost three figures walked up to Charlie and greeted him with a kiss.

"You look wonderful," Mark said and glanced down at the papers in his hand. "Are you ready to go or do you need some more time?"

"No, we're all done here. You remember Tim, don't you? He's the *Shopper*'s ace reporter."

Mark offered him his hand and Tim shook it. "Of course. Good to see you again, Tim."

"You too. Charlie was telling me about your plans. I hope you guys have fun tonight."

"Oh, I think we will," Mark said. "We're heading over to Akron to see a production of *Wicked*. Charlie's never seen it and the touring company performing this evening is simply amazing." He turned to the publisher. "You're going to love it so much."

Tim smiled. It was good to see his boss happy. He didn't have much family that lived nearby, just a brother and sister, both of whom lived out of town. When he'd been shot they'd made the flight out but both had their own lives. Tim and Amy had ended up helping him quite a bit.

"You kids go have fun," Tim said. "I'm exhausted, so I'm heading home."

The two older men climbed into the Mercedes and Tim watched it speed off.

5

iles away, under that same late afternoon sun, Larry Coogan knelt down on the narrow dirt road behind the Beer & Bait that led to the gas well. The road was really just a couple ruts running through the woods where a bulldozer had come along and cleared the trees so a drilling crew could set up a rig to frack the natural gas deposits in this corner of the Marcellus Shale. The paved road leading to the lake was a quarter mile back the way they had hiked in from. A pair of Ohio State Patrol troopers accompanied him and his partner, Darren Lewis.

The staties had a tape measure out to record the width of the wheel base in the soft dirt. They used the measurements to determine what kind of vehicle the killer had driven to the scene. It was wide, so Coogan figured it would come back as an SUV or pickup truck.

Lewis stood near the path they figured the guy had followed to get to the rear of the Beer & Bait. Coogan stood and his knees popped, a sign that the years were passing faster than he liked. He moved over to Lewis and followed his partner's line of sight.

"There are some footprints near the tire marks," Coogan said, pointing to the area where the killer's vehicle had been parked. "The troopers will get photos and plaster casts."

Lewis nodded toward the store. "Do you want to take a walk?"

"I do."

They walked the path looking for anything that resembled a clue, but they didn't see anything. Mosquitos and gnats haunted them, buzzing around their sweat-soaked skin in the humid air. It was the kind of afternoon you'd trade hard money for in January but by August the novelty had worn off. Coogan slapped a mosquito on his forearm where his rolled-up shirtsleeves left some skin exposed. "I'm starting to see why this guy favored jeans and a hoodie on a hot night," Coogan said.

"There's some repellent back in the car," Lewis said.

"I'll be fine."

They stopped when they came to the end of the path. It was at the top of a low rise that looked over the rear of the convenience store. From here it was just beaten-down grass and scrub brush to the cracked blacktop of the parking lot.

Coogan looked intently at the ground around them. It took a moment but he found what he was looking for in a rounded bare spot. Five cigarette butts and some shoe prints in the soft soil. An empty quart bottle of orange Gatorade lay a few feet away. He took his cell phone out and snapped photos. He could hear Lewis calling in the find so the BCI crime techs could get up here to document and collect the evidence, but this way he had his own photos.

"I bet he came early and staked out the place," Coogan said. "You can see just enough of the front parking lot from this angle to see cars come and go. He would have known if anyone else was in the store."

Lewis nodded and looked at the butts on the ground. "So, he gets here a little before closing, smokes these cheap-ass Basics, and stays hydrated by guzzling Gatorade."

"Hydration is important," Coogan said.

"Do you think he bought this stuff in the store or did he bring it with him?"

Coogan sighed. "Since there are no cameras in the store, we'll have to ask Amber." The clerk was currently in a Youngstown hospital with a police officer on her door. No one thought the robber would really try anything at the hospital, but then again, no one thought he'd kill two people in a convenience store at Lake Trumbull, either.

"It should be a crime to run a store without video cameras," Lewis said. "Cheap as they are now? That asshole owner could afford them."

Coogan knew Lewis's anger was more about not having one more lead to go on rather than thinking cameras would have helped the clerks. They both knew a killer bold enough to accost two women in a public place wasn't going to be deterred by a couple video cameras. They shuffled down the low rise to the parking lot and took a look around.

"He must have come around this way," Coogan said, pointing to the right side of the building where the lot wrapped around. "The other way over by the dumpster has trees and brush all along it."

They walked along the side of the store, examining the ground. It was so littered with cigarette butts, empty pop bottles, and discarded food wrappers they knew it would probably be impossible to get anything useful, but they would collect it all anyway. A concrete sidewalk fronted the building and led directly to the entrance. Convenience store artifacts were lined up against the front of the store: a rack of propane tanks, an ice machine, and a Redbox DVD kiosk.

They stopped when they came to the double glass doors, examining evidence of last night's carnage. Blood still coated the glass of one door and it was cracked where a bullet had struck after passing through Carol Jackson. They entered the store through the door that was still clean. Other members of the task force were spread out around the store's interior working the crime scene.

"Given what we've seen so far," Coogan said, "I'm guessing our guy waited up near the tree line until it was closing time and slipped down here before they locked up. He came in, subdued the first victim, Linda, with the gun and tried to get Amber to tie her up."

"Which is strange, right?" Lewis said. "I mean, how many robberies you work where a guy subdues the store clerks instead of just getting the money and bolting?"

"You think this wasn't just a robbery?"

"Two females all alone out here?" Lewis said. "And this guy comes in with his own restraints? Hell, he didn't even take the money from the register. No, this wasn't a robbery."

Coogan nodded. It was the same conclusion he'd come to. "I think his plan was probably to march them out the back, up the path, and do whatever he was planning."

Darren nodded. "Yeah, and then Linda's mom showed up and screwed his plan."

Coogan looked at the sales counter from his vantage point near the door. "The gun was just to control them. I think he knew there were two women in here and he was afraid he would have trouble with them, so he brought a gun."

"So why shoot Carol?" Darren said. "Is it just because she surprised him?"

"I think so. There's a lot going on here, from his perspective. He's accosting two victims. That's probably new to him, if this is his first attack. I'm guessing we're going to eventually find out that he's been scoping this place out for a while, not just last night. For whatever reason, the idea of getting two women up in the trees appeals to him so he plans this out. He's all amped up and ready to go. He's been fantasizing about this and tonight's the night it's all going to happen. Up until the point Carol walks in, it's going just like he's planned. It's late, there's just Linda and Amber in here, and he's got everything under control. One woman is restrained and the other will be in a minute. Then that door opens and in walks Carol."

"You're thinking he panicked?" Darren said. "Because that's what I think. He didn't know what to do."

Coogan pointed a finger at him and nodded in agreement. "Exactly. This asshole is suddenly confronted by something not going according to plan. Who is this lady? Why is she here? What do I do? I think in that split second he thinks shooting her is easiest."

Coogan turned toward the door and raised his arm, finger extended like a gun. "Just like you said, he panics. Bang, he shoots Carol, then he turns back to the clerks and problem number two presents itself. Amber is hauling ass out the back door. Linda is screaming her head off because she's just seen her mother murdered. Now what's he going to do? The gun isn't giving him control of the situation because Linda probably won't shut up and he has to make a decision to take her or chase Amber. His adrenaline is up, the plan is blown, and this is nothing like his fantasy."

He turned back toward the counter. "Linda is bound and can't escape like Amber so he takes out his anger and frustration on her." His hand came up again and aimed across the counter, right at a bloodstain on the wall covering a cigarette display. "He kills her and vaults over the counter, knocking all these displays and shit to the floor. Maybe he even trips and slides around on it before following Amber out the back door. Maybe that buys her a few extra seconds before he gets to the back door.

"By that time, though, she's gone. What he thought would work for him, the wooded setting, is now working against him. He doesn't know where she's gone and he can't spend time looking for her. He's fired his gun twice and while this is a secluded area, someone may have heard it. Plus, Amber may already be on her cell phone calling for help.

"So, he takes the only option left open to him and escapes. Sure, he's left a witness behind but what has she seen, really? A guy in a hoodie and a ski mask."

"Makes sense," Darren said. "I wonder why he didn't block the back door from outside and contain the girls in the building?"

"He may have been planning to use it," Coogan said. "Taking them out the back is less visible than marching them around the building."

The air in the store was becoming stifling so they walked out to the parking lot. A few news vans were still hanging around, looking for updates.

"We have to catch him," Coogan said. "If we don't he's just going to do it again. This guy will not stop on his own. What I said earlier, about him fantasizing about all this? He didn't get the satisfaction he was looking for." He sagged, bent over at the waist, and put his hands on his knees. "We can't let this go unanswered."

Darren squeezed his shoulder. "He ain't getting away with shit. Now come on, man. We've got work to do."

6

Around eleven on Friday morning, Tim found the house he was looking for in one of the older neighborhoods of Hogan. It was a cheery yellow two-story American Foursquare that still had wood siding lovingly cared for in a time when most people had switched to vinyl. Many homes in the older neighborhoods were of this type, built in the early twentieth century near the center of town, so people could easily walk to the businesses downtown or catch the old bus lines that ran out to the steel mills in the larger surrounding cities.

The houses had large front porches, allowing families to sit outdoors in the evening so they could watch the kids play or commiserate with neighbors. The roof over the porch at the yellow house was held up with thick wooden columns painted white to match the trim. A green metal swing hung from the ceiling at the end of the porch farthest from the front door. This was clearly a house that was a home.

Despite the police not yet releasing the victims' names from the Beer & Bait robbery, Tim had them. He had a source at the hospital in Youngstown, where all three had been taken. He knew a clerk who still did admissions at an age when she should have been retired, but like so many elderly people around here, she couldn't afford it. She helped him out for a hundred bucks a pop when he needed it. He'd met her when Charlie was being treated for his gunshot and they'd hit it off.

Tim raised a hand to knock on the screen door but it opened before his hand fell on the aluminum frame. A man of about fifty with a solid build stood in the doorway looking at him.

"Can I help you?"

Tim gave him his best smile, trying to keep things light. "Mr. Prentice? I'm Tim Abernathy from the *Hogan Weekly Shopper*. I think we spoke earlier on the phone." Tim held his hand out, feeling oddly like he was here to pick up a date rather than interview the victim of a violent crime.

The older man nodded and took his hand. "I'm Robert Prentice. Please come in."

Tim followed him into the house. The small foyer led into a living room, where a pair of wingback chairs covered in pink-hued pastel fabrics sat against a picture window overlooking the front porch and street. An oval cherry-wood coffee table sat in the middle of the room and a sofa that matched the chairs sat against an interior wall.

A woman about the same age as Robert, with blonde hair in a short cut, occupied one of the chairs. She sat arrow-straight, her manner prim and proper. A young woman with matching blonde hair sat on the couch under a red-and-pink crocheted afghan.

"This is my wife, Julia," Robert said.

The woman nodded curtly and said, "Hello." The look on her face was stern and anything but inviting.

"And this is my daughter, Amber," he continued.

The young woman smiled and gestured to the other end of the couch. "Would you like to sit down?"

Tim returned the smile. "I would. Thank you."

She pulled her legs back to make room and tucked the afghan under her feet. He sat down in the cleared space and pulled a long, slim, spiral-bound reporter's notebook from his back pocket.

Looking at Amber, he said, "I want you to know my publisher, Charlie, and I appreciate you taking the time to meet with me. We understand this is a difficult time for you." In reality, he'd only called Charlie after he'd gotten Amber Prentice's name and called her folks' house to arrange the interview. He had strict instructions to be respectful, but get the story if he could.

The young woman nodded and said, "Thank you. I appreciate that."

Tim drove forward, not wanting to give silence a chance to fill the space between them. Interviews like this were difficult; the bottom could drop out at any time when crime victims started recalling the horrific events he needed to ask about, especially when those events had taken place less than two days ago.

"Just so you're aware, I've interviewed some of the officers involved with investigating this crime, so I have some awareness of what went on. What I'd like to do today is speak to you about the attack so the public has an idea of what it is they are facing."

Amber pulled a pink throw pillow close to the chest. "All right."

Julia Prentice coughed slightly from her chair. "Honey," she said, "you don't have to talk if you don't want to."

"I know, Mom."

"Julia," Robert said, his voice low, like he was in a library, "she wants to."

Julia sat back in her chair and crossed her arms, looking down her nose at Tim. "I just don't see what good it will do. Our daughter was attacked. Now the press wants to talk to her about it. I don't see what dredging it up will accomplish. She needs rest and privacy to get over it."

Tim turned to her, unsure if he should say anything, but feeling like he should. "Mrs. Prentice, please understand, I'm trying to inform the public about what happened. In the absence of good information, rumors will fill the void. Amber can use this opportunity to tell her story."

The woman's face screwed up. "It's no one's business but Amber's. She was the one almost killed by this maniac. It was her friend and her poor mother who were actually murdered." Her voice hitched on the last word and she reached for a linen handkerchief lying on the end table between their chairs. "I just don't see the point of making a spectacle of it."

"I want to do it, Mom," Amber said, her voice rising a little. "It's my choice. If the police don't stop this guy, he's just going to do this again. Do you understand? Some other woman working the night shift is going to see him walk through the door." She paused and took a breath. "If I can help stop him, I should."

Julia Prentice stood up from her chair. She was a thin, small woman but she came across as a five-foot bundle of indignation and fear. "If you go around talking to everyone about him, how do you know he won't come after you again? Have you thought about that? You escaped once. Isn't that enough?"

"Mom, please. Just let me do this."

Julia walked from the room without another word, the sound of her low heels clicking against the polished hardwood floor the only sound. Tim heard a door open and close sharply. He turned back to Amber.

"I appreciate you speaking with me. It's very brave."

She shrugged. "Linda was braver than me. Telling people about her is the least I can do."

Tim glanced at his notebook and decided to start with some easy questions. "How long have you worked at the Beer & Bait?"

"I started last year at the beginning of my senior year, so almost a year."

"You graduated this past spring?"

"That's right."

"Is it a good job?"

She smiled and shrugged. "I guess I like it. It let me save up some money and move out on my own. I like being out by the lake."

Tim looked up. "You live out there?"

"Yeah, I rent a little cottage on the east side of the lake. It's the end that's kind of swampy so it's pretty cheap."

"It's a shack," Robert said, but when Tim looked at him he saw the man was smiling. He got the feeling Dad was willing to let his daughter grow up a little more than Mom.

Amber grinned. "It's not that bad, Daddy." She turned back to Tim and gave him the address. "Anyway, my boyfriend, Jerry, keeps his jet ski out there, so we spend a lot of time in the water when we're not working."

Tim had a feeling Jerry was sharing the lake cabin with her but rather than bring it up in front of her dad he moved on. "Do you feel safe out there?"

"What do you mean?"

"At your cabin. Do you ever have any trouble? Does anyone ever come around who shouldn't be there?"

She shook her head. "No, nothing like that. I mean, I've only been there a couple months, since the beginning of summer. It's pretty quiet."

"What about the Beer & Bait? Any trouble there?"

"Not really," she said. "Ronnie, the owner, doesn't let anything go on. I mean, sometimes we get some rowdy folks in who have been partying all day but they're easy to deal with. We've never been robbed or anything, if that's what you mean."

"Ronnie Verlander, right? He's the owner?

She nodded.

"Was he there that night?"

"No, he usually opens at seven in the morning and hangs out until five or six. Linda and I work the afternoon shift."

Tim cleared his throat and decided to get into it. "Where were you when the man entered the store?"

She settled back in her corner of the couch, like she was bracing herself against the memories of a man trying to kill her by hugging a pillow. "I was in the rear, stocking the coolers. When you're back there, it's hard to hear what's going on out front. There are all kinds of fans running."

"How long were you back there?"

Her face scrunched up as she thought about it. "I'd guess about fifteen minutes. It takes a while to pull all the milk and beer from the walk-in fridge to the coolers, especially when it's as hot as it's been. Boaters and campers out at the lake really drink when the weather gets like this."

"I'll bet," Tim said. "So, you didn't hear the robber come in?"

She shook her head. "No. I didn't see him until I was finished. I wanted to see how Linda was making out with her part of the closing list. That's when I saw him holding a gun on her." A tear appeared in the corner of her eye and she wiped it away. "She looked so scared, you know? I mean, she was just getting ready to start her senior year of high school and some guy in a ski mask was sticking her up."

"He was there for the money?"

Amber's face went dark, and Tim knew something he'd said was incorrect. She shook her head, slowly. "No, he wasn't there for the money."

Tim looked down at his notes in confusion. Nothing in them made him think this was anything more than a robbery that had gone terribly wrong.

"What was he there for?"

Her foot was shaking under the afghan, hard enough that Tim could feel it. "He was there for us." She swallowed hard. "I mean, yeah, at first I thought he just wanted the money in the register, but then he told me to tie up Linda and I saw there were zip ties on the counter." She bit at her lower lip, clearly thinking back to that moment. "That's when it occurred to me something else was going on. Something worse than a robbery."

"That sonofabitch," Robert said from his chair. The easygoing dad trying to be strong for his daughter seemed to be giving way to a man who wanted nothing more than to protect her.

"Did he ever ask for the money in the register?"

Her head gave a small shake. "No. I kept offering it to him. I kept saying I would give him the money because I thought if he took it he would go, and I wanted him gone." She pulled the throw pillow closer to her face, rolling the frilly edge up in her hands. "More than anything else in the world I just wanted him to be gone, for things to be the way they had been.

"I kept thinking about what Ronnie had told us to do if someone held us up. 'Just give them the money,' he'd say. 'Don't do anything else, nothing is worth getting hurt over.' He always told us just hand over whatever they wanted and let the cops deal with it, but this guy," her voice choked a little, "this guy didn't want the money."

Her voice became tighter but she kept talking. "He had me tie her hands. I didn't want to do it but I kept thinking that if I went along with him, there would be a chance to get away. The store has a back door right through the stockroom behind the register. I thought he'd get distracted or make a mistake and then we'd be able to run. We're both in good shape and he was kind of a big guy and he sounded older, like maybe in his late thirties. I saw the door and I just knew we could outrun him."

"Amber ran track last year in high school," her dad said, a proud smile creeping back onto his face. "Cross country."

"So, you tied Linda's hands?" Tim prompted. He was afraid of the conversation veering away from what happened that night. It would be easy to start talking about Amber running track, and to reminisce about happier times. He didn't want that, not now.

She chewed her lower lip. "I didn't want to, but yeah, I did."

"What happened next?"

"Carol, um, Mrs. Jackson walked in. She was there to give Linda a ride because her car broke down and her dad was looking at it." Amber drifted off for a moment and Tim was about to say something but then she started talking again. "It happened so fast. I think Carol scared him. He swore and then he turned around and shot her. I've never seen anything like that before. It wasn't like the movies at all. One minute she was standing there and then there were these super loud gunshots. I mean, when that happened I couldn't hear anything. Mrs. Jackson just went down like a puppet whose strings had been cut."

She reached out with a trembling hand and took a sip of water from a glass on the small end table beside her. It seemed to calm her enough to keep going. "That's when I ran. I was so scared that it was just instinct. I bolted for the back door just as fast as I could and went right through it. I kept thinking that I could outrun him if I had the room."

"You did, honey," Robert said from his wingback chair. "You ran him into the ground."

She smiled at him. It was thin and Tim could tell she was trying to make her dad feel good, even as he was trying to comfort her. "I know, Dad, but I left Linda behind and he killed her." This time the floodgates opened and she started sobbing. "I just left her there and he shot her in the head."

Robert Prentice rose from his chair and hugged his daughter, kneeling down on the floor in front of the sofa. "You survived, Amber. That's the only thing that matters. If you'd tried to do anything else you'd be dead, too."

He turned his head to Tim. "The counselor at the hospital and the police told her as much but they said she has survivor's guilt."

"We can stop now, if you'd like," Tim said.

Amber wiped her eyes with a tissue. "No, it's all right. Do you have more questions?"

"Do you think he knew you were in the back of the store?"

Her eyes narrowed as she thought about it. "I don't know. I guess so. What makes you say that?"

"You said the zip ties were laying out on the counter when you came out of the coolers. He'd already put them there?"

"Yeah."

"So, he must have been expecting you."

Her brow furrowed. "I suppose so."

"Do you think he's been in the store before? Is it possible he knew your closing patterns?"

"The police asked me the same thing," she said. "He was wearing a mask. I mean, I couldn't even see his hair. It was just a normal night. The regulars came in playing the lottery or buying beer. I don't think he was in the store that night, but I can't really say."

"And since you and Linda usually do the closing, you pretty much know all the regulars?"

She nodded and dabbed her eyes again. "Yeah. I don't think it was any of them."

Tim made notes and looked up at her again. The poor woman looked spent. Putting her through this had to be emotionally taxing, so he decided to wrap it up. "I just have one more question. Is there anything you'd like to tell me? Anything we haven't covered?"

"About him?"

"Sure."

"When I made it outside into the woods and hid, I could see him when he followed me out. He came through the door like a bulldozer, just fast and big. I watched as he looked around, and I was just so scared he was going to see me up in the trees or hear me breathing. If he had come in my direction I was ready to run again. There are some campsites about a mile from the store through the woods in that direction and I was going to run for them. That was my plan. Just run until I lost him again."

"But you didn't have to, right? What did he do?"

She swallowed hard, remembering. "He stood there under the parking lot light, turning all around, looking for me, just as cool as could be. I knew he'd shot Carol, but I didn't know about Linda, not yet. He knew, though. He'd killed two people and he wasn't in a hurry. He didn't rush around looking for me. I think he regrouped himself while he was standing there."

She paused for a moment before continuing, like she was collecting her thoughts.

"I saw his head tilt," she said, and then cocked her head like she was imitating what she was remembering. "I think he was listening for me, trying to hear if I was crashing through the brush so he could chase me. I think he would have, too, if he'd known which direction to go, but once you're in those woods you can go a few different ways. I sat there as quiet as I could be, praying he wouldn't come in my direction, and my prayer was answered. You know what was kind of weird, though?"

"What?"

"I lost track of him and that scared me more than anything. I was behind a tree stealing looks at him and I had to duck because he started to look in my direction. When I looked back, he was gone. It was like he turned invisible."

"You didn't hear him or see him walk away from the parking lot?"

She shook her head. "Not at all, and that's what made me so scared. As long as I could see him, I knew I could run away from him. Once he vanished, I didn't know what I would do. He was so quiet. I was afraid he was going to walk right up on me and I wouldn't see him."

"What did you do?" Tim asked. He felt bad dragging the interview out but Amber clearly had more to say.

"I just sat there in the dark, listening for him. I didn't hear anything until a car started up over on the access road and I saw the headlights pull away. That's when I finally felt like I could call for help."

Tim risked another question. "When he came out the back door after you, it sounds like his movements after the shooting were deliberate. Is that how you would describe it?"

She nodded slowly. "That's a good way of putting it. It was like he thought of me as a loose end to tie up and if he couldn't, well, he seemed okay with that."

"It took eight minutes for the police to get there," Robert said, growling, like he was thinking of his daughter hiding alone in the woods from a killer. "That's a story you should write up. Why it took so damn long for them to get to a double murder."

Tim nodded. "I'm sure it will come up, sir." He looked back to Amber. "Is there anything else before I go?"

"I'd like to know how many of us he gets to kill before they catch him."
Her father held her hand in his. "Amber, don't get worked up."

She turned toward him, eyes blazing. Now that she'd gotten through the hard part of remembering, anger seemed to flare up in her. "Don't get worked up? This guy killed two women and he's still running around." She turned to Tim.

"I had to move back in with my parents because I'm too afraid to stay out at my place by the lake. I can't ever go back to work at the store. He's taken my whole fucking life from me while I have to sit here and wonder if he's coming back for me. And you know what the worst part is?"

Tim shook his head.

"Linda doesn't even have it that good. She doesn't even get the option of living a shitty life where she jumps at every noise and swallows tranquilizers just so she can sleep for a few hours. He stole everything from her and she was seventeen, for Christ's sake. She didn't get to go to senior prom or graduate or go to college or anything. All she did was go to her part-time job and she was murdered for it. That's all. That's what happens to women. Some man gets angry enough and we die. Women shouldn't have to live like this. I shouldn't have to live like this."

Tim stood and slipped his notebook into his back pocket, unsure of what to say. He felt awkward, like he should apologize for his whole gender. "You're right, and I'm sorry."

He moved toward the front door, preparing to leave, but she leaned forward. "One more thing."

"Sure."

"Make sure you write about Linda. She was funny and loved to tell dirty jokes. She didn't mind running the lottery machine and I hated that shit, so she did it." She paused for a moment and took a deep breath. "I liked working with her and I would give anything to be going to work tonight for my regular shift with her. I'd give anything at all."

Tim smiled. "I'll remember that. Thank you for speaking with me. I really appreciate it."

Amber hugged her dad and said, "Anything that helps catch him."

Tim nodded and left.

7

Saturday morning, Paulie Carmichael was eighty miles away from Hogan, near Cleveland, sitting in a mall parking lot watching the motel across the street. The Drop Inn was a shabby two-story deal where the rooms wrapped around a courtyard with a pool.

She had binoculars trained on the ground floor door of a hot tub suite. Fifty years ago, the motel had probably been hip, but now its clientele appeared to be those who didn't mind their motel room doors opening to the outside instead of an interior hallway.

The target of Paulie's attention was still in room 102. The black luxury sport utility vehicle he'd arrived in sat in the same spot it had occupied since eleven thirty last night. He was the owner of a local trucking company and the woman who had exited the Mercedes GLS with him was not his wife, not by decades. In fact, Augie Pastolli's wife, Miranda, had hired Paulie to see what her husband was up to since he had been traveling for business more than usual over the past year. Sure enough, it seemed like Augie was messing around with a tall, leggy brunette.

She'd been following him for a few weeks now, but yesterday Miranda had alerted her to an overnight business trip, so Paulie trailed him when he left his large house. He drove to a four-plex apartment building in the middle of town and she watched as he picked up Little Miss Short-skirt-with-a-long-jacket. She followed them all the way to Cleveland and watched while they had dinner at a Lake Erie waterfront restaurant. Then it had been over to a downtown Cleveland casino for a little gambling (where parking had been an absolute bitch), and they'd finished the night here.

Paulie yawned and wondered what was taking the couple so long. She'd been following the guy long enough to know that sixty-three-year-old Augie was carrying about forty extra pounds, despite hitting the gym a few times a week. She had to give him credit, though. His rowing machine workouts were strenuous enough to make her sweat in sympathy on the times she'd observed him through the gym's floor-to-ceiling windows.

While she sat in the mall parking lot, Paulie checked out the address where Augie had picked the woman up. The olive-skinned brunette was a trainer at his gym and a former Miss Ohio contestant named Trish Mostello. She was also thirty-five years younger than Augie, so if they were still going at in the ground floor suite he must have packed some little blue pills in his overnight bag.

She looked at the picture of Trish on her phone. It was from a Miss Ohio competition a few years back where the girl strutted on stage in a one-piece red-hot bathing suit with matching four-inch heels. Paulie sighed. Her twenties were a couple decades behind her and even then she would never have been able to pull off the look this young woman had achieved. Paulie rocked a five-four frame and tipped the scales at just shy of two hundred pounds.

Her surveillance log was updated and the high-end Nikon digital camera on the passenger seat of her Saturn Vue had all the photos she would need to put this case to bed for Miranda Pastolli. It was too bad, and she hated to give spouses bad news, but Paulie had a feeling the woman knew. After all, she hadn't been hired because things were going great in the Pastolli marriage. It was funny; men always thought they were being so damned clever when they stepped out, and in her experience the wives almost always knew.

Paulie popped the door open and stepped out of the small SUV to stretch

in the parking lot. She was dressed for comfort in a red Hawaiian blouse decorated with bright orange flowers, a pair of jeans, and white sneakers. She'd
snuck over to the Panera Bread at the far end of the lot an hour ago to use the
restroom and score a bagel and coffee. Now she was just bored.

Then sirens split the morning air.

The motel was across a four-lane road but traffic was light and she had
a good view of the door to the hot tub suite. The first emergency vehicle to
arrive was an ambulance. It was a big white box with a yellow stripe down
the side, and it wobbled as it mounted the small ramp leading to the motel
entrance. The door to Augie and Trish's suite opened up and the gym trainer
raced out dressed in a short white robe.

"Over here," she yelled loudly enough for Paulie to pick up across the
distance. "He's in here! Hurry!"

Paulie reached into the Saturn for the Nikon and sprinted across the road.
By the time she climbed up the short grass embankment she was out of breath
but she had the camera up and working, snapping digital photos of the young
woman in the robe directing the paramedics into the room.

A black-and-white police cruiser arrived next, fishtailing into the lot with
its lights and siren going. The noise cut off as a young officer bounced out
with too much exuberance for a medical call. He took a quick look around the
lot and followed the medics. Doors all along the ground floor were opening
up now as hotel guests peeked out at the commotion. Paulie captured it all
on her camera.

"Hey," someone said from behind her. "Who are you?"

Paulie turned and saw a college-aged blonde woman staring at her. She
was dressed in a nice white blouse and dark slacks with a gold name tag that
read "Brenda." Paulie decided to go with the truth since the situation was
quickly disintegrating.

"I'm a private investigator. Can you tell me anything about the man in
that room and what's going on over there?"

The girl shook her head. "Sorry, I'm not allowed to discuss the guests."

Paulie dug in her jeans pocket and pulled out some folded cash. She
peeled off a twenty and handed it to Brenda. The bill disappeared into a pocket and she pointed at the hot tub suite.

"You see that hot chick in the robe?"

Paulie nodded.

"I'm pretty sure she fucked that old guy to death."

"If you can't tell me anything more than that I want my money back."

"What else is there to tell?" Brenda said. "He called ahead yesterday and had us put a couple bottles of champagne on ice for him in there. You're not really supposed to drink in a hot tub, by the way, especially if you're a hundred years old. Anyway, he grabbed the key from me at the front desk late last night while she waited by the car. Then they went over to the room."

Paulie pointed at Trish, who was now standing outside the room watching the medics do their thing through the open door. She seemed disheveled and less confident than she had last night. Her hair was in disarray and without her heels and makeup some of the allure was gone. "Did you talk to her?"

Brenda nodded. "Just for a minute. She called the front desk and said her date had a heart attack and that she was doing CPR on him. I called 911 and now I'll be stuck here past the end of my shift explaining all this to my manager."

"This doesn't seem to be bothering you very much."

The clerk shrugged. "I've been working here a little over a year. We call for an ambulance about once a month. If it's not a heart attack, it's drugs."

"Is your manager here now?"

"No, why?"

"I'd like a copy of their room registration. Can you get it for me now before that rookie cop gets his shit together and comes over here to talk to you?"

Brenda considered it for a moment. "That will be forty. I could get in serious trouble."

Paulie nodded and they walked into the office. She saw a Zips sweatshirt hanging on a coat rack behind the counter. "Do you go to school?"

"Yeah, I'm pre-law at the University of Akron." She printed off a copy of the registration and handed it to Paulie.

Paulie slid a couple twenties across the counter and checked the document. Thinking of how quickly the young woman was making her money disappear, she said, "Good luck at school. I think you're going to do well as an attorney."

An hour later she was almost home and had just finished giving Miranda Pastolli the bad news when she decided to stop at the grocery store and pick up a few things. On her way out, she grabbed a copy of the *Hogan Weekly Shopper* and stuffed it into a bag.

Back at her old house on the south side of Hogan, she unpacked the groceries and flopped down on a couch in her upstairs apartment. The downstairs served as her office.

She turned on the TV and put a news channel on for background noise as the paper she'd picked up caught her attention. The headline jumped off the page with news of the killings at the Beer & Bait. Paulie read the article through heavily lidded eyes as her late-night shift caught up to her. When she got to the second article, though, she sat up straight. This one was an interview with Amber Prentice, the surviving clerk from the store.

Adrenaline surged through her and she got up, hustling down the stairs to her office. If the details in the paper were accurate, if the interview with the witness was truthful, then Hogan had been visited by the devil and no one but her knew it.

She grabbed her cell phone from its charger on her desk and Googled the website for the paper. There was a contact page listing email addresses and a phone number. She took a deep breath and forced herself to calm down. What she had to say was going to sound insane enough without her rattling it off faster than anyone could understand. After forcing herself to count to ten, she thumbed the "Send" button and made the call.

It rang enough times that she thought it was going to go to voicemail and then she remembered it was Saturday. The *Shopper* was a small town freebie newspaper available in stacks at the grocery store. They probably didn't staff on the weekends. Then she heard a click and the tone of the ring changed. A voice answered.

"*Hogan Weekly Shopper*, Tim speaking. How can I help you?"

She was surprised for a moment but then she caught a good breath. "Hello, my name is Paulie Carmichael and I'm a private investigator here in town. I just read your article on the Beer & Bait and I think you need to know, it probably wasn't a robbery. I think the assailant is a serial killer, and this isn't the first time he's been in Hogan."

8

A little before two that afternoon, Tim found Paulie's office along Main Street at the edge of town. A red-and-blue metal sign by the road declared he had arrived at the office of Carmichael Investigative Services. It was a repurposed two-story house with part of the front yard paved over to create a parking lot. Tim pulled his Jeep Wrangler in and parked next to a white Saturn.

The house looked well taken care of, with blue vinyl siding. He mounted the three steps to the front porch and raised a hand to knock but a voice from inside called out, "Come on in."

Tim opened the screen door and entered. The interior of the house had been converted into office space. The first floor was split by a staircase leading to the second floor. The former living room to his left was now a waiting room with glass pocket doors pulled closed, but it looked very much like what it had been, with a sofa and chairs neatly arranged on a hardwood floor. A TV hung on one wall but the screen was dark.

"In here," someone said from behind him.

He turned to his right and saw a woman in what had once been the dining room. She sat behind a sturdy gray metal desk, a couple filing cabinets lining the wall behind her. Tim walked over and she rose, shaking his extended hand. "You're Tim Abernathy?"

He nodded. "That's me. You're Pauline?"

"Call me Paulie," she said. "I never cared for Pauline too much. Have a seat." She waved at a thickly padded scarlet-and-gray chair on his side of the desk decorated with the Ohio State Buckeyes logo. Tim sat down.

Paulie studied him. "You wrote the story about the Beer & Bait?"

"That's right," Tim said. "Did you mean what you said on the phone? About the guy being a serial killer?"

"I did."

Tim looked at her, and then glanced around the office. It all looked perfectly ordinary, not at all like the lair of a conspiracy theorist who was given to thinking the Earth was flat or the moon landings were faked.

"I'm not crazy," she said and gave him a look of disgust. "I know what you're thinking. 'Why does this chick think a serial killer is stalking around when no one else does?'"

Tim shrugged. "The thought had crossed my mind." Paulie started to say something but Tim held up a hand. "Hold on, before you get too excited."

Paulie eyed him with suspicion but remained silent.

"After you called, I spoke with my publisher, Charlie Ingram. He's never met you but he knows you by reputation. There was an incident a few years ago where you found a little boy kidnapped by his father down in West Virginia. That was you, right?"

"It was," she said. "The parents had a messy divorce and Dad ran when it was his turn for visitation. It took me three months to find them. They were up a hollow in a little town about twenty miles outside of Weirton."

"Charlie said you recovered the kid and helped put the dad in jail."

She nodded. "They were in a little hunting cabin. No electricity, no running water. I had to dig through property records for his whole damn family before I found the deed showing one of his uncles owned the place. Then I had to go out there and watch the place for two days before he finally poked his head out. I called the cops and they did the rest."

"Charlie says that makes you a serious person and that if you have something to say, I should listen to you. So, I'm here."

"Well, thanks for coming on a Saturday. I appreciate it." It was her turn now to give him the once-over. Her eyes studied him, and he felt vaguely uncomfortable, like he was at a job interview. She must have approved of what she saw because she finally nodded and spoke. "Do you know who Kelly Dolan is?"

Tim thought about it. The name sounded familiar, like he should know it. The problem was, in this job you spoke with so many people it was difficult to keep names and faces straight. Then it came to him.

"The woman who vanished? What, like ten years ago?"

Paulie nodded and opened a manila folder on the desk in front of her. She slid a four-by-six photo out from under the paper clip holding it and held it out to him. He took it and looked it over.

The woman was young, in her early twenties, and pretty. She had red hair, laughing green eyes, and a radiant smile.

"That's Kelly Dolan," Paulie said. "She vanished over Labor Day weekend in 2010. She was twenty-three, five foot four, one hundred ten pounds. I believe she was kidnapped from her home and killed by a serial offender operating in northeast Ohio."

Tim handed the photo back. "What's your interest in the case?"

"Her sister, Quinn, hired me about five years ago, after the police failed to locate her or the person who took her."

"I've never heard anything about a serial killer," Tim said. "Nothing in the police blotters and nothing in the media."

The accusation hung in the air between them, even if Tim hadn't come right out and called Paulie crazy. If a serial killer was hunting in this part of the state, and had been for at least nine years, why was Paulie Carmichael the only who knew?

The private investigator leaned across the desk. "Look, I know you have to be skeptical. I understand it's a big part of your job. I'm just asking that you don't treat me like I'm some crazy person mumbling to myself about 9/11 conspiracies in the town square."

Tim held his hands up. "I'm not doing that."

She cocked an eyebrow at him and gave him a look that was probably successful at cutting through whatever bullshit people usually tried to give her. "You need a better poker face, kid." She twirled a finger in the air between them. "The look you have right now is saying something different."

He smiled, embarrassed that she was so able to read him so easily. "Like you said, it's my job to be skeptical."

"I don't blame you," she said. "It sounds nutty to me, too, but as far as I can tell I'm right about this, even if no one else thinks so."

"Okay," he said. "Let's hear it."

Paulie cleared her desk, moving her blotter calendar, phone, stapler, and a mug full of pens to a side table. The metal desk looked like it had once used by a clerk in one of Youngstown's steel mills. Tim had no problem imagining some guy sitting behind it, sweating out the heat of summer on a shipping dock.

She laid four manila folders in a row across the top of the desk and flipped them open. The folders were thick with documents but a photo was on top of the stack of paper in each folder, so that a face was the first thing you'd see when you opened them. Paulie's hands were thick and strong but her fingers moved lightly, quickly arranging things the way she wanted for her presentation. Tim had the feeling she'd done this before.

"My involvement with this case began about five years ago," Paulie said. She jumped right into it without preamble. "A woman named Quinn Getty contacted me about finding her sister, Kelly Dolan."

"Kelly was from Hogan, right?" Tim said.

"Not quite. She grew up in Berry Creek but lived in Hogan," Paulie said. She dug inside a drawer and came out with a pack of Camels. She nodded at Tim. "You mind?"

"It's your office."

She lit the cig with a practiced flourish from a chrome Zippo and snapped the lid closed with a loud click. "Someone took Kelly Dolan. Let me be very clear about that. In fact, let me emphatically state without hesitation that someone is responsible for making her vanish."

"As opposed to her up and leaving on her own?"

"Exactly," Paulie said.

"What makes you say that?"

"When you meet with her sister and her friends, the people she grew up with—because you're going to end up doing that—you'll know what makes me so certain."

"Let's not get ahead of ourselves. Why don't you tell me a little about her?"

She waved the cigarette as she spoke, leaving a nicotine contrail in the air above her desk. "Kelly had a hard life. The whole bit: single mom, an absent dad, and abusive boyfriends. Her whole life was a series of cable TV movies. She had every right to end up as a junkie or in jail for thieving but that wasn't her. She made something of herself."

Paulie paused a moment and Tim nodded, reminded of Amy and what she had been through. Parents killed in an accident, brother murdered by a psychopath, and still she had persevered and succeeded. "She made it out?"

"You bet. She worked hard, with Quinn's help, to get through high school and then college in Bowling Green, where she finished up with a BFA in digital arts."

"Was she good at it?"

Paulie chuckled. "Good? I've seen her portfolio. Yeah, she could do things on that computer that looked amazing. The people around her, the ones I spoke with, all said she had that way about her that was going to lead to success. You know what I mean?"

Tim smiled, picturing Amy's face. "I think I do."

"Some people, you can tell they're going to make it, like they have the skills or the smarts to take care of themselves without handouts or someone taking care of them. That's why I'm sure someone took that girl. She was on her way." Paulie paused a moment and stubbed out her Camel in a stamped metal ashtray sporting the logo of Brinco, a local auto parts manufacturer. "When people have that kind of momentum, they don't just stop. They don't just up and vanish on their own. No, it takes someone else to fuck up their lives. Some prick did her in."

"It sounds like you think it was a man. Is that right?"

Paulie barked out a short laugh. "Well, hell, Tim. If this life has taught me anything it's that behind the troubles of every woman there's usually a man."

She held up a pre-emptive hand. "Don't get me wrong, I know it goes both ways. Plenty of women make trouble for men, too, but in this case it's a beautiful young woman who is missing." She took a deep breath and sighed. "Yeah, I think it was a man, the same one who killed a whole string of women."

"Your phantom killer?"

She looked across the desk at him with venom in her eyes. "Oh, he's real all right. Let me ask you something;. Is Larry Coogan the lead investigator on the Beer & Bait case?"

"He is."

She chuckled a wry little sound that told him she wasn't a fan of the detective. "Larry Coogan is good at playing like he's just a simple beleaguered civil servant trying to keep us all safe but the reality is that he feels like he screwed up Kelly's case."

"What do you mean? Did he make a mistake?"

"Kelly is still missing, isn't she?" Paulie picked up an orange foam ball and began to squeeze it. "That pisses him off. Don't get me wrong, Larry is a good cop, but this one is stuck in his craw. Pretty soon we're going to be at the ten-year anniversary and for a week or so the disappearance of Kelly Dolan is going to be back in the news. He doesn't want to have to deal with the fact that he was there from the very beginning and still hasn't found her."

Tim slumped back in his chair and considered what Paulie said. Coogan could be irritable about little things, so he couldn't imagine what it was like for him to stare down a failure of this magnitude, especially if it played out in the press.

Paulie opened the second file on her desk and pulled out a thick sheaf of high-resolution color photos held together with a thick black binder clip. She pulled it off with a snap and spun the photos around on the desk for Tim to see.

"These were taken the day after she disappeared when the state crime lab sent investigators up from Columbus. As you can see, there are a lot of woods around Kelly's house. It's a rental out in the township."

Tim leaned in and examined the photographs. Kelly's little house was a green ranch with white trim. It wasn't shabby, but it needed some maintenance. An address was printed on a tag stuck to the photo and he was familiar with the area out in the township. It was full of houses like this, plunked down in large open areas surrounded by thick woods.

"Do you think she's in those woods, Paulie?" Tim said, pointing at the trees in the background.

The private investigator shrugged. "I give it fifty-fifty odds. I mean, we know she was at work that Friday. I've spoken to enough of her coworkers in Akron to place her there. She made two calls on the way home, the first to a friend and the second to her sister. Both of them related their calls to me and they were essentially the same. She complained about work and confirmed she would be at a Labor Day party Quinn was hosting the following Monday."

Tim chewed the top of his pen. "You said she complained about work. What was going on? Was something specific, or someone, bothering her?"

Paulie consulted a note sheet stapled to the inside of the manila folder. "Her boss didn't like something about her work and requested changes. She told Quinn that she was going to hole up for the weekend and knock out the designs he wanted and then go to the party. She never showed."

Tim nodded slowly. "So, when she didn't show, Quinn became concerned?"

"That's right," Paulie said. "They went over on Labor Day when she didn't answer her phone. She didn't answer the door, either, so they called the police. Coogan was the responding officer."

She leafed through the photos and pointed to one showing the outside of the house. "As you can see here, her car is parked in the driveway. This one," she said as she pulled another from the stack, "shows her keys, purse, and cell phone on the dining room table." She looked up at Tim and tapped the photo. "To me, this implies that Kelly made it home Friday and sometime before Monday, someone took her from her house. Even if she went out with someone, she wouldn't have left her things behind."

Tim moved the photo aside to reveal one that showed the woods behind Kelly's house. "I assume the authorities have been all over these woods?"

She nodded. "You bet. They've been searched thoroughly by the cops, firemen, her friends and family, and even a volunteer search group from out of state that uses horses. Hell, I've lost count of how many afternoons I've spent out there."

Tim looked up at her. "You went out there?"

She raised an accusing eyebrow at him. "Are you trying to imply something, Tim?"

He grinned and held his hands up defensively. "No, nothing like that. You just surprised me. I thought private investigators did divorces and background checks."

Tim pulled the photos of the home's interior closer and examined them, sliding them aside one by one. The house in the pictures was neat but not so much you couldn't tell someone his age lived there. Clothes lay on the floor beside the queen-sized bed near a white wicker hamper. A cell phone charging cable was coiled on the nightstand next to a small brass lamp. The closet had clothes hanging from a rod near the top while shoes tumbled across the floor like they'd been kicked off and left to lay. A small dresser occupied the wall facing the bed. The drawers were shut but makeup bottles and hair brushes littered the top. He found it easy to imagine her sitting at the foot of her bed each morning, getting ready for the day.

The next photos were of the living room. He didn't see much there beyond some furniture that looked like it probably came with the house. An olive-green sofa with thick, deep cushions sat in front of the picture window overlooking the front porch and the driveway beyond it. An old coffee table made of a light-colored wood sat in front of it. An afghan was folded over the back of the couch, crocheted in autumn waves of orange, brown, and yellow. A few magazines were spread across the coffee table but otherwise the room looked neat. He slid the photo aside and the next one revealed the only other furniture in the room, a chair upholstered in hideous muted pink fabric that looked scratchy. An end table sat beside it holding a black, wrought-iron lamp.

The dining room had a small table with chairs. A small, cheerfully painted bowl sat in the center, holding a set of keys and a cell phone. A small black purse leaned against the bowl. In one of the corners facing the other picture window a small desk with twin monitors was set against the wall. It looked like a workstation.

The last photos in the stack were of the small kitchen, which appeared to be spotless. Lightly stained wooden cabinets lined one wall. An empty stainless-steel sink was set into the dull yellow countertop. Darker, scuffed yellow linoleum lined the floor. It appeared that Kelly liked a clean kitchen.

The door leading out to the backyard was set into the wall at the rear of the kitchen. The woods beyond were visible through the small windows in the door and an ominous chill rolled down Tim's spine. If something happened to Kelly here, in this house, it was easy to see why the search had moved immediately to the trees beyond her home. He could imagine how easy it would be to step over a clue and not see it. Now that so many years had passed it would be even more difficult to see something.

He pointed at the photo. "You think she's out there, hidden in the trees somewhere? Is that what you're telling me?"

Paulie took a deep breath. "Maybe, but until someone finds her we're not going to know. She could literally be anywhere except inside that house. It's been searched too thoroughly for her to be there. Everywhere else is still on the list."

She put her hands on the other folders, fingers splayed across them like she wanted to make sure they were all included. "I've been doing some research into the Woodsman's MO, and Kelly's disappearance seems to fit. She was alone and taken from her home."

Tim shook his head. "Who is the Woodsman?"

"Sorry," she said. "That's what I call him. The Buckeye Woodsman."

He rolled that around for a moment. "Why do you call him that?"

"Because of the locations where his crimes take place," she said. "He prefers rural locations near wooded areas. My theory is that the woods allow him to observe his victims prior to the attacks. He approaches the locations via access roads leading to gas wells and utility infrastructure."

She tapped the folders in turn. "In each of these cases the women lived in isolated, rural areas bordered by woods, with access roads within a mile of their residences."

Tim glanced down at the folders. "Where did you get this information?"

"Being a licensed private investigator allows me to have access to police records that others don't have. I've also developed connections with police agencies and the media all over the state." She placed a hand flat on a folder. "This is all good data."

"Okay," Tim said, and waved a hand at the documents on the desk. "How did you get from Kelly Dolan vanishing to all this?"

Paulie held up a single finger. "Now that's an excellent question. When Quinn contacted me, Kelly had been missing for about four years without the police getting anywhere. I went over all their files and couldn't find anything out of the ordinary. It looked to me like they'd done a thorough job. I'll give Coogan that much."

"But they haven't found her," Tim said.

Paulie shrugged. "It doesn't mean they did anything wrong. It just means they haven't caught the break they need. Investigations are difficult, you know that."

Tim did indeed. "Okay, so what turned you on to all this?"

"I'm an investigator, not a cop, so I can let my mind wander a little farther than they can. I don't have the burden of making a case that will stand up in court, not when I'm starting out, anyway. I can play a little fast and loose with the rules.

"This case was weird. I could see that right off the bat. People don't just go missing like this. When a woman is harmed, you immediately look to the people in her life. You look at the people who don't like her but you also look at the people who love her. Murderers kill because of motivation and most of the time, that motivation is money, sex, or revenge. So, like any good investigator, that's where I started."

Tim looked at the photo again. "She's pretty. I assume there were boyfriends?"

Paulie followed his gaze to the photo. "Not as many as you'd think. Sure, she dated, and I talked to all of them, but only one guy stood out. His name was Barret Dedrick and he's a first-class asshole."

"What makes you say that?" Tim said.

"They were on again and off again from the time they were in high school, so they had some history. Most of it was bad. The friends I interviewed said he was emotionally abusive. The cops liked him for it but they could never make a case against him."

"What about her family? How did they feel about him?"

"Quinn thinks the stories about him are overblown and that he never laid a hand on his sister. I got the impression that she thought Barret brought a stability to Kelly's life that was missing."

"How about you?" Tim said. "Did you like him for it?"

Paulie nodded and sighed. "I did at first. I mean, it just made sense. They'd been together for a while, these rumors were swirling around, and once I met him . . ." Her voice trailed off for a minute. "I'm going to admit something to you that's hard for me to say. This guy was such a cocksucker that I just wanted it to be him. It's dangerous to have that kind of bias in your thinking, but after talking to him for a while he just rubbed me the wrong way. No, it was more than that, I have a visceral reaction whenever I'm around him." She was quiet again, drifting back, he assumed, to her interaction with this guy.

"I spent the better part of a year trying to build a case against Barret," she said, "even though Quinn didn't like it. I couldn't make it work. The evidence just wasn't there. I don't mind telling you it took a lot for me to let him go. Then I forced myself to start over and look at everything with fresh eyes. That's when I came across Alissa Moldanado. Are you familiar with her case?"

Tim shook his head. The name didn't ring any bells.

She opened the folder and flipped past the photo to the stack of papers underneath. Tim saw a page of typed notes. "The first attack was in Mogadore. You know where that is?"

He nodded. "It's between here and Akron."

"That's right. In May 2008 a twenty-eight-year-old nurse was taken from her home while her husband worked the midnight shift at a lighting factory. They found her two days later near a natural gas well a mile from her house. She'd been stabbed to death. Her name was Alissa Moldanado." Paulie pulled the photo from her file and laid it on the desk. Alissa had been a pretty brunette with a great smile.

"Jesus," Tim said. "How did you find this?"

"The manner of Kelly's disappearance bothered me," she said, sitting down behind the desk and settling into her explanation. "There was no sign of a struggle in her house. No overturned furniture or broken knickknacks. It was like someone just plucked her right out of that house. I figured that if someone could do that, it might not be their first time. Serial offenders get good at what they do, just like everyone else. They plan and they practice."

"So, you figured Kelly wasn't his first victim," Tim said.

She nodded slowly. "Exactly. I started looking for unsolved kidnappings or homicides involving women within fifty miles of Kelly's attack in a time frame of about five years. I filtered them by an unsolved status because if the perpetrator had been caught, he wouldn't have been around to attack Kelly."

"That makes sense," Tim said. He was paying attention now. Facts always got his attention. Having a conspiracy theory was one thing, but backing up such a theory with data moved Paulie from the "nutjob" column to the "hey, maybe we should look at this" column.

"The similarities between Alissa and Kelly checked a lot of boxes," Paulie continued. "Both were young, pretty women living in rural settings near wooded areas with access roads nearby. They were both alone at the time of their attacks, and neither home showed signs of a struggle."

"You said they found Alissa Moldanado, though, right?" Tim said.

"That's correct, out on the access road in the woods behind her house."

"But the authorities haven't found Kelly. Does that hurt your theory?"

"I don't think so," Paulie said. "He may have just done a better job of hiding her."

"Or he could have taken her."

"Maybe," Paulie said. "I'll know when I find her. You should understand something about me, Tim. I only believe what I can prove." She waved her hands over the folders. "I know this is only a theory. I'm not stating it as fact, but right now I believe it's the best lead I have to finding Kelly Dolan."

"I understand," Tim said, and he gestured to the other folders. "What about these others? Do they fit your pattern as well?"

"They do," Paulie said. "Understand, I've looked at hundreds of homicides in my time frame and Alissa was the only one who fit. Then I expanded the time frame forward to the present day. I figured if this guy killed Alissa and was responsible for Kelly's disappearance, he was probably still active." She tapped the next one in line. "That's when I discovered Debbie Jo Biggle."

Tim felt his stomach churn when he examined the picture. It was a wedding photo, and Debbie Jo looked like she was about five feet even and a hundred pounds. It was one thing to hear about a murderer's body count, but these were real women, with families. Their smiling faces looked up at him from Paulie's desk.

"She worked in a small town southeast of here called Berlin Center."

"I know where that is," Tim said. "It's a nice place."

"It is, but in August of 2012, Debbie Jo was working the late shift alone at a gas station and convenience store. Her relief came in at six a.m. and found the store empty. This is a weird one in that the last pre-paid cash sale was at four thirty a.m., which is the last time thirty-two-year-old Debbie Jo Biggle was seen alive. A customer paid her inside the store, so we know she was alive at that time."

"Okay," Tim said. "So, whatever happened occurred between four thirty and six."

"Correct. However, three other customers pumped gas in the following ninety minutes. They all used credit cards at the pumps to pay for their gas, so they never entered the store."

"The store was empty and none of them knew it?" Tim said.

"That's right," Paulie said.

"Damn," Tim said. "Where did they find her?"

Paulie didn't need to look at her notes. "A week later a farmer called the police to report that one of his dogs had dropped a human forearm on his back porch. Other animals had gotten to her but they found her on a nearby access road leading to a line of electrical transmission towers. You know, the great big steel ones carrying high-tension lines?"

"Yeah, I know what they look like," Tim said.

"Her boss said she was probably abducted from behind the store when she took garbage out to the dumpster."

Tim turned that over in his mind. "That sounds an awful lot like the Beer & Bait."

Paulie pointed a finger in his direction. "That's exactly what I thought when I read your article. He hasn't limited himself to residences. If he hit this gas station, why not a convenience store here in Hogan?"

Tim didn't want to get on board the crazy train just yet. Paulie made a compelling case for stringing together unsolved mysteries, but other than similarities between the settings and victims, she hadn't provided any hard evidence that would be considered irrefutable. All of these incidents were terrible, but he couldn't let the shock of them cloud his judgement. It was important to maintain his objectivity.

He pointed to the last folder with dread, knowing what it contained, even if he didn't have the particulars. "Who is that?"

Paulie picked up a photo and held it up for him. This woman looked older than the rest, but not by much. "This is Julie Silverstein from Twinsburg. She was a secretary who lived on a cul de sac. She and some friends had a standing card game every Thursday night. Just four ladies getting together to drink a little wine and play bridge. The host lived on the same street, so Julie just walked home from the game. It was less than a block to her house but no one ever saw her alive again. This was in 2016."

Tim just shook his head without saying anything. It was useless to express his horror vocally anymore.

"She was divorced with no kids, so no one missed her at home. Her boss and a coworker at the small real estate company where she worked went looking for her when she didn't show up at work the next day. They found her keys on the front porch, with a can of pepper spray on the ring. It hadn't been used." She laid down another picture, this one showing a pink pepper spray key ring with a collection of keys on it.

"He took her by surprise," Tim said.

Paulie nodded and laid out another photo, this one of a small, neat white house with a black front door and a picket railing around a small concrete porch. Hedges ran along the front of the porch. "They think he waited for her in the bushes."

"In front of her house?" Tim said. "That's bold, isn't it?"

"It is. I think it shows he's becoming more confident in his ability to blend in and be unseen in these suburban and rural environments." She paused for a moment and pulled another cigarette from her pack. After lighting it, she pointed to the photo. "Clearly he had been scoping her out for a while, learning her routine."

Tim pulled the picture of the front porch toward himself. The bushes needed a good trim, because they grew up over the edge of the porch. "These hedges don't offer a lot of concealment, even as overgrown as they are. He had to know generally when she would return home so he could grab her."

"I think so, too," Paulie said. She blew smoke up toward the ceiling of her office. "It took three days for them to find her on an access road used to reach a nearby dam."

Tim shifted uncomfortably in his chair and considered that the trailer park he and Amy lived in was surrounded by woods. He'd never look at them the same way again.

Paulie dropped the photo of Kelly on the desk in front of him and the smiling redhead with green eyes looked up at him. He touched it, stroking the edge to make it more real.

"He's killed two women since Kelly," Paulie said. "Well, four now, I guess, considering the two from the Beer & Bait. That's six women in twelve years."

Tim looked at the photos arrayed across Paulie's desk. It was almost too much to take in. "It's incredible to think one man has killed this many women and hasn't been caught yet."

"Incredible is one word," Paulie said. "Terrifying is another. Remember, no one is looking for him because as far as the police are concerned, he doesn't exist."

He spread his hands over the photos. "How does that work? Why are you the only one who sees this? How could the police not have a task force looking for this guy? Have you spoken to them? I mean, if this is true, this kind of evil is enormous."

"Yeah," she said, "that's true, but remember, he's had time and distance on his side. To answer your question, yes, I've spoken to the police, but no one is listening to me. Hell, I couldn't even get Larry Coogan to sit with me for more than fifteen minutes."

"They don't see it your way?"

"They don't want to believe it so they don't listen."

"But that doesn't make any sense," Tim said. He wasn't fully on board yet, not without sitting down and going over the evidence himself, but there was enough here to pique his interest. "How can they write this off?"

Paulie gave him a wry smile. "You're in the news business, so I'm going to assume you're pretty well informed. What happened in Cleveland today? Did anything bad occur in Pittsburgh? Was anyone murdered in Akron that you know of?"

"I don't know," he admitted.

"Right, and I think that's what this offender is counting on. It can be difficult to investigate something when you don't know it's happening."

Tim sat quietly for a moment, drinking it all in, and then he slid a couple pictures aside so Kelly's was on top. "They never found Kelly?"

Paulie shook her head.

"That's odd, right? I mean, they found all the others, but not her? I assume they've been all over that gas well access road?"

"Many times, and through the woods. They went back over the area with a small army of searchers. No trace of her has ever been found."

He took a deep breath before asking his next question. "I understand this is a lot of work and you've put together a compelling argument, but do you believe she was one of his victims? I mean, there's an abusive boyfriend in the picture and you said yourself that the perpetrator of a murder is usually someone close to the victim." He pointed to the folders. "This kind of stranger-on-stranger crime is very rare, and even more so if a serial killer is involved. The safe bet is the boyfriend but you're excluding him."

Paulie studied him closely, her eyes boring into him, but he didn't back down. She was peddling a story that was hard to swallow and it was on her to prove he should buy in.

"Yes, Tim, I believe Kelly Dolan is the victim of a serial offender. I certainly don't have any evidence to the contrary. I mean, just look at how well it lines up with his behavior."

"You keep saying that, as if his very existence isn't a theory," Tim said. "Nothing here proves that."

"The thing is," she said, leaning back in her chair, "I believe what I can prove, so I'll know what the answer is when the case is solved. As you look into this, you're going to hear a lot of theories and ideas about what happened to Kelly. Everyone in town seems to have one. The only way to solve this clusterfuck, though, is to follow the evidence to wherever it leads and I've done that to the best of my ability. I simply don't know what happened to this girl. Yet."

"So, you still believe she will be found?"

Paulie nodded. "I do."

Tim flipped back to the beginning of Kelly's file, where photos were clipped to the front of the folder. Kelly was on top and he lifted it, revealing another woman who looked a little older than Kelly. They had similar features: red hair, green eyes, and smiles that made them look like they had an inside joke. He tapped the photo.

"This is her sister, Quinn?"

Paulie nodded. "That's her. Getty is her married name."

"What can you tell me about her?"

"She's good people. From what I gather, Kathleen Dolan wasn't much of a mother. Besides the drinking, her other hobbies included collecting loser boyfriends.

"As the girls were growing up, Kathleen struggled with work and had a hard time making ends meet. That led to her shacking up with guys to help pay the rent. I don't know all the details, but from what Kelly's friends tell me, the situation was less than ideal."

"What about their dad? Was he around?"

Paulie shook her head. "He walked out a couple years after Kelly was born. They didn't hear from him often."

"Did any of these guys abuse the girls?"

"Not that I know of, but that's probably something Kelly's friends would know better than I would."

"So, the girls were left alone sometimes?"

Paulie grunted. "Oh yeah. What I've heard is that Kathleen and her boyfriends would spend a lot of time and money in bars. Quinn kind of became a surrogate mom to Kelly. She would make her dinner, make sure she got up for school, help with her homework, you know, that kind of stuff."

"That sounds like a lot of responsibility."

"There was more to it than that," Paulie said. "Quinn told me that she helped Kelly get through college."

"You mean she helped pay for it?"

"That's right, her and her husband, Roger. Kelly qualified for some grants because her mom didn't have much in the way of income, but it wasn't enough."

"You can say that again. I'm going to be paying off student loans until I'm in my thirties."

"See, Quinn didn't want that for Kelly. She wanted her little sister to start life without any more baggage. The way she thought about it, the two of them had already been through a ton of shit and that was enough. Anything Kelly needed to get through school, Quinn made sure she got it." Paulie got a faraway look in her eyes and fell silent.

Tim waited quietly, wanting to give her whatever time she needed. Charlie had taught him that listening and being patient could be half the job sometimes. Finally, Paulie spoke up again.

"She had just graduated the previous spring. Did you know that?"

Tim shook his head. Paulie was almost solemn when she spoke about Kelly. He started to get the idea that she'd be investigating her disappearance whether there was a retainer or not. "No, I didn't."

"All that hard work, all that effort by both sisters to get to a point in life where they could be free and do what they wanted. They did that through sheer force of will and hard work, on their own, just the two of them. Then, a few months later Kelly just up and vanished."

"How did Quinn take it?"

Paulie licked her lips and fired up another smoke. The metal chair creaked a little under her weight. "It devastated her. That's why she got me involved when the cops weren't making progress. We spoke about once a week. She was full of good ideas and worked hard to keep people interested in her sister's case.

"I explained to her that someone was responsible for Kelly's disappearance and the key to finding her was getting someone to talk, to give us that break we needed. She did interviews on TV and for the newspapers but after a while, other things came up and it got harder and harder to keep people's interest. Eventually, it just got quiet and when that happened, all the leads dried up."

Tim was busy scribbling notes and the only sound was his pen scratching against paper. He knew how fast the world moved and the impact it had on news cycles. Kelly had been gone for nine years. Even if the case was fresh, he doubted she would even trend on Twitter or rate a mention on a news website outside the region. After a week people would lose track of the story completely, their attention consumed with whatever manufactured outrage the internet could gin up or a celebrity wedding. A missing girl in a small town like Hogan didn't stand a chance against those odds.

He looked up and saw Paulie staring at him. "All caught up?"

"Yeah," he said.

"What's really heartbreaking about the whole thing," Paulie said, "is that she had a good job lined up. A firm in Boston had offered her a position. It was just entry level, but it was something. A way to build a portfolio and something to put on her resume."

"A step forward," Tim said. "A first step toward something greater."

Paulie nodded. "You got it. That's why I know someone did this to her. She had it going on and was going to make it, not settling for some job around here where her talents would be wasted. All that work paid off and it was stolen from her. All her effort turned out to be so much piss in the wind."

She tapped her cigarette over the ash tray. "You know, those two could have been hellions, given how they were brought up, but that's not what they did. It's almost like Quinn rebelled by being normal, by being more mature than everyone around her."

"By helping her sister," Tim said.

"That's right. Quinn's got a way about her. She gets things done. I think her greatest fear is that her or Kelly would end up like their mother, weak and dependent on some man. Her and her husband, Roger, do pretty well. You should see the spread they have over in Berry Creek." She held hands about two feet apart. "Nice big house in a development and a couple of great kids."

"That sounds fantastic."

"I think it mostly is, but this thing with Kelly," Paulie paused a moment. "It eats at her. For someone who likes to manage things, who doesn't like loose ends, well, I think it drives her just about out of her mind when she lets herself think about it. If you talk to her, don't get her hopes up. I don't think she can take it."

Tim nodded slowly, thankful for the advice. "I'll do that." He rose from his chair. "If you don't have anything else I think I'll stop taking up so much of your time."

Paulie stood and set her cigarette on the edge of the metal ashtray. The bluish smoke curled up in whorls and loops. "Are you going to look into this theory of mine?"

"Yeah," he said. "I'll run it by my publisher, but I think it's definitely worth a look."

"Let me know if you find anything, okay? This sharing thing is a two-way street."

"You got it."

9

Let me get this right," Charlie said. "You met with a private investigator who thinks a serial killer has been stalking this area of the state for the past decade, who is responsible for a missing woman here in Hogan, and who also killed the two women out at the Beer & Bait last week. Am I understanding you correctly?"

It was Monday morning and Tim had spent Sunday deciding whether he actually believed Paulie. He'd spoken with Amy about it because her mind was logical and he needed someone he trusted. They'd laid in bed together with nothing else going on and he'd explained the whole thing. Their lazy Sunday morning turned into a lazy afternoon and they'd finally given into hunger and had lunch at the Yankee Skillet, a pancake joint off the beaten path near one of the local highways. The conversation drifted away from the topic as they shopped in a local factory outlet mall, but always circled back around and by the time they'd been ready to turn in that evening, neither of them could come up with a reason why Paulie's theory was implausible.

Tim looked at Charlie and saw the publisher staring him down. His slate-colored eyes were full of disbelief. Whatever magic Paulie had been able to weave in her tale, Tim seemed to lack. He finally nodded.

"Yeah, it seems like you understand it," Tim said. "You don't think there's anything here?"

"Tim, come on. What do you want me to say?"

He swallowed. In all the time they'd worked together, Charlie had never waved him off a story. Their usual process was to talk it through, chase it down, and see what they could find. This kind of rejection was new, and Tim didn't like how it felt.

"I know this seems kind of far-fetched, but someone took Kelly Dolan, and whoever hit the Beer & Bait was clearly after the women who worked there, not the money in the register. My interview with Amber and the evidence found at the scene suggests as much. There's no reason it couldn't be the same guy."

Charlie raised a disbelieving eyebrow and his gaze bore into Tim. "There's no reason to think it's the same guy. The crimes aren't even that similar. Ignoring the fact that almost a decade has passed since Kelly went missing, she was taken from her home, not a business. If I let you pursue this, how would you even proceed? There's not a single link between the crimes."

This was a question Tim was prepared for. After speaking with Paulie, he'd spent hours considering how he would go about chasing the story, figuring out how to build it if he dug up the right information.

"I want to start with Kelly Dolan," he said. "She's our hometown victim, the woman who was taken and never found. I want to talk to her family, the police, and anyone else who can bring her back into the spotlight. If I shake that tree hard enough who knows what will come loose?"

Charlie leaned back in his chair, staring at him across the two desks separating them. Tim could see the gears inside his head spinning, calculating the odds of there actually being something to this.

"And then what? Say you do a profile on Kelly, speak to her family, and nothing ties the crime against her to the Beer & Bait. Will you be back in here asking me to pursue some other angle?"

It was a fair question, and Charlie had a point. Having similar aspects wasn't the same thing as having irrefutable proof. There was no physical evidence that tied the two crimes together. All he had was Paulie's theory.

"Well, actually, I think I'd like to speak to all the families on Paulie's list. After all, those cases are still open and as you noted, some of them go back a decade. At the very least, we'll be able to question the authorities and see about the status of the cases."

"No," Charlie said, shaking his head. "We are not going to peddle some half-assed theory about a serial killer to people who have lost their loved ones in the most brutal manner possible. All we'll accomplish is making them more upset."

"Charlie, that's not what—"

He held up a hand to cut Tim off. "No, Tim, just hear me out. It's not fair to make them think there's a new lead in their cases. I've dealt with cold cases. The families make a point of staying in touch with the police. They mark it on their calendars and call detectives on a set schedule. As long as a family is involved, those victims are not forgotten. Now, it's different if there's no family or the victim is unidentified, but what you have there, in your file, are women whose families are involved in their investigations. To go to them with this would be cruel."

Tim opened his mouth to respond but stopped. Charlie had a good point. If he couldn't find something solid, some evidence that these cases were at all connected, what was the point of getting the families riled up? He glanced down at the folder containing all of Paulie's notes. Was there an answer in there or was it just the beginning of something?

"Charlie, I understand what you're saying but I have to disagree with you. I can speak to Kelly's family and the others without drawing a connecting thread between their cases. I understand your concerns, but these families are all looking for justice and they aren't getting it. There's nothing unethical about interviewing them and bringing attention to their cases."

The publisher leaned forward. "There's nothing unethical about interviewing them under false pretenses? Is that what you're telling me? Because it sounds an awful lot like what you're saying is that you want to go on a fishing expedition to see if Paulie Carmichael's theory is sound, and you want to do it without telling the victim's families why you're doing it. Are you going to tell them you plucked their names from a hat?"

Tim swallowed. When Charlie put it that way, it did seem like he was hiding something. He tapped a pencil on the folder. "Look, Charlie. It would be very difficult to proceed with an investigation like this if I didn't interview the families."

"You're a smart guy," he said. "You'll find a way."

They stared at each other, the silence growing between them. Tim didn't like it. What he wanted to do was rant and rave, argue as loudly as he could to make his point, but that would be useless and so unprofessional that Charlie would probably send him home. In the end he just shook his head.

"Okay, I'll see what I can discover without approaching the families."

Charlie nodded and his shoulders relaxed. It was nice to see he had been feeling the tension. too.

"Tim, I think it would be a good idea to interview Kelly Dolan's family."

He swiveled in his chair. "Didn't you just say we weren't going to do that?"

"I said we're not going to pursue the serial killer angle," Charlie said. "However, Kelly Dolan has been missing for nine years and the case is still open. I think it's in the best interests of the community for us to get an update on the case."

Tim smiled. "I can do that."

Charlie wagged a finger at him. "That's all you're going to do, though. I want a story that profiles Kelly and gives us a status update on the progress of the investigation. I don't want you writing a word about serial killers or connected cases."

Tim deflated a bit. He'd thought maybe Charlie was giving him a wink and a nod to pursue Paulie's theory but he had just expressly forbidden it. He nodded his agreement.

"No problem. I'll talk to her family and the police. Give me a few days to get it done."

Charlie held up his hands. "I'd like it to be in next week's edition, if that's possible."

"Okay," Tim said. "You'll have it."

● ● ●

That night, Amy actually beat Tim home. When he rolled in from the office around six, she was in the kitchen putting the finishing touches on dinner: cheese ravioli and a salad. They'd been trying to save money by cutting down on eating out and if either of them had the opportunity to cook, they tried to take it. It was usually a failing endeavor because of how busy they were, but tonight she'd stepped up.

He dropped his laptop bag on the living room floor and collapsed on the couch. Amy followed him and handed him a cold beer from the fridge. She had another in her opposite hand that was already half empty.

"Rough day?" she said.

He looked at her. It was the height of summer and her skin was tan from weekend afternoons spent laying out by the trailer park pool. He smiled at her and toyed with a loose strand of blonde hair near her ear. It was several shades lighter than normal thanks to the sun.

He leaned over and gave her a small kiss. "It was a little rough, but it's better now."

"Want to talk about it?"

"How long until dinner?"

"About ten minutes."

"Good," he said, and told her about his conversation with Charlie.

"I don't understand," she said. "Paulie's theory isn't just some conspiracy theory she pulled down from the internet. I mean, sure, it's all circumstantial evidence right now, but doesn't that mean it should be looked into further? I've seen you start stories with less. That's all this is, the beginning."

He exhaled. "I know, but I can't get Charlie to buy it. He's convinced that even talking to the families of these women will disturb them. He also doesn't want the *Weekly Shopper* to be seen as a tabloid."

She curled into him and he put an arm around her shoulders. "So, what are you going to do?"

"I'm going to do the story on Kelly Dolan," he said. "Between the family and the police, you never know what that will shake loose. There may be something there that's been overlooked. Time can erode people's memories but it also allows for things to surface."

"You may get lucky," she agreed. "Someone has to know something, after all, and if you ask the right questions, an answer could pop loose."

"After that, though, I'm looking into Paulie's theory."

Amy untangled herself from him and sat up. "Yeah?"

He shifted around and looked at her. "I think she's on to something and I think Charlie is just wrong. He's too scared to go after it because he's trying to build the *Weekly Shopper* into something new, which I totally understand, but there's something here. Like you said, it's the beginning of something. It will take some hard work to figure out if it really means something."

"Charlie will be pissed if he finds out you went behind his back."

He shrugged. "I'll deal with that if it becomes a problem. This needs doing."

She smiled. "So, the game is afoot, eh?"

He put his arms around her and gave her another, longer kiss. "Hell yeah, Dr. Watson. You want to help out?"

"Yes," she said, but her face held a look of disappointment. "Work is still busy as ever, but I'll do what I can."

"That's fine," he said. "It's just as well, anyway. At least you'll still be bringing home some money if I end up fired."

She tapped her beer against his. "Here's to poking around where you don't belong. Don't get caught, though. I don't make much."

10

Tim spent the rest of the evening reviewing the files on Kelly Dolan's case. Charlie had clippings and notes from the time of her disappearance, which gave him a place to start. The next morning, he kissed Amy goodbye as she left for work and then picked up the phone to make an appointment with Larry Coogan, but thought better of it. Why give the detective an easy way to blow him off by refusing to see him? He jumped in his Jeep and drove into town. It wasn't like he could be locked up for dropping by.

Tim drove over to the City of Hogan's administration building, a sandy-colored brick building off of Independence Street. The small police department shared the building with the rest of the city's municipal departments. The parking lot near the police entrance was empty except for a black-and-white cruiser and the silver, four-door Dodge Charger that Tim knew to be used by the department's two detectives.

In the small lobby, he signed in with the uniformed officer sitting behind glass at the front desk and asked to see Larry Coogan. The grumpy detective and Tim had sort of worked together earlier on the letters case. Coogan had come close to figuring out who had killed Amy's brother, Boyd, but Tim had gotten the answer first. Of course, it hadn't been soon enough to save Charlie from taking a bullet. Sometimes Tim still thought about that night, and how it had ended with violence and blood in the snow on Main Street.

The glass door to the waiting room opened with a loud electronic buzz, rousing him from his memories. Larry Coogan stared at him from the doorway with tired, bloodshot eyes. The detective looked like he hadn't slept properly for days. He shook his head at Tim.

"Whatever you're here for, Abernathy, I just don't have the time. Make an appointment."

Tim jumped up, eager to keep him from closing the door. "Hold on, it won't take long. I promise."

"You lie."

Tim held up a brown paper sack. "I brought you breakfast. Coffee and donuts from Jake's Bakes."

Coogan raised an eyebrow at the thought of caffeine and sugar from Hogan's oldest and finest bakery. "All right, come on."

He waved Tim into the back offices, so he followed. The detective was shorter than Tim and stouter, carrying a lot of weight in his barrel-shaped torso. He looked unkempt, which was out of character for him. He needed a shave and the tail of his dress shirt was untucked. The collar of his shirt was open and his tie was missing.

"How are things going, detective?"

They walked through an open room filled with beige cubicles. The carpet was the kind of dark brown Berber you saw in hotel lobbies, designed to hide dirt. Coogan swung into a cubicle and pointed to a black metal chair with worn gray padding that looked like it had started life in a middle school office waiting room. Tim sat down and Coogan collapsed into the chair on the other side of the desk. He took the bag from Tim and dropped a couple cream and sugars into the tall cup of coffee before answering.

"Things suck, Abernathy. I've been working sixteen-hour days because I've got two dead bodies out by the lake. Oh, and I still have to solve all of these."

He pointed to a teetering stack of manila folders on his desk. "That's the largest my caseload has ever been and it's just going to get worse since people can't stop using heroin, selling heroin, or robbing other people to buy heroin." He rubbed his red eyes with his knuckles. "It just won't stop."

Tim's head spun from the sudden onslaught of information but that was just the way Coogan spoke, in furious bursts packed with detail. In the time he'd known the detective, the officer had never had a moment to spare. His whole life seemed to be about crossing one item off his mental list and getting onto the next one. Tim pulled out the steno pad he used for notes and uncapped a pen as Coogan grabbed a chocolate long john from the bag and bit off a third of it.

"I'm here about Kelly Dolan."

The detective slumped down in his chair with an air of defeat around him. "Come on, Abernathy," he said around a mouthful of donut. "Why are you doing this to me?"

"I'm here because what happened out at the Beer & Bait jogged our memory about Kelly and we thought it would be a good idea to do a profile on her. Part of that is asking you about the status of her investigation."

Coogan shrugged and kept eating. "What do you want me to say? If there was something new you and everyone else would know about it."

"Do you think she's dead?"

The detective swallowed the donut and sipped his coffee before answering. "No, I don't think she's dead. She's missing and that could mean she's dead, but I'm not convinced yet."

"Why not?" Tim said. "She's been gone for nine years."

Coogan gave him a look like he was a teacher wondering how one of his students could be this stupid. "I don't think she's dead because I haven't seen a body, Abernathy. What is this, your first day?"

Tim flushed, embarrassed that he'd simply made the assumption the young woman was dead when there really wasn't any proof.

"Sorry, I shouldn't have said that. It was a mistake."

"Yeah, it was." He raised an eyebrow. "Look, Ms. Dolan's case is stone-cold dead right now pending any new information."

"Can I quote you on saying that the current status of the case is that it's 'stone-cold dead'?"

Coogan sighed. "You want a quote? Okay, here's your quote: The Kelly Dolan investigation is active and being worked diligently by the City of

Hogan Police Department and our law enforcement partners in Humboldt County and the State of Ohio. We have no updates to provide at this time."

Tim was taken aback by the speed with which the exhausted Coogan rattled off the statement. "Come on, Larry. I'm writing a profile about her and her disappearance. That could be good for you. Can't you give me an update on the investigation?"

"Sure. The Kelly Dolan investigation is active and being worked diligently by the City of Hogan Police Department and—"

Tim waved him off before he had to hear the whole spiel again. "Yeah, yeah, I get it. Can you give a summary of what is known?"

"It's all been written up, Abernathy, and I have a double homicide to solve. Go do your own homework."

Tim sat quietly for a moment, looking at the detective. He needed something to get him started and Coogan was just the thing. Charlie's first articles on the disappearances listed a younger Officer Coogan as being there at the beginning. He only had one card to play.

"I'm trying to help," Tim said. "Is there anything you can tell me about her disappearance that would help jog people's memories? I mean, when is the last time someone walked in here and even asked about her?"

Coogan stared at him for a long moment and Tim started to feel uncomfortable. He couldn't imagine what it would be like to sit in an interview room as a criminal being questioned by him. Finally, the detective let out a deep breath and nodded.

"Okay, what do you want to know?"

"The first day, when she vanished? You were there. What can you tell me about that?"

The detective leaned back in his chair and took a deep breath. At first, Tim thought he might renege and send him on his way. Then he began talking. "It was Labor Day and I was still in the patrol division, which meant holiday traffic duty . . ."

11

Coogan was sitting in a Hogan PD black-and-white Crown Victoria in the parking lot of Mulligan's Drug Store at the intersection of Independence and Main Streets. It was a gorgeous day, sunny and bright with almost no humidity, so he had the windows down. A light breeze moved the air just enough to keep things comfortable. His radar gun was locked into the dash mount and aimed at the westbound lane of Independence so he could ring up any speeders coming down the hill into the city from the township.

He glanced at the clock and saw that the afternoon was creeping up on two o'clock. His shift ended at four and he had plans to see his girlfriend, Brenda. The radar unit blared obnoxiously and interrupted his thoughts. A pickup was coming down the road at eleven miles per hour over the twenty-five mile per hour speed limit. He put the car in gear and reached for the switch to fire up the lights and siren, but his radio squawked.

A dispatcher said, "Three-Baker-Two."

Coogan sighed, put the car in park, and picked up his dashboard mic. "Go for Three-Baker-Two."

"Can you handle a ten-seventeen at thirty-two Caldwell Road?"

"Ten-four." Coogan put the cruiser in gear and rolled out of the parking lot, heading up the hill he had spent the last hour watching. The address was out in the township and the radio code was for a welfare check. "Dispatch, is anyone at the address?"

"Affirmative. Family members are at the residence."

Eight minutes later Coogan was driving down Caldwell Road. It was a typical township two-lane blacktop with gravel shoulders. Thick, green woods grew right up to the drainage ditches on either side of the road except where houses had been built. Two women waved to him from in front of a little one-story house with peeling green paint and white shutters. Two cars were in the driveway, a little blue Honda Civic coupe parked near the house and a red Dodge Caravan minivan. Gravel crunched under his tires when he pulled into the driveway behind the van.

The older of the two women approached his cruiser, so he exited quickly and radioed in his status using the lapel mic on his shoulder. She moved to grab him and he put a hand out to keep her at arm's length. She appeared to be in her late fifties and was unhealthily skinny in that way some people get as they grow older and drink more than they eat. Her hair was tinted red but it had been a while since her last dye job and silver roots were gaining ground. The green blouse she wore was baggy on her, as were her jeans.

"My daughter is missing," she said, slurring her words. "She didn't come to the barbecue and she should have been there."

"Okay, ma'am, calm down." He looked to the younger woman, who was considerably calmer. She was younger, probably in her mid-twenties. She was also a redhead, and her hair curled down over her shoulders in loose springs. She was more fit and the blue tank top she wore showed off well-defined arms. The legs peeking from beneath her khaki mom shorts were toned. "Can you tell me what's going on?"

She put her arms around the older woman and hugged her. "Mom, please relax. You're not helping the situation. Come on, just come over here." She walked her back toward the van and leaned her against it, steadying her like a mop that might tip over in a kitchen. Then she walked back to Coogan.

"I'm sorry," she said in a low voice. "My mother has a bit of a drinking problem and we had a barbecue today, which means she's been at it for a while."

Coogan looked at the older woman, whose eyes were riveted on him. He turned back to the daughter. "Is this your house?"

She glanced back at it. "No, this is my little sister's place. Her name is Kelly Dolan."

"What's your name?"

"I'm Quinn Getty and that's my mom, Kathleen Dolan."

"What's going on with your sister?"

"Well, like my mom said, we were having a Labor Day barbecue and my sister didn't show up. We called her but she didn't answer, so we came over to check on her. The house is dark and locked up."

Coogan's eyes roamed the property while she answered, checking things out, looking for signs of a disturbance. The windows were intact and the door was standing straight in its frame, so it didn't look kicked in. Green moss grew on the roof in the shade of a couple big maple trees that grew too close to the house.

"Have you spoken to any of her friends or other family members?"

"My mom and I are her only family," Quinn said. "She only has one close friend and she said she hasn't spoken to Kelly since Friday."

"Boyfriends?"

She shook her head. "Right now she's not dating anyone, as far as I know."

He pointed at the Honda. "Is that her car?"

She nodded. "Yes, that's what has us nervous. If her car is here, she should be, too, and she isn't answering the door."

Coogan keyed his mic again, and in a quiet voice, radioed in the license plates of both vehicles and the names of the women, checking for warrants or outstanding violations. While dispatch checked for him, he walked around the little Honda without touching it, peering through the windows. It was empty and nothing looked out of the ordinary.

There was no garage near the house so he walked toward the front door. A covered porch ran the length of the house. Some of the stiles were missing from the waist-high railing. There were wildflowers growing in the dirt and none of them looked disturbed. He mounted the two steps leading to the porch and banged on the door. There was no answer.

"She's not answering," the mom said from the back corner of the van. "Where is she?"

Dispatch got back to him with his records check. The women were clean and the cars were registered with no outstanding violations. There were two picture windows facing the road, one on either side of the door. He cupped his hands and looked through the one on his right. A small dining room was visible inside the house through the sheer curtains, and beyond that he could make out a galley kitchen. He moved to the other side and looked through the window to the left of the door. There was a living room with a couch, TV, and an upholstered chair.

There was no sign anyone was inside. He turned to look at the women. Quinn was hugging Kathleen near the van, trying to keep her mother calm.

"I'm going around the back," he said. "Please wait here."

Coogan walked around the house to the backyard. As neglected as the dwelling looked, the yard appeared to receive regular attention. The grass was cut and the weeds were trimmed along the little concrete patio near the back door.

The house wasn't big. He saw three windows at the back, and one was smaller than the other two. Curtains and blinds hung in each of them but he was able to see inside enough to tell that the two larger windows were for empty bedrooms and the smaller one was for a bathroom with no one in it. As far as he could tell, the house was empty.

He opened the white aluminum screen door with a loud squeak and tried the back door. It was a blue nine-lite model, and all of the glass panels were intact. The locked knob refused to turn under his hand and the door was tight in the frame when he tried to rattle it.

A small, raggedy shed stood at the back of the property near the tree line. He walked toward it, approaching from an angle that let him see behind it and into the woods. The boards of the shed had once been the same green as the house, but the paint had been mostly worn away by untold seasons of sun, rain, and snow. The doors were secured with a dull brass padlock, and he could tell the hasp was screwed tightly into the wood of the door when he yanked on it. One side of the small outbuilding had a tiny window. He looked inside, but it was too dark to see anything. He pulled a small flashlight from his belt and shined it inside. Dusty particles drifted lazily in the bright beam of the flashlight but the only thing he saw was a narrow worktable mounted along one wall. The rest of the small building looked empty.

He noticed a brush pile at the tree line, so he approached it. Tall weeds moved in the light breeze around the pile of old branches, but nothing else caught his attention. He straightened up and looked into the woods behind the house, swallowing hard. If something bad happened to Kelly Dolan here, there were thousands of acres of woodland all around him.

Dispatch had said she was only twenty-four when he called in the car parked in the driveway.

He reached for his lapel mic. "Dispatch, Three-Baker-Two. I'm going to need some help out here."

⊕   ⊕   ⊕

Half an hour later, another cruiser and the supervisor's Ford Explorer lined the edge of Caldwell Road in front of Kelly Dolan's house. Coogan was talking to his shift commander, Pete Webster. The sergeant was in his mid-forties and his remaining blond hair was cut high and tight. The other Hogan officer, Darren Lewis, a young man with chiseled good looks, was re-interviewing Quinn and Kathleen in the driveway near Coogan's cruiser.

A car pulled up behind the police vehicles and a young man got out. He waved toward Coogan and his sergeant and hopped across the drainage ditch that ran next to the road. The man looked to be in his early thirties, had long dark hair, and wore jean shorts, beat-up white Nikes, and a black Green Day t-shirt.

Coogan approached him. "Are you the landlord?"

The young man shrugged. "Sort of. My dad, Richard, owns the houses, and I work for him taking care of them. I'm Harvey Reynolds." He held his hand out and Coogan shook it.

"Well, Mr. Reynolds, we need you to let us in. Did you bring a key?"

"Yeah. Is Kelly all right?" He looked back at the police cruisers. "Did something happen to her?"

"We're conducting a welfare check for her family," Coogan said, "so we really need you to open the door for us."

"Yeah, sure."

All three of them walked across the yard and up onto the porch. Coogan turned to Harvey as he pulled a ring of keys from his pocket and thumbed through them. "Is there a basement in the house?"

The young man shook his head. "No, it's on a cement pad. No second floor, either, but I guess you can see that." He looked back at his keys. "It's this one," he said holding the ring up by one key. "Do you want me to open the door?"

Coogan took the key ring. "I'll take care of it. Why don't you step back and wait here?"

The key slipped into the lock and Coogan opened the door. He and Webster stepped into the dark living room and his eyes went to the corners out of habit, checking to make sure no one was waiting for them. He didn't see anything out of the ordinary and the house was silent. It was the quiet of an empty house, not just a dwelling where there is no sound, but a home devoid of presence. A shiver moved through Coogan and he let it ride, just to get it over with.

They walked from room to room, careful not to disturb anything but leaving nothing unsearched. Coogan disliked this part of the job, moving through a person's home and picking through their personal belongings. There was nothing that tripped him up, though. No drugs, no bongs, needles, or blackened spoons that would lead him to think about drug use. He didn't even see ashtrays.

Webster moved through the dining room into the kitchen after they finished with the bedrooms, but Coogan stopped and looked at the small four-chair table in the center of the room.

"Hey, Sarge? Take a look at this."

Webster turned to look and Coogan pointed at a ceramic bowl in the center of the table. It was white with violets and yellow daisies painted around the edge. A cell phone and keys lay inside. A small black purse leaned against the rim. Coogan pulled a stick pen from his breast pocket and fished the keys from the bowl. They were for a Honda.

"She was here?" Webster said.

Coogan looked around the house again, eyes traveling from the kitchen to the living room and back again. "I don't know."

"Her stuff is here," Webster said as he looked through her purse. He removed a wallet and flipped it open. The driver's license under a plastic window belonged to Kelly Dolan. He sighed. "You know a woman who leaves the house without her purse or cell phone? Even if she was going for a walk, she'd take her keys. The house was locked up."

Coogan gave him a small nod. "Yeah."

"I don't like this," the sergeant said.

"I don't either," Coogan said, thinking of the woods behind the house. "Let's get some bodies out here and do a walk-around."

"What makes you want to do that?"

Coogan was sure the sergeant knew why, so he felt like he was being tested. He wanted to know why the younger officer was thinking the way he was. Webster did that sort of thing often, making the younger guys defend their decisions. Coogan pointed at the bowl and its contents. "Right now, this is all we have, so we may as well start here, but I have to tell you, it feels wrong. That's all I can tell you."

Webster paused for a moment like he was considering what Coogan said. Then he nodded. "All right. I'll make some calls, but don't get ahead of yourself. Before we go all in on this, let's take some prudent steps. We're going to lose the light in a couple hours."

Coogan pointed toward the driveway. "We need to start with the trunk of her car."

Webster nodded and they looked outside. Darren Lewis still had the ladies near Coogan's cruiser with their van between them and the Honda. "I'll go outside. When you see me near the car, hit the release on the remote."

The shift commander walked outside and stepped behind the car. He nodded and Coogan pressed the button. The trunk lifted a few inches and Webster looked inside. For a second, Coogan thought his shift commander had found something. Then he closed the trunk and shook his head toward the house. Coogan dropped the keys back in the bowl and walked outside.

●   ●   ●

The sun was lower in the sky by the time reinforcements arrived in response to Coogan's request for help. Two Humboldt County sheriff's deputies, a few Hogan firefighters, and a pair of patrolman from nearby Berry Creek were in the woods behind the house, beating the bushes. Their vehicles were lined up on the road in front of the house, like a parade had come to a halt. Webster and Lewis were directing the search while Coogan watched the front of house and the road.

Coogan worried about the light. It was a little past seven now and he'd called Brenda to tell her that he was going to be late tonight. The sun was low but still visible where he could see sky. However, under the canopy of trees, dusk was settling in. Several flashlight beams were already bouncing around further back in the woods.

"Excuse me, officer . . . ?" Quinn said.

He turned toward her. "It's Coogan, ma'am."

"Right, I'm sorry." She swallowed hard and he could see her fighting for control. "I'm going to take my mom home. She's exhausted. I'll come back after."

He scratched at a mosquito bite on his ear. The whole place was lousy with them. "You really don't have to do that. There's nothing you can do here. We'll call you when we find something."

She nodded and he saw that her eyes were swollen from crying. "I appreciate that but I'd feel better if I was here, helping."

"Mrs. Getty, it's going to be dark soon and we don't even know for sure your sister is out there," he said, pointing at the darkening woods. "You've had a long day. Maybe you should get some rest yourself."

She looked back toward the woods. "You have a lot of people looking back there for not being sure."

He nodded. "It's just a precaution. Is there anyone I can call for you? Your husband maybe?"

She shook her head. "Roger is watching the kids. I talked to him earlier and told him to stay with them. They don't need to be out here."

Coogan didn't know what else to say so he walked her to the driver's side of the van. He held up his notebook. "I have your contact information. I promise we'll call as soon as we know anything."

She dabbed at her eyes with a tissue. "Thank you."

He opened the door for her and saw that her mom was already buckled in the passenger seat, her head lolling against the window with her eyes closed. Quinn climbed inside and started the van. He waved as she backed out onto the road and pulled away.

●　　●　　●

". . . and I didn't call her with good news that night," Coogan said. He had a faraway look in his eye, so Tim sat patiently. After a moment the detective leaned forward. "Not that night or any other night. My news to Quinn Getty is always bad. Is that what you wanted to hear?"

"The story? Yeah," Tim said. He looked down at the notes he had taken, scribbling furiously as Coogan laid out the story for him. "You suspected a kidnapping before you even called for your supervisor, didn't you?"

Coogan looked at him with bleary eyes and shrugged. "All I knew at that point was that the circumstances fit a certain profile we're trained for. You have to understand, when you're at a scene like that, it could be so many things. Maybe she was out with a boyfriend. Maybe she'd gone for a walk to clear her head and gotten lost or injured. She could have been out with friends. We just didn't know. You have to run all those down, eliminate the obvious things before you jump to kidnapping. It isn't like the movies where we just know what's going on."

"I understand that. Is there anything else you'd like to tell me?"

"Not really." He leaned back and rubbed his red eyes. "There was a time when we had more leads than we knew what to do with. Nothing that mattered, though. We never got anything that led us to her." He looked at his cell phone. "I have stuff to do, so you need to clear out."

They stood and Tim spoke, offering up the words almost without thinking about it. "There's a theory being floated around that Kelly Dolan is a victim of a serial killer. Is that an avenue your investigation has looked into?"

Coogan stopped tucking his shirt in and looked at Tim. He thought the cop was gearing up to take his head off for asking such a question but instead he grinned.

"Oh man, you've been talking to Paulie Carmichael. Christ, Abernathy, go peddle that shit in some online forum, okay? I've got no time for the tinfoil hat legion."

Tim felt a defensive response rise up, but he bit it back. He had to be objective. "Look, I'm not on board with everything she's saying. I just think that she's very persuasive in her beliefs and I thought I'd ask you about it."

The detective finished straightening his clothes and slipped on a brown sport coat. He looked halfway decent again. "What? That a goddamn boogey-man is haunting northeast Ohio? Some phantom that none of us have ever suspected? You've been watching too many movies. Get a grip on yourself."

"I take it you've spoken to Paulie?"

Coogan laughed and Tim felt the heat of embarrassment creep into his face. He only hoped he wasn't turning red.

"Yeah, I've spoken to her, more times than I'd like to admit. She can't stop jabbering about her nutty theory." He picked up a leather portfolio, the same one Tim had seen him carrying at crime scenes. They started walking toward the front of the building.

"Let me tell you something about Paulie," Coogan said. "She's failing her client by not finding Kelly, so she concocted this wild-ass idea about some guy going around killing women. It's bullshit. Don't get sucked into it or your career will start circling the drain, just like hers."

"You have to admit," Tim said, "her evidence paints quite a picture. There are a lot of open cases with similarities."

Coogan shrugged as he opened the outer door and they stepped into the sunshine. "Big deal. If I turned you loose with the unsolved files of a dozen police departments and told you to examine their open cases for similarities, you'd find patterns, too. Over a long enough time frame, like a decade for example, it's easy to cherry pick some cases and come up with a theory like a serial killer on the loose. There's a reason she's a PI and not a real cop."

"She's also convincing."

Coogan held his hands up. "If you say so. I think that just makes you sound gullible."

"So, this isn't something you're interested in investigating?" Tim said. "That's what you're saying?"

Coogan's eyes narrowed and his mood shifted. "No, I'm not, and let me tell you something, Abernathy. I've dealt with Kelly Dolan's case since the day she vanished. No one takes this more seriously than me. Not you, and certainly not some private investigator who is one step away from being the kind of freak who hosts a true crime podcast. I'll chase down any lead that can help me solve this case, but this ain't one of them."

Tim held his hands up. "Take it easy, I'm just asking. I wanted your opinion, that's all."

"Well, if this is the kind of journalism you're practicing, you're going to hurt a lot of people," Coogan said, pointing a finger at his chest. "If you start going to families and selling this serial killer bullshit, you're just going to tear open a lot of old wounds and waste the time of a lot of police officers. I've got enough to do without answering a hundred calls from concerned family members who think we've got some new course of investigation."

"I said, I understand," Tim said, more loudly than he meant to. Coogan stepped back and raised an eyebrow. Tim held his hands out. "I'm sorry, I didn't mean to shout. I just don't feel like getting lectured."

Coogan ran a hand through his hair and shook his head. "I don't have time for this." He walked toward his car and Tim watched him go, frustrated with himself.

12

Visiting the hospital always depressed Quinn Getty. The antiseptic smell of the chemicals used to keep the ward clean masked the undercurrent of odors patients produced as they went through withdrawal or long-term rehab. Every time she visited the Stoneside Substance Abuse Rehabilitation Center her heart dropped as soon as she caught of a whiff of the contradicting odors. It didn't seem to affect others as badly. Her husband, Roger, and their kids, Claire and Patrick, never seemed to notice it on the rare occasions they came to visit her mother. The long-term care ward was in the rear of the rehab center, away from the noise generated by those going through withdrawal.

This was one of Kathleen Dolan's bad days, Quinn noted as she sat in a low-backed chair near the window in her mother's room. The room was small, with a single bed. It had an odd decorative theme split between a hospital room and a motel room. The walls were institutional adobe tan. A few landscape prints of the type found in waiting rooms hung on the walls. Rather than giving the room the desired homelike feel, it conveyed the confusing atmosphere of a bed shoved into a Holiday Inn conference room. Quinn didn't know how anyone would ever feel comfortable here.

Kathleen lay in bed, eyes half open, staring at the ceiling. At least Quinn thought she was staring at the ceiling. This happened sometimes due to the alcoholic dementia she suffered from. Decades of abusing alcohol had left her in a state where she sometimes lay there unresponsive to outside stimuli. The hard days were when it happened for the entire time Quinn sat in the room with her. Other times Kathleen was quite lucid, if not wholly in the moment. Quinn reached out and placed a hand on her leg under the thin hospital blanket and gave it a gentle squeeze.

"Mom, how are you doing today?"

Kathleen continued to lie still. Quinn noted that the rhythm of her breathing didn't change with her touch. She slid the little chair closer to the bed and held her mother's hand in both of hers.

"Mom, I wanted to tell you about Claire. She's doing so well with her swim team. They finished the season with a trip to Columbus for state finals. Roger and I were so excited for her. She's sixteen and she's so beautiful and smart and just so capable. We couldn't be prouder."

The smile fell from her face when she noticed a string of drool slip from the corner of her mother's lower lip. She turned and pulled a tissue from the nightstand next to her mother's bed. Quinn wiped the spittle away and dropped the crumpled wad into the wastebasket. She ran a hand over her mother's hair. It was gray now that it wasn't dyed the brilliant red that she had been so proud of when Quinn was younger, the same shade she and Kelly had inherited.

She bent and kissed her mother's forehead. It was cool and dry. Quinn moved to the closet in the room and pulled down another starchy white blanket and laid it over her. The weather outside might have been humid and in the eighties but the hospital's air conditioning had an arctic feel.

Her phone beeped with a text and she pulled it from her purse. It was her fourteen-year-old, Patrick, asking what they were having for dinner and what time. She sighed. Sometimes it seemed like that boy could eat a side of beef and ask for seconds. The time stamp on the message was three twenty-four, which meant it was time to get home and check on the meatloaf simmering in the slow cooker. It was probably the smell of her mixture of beef and pork that was making Patrick hungry. She sent him a message back telling him to find a snack but to not ruin his appetite, as if such a thing were possible.

Her hand found her mother's and she squeezed again. "I'm leaving now, Mom. I have to get dinner ready for the kids and Roger will be home soon. You take it easy, okay? I'll be back the day after tomorrow."

Kathleen continued to stare at the ceiling through half-closed eyelids.

Quinn lifted her purse and slung it over one shoulder of her short-sleeved black blouse. With the heat the way it was, she enjoyed the light material of the top and wore it with a gray skirt that fell to her knees. She pulled her key fob from her purse and clicked the remote start.

A young orderly gave her a quick once-over and nodded at her with a small smile as Quinn made her way past the nurses' station to the parking lot exit. Once he was behind her, she let a smile of her own cross her face. It might be vain, but she appreciated the looks she still got from younger men at thirty-four. *Nice to see those hours at the gym are paying off,* she thought.

In the parking lot, Quinn opened the door to her black Lincoln MKX and stepped up behind the wheel. She pulled a pair of Tom Ford butterfly sunglasses from a case in the center console as the air conditioning succeeded in beating back the heat.

Roger was doing well at the engineering consulting firm he worked for near Cleveland. He would be leaving about four and getting home at about five fifteen. They could live closer to his job but her mom was in Stoneside near Warren, so they settled in her hometown of Berry Creek.

Twenty-five minutes later she was out of the city and cruising through the suburbs toward home. A wooden sign painted with an idyllic stream winding through a stand of trees beckoned to her from the entrance of the development her family called home, the Banks at Berry Creek. She followed a wide lane around an area of communal green space toward the back of the development and pulled the Lincoln into the two-car garage at the end of the driveway. The other side would hold Roger's Chevy Impala when he got home. The back of the garage was extended and held sports equipment for the kids: bicycles and bins full of soccer balls and basketballs.

The house was only a decade old and they were the first owners. It was just under three thousand square feet with five bedrooms and three bathrooms. The front of the house facing the road had a stone façade topped off with vinyl siding molded to look like clapboards. The vinyl wrapped all the way around the back and down to the lawn that was turning brown in the summer heat.

It had taken all of her persuasive abilities to make Roger understand that they couldn't live this well if they moved farther north. The same money that bought this house would have gotten them half as much in some Cleveland suburb. No, this was where she wanted to be, so this was where they were staying.

She was in the kitchen when her cell phone rang. The caller ID said "Abernathy." She slid the answer icon with her thumb and said hello.

A voice said, "Quinn Getty?"

"This is she."

"My name is Tim Abernathy. I'm a reporter for the *Hogan Weekly Shopper* and I'd like to speak with you about your sister, Kelly."

❀   ❀   ❀

At eleven o'clock the next day, Tim arrived at the coffee shop in Berry Creek that Quinn had specified on their call. Despite there being just a few miles between the two towns, Tim noticed quite a difference between them. He might be biased, but it seemed like Hogan had a worn charm and scars it wasn't afraid to show. Berry Creek, on the other hand, seemed busy erasing anything that showed the slightest bit of age.

Where Hogan had a crowded main street lined with small shops, Berry Creek had embraced modernism by expanding its retail sector to become the shopping center for the region. Wide avenues lined with layers of strip malls spread out from the center of town. The trendy shops all had newly constructed storefronts with tan paint and a mixture of glass and colored brick. Chain restaurants and niche shops sat side by side. To Tim's eye, the whole stretch looked like it could be picked up and dropped down anywhere in America.

There was no history here and there never would be as long as retail chains could swap out old storefronts for new like a fashionista changing outfits. Berry Creek seemed like the kind of place that ached to be trendy by looking to the West Coast two thousand miles away and back in time three years. They wanted to be hip and cutting edge, but only after others had blazed the trail and proven what was successful. Nostalgia here would be remembering when the dry cleaners used to be a Jamba Juice, and something else even before that. In Tim's estimation, Berry Creek didn't realize authenticity could only be earned, not copied.

All About the Beanz was a coffee shop sandwiched between a yoga studio and a big box craft store that was the anchor for this particular plaza. He walked through the door and scanned the tables and booths. A redhead sitting at a small table waved to him. Her hairstyle had changed in the intervening years, but Quinn still looked very much like she had in the news footage of Kelly's disappearance he had reviewed. Tim smiled and walked over.

She rose from her chair and he saw she was wearing black yoga pants and an oversized pink t-shirt with "Mom" spelled out in silver glittering letters. Her curly red hair was pulled back with a scrunchy and she had a light sheen of sweat on her neck. A pink athletic bag hung from the back of her chair. He shook her outstretched hand and she said, "Are you Tim? I'm Quinn Getty."

"I am. Thank you for meeting with me. I really appreciate it."

They sat down at the table and she held up a clear plastic cup swirling with coffee and small ice cubes. "Would you like to get something? They have great iced lattes here."

That sounded like a good idea, so he said, "Yeah, you know, I think I would. You don't mind?"

"No, not at all."

"Can I get you something to eat? Maybe a muffin?"

"No, I'm fine. I just came from a yoga session next door so I don't want anything too heavy."

He went to the counter and ordered. While he waited, he glanced back at Quinn and took the opportunity to observe her. She seemed relaxed, looking out the big glass wall toward the parking lot and the road beyond. One black-clad leg was crossed over the other and a white Nike on her foot bobbed up and down lightly. She had kind of a Jessica Chastain thing going on. The barista called his name and he picked up his drink.

When he sat down again, he pulled out a notebook and a pen. "I'll try not to take up too much of your time."

She smiled again. "No problem. Anything that brings attention to Kelly's case is very welcome. I spoke with Paulie Carmichael after you called me. She told me that the two of you talked about her theory, about the man she calls the Buckeye Woodsman."

"That's right," Tim said. "She can be very persuasive."

"Is your interest in Kelly's case due to what Paulie told you? That she believes what happened at that store is tied to Kelly's disappearance?"

"Not exactly," Tim said, and he saw the look on her face change to something more rigid. "My publisher isn't entirely convinced, but he thought it would be a good idea to touch on Kelly's story again because her disappearance occurred in Hogan. You know, shake the tree and see if anything comes loose."

A dejected look crossed her face. "It was just terrible about that girl and her mother. I wish they would just catch the sonofabitch. It's been almost ten years since he killed Kelly."

"I'm sorry if I've upset you," Tim said. "Is it safe to assume you believe Paulie's theory? I'd just like to know how to proceed here."

"It took some convincing, but like you said, Paulie is persuasive. Yes, I believe she's on to something. There's just too much evidence to believe otherwise."

"You mentioned Kelly being killed. Does that mean you believe your sister is dead? I only ask because she hasn't been found."

"It's very frustrating to live with something like this. The years go by and you think you're moving forward with your life but then you're right back there, stuck, waiting for something to happen. To answer your question, yes, I think Kelly is dead. I see no evidence to the contrary. After all, if she were alive, she would have gotten in touch with me somehow. Her body is just hidden very well. I do believe we'll find her someday, though. I firmly believe that."

Tim paused for a moment and let Quinn collect herself. "If this is too difficult, it's okay to ask me to stop."

She wiped a tear from her eye with a finger. "No, it's all right. What can I tell you about my sister?"

"What I'm looking for is some deep background on Kelly. I'd like to paint a portrait of her that's very personal. My editor and I think such a profile will remind our readers that she was a person before her disappearance, just like them."

"And not just a victim? You think that will help?"

"It's our hope that it will. Whether someone took Kelly or she vanished through other means, chances are good that someone knows something. We would like our article to draw that information out. It's possible that someone has dismissed some bit of information they have as being insignificant when in reality it may be a very important piece of the puzzle. If we succeed in raising the public's awareness, someone may come forward. If that leads to establishing a connection between Kelly and these other women who have been killed, that's a bonus."

Quinn took a sip of her coffee and seemed to be considering everything he said. "I've been down this path before, you know. Using media portrayals to make sure the public knew she was a real person and not just a missing person. There was a time when it seemed like all I did was interviews on TV. It didn't mean much."

Tim gave her half a smile. "I have a little experience with TV newsrooms and I can tell you that I'm sure they did a good job, but ultimately I think a written portrait may be more effective."

She cocked her head and raised an eyebrow. "Why?"

"When you did TV interviews, I'm guessing they were generally of two types: short ones out in the field or longer ones in the studio. Am I right?"

She nodded. "Is there a problem with that?"

"Each has their merits and drawbacks," Tim said. "The ones in the field let you use a background relevant to the topic, in this case Kelly's house. Did you do some from there?"

"I did."

"See, that helps viewers get a visual. Even if they don't know exactly where that was, it looks like someplace they are familiar with. The house, the woods, the road, all of it is familiar. The trouble is, they are thinking about that or talking about how they know just where it is while you are trying to tell them about your sister. Those types of interviews also generally last less than a minute. That's not enough time to say what you want about Kelly."

She nodded. "I've actually thought that, but that's why we did the studio interviews."

"Right, and those are better for what you want, but those are often done in the morning, right?"

"They were," she said.

"No offense to my broadcast journalism colleagues, but those segments are squeezed between weather on the fives and traffic reports because that's what people are really interested in at that time of the day. Viewers have the news on, but it's the background noise to their morning routine. They're busy getting the kids ready for school or getting themselves ready for work. For a story to interrupt that routine and get them to pay attention, it has to have flashy video. You sitting on a sofa with a morning anchor talking for a few minutes, at most, isn't going to do it."

Quinn sat back in her chair. "So, all my efforts have been for nothing?"

Tim shook his head. He wanted to be careful here, he realized. The last thing he needed was Quinn angry or feeling inadequate. "Not at all. I'm just trying to explain some of the limitations of broadcast news, chief of which is time. Newspapers don't have that problem."

"What do you have in mind?" Quinn said.

She was still interested, Tim noted. "A series of articles on Kelly, her disappearance, the investigation, and how it may tie into the attack at the Beer & Bait. I'd also like to focus on how her absence has affected the lives of the people who knew her, like her friends and family. I think we get it all out there in detail and readers can absorb it at their own pace. We can take the time to talk about Kelly in the way that you knew her, the things that only a sister or friends would know. The pace is slower and the articles are more in-depth. We'll be able to communicate your message more effectively."

Her eyes narrowed. "Tim, it sounds like you're trying to sell me on this. I may not know much about the media but I know you can write this story whether I want you to or not. You don't need my permission."

He smiled. "That's true and I didn't mean to come on like a salesman, but I think the articles will be more effective if you are on board. If we can show how much Kelly's family misses her we'll get readers to give us the time we want. Believe me, if we can rekindle interest in her story, I think we'll have a good shot at generating some leads."

Quinn took another sip of her coffee and tried to hide the fact that her eyes were welling up with tears. Then she gave up and dabbed at them with one of the brown napkins from the holder on the table. "I'm sorry."

Tim didn't know what to do. Comforting people always made him feel uneasy. "Hey, it's okay. Don't worry about it. I didn't mean to upset you."

She shook her head, which sent her red curls to bouncing, and gripped his hand. "It's not you. Someone did this to her and it's been hard not knowing who or why. Now I believe he's done it again. Another family has to go through what we're going through. It's not right."

Her proclamation echoed Paulie Carmichael's sentiment that the Buckeye Woodsman was responsible for Kelly's disappearance. He became self-consciously aware that he was still holding Quinn's hand and let it slip from his. "I'd like to move forward with a series of interviews, if that's all right with you."

She nodded and inhaled deeply, her eyes redder now than they had been before. "That would be fine. Is there an office where you would like to do this?"

"I'd like you to feel comfortable, so anywhere is fine with me. We could just come back here, if you'd like."

"I'd hate to make you drive all this way."

He chuckled. "Don't worry about it. The paper picks up my gas."

"Maybe my house, then?" she said. "That would let me keep an eye on the kids and get some stuff taken care of while we talk. How would that be?"

Tim thought about it for a moment and couldn't find a reason to say no. "That would be fine, but I'd hate to impose."

She reached for his hand again and grasped it tightly. "You're helping my family. When should we begin?"

"Tomorrow afternoon? Would that be okay? I have some work to take care of at the office in the morning."

She smiled. "Tomorrow at one." She let go of his hand. "Thank you for this."

13

The next day, Tim drove to Quinn's house. The neighborhood was much nicer than most of its working-class counterparts in Hogan. Instead of side streets with early twentieth-century houses packed so close to one another neighbors could hear each other's conversations on nights when they left their windows open, these homes were situated on grassy half-acre lots.

He smiled as he approached the entrance to her development and saw the sign. The houses here might start at a quarter-million dollars, but there was a similarity between the Banks at Berry Creek and the West Wind Mobile Home Park that didn't escape him. He imagined that instead of a mobile home park manager checking up on their tenants, the Banks had a homeowner's association keeping an eye on how high the grass grew.

The house was nice, the sort of place that he'd like for Amy someday. He could tell the siding was molded vinyl rather than real wood clapboards, and the stone façade appeared to be more of the same, but after living in a mobile home he didn't think she'd mind.

He pulled all the way up in the driveway to use the back door like Quinn had requested. He had eschewed jeans today, instead wearing a pair of dark mustard-colored chinos and a blue button-down shirt with a pair of brown leather Rockports. He felt like an interview in someone's home was a good opportunity to treat his profession a little more seriously.

The backyard was hidden behind a tall, pressure-treated cedar fence that had the corners of the pickets clipped off to give them a touch of style. He could hear splashing behind the fence so he assumed there was a pool behind it. A closed gate faced the driveway and he headed toward it.

He opened the gate and saw his guess had been right on the money. The backyard did indeed have a pool. It wasn't the aboveground circular type that was so common in Hogan, though. This was a large, in-the-ground kidney-shaped deal with a wide cement apron surrounding it. He also noticed there were three teenage girls splashing around in the water, two blondes in colorful bikinis and a redhead sporting a blue one-piece suit.

"The one in blue is my daughter, Claire," Quinn said from a metal table under a blue-and-white umbrella. Tim hadn't seen her there and he turned toward her awkwardly, afraid she'd assume he'd been checking out the girls.

She rose from the table and he saw she wore a white-and-red paisley sundress with her red hair down over her shoulders. He couldn't help but notice she cleaned up well.

"Good afternoon, Quinn," he said, and held out his hand. She shook it and invited him into the kitchen through a set of French doors, then gestured to a round white table surrounded by four chairs.

He took a seat and she went into the kitchen, returning a moment later with a pitcher of lemonade and glasses on a wooden tray. He rose to help her but she slipped past him and set the load down on the table.

"It looks like they're enjoying their summer vacation," Tim said. The table had a full view of the patio and the pool. He imagined you could throw an excellent party here if you wanted to.

Quinn sat down in the chair to his right and swiveled toward him, crossing her legs as she did so. "They are, but they're also doing a little training. Claire and her friends are on the swim team, so they practically live in the water. Were you a swimmer in high school? You have the right build for it."

Tim shook his head and felt a little heat rising in his face at the compliment. "Thanks, but no, sports weren't my thing. I was all academics."

Quinn continued looking outside. "Oh, she does well with her grades, too. If she keeps going the way she is there's a chance you might be looking at a girl who gets a full ride to OSU in Columbus. It all depends on her senior year. I'm sure you remember how much pressure you could be under."

"I do, and it only gets more intense when college begins." He got the feeling Quinn was the kind of mother who could chat about her kids all day if you let her. "You don't mind if we get started, do you?"

"Sure, that's fine," she said and put a glass of lemonade in front of him.

He lifted his bag and pulled out his digital recorder and a spiral-bound notebook. "I'm going to be taking notes for accuracy. Please don't mind the recorder. Just act like it's not here."

"Don't worry, this isn't my first interview. Where would you like to start?"

"I was thinking you could tell me a little bit about where you grew up and what that was like for you and Kelly."

The smile faded from her face and the look that replaced it was one he'd seen many times before, like in Amy's eyes when she spoke about her murdered brother, Boyd, or the parents she'd lost to a car accident. That look was loss.

"I guess our story begins here in Berry Creek," she said, "but not in a place as nice as the Banks. No, we started out across the tracks in a neighborhood on a dead-end street . . ."

●　　●　　●

Summer 2001

Quinn Dolan was pissed. There was no other way to describe how angry she was. As if she didn't have enough to do, like cleaning the house and getting dinner ready before her mom got home from work, now she had to hike out to the middle of goddamned nowhere to find her little sister. Kelly was supposed to be doing her half of the chores, which amounted to nothing more than running the vacuum cleaner and cleaning up her room, and she couldn't even do that. No, instead she had snuck out with her loser friends. Now Quinn had to drag her home.

Their neighborhood was on a street that dead-ended into some woods, and their yard backed up against a cornfield. Beyond the field lay undeveloped land thick with every kind of tree, bug, and critter that crawled, slithered, or flew in northeast Ohio. Quinn clipped the generic CD player she'd bought at Kmart to her cutoff jean shorts and pressed "Play" on No Doubt's *Tragic Kingdom* CD.

Her anger subsided a bit as the ska beats of "Spiderwebs" started up. She began to jog the dirt trail that ran along one edge of the cornfield. Listening to Gwen Stefani's voice always calmed her down because Gwen was the fucking bomb. She didn't take shit from anyone. Quinn had never actually met the singer, of course, but she got the impression that anyone trying to take advantage of her would find a chunky black-and-white sneaker lodged in their ass.

She had started running track last year and now she could keep a pretty good pace for longer distances than when she started. It used to take her fifteen minutes to walk to where Kelly and her friends hung out but now they fell into view as "Just a Girl" was ending, which meant she had shaved about four minutes off her time. The dirt path she ran curved around the long end of the cornfield and gave way to ankle-high grass. Her pace slowed to a walk and she pushed a few sweat-soaked strands of hair from her eyes as she started to cool down. Fifty yards from where she stood lay Paradise.

Personally, she thought it was a stupid name, but apparently that's what the area had always been known as. It was probably just kid lore handed down from generation to generation. For all she knew, some stoner in the seventies had called it that after getting laid there and the name had stuck. There wasn't anyone to ask in the neighborhood because no one's roots actually went back that far. The houses were all rentals where no one seemed to stay more than a few years before moving on.

As she drew closer, the main attraction of Paradise came into view. The grassy field dropped off into a steep ravine with a creek at the bottom. This was where kids from the surrounding neighborhoods came to party. Occasionally, kids with dirt bikes would make runs up and down the ravine, so deep ruts tracked up and down the steep walls.

The green fiberglass fence of a junkyard was visible through the trees on this side of the ravine. Over the decades, kids had salvaged all kinds of things from inside and dragged them to the edge of the tree line. A rusted burn barrel full of holes lay in the center of a circle made up of old truck bench seats, wooden crates, and a couple old kitchen chairs with ripped orange vinyl upholstery.

Quinn slipped her headphones down to her neck and looked at the group of kids crashing around the burn barrel. There were about a dozen of them and someone had a radio blaring Eminem into the thick trees.

She finally spotted her fourteen-year-old sister on the torn fabric of an old car seat making out with that asshole Barret Dedrick. Pissed, she stomped over and yanked on the ponytail sticking out of the back of his green and black BP baseball hat. A chorus of "Ooooohs" rose up from the kids assembled around the burn barrel.

He jumped up and said, "Hey, what the fuck?" Barret was only sixteen, but he was already a couple inches over six feet tall. His shoulders and arms bulged under a tight t-shirt emblazoned with the logo and phone number of his dad's garage. His muscles were a testament to the work he did for his daddy in that garage. His Levi's were worn thin enough that they looked comfortable and he had on hiking boots. It was the same outfit all the motorheads wore around here. If he expected Quinn to be intimidated by his size, though, he was sorely mistaken.

She took a step toward him. "What are you doing, Barret? That's my little sister."

He smiled and crossed thick arms over his broad chest. "So?"

"So, she just finished eighth grade, asshole. She's fourteen and you're too old to have your hands all over her."

He cocked an eyebrow up and looked at her, his gaze traveling over her sweat-soaked t-shirt and lingering on her cutoffs. She wasn't deterred, though, and stood her ground with her hands on her hips. After all, she wasn't doing anything wrong. Barret was the one pawing at her sister.

"What's the matter?" he said. "Jealous?"

She was flustered for a moment, caught off guard by the question. "Wait, what? Are you insane? Of course I'm not jealous. I just want you to stay away from her."

A smile creased his face, perfect white teeth set into deeply tanned skin. She considered him for a moment. It wasn't that Barret didn't have his charms, it was just that he didn't need to be plying them on her kid sister.

"Why don't you ask her what she wants," he said, jerking his head at Kelly. "After all, she started it."

Quinn looked down at her sister, sitting there in a cropped black-and-white halter top and stretchy black shorts with dirty sneakers curled under her, all of which Barret seemed to find attractive.

"Quinn, why don't you just go home?" Kelly said with an exasperated tone. "We're just hanging out and you're a major buzzkill."

A wave of anger welled up inside her and dragged her down in a sea of resentment. Like she was the problem here, instead of the one trying to get things done. Without thinking about it, she reached out and grabbed Kelly by one thin wrist and yanked her off the car seat.

"You're coming home with me," she said. "There are chores to do before Mom gets home and I'm not doing all of them."

Kelly twisted her arm around until she found Quinn's thumb and she pulled hard against it, breaking her grip. "Who cares? Mom will be out drinking until midnight and when she does get home, she'll be so in the bag she won't notice a sink full of dishes."

Undeterred, Quinn reached out again and grabbed her younger sister by the upper arm, getting a better grip this time. "I'm in charge and you're coming home with me."

The younger girl's eyes flicked to Barret, who stood there watching with an impassive look on his face. She turned back to Quinn.

"I'm not going anywhere," she said and pushed at her sister.

"Cat fight!" someone in the group hollered.

"Knock it off, you guys," another girl said. She disentangled herself from the lap of the boy she was sitting with and stood up. The girl was about the same age as Kelly, with dark brown curly hair and skin tanned darker than Barret's. "You're making a fucking scene."

She stepped between the sisters and faced Kelly. "Come on, I'll walk back with you guys. I have stuff to get done before my mom gets home, too."

Kelly nodded and looked at Quinn as she spoke. "All right, Vanessa. I mean, since you asked."

"Bye, Kelly," Barret said. "Looking forward to seeing you again."

Quinn spun to say something but Kelly was quicker. "Nice to see you, too. Meet me here again tomorrow."

Quinn gave her a shove down the path. "You are not coming back here to meet up with him."

"I've already got one mom, Quinn, and you're not her. I'll do whatever I want and you can't stop me."

"Fine," Quinn said. "We'll see what Mom has to say about it."

"She ain't gonna say shit," Vanessa said. "You know that, Quinn."

"This doesn't concern you."

"She's right, though," Kelly said. "You know it, too. Why do you insist on living like our life is normal? Dad's gone and I don't think Mom remembers we're around unless we're standing right in front of her."

"That's not true."

"The hell it isn't," Kelly said. "You're marching me home to clean up the house and she's the one who messes it up."

"Again, not true."

"Oh sure, those are my wine bottles under the couch and I'm the one who puked on the living room rug."

Quinn shot her a look. "You don't need to say all that in front of your friend."

Vanessa's eyebrows dipped quizzically. "Do you really think people don't know your mom is a drunk? Everybody who lives on this street knows it."

"No, they don't," Quinn said. "That's bullshit."

"Are you serious?" Vanessa said. "She crashed her car into a telephone pole."

Quinn's eyes darted away from the others. "That happened because it was icy, not because she was drunk."

"It happened in April."

"My sister is delusional," Kelly said. "She wants to project this image that we live a perfectly normal life like all those TV shows she watches. All she wants is to be the Cosbys or some shit. The last thing she wants to do is admit that we're all fucked up."

Quinn felt heat flush up into her face. "That's not true. You're the one who makes it all so hard. It's you who barely passed school last year and it's you who's out here slutting it up with Barret Dedrick. You couldn't cut it as a Cosby kid."

"Oh my God," Kelly said, exasperation creeping into her voice. "I was just making out with him a little. I didn't fuck him."

"Yet."

"He's right. You are so jealous."

"Of what? Him? You think I couldn't get some loser like Barret if I wanted? Please."

Kelly traded a look with Vanessa before turning to her sister again. "You totally want him."

"I don't. Barb Regan dated him and said he was an asshole. Everything always has to be his way and he can't keep his hands to himself. He was too pushy."

Kelly was quiet for a moment and tilted her head. "Well, what's wrong with that? It would be nice to be with a guy who knows what he wants."

"You have daddy issues," Vanessa said. "Barret is fine, no doubt, but he's too bossy. You can tell he wants everything to be his way."

Kelly pushed her playfully. "Shut up. I don't have daddy issues."

"Whatever you say, girl."

They were back on their street now and Vanessa peeled off for her house. "Call me later when you get your chores done."

"Yeah," Kelly said.

They walked into their house and Quinn pointed at the kitchen. "We can knock this out quick, okay? I'll do the dishes and you straighten up the living room."

"Whatever."

Quinn paused by the entrance to the kitchen. "I don't like that we fight all the time. You're right. We don't have the perfect life."

"Then stop pretending we do," Kelly said.

Quinn nodded and stepped into the kitchen. Then she turned. "I'm right about Barret, though. That guy is bad news. You should stay away from him."

Kelly rolled her eyes. "Are you serious? Did you see the arms on that guy? I'm just having some fun with him."

"He may not know it's just fun."

Kelly tossed a throw pillow at her from the couch. "You worry too much."

⬤   ⬤   ⬤

". . . and that was our relationship then," Quinn said, her voice soft with nostalgia. "Fighting about boys one minute and making up the next. Do you have any brothers or sisters?"

"None that I grew up with, exactly. My situation is complicated."

Quinn laughed. "Too bad. You'll never fight with or love someone as much as your siblings."

"Did Kelly end up dating Barret?"

The light fell away from Quinn's face and she licked her lips. "Not so much that summer. He was two years older and someone else caught his eye. Something about him stuck with her, though. A couple years later, when Barret and I graduated, she turned sixteen. My mom's behavior was even worse and I was making plans to go to college. With no eyes on her, Kelly went after him like a lovesick puppy, following him around, showing up at all the places he'd be. By late July they were going together pretty hot and heavy."

"It sounds like you didn't approve."

"Well, he turned out to be the asshole I always thought he was but you couldn't talk to Kelly about it. She turned a blind eye to everything he did." Quinn drained the lemonade from her glass and poured another glass, then topped up Tim's.

"By the end of that summer I had other problems to worry about."

"Starting college? That can be a crazy time."

Quinn threw him a sneaky little smile and nodded toward the pool, eyeing her daughter. "That was the summer Roger got me pregnant with Claire."

Tim chuckled. "I could see why that would be distracting."

"That's putting it mildly," Quinn said and then she sighed. "Being eighteen and pregnant, with an alcoholic mom and a younger sister, I found out there's only so much you can do. We worked with Roger's parents and decided he would go to school and I would take care of the baby."

"That must have been difficult."

She gave him a little shrug. "It really was the best thing. He turned out to be one of the good ones. It wasn't easy, but he studied hard and graduated with his engineering degree. Things have been good ever since. A girl in my position could have ended up in worse places than this."

Tim thought about women he'd known in similar circumstances and silently agreed with her. The trailer park he lived in had quite a few single moms and young families struggling to get by.

"Kelly wasn't wrong about my mom," Quinn said. "She drank a lot. And when I say that, I mean she drank more than any three people you know. You can't do that and be a good mother. Things slip by no matter how hard the people around you try to pick up the slack. I did my best to keep Kelly on the right path but once I got pregnant, I'm ashamed to say Kelly kind of fell through the cracks. Roger and I had been dating for about a year when we got sloppy."

"That happens," Tim said.

"It does, but . . . look, I don't want this in the story, okay? This part right here? It's just so you know the background of what was going on at that time. I don't want my daughter to think she was a mistake or that I gave up anything."

Quinn twisted a napkin in her hands, winding the linen one way and then the other. "Anyway, I love my daughter, but I had plans. I was going to go to school, be a teacher and have a career. I wanted kids but I always thought I'd do it on my own time and then, suddenly, I was pregnant."

Her attention drifted back to the pool and Tim followed her gaze. The girls had gotten out of the pool and were lying on chaise lounges, bronze bodies soaking up the sun. Tim smiled. Back in high school these were the girls who would have captured his attention even as he was too shy and embarrassed to speak with them. Now, they seemed too young to even be worth a second glance.

"They have their whole lives ahead of them," Quinn said. "They have no idea how beautiful they really are and how much potential lies within them. They just need someone to watch out for them, to steer them in the right direction. All they need is for someone to pick them up when they fall."

He looked back to Quinn, aware that she was projecting her life onto her daughter and her friends. "You didn't have that, did you?"

"Not really. By then my mom was pretty well living the pickled life. Her job prospects were pretty much zip because she couldn't hold it together enough to clock in on time or work straight when she was there. It was just tough, and when I found out I was pregnant, well, I had some choices to make. I'd seen what a terrible mother was like and I definitely didn't want that for my child, so I made up my mind to be the best I could be. It really wasn't that hard to decide to help put Roger through school and become a stay at home mom."

As fascinating as this was, Tim really wanted to hear more about Kelly. One thing he'd learned was that people loved talking about themselves once they got rolling. Keeping them on track could be like riding a bull. "So, what can you tell me about Kelly's relationship with Barret? It sounds like it wasn't working out the way you'd like."

She shook her head, like she was trying to drive away the memories. "He wasn't someone I wanted to see her with."

"Did he hit her?"

Quinn cocked an eyebrow and looked at him. "No, it was nothing like that. Did you hear that from someone?"

"Then what was it?" Tim said, ignoring her question. "It seems like you weren't crazy about the two of them being together."

"Look, I don't want to sound like a bitch, but I'm going to tell you the truth. Barret is going to live in Berry Creek his whole life because this is where he feels safest. He's the kind of guy who would never take Kelly to a nice restaurant in a suit. His idea of dressing up means putting on his nicest Cabela's hoodie with his best jeans. I mean, if you live here because you want to, that's fine. There's nothing wrong with that. Roger and I stay because I have to take care of my mom, but we could live near Cleveland if we wanted to. We'd be closer to his work and I would certainly like to live in one of the suburbs up there.

"Barret, though, is a different story. He worked in his daddy's shop when he was a kid and he made up his mind a long time ago that was going to be his career. There was never a time when he seriously considered going to college or joining the army. Exploring was stuff other people did. Going to technical school to learn about cars was as exciting as his life got."

Tim smiled, and deep inside he knew her description of Barret could fit him as well. He'd never had a desire to live in a city. He'd visited a few and they weren't for him. Cities had too many people, which just made it hard to go anywhere and resulted in too much noise. He liked driving anywhere he wanted to without sitting in traffic and sitting on his patio at night with nothing to hear except the crickets.

"I know people like that," he said. "Sometimes they're just happier in a small town."

"Well, I wanted more for Kelly. I didn't want any restraints on her. Barret could become a center of gravity in her life, trapping her here in his orbit. She had too much going for her to settle for some guy who peaked at eighteen."

"Were they still together when she disappeared?"

Quinn glanced outside again and shook her head. "No, they were over by then. They had been broken up for a few years."

"Was he a suspect in her disappearance?"

Quinn took a deep breath. "He was, but you need to understand something about him and the police. It was easy for them to narrow in on him as a suspect because he was known to them."

Tim gave her a puzzled look. "What do you mean?"

"He'd been picked up a few times, the most serious of which was for a DUI. I think there may have also been an assault because of some trouble out at his daddy's garage. The thing is, the cops around here aren't very good. Once they knew Barret and Kelly had a relationship, they focused on him to the exclusion of everyone else."

"You think they made a mistake?" Tim said as he sipped his lemonade.

"Hell yes they made a mistake," she said. "They've never arrested anyone for her disappearance or found her body. Their incompetence is why I still don't know where my sister is or what happened to her. All they did was hound poor Barret until his attorney threatened to file suit against them."

"You sound somewhat sympathetic to him. Is that how you feel?"

She pursed her lips, taking a moment before answering. When she finally did, Tim could tell she was growing angry thinking about the situation.

"It's not that I have sympathy for Barret as much as I detest the time police wasted badgering him when they should have been looking elsewhere. They've let years go by without generating a single usable lead."

Tim scribbled notes and looked up at her. "Is that why you hired Paulie Carmichael?"

She nodded. "I needed to feel like I was doing everything possible to discover what happened to Kelly. So, I asked around, and Paulie had a good reputation."

"Do you agree with her serial killer theory?"

Quinn looked up at him, her green eyes meeting his. "I do. Paulie makes a compelling case for Kelly being one of his victims."

"The police don't agree with her. They think it's a conspiracy theory. Does that bother you?"

Quinn smiled. "No, it doesn't. They haven't been able to solve the case, so they're threatened by her. She's more of a professional than any of them. Do you believe her?"

Tim hesitated, mindful of Charlie's advice about getting anyone's hopes up. "I'm intrigued enough to ask some questions about it. My focus today is Kelly."

Quinn reached out and gripped one of his hands. "I believe Kelly was killed by the Buckeye Woodsman, not Barret or some drifter or any of the other ridiculous theories that have been floated by the police. She's the victim of a serial killer and no one but Paulie Carmichael is looking for him. She could use some help."

Tim looked into Quinn's eyes and drew his hand back. "I'll see where my story takes me. That's the best I can do.

Quinn's mood seemed to change, as if his assurance to follow the story where it led wasn't enough. "My sister wasn't perfect, especially where Barret was concerned, but I know that during the time they spent together, they were convinced they were in love. I really don't think he had anything to do with her disappearance."

"I understand."

"I'm telling you that because the last thing I need is for people to assume he's guilty and getting away with it. We've wasted enough years going down that path."

Her cell phone chimed and she glanced at it, reading a text message. "I'm sorry, but we're going to have to cut this short. My husband needs me to run an errand. Can we schedule another time?"

Tim thought she was making an excuse but played along. "Of course. I'm tied up tomorrow, but how about the day after?"

She stood up and nodded. "That's fine. I'll see you here. Is the same time good for you?"

"Absolutely. I'll see you then. Oh, one more thing."

"Yes?"

"I would also like to talk to some of Kelly's friends to get as complete a picture of her life as possible. Can you think of anyone I should talk to? Maybe the girl you mentioned?"

Quinn looked at him for a second, as if she were caught off guard. Then she grinned. "Of course. Kelly didn't have many friends, but she was close with a neighbor named Vanessa Lipton. I think she still lives in Berry Creek, but I don't have her number."

Tim scribbled the name in his notes. "That's okay. I'm sure I'll be able to find her."

They stood up from the table and Quinn's cell phone rang. She turned to take the call and he glanced out at the pool. Claire's friends were heading through the gate, dressed in shorts and t-shirts. She walked in through the French doors with a towel wrapped around her waist.

"Hi," she said, glancing at her mom. "Who are you?"

Tim introduced himself. "I'm writing a story on your Aunt Kelly."

Claire glanced at Quinn, who had retreated into the kitchen and was taking the call with her back to them.

"Do you remember your aunt? You must have been young when she disappeared."

Claire's eyes flicked to her mother again. "Do you have a card?"

Tim nodded and fished one out for her. She took it and slipped it into the towel where it was knotted at her waist. "It was nice to meet you," she said, and walked out of the kitchen.

Tim turned back to Quinn, who was finishing her call. She had her arms crossed over her chest and was staring at him.

"I'd rather you only spoke to me," she said. "It's not that I don't trust you, I just want to minimize her exposure to this business with Kelly. It's frustrating enough for me to deal with. Claire and her brother shouldn't have to worry about it."

"No problem," Tim said as he moved toward the door. "Thanks for your time. I'll be in touch."

She shook his hand. "You're quite welcome. I hope this turns something up."

He nodded and walked back to his car, thinking about Claire. That interaction had been strange. Maybe she had more to say?

14

It took Tim almost no time to find Vanessa Lipton and give her a call. The woman had been happy to talk about Kelly, almost eager in fact, and had invited him right over. She still lived in the same neighborhood where she and Kelly grew up.

He pulled into the blacktop driveway of her house and parked. It was a nice ranch with pale yellow aluminum siding that dated it, but it was also neatly kept, especially compared to the rest of the neighborhood. The other houses looked worn and in need of maintenance. He recalled what Quinn had said about most of them being rentals and thought the landlords could be doing a better job of keeping up on their properties.

He closed the door of his Jeep, walked up the driveway to the front porch, and was met by a stern-looking little girl who appeared to be about six years old. She looked up at him with a yellow piece of sidewalk chalk in her hand and various other colors of chalk scattered around her. Drawings of Sponge-Bob and Bikini Bottom buildings covered the painted wood of the porch.

"Are you a stranger?" she said.

Tim smiled and looked down at her. "Since we don't know each other, I suppose I am. Is your mom home?"

The little girl shrugged and went back to drawing on the porch. A voice came from inside the house.

"Deanna, who are you talking to?"

The little girl paused and hollered back. "A stranger."

There were a few seconds of silence and then rapid footsteps approached the door. "What did you say?"

The white aluminum storm door creaked open and a woman stepped onto the porch. She had dark, curly hair and was a little on the thick side, wearing mom jeans and an oversized black-and-gold Steelers jersey that looked like it might have been borrowed from her husband. She looked at the little girl first and then at Tim. He raised a hand in greeting.

"Hi, I'm Tim Abernathy. If you're Vanessa, I think you're expecting me."

She smiled and waved him up. "Vanessa Lipton, like the tea but without all the money. Sorry about Deanna. We're learning all about stranger danger."

He mounted the steps, walked around Deanna's drawings, and followed Vanessa into a small living room. "Well, you're doing a good job. She stopped talking to me as soon as she knew I was a stranger."

Vanessa pointed to an armchair and he sat down. She took a seat on the couch nearest him. "On the phone, you mentioned you were doing a story about Kelly. Is that right?"

"I am," Tim said.

"That's good," she said. "It's been so many years since she was killed and they still haven't caught whoever did it." She looked down at her hands. "Sometimes I'm afraid that no one besides me and Quinn remember her or care."

"Then you assume she's dead? I only ask because officially she's a missing person."

She gave him a questioning look, the same one he saw when people realized they were talking to a reporter and not just some guy who was there to shoot the breeze. He saw it whenever they realized the things they said to him could wind up printed in a paper or online for their neighbors to see. It was the look of the guarded.

"Yes," she said. "I assume Kelly's dead. She didn't have any reason to run off and hide or some dumb shit like that. It ain't like she had a suitcase full of money squirreled away to finance a new life." She looked down for a second, considering, then her eyes rose to stare at him. "The cops can call her a missing person if they want. It just means they haven't found her body."

Her voice was devoid of hope and Vanessa clearly wasn't waiting for some miracle, that Kelly would be found somewhere living a happy life. She seemed to be a realist.

He paused, anxious to speak about Kelly. He needed comments and anecdotes about her for the profile Charlie wanted and aside from Quinn Getty, Vanessa appeared to be Kelly's only friend.

"For the story I'm working on, I'd like to know more about Kelly's background."

"You've come to the right place, that's for sure. What are you looking for exactly?"

"The kinds of things that friends know. It's been my experience that our families, no matter how close, don't always know us quite as well as our friends. Those are the people we choose to confide in."

Vanessa considered that for a moment. "I think I know what you mean. Well, we grew up right here in this neighborhood."

"Quinn mentioned that."

Vanessa sighed at the mention of Kelly's sister. Tim gave her a puzzled look. "What's that all about?"

"Look, I feel for her. She hasn't had an easy life and her mom is in bad shape up there at the rehab hospital. You'd have to be heartless not to pity her, but she makes it damn hard."

"What do you mean?"

"She's given interviews playing up how terrible it was for Kelly to grow up here but it wasn't all that bad. Not really. I mean, sure, her mom drank and they were alone but Kelly kept her shit together for the most part. She didn't turn into a meth head or anything. That girl did better than I did and both my parents were in my house growing up."

Tim studied her and saw that she clearly believed what she said. The tale of woe Paulie spun and what he'd learned from Quinn didn't seem to jibe with Vanessa's recollection.

"I've been given to understand Quinn pretty much raised Kelly because their mom was incapacitated. Is that correct?"

"I guess so," Vanessa allowed. "Quinn was a cast-iron bitch back then, always telling Kelly what to do, checking up on her boyfriends, making sure she wasn't having too good of a time."

"Isn't that what you'd expect from an older sister?"

Vanessa shook her head and laughed. "Hell no, man. Come on, what sixteen-year-old is that serious all the time? Quinn went from being a kid to an adult with nothing in the middle." She raised her hand from low to high as she spoke. "She was a huge pain in the ass. Every time Kelly and I were on the verge of having fun, Quinn would show up and spoil it."

Tim grinned. "Yeah? Like how?"

"We were down in my basement with some friends when we were about fifteen, just partying a little bit because my parents were out and sure enough, old Quinn comes stomping down the steps yelling for Kelly to get home. That poor girl had one mom not worth a damn and another that wouldn't leave her alone."

"I heard some stories about a place called Paradise. Can you tell me about that?"

She threw her head back and let loose with a laugh that verged on squealing. "Oh, man, I haven't thought of Paradise in almost forever. That was where we'd go to party when the parents were around. I mean, it was nothing serious, just a place to be by ourselves where we could listen to music without being told to turn it down and maybe drink some beers if someone could sneak them from their folks."

Tim made a show of looking at his notebook. "I heard that's where Kelly would meet up with a guy named Barret. Was he in your group?"

This time there wasn't any laughter in Vanessa's response and her face sobered up. "Oh, yeah, that guy. He was definitely around. Whoever told you about him, they told you he's kind of a dick, right?"

Tim decided to play a hunch. "Was he abusive toward Kelly?"

Vanessa snorted. "He's an asshole to everyone, and he's been known to hit all kinds of people, not just the women in his life."

"What do you mean?"

She sighed. "I'm not in touch with him anymore, but Berry Creek is a small town so I hear things. Anyway, he's had the cops called on him a few times for fighting in bars and out at the garage he owns. I've also heard he's hit a few girlfriends. The man may be in his thirties but he still thinks he's a teenager."

Tim nodded and made a note to look up any criminal history on Barret. It was weird, though. Quinn had made similar comments about him being one of the teenage forty-year-olds the area had an ample supply of, but she'd emphatically stated he never hit Kelly. "Is there anything else you can tell me about him?"

"He's a controlling sonofabitch."

"Yeah?"

She leaned forward on the sofa, seemingly eager to dish a little dirt. "When they dated, he had all these stupid rules Kelly had to follow and she just went along with them. At first, I was kind of jealous, if you can believe that."

"Why?"

"He had a lot going on, especially if you were a girl who didn't have much. He was tall and built, really strong from working in his dad's garage and salvage yard. If I'm honest, he looked good; handsome, I mean, and he had that whole bad boy thing going on. He always had loud cars and motorcycles. That kind of stuff."

"Did Kelly like that about him?"

She gave him a sly grin. "All the girls liked that, but yeah, Kelly definitely did. He'd put her on the back of his bike and they'd go tearing around the woods. I think he made her feel safe, like as long as she was with him, nothing could hurt her. Nothing except him."

"Do you have any idea why he was like that?"

Her lips pursed as she considered the question. After a moment she shook her head. "For everything he had going on, he also seemed insecure. You could see it, especially when he would get jealous of anyone Kelly paid attention to, men or women." She paused for a moment, and her eyebrows knitted together as she considered the past. "He would get this look on his face, like he was struggling with the way he was acting, and you could tell his better angels didn't win many of those battles. He would just get dark. People said his father was mean, but I didn't know anyone else in his family. Maybe that was it. After all, you carry your parents' baggage more than you think.

"If he and Kelly weren't together, he wanted to know who she was with and why. He'd get into fights with guys who talked to her if they flirted and, really, at that age, what guy doesn't flirt with every girl he's around? Barret, though, he couldn't handle it. I can't tell you how many guys he threatened to beat up or actually did swing on."

"Sounds charming."

"Mmmm . . . he could be," she said, smiling a little. "That's why Kelly stayed with him. I think she got good at figuring out what his triggers were. She could steer him out of situations that might set him off.

"When they were together and he wasn't being a prick, he made her laugh, and that's something she needed. Between her mom and sister, Kelly wasn't having a good time at home, so here comes this handsome guy and he pays attention to her, and he had money from working in his dad's shop so he could take her out and show her how special he thought she was. We were all too stupid to understand what was going on."

"Like what?" Tim asked.

"Kelly was never a big girl but Barret would give her these backhanded compliments about her weight that made her self-conscious as hell. By the time she finally broke up with him she was a size two. I don't know if you know what that is, but it's ridiculous. I hadn't noticed her decline because by that time she wasn't allowed to hang out with me."

She paused for a moment, taking a deep breath before she went on. Her voice sped up, as if she had to get it all out before some part of her hit the stop button. "I should have been a better friend but I didn't understand what was happening. I'd never had a boyfriend, not a real one, so I just thought it was normal for her to spend less time with me because she was with him."

Tim nodded and felt sorry for the woman. Clearly, she was still feeling some guilt even after all this time. "That doesn't sound like it was your fault."

She shrugged and silence filled the living room. Tim started to fear their time was up but Vanessa surprised him.

"Would you like to see it? Paradise, I mean?"

"Sure."

"What are you driving?"

"A Jeep."

"Perfect, because I don't feel like hiking all the way back there." Vanessa stood up and walked to the hallway. "Margaret, watch your sister for a little while, okay? I'm going to run an errand."

A teenage voice grunted agreement from the back of the house.

Tim stood. "If it's a bother, don't worry."

She blew him off and slipped on a pair of sneakers. "Don't worry about it. I need a break from mom duty for a little while and she babysits all the neighborhood kids."

They walked out the front door and Vanessa told her youngest to listen to her older sister, then they got in his Wrangler. She pointed up the road and said, "Go that way."

As they drove, she pointed to a house across the street and about three houses up from hers. "That's where Kelly and Quinn used to live."

Tim slowed to a stop and took it in. The house was a little two-story Cape Cod with dented white aluminum siding. A garage with a crooked door sat at the end of a blacktop driveway. The yard needed to be cut and the bushes in front of the living room windows needed a trim.

"There's an older lady living there now," Vanessa said. "Her son comes over twice a month to do the yard work."

Tim nodded and kept driving. About two hundred yards up, the road veered to the right and led out to the larger two-lane blacktop he had driven on to find the neighborhood, but Vanessa pointed left toward a dirt trail. A wooden gate with peeling white paint hung across the entrance. She jumped from the Jeep, swung the gate wide, and got back in.

"Nobody cares if we go back here," she said.

"Then why is there a gate?"

She shrugged. "Maybe they just want to keep people away from the corn-field, but we're going past that." Her head bobbed toward the trail. "Let's go."

Tim slipped the Wrangler into four-wheel drive and followed the twin ruts worked into the dirt by years of tractor tires. She told him to turn left at the edge of the cornfield and he did. After a few minutes the field gave out and they passed a pond, and then he drove up into some knee-high grass and parked.

Vanessa swung down to the ground and looked around. "Jeez, nothing's changed."

Tim saw a rusty burn barrel like the one Quinn had described and the circle of makeshift furniture surrounding it. Vanessa walked over to it and pointed at a sofa parked beneath a tree.

"That couch is new," she said. "How the hell did someone drag that all the way back here?"

"Probably in the back of a pickup truck," Tim said. He looked around at the trees and took in the seclusion of the area. "This is where you all used to hang out, huh?"

Vanessa nodded and smiled. "Yeah, this was the place to be. No parents, just us, music, and a cooler. Back then it was all we needed to be happy."

Tim pulled his cell phone and snapped a few pictures. He had a single bar on his connection.

"I'm surprised kids still come back here," he said. "The cell service sucks."

Her fingers traced the back of an old truck bench seat. "The kids aren't out here for Twitter. They're out here to be alone with each other, without parents knocking on doors or walking in on them while they're sucking face."

"Quinn told me she found Kelly and Barret out here doing just that."

A small laugh escaped Vanessa. "Yeah, but everyone was out here messing around, not just them. I kissed a couple of toads sitting out here around this barrel." Silence lingered for a moment and then she said, "Kissed them and more. Once the sun went down you couldn't see much. I imagine not much has changed."

Tim cast a glance over at the ravine. "That's the main attraction?"

Vanessa walked toward the edge of the drop-off. "Yeah, we would climb down there and up the other side."

Tim peeked over the side. It was just packed earth at a steep angle that dropped about twenty-five feet to a flowing creek full of crystal clear water. He pointed toward it. "You climbed down there?"

She laughed and then sighed. "Oh yeah, back in the day we'd do it without even thinking about how dangerous it was. I wouldn't do it now, of course, but back then I could scramble right down with nothing more than a pair of Skechers on my feet."

He pointed to a worn trail full of narrow tire tracks leading down one side, through the creek, and up the other side. "Looks like they still ride dirt bikes back here."

Her eyes lit up. "That's never going to go out of style with the kids around here. I used to date this guy named Jeff and he would scare the hell out of me. I'd climb on the back of this Yamaha his parents bought him and we'd go all through these woods. They're full of trails so we'd just ride all around. Every once in a while, he'd just take us right over the edge and I'd scream my damn head off. Kelly said she could hear me over the sound of the bike." She looked down and pointed. "It was bad enough going down, scarier than any roller coaster at Cedar Point, but then you'd feel the creek water on your ankles and hear the motor rev as he attacked the other side. Then? Oh, holy shit, my heart felt like it was beating out of my chest when he'd gun that motor. There would be this point where it felt like gravity was going to win and dump us backwards into the creek, then we'd shoot over the top. Goddamn, I haven't felt a rush like that in years."

Tim noticed she was breathing hard just thinking about it. "Did Barret and Kelly do stuff like that?"

She nodded. "Oh yeah. Barret wasn't going to let anyone do anything better than him if he could help it. If I'm remembering correctly, he had a Honda he'd rebuilt and the two of them would race all over around here."

Tim glanced over the edge again. "That's a pretty good drop if you don't make it. That ever happen? Anyone ever get hurt?"

Vanessa shrugged. "Maybe other people, but not me. The only bad thing that happened after going up the other side was disappointing sex with Jeff back in those trees."

Tim laughed. "Sorry, didn't mean to bring up bad memories."

She grinned and waved him off. "It wasn't your fault. I just hope he got better over the years, but I guess he'd have to. He certainly couldn't get worse."

Tim laughed again. He could see why someone like Kelly, who had it rough, would hang out with Vanessa. She was funny and didn't seem to take herself too seriously.

"It wasn't all good times back here, though," she said.

"What do you mean?"

She took a deep breath. "Barret came back here once and saw Kelly hooking up with this guy from our neighborhood. His name was Juan and he lived a couple doors down from Kelly. His family was from somewhere in Central America, I don't know which country, and they didn't stay long. Anyway, he was a good-looking kid with curly dark hair and gorgeous brown eyes. Kelly started up with him during one of those times when her and Barret were on again, off again."

"Did that happen often? The two of them breaking up and then getting back together?"

She walked along the edge of the ravine, looking down at the creek. "It did. Barret would do something that made her angry and she'd swear they were done and then a week later they'd be back at it, hot and heavy. This time, though, we were all back here around sundown. I was with Jeff and Kelly brought Juan. He was a skinny little thing and a year younger than us. Hell, he was still learning English. He was new and this pretty girl was paying attention to him, so he did pretty much whatever she said."

"What happened?"

She looked back over her shoulder and pointed. "You see that green fence through the trees?"

Tim looked and squinted. He could just make out corrugated green fiberglass fence panels wired up to a frame of steel pipes. It stretched wide in either direction. "Yeah, I see it."

"Well, that's Dedrick's Salvage Yard."

"Barret's place?"

Her head dipped in agreement. "It is now that his dad passed away. Don't let the look of the place fool you. He does very well for himself between the salvage and the attached garage. That prick has a dozen guys working for him and a couple hundred acres fenced in."

"I see," Tim said. He made a note to check on the property in county records before interviewing Barret and then turned back to Vanessa. "What happened with Juan?"

She gestured toward the woods between the salvage yard and the burn barrel. There was a trail there, he saw, leading back toward the salvage yard.

"Barret came up through the trees, like he would, and he saw Kelly kissing Juan and just lost his goddamn mind."

"This is when they were broken up?"

"They were, but I think Barret's one of those guys you can never really break up with. I don't know if you get what I'm talking about, but some guys, they just think they own you once you've gone out with them."

"So, what happened?"

"Ah, hell, I wish I still smoked," she said. "I could really use one." She paused for a moment and then said, "Barret came out of the trees over there and said . . ."

●   ●   ●

"What the fuck are you doing?"

Vanessa's head snapped around at the outburst and left Jeff's face in mid-kiss, looking like a fish gulping air. Barret stood in the trees with an angry look on his face. Then he started marching toward them.

Juan and Kelly disentangled themselves from their embrace on the bench seat on the other side of the circle. Juan jumped up and put himself between Barret and Kelly but Barret had almost a hundred pounds and six inches on the fifteen-year-old. He pushed the smaller kid aside and he tumbled into the grass.

Vanessa saw Kelly stand up and one of Barret's giant hands shoved her back down onto the bench. The girl bounced against the back of it and the seat threatened to tip over. "What the fuck are you doing, Kelly? This is how you treat me?"

Kelly put up a hand defensively, "We're broke up, Barret. What I do isn't any of your business."

He pointed a thick finger at her. "We're not broke up. We're just working some things out."

Vanessa saw a flash of movement and Juan slammed into Barret, knocking him off balance. The two tumbled into the grass and rolled around, each trying to get the advantage of the other. Vanessa nudged Jeff.

"Do something. Make them stop."

Jeff rolled his eyes and stood up. With his hands on his hips he said, "Come on, guys, knock it off."

Barret succeeded in using his bulk to flip Juan and crawled on top of him, pinning him to the ground. One meaty fist slammed into the skinny kid's face and Vanessa realized that Barret might actually hurt him. She leapt from her folding chair and shouted, "Cut it out, Barret! He doesn't even know you!"

Barret landed another punch and blood flew into the air. Juan screamed but Barret drew back again. He stopped, fist in the air, and looked at Kelly. "Is this what you want, slut? You like to see me like this?"

She got off the bench seat, hands held out in front of her. "Barret, please stop. He doesn't know anything about us. Don't hurt him anymore. Please."

Vanessa looked back to Barret and she wasn't sure it was getting through. His eyes were full of rage and his fist was still in the air. She looked at Juan and saw the poor kid was helpless. Barret had his arms pinned with his knees and even though he was squirming, she could tell Juan wasn't getting loose unless Barret let him up.

After a silent moment, the big man stood up and Juan curled up into a protective ball. Barret reached down and grabbed him, pulling him to his feet. The kid put his hands up to ward off another blow, but Barret reached past them and grabbed him by the throat.

Vanessa watched in horror as he dragged Juan to the edge of the ravine. He turned back to Kelly.

"What do I have to do to prove I love you? What will it take?"

Feebly, Kelly said, "Please, don't. Let him go."

"You either love me or you don't, Kelly. You can't keep playing these games like this, using these other guys to make me jealous."

Vanessa saw Juan's feet kick up dirt and loose stones as he struggled to keep his balance on the edge. He teetered there, struggling to breathe, as Barret yelled at Kelly.

"I'm not playing games," Kelly sobbed. "We're broke up. I wasn't trying to make you jealous. I swear. I mean, I thought we were broke up."

He stood there, one cantilevered arm the only thing keeping Juan from falling into empty air. "You do this to me all the time. How am I supposed to act when you keep doing shit like this?"

She gestured to him. "Just let him go, babe, and come over here. We'll talk, okay? We can work it all out."

"Yeah?"

"I promise. Just don't hurt him."

Barret looked at Juan like he'd forgotten he was there. He pulled him away from the edge and dropped him like a pile of laundry as he walked over to Kelly. "I've missed you so much, baby. Please don't ever leave me again, okay?"

Vanessa pulled Jeff over to Juan and they looked him over. In the setting sun she could see blood was crusted on his upper lip and his left cheek was swollen. She turned to Jeff. "We need to get him out of here," she said.

Jeff nodded and pulled Juan to his feet. The kid was unsteady but stayed up. Vanessa turned to Kelly and saw Barret hugging her. "Kelly, we're taking Juan home. Are you coming?"

She waved them off. "It's okay. I'm going to talk to Barret for a while. You guys go ahead."

Vanessa's brow furrowed. "I really think you should come with us."

Barret turned to her, his face flush with color. "I'll take care of her." There was menace in his voice, like maybe the evening's violence wasn't done.

Jeff tugged at her arm. "Come on, honey. Let's go."

⬤   ⬤   ⬤

"So, we took Juan back to my house and cleaned him up before taking him home," she said to Tim.

They stood there in the ankle-high grass, and Tim slapped at some insect biting his exposed forearms. He wished they were back at her house, out of the damned woods, but this was where she appeared to be comfortable talking so he kept going.

"Do you know if Juan's parents ever filed a police report?" It would be great if he could find some documentation on Barret.

She shook her head. "I don't think so. If they did, I never heard anything about it. They were all new immigrants, so I got the impression they didn't want trouble. I remember they moved away not long after."

Tim made a note to check anyway. He could see why Barret would be a suspect in Kelly's disappearance. "Do you think Barret was abusive toward Kelly?"

Vanessa crossed her arms and looked at the spot on the ravine where she
said Barret had dangled Juan. "He was emotionally abusive, that much I know
for sure. He was manipulative and mean to her when he didn't get his way."

She ran a hand through her dark curls and turned away from him. He had
a feeling that she wasn't going to speak more about it. He shifted directions.

"When I spoke with Quinn, she said she didn't know of any incidents
where Barret was abusive toward Kelly, and said that his reputation in that regard was blown out of proportion. Can you think of any reason Quinn would
have such a different interpretation of their relationship?"

"I don't know for sure, but I can take a guess," she said. "Quinn likes to
put a good face on things. Even when she was a teenager she liked to pretend
that things at home weren't as bad as they really were. She believes that dirty
laundry should stay in the family and not be aired in public. Since the police
have never been able to pin anything on Barret about Kelly's disappearance,
Quinn would rather just ignore that part of her sister's life and get on with
looking in other directions."

"Do you agree with that?"

She shrugged and looked toward the salvage yard. "I'm not going to lie
to you, I wouldn't be heartbroken to see a little trouble come his way just
because of the way he treated Kelly when she was alive. Maybe Quinn's way
is right, though. If there's nothing there, maybe it's time to let it all drop and
concentrate on finding whoever is responsible."

Silence lingered between them for a moment and the afternoon was
drawing late, but Tim still had questions. He consulted his steno pad. "You
spoke to Kelly on the Friday before Labor Day. Can you tell me what you
spoke about?"

"It was nothing much, really," she said. "I know everyone wants to dig
some clue out of that conversation, something that will tell us all where Kelly
is, but it was just a normal phone call, the kind you have with your friends."

"What did you talk about?"

She shrugged and he got the feeling she was growing tired of answering
questions. "Her job, mostly. Kelly had some work to get done over the week-

end but she was fixated on her new job, the one she had coming up."

"The one in Boston?"

"That's right. She was going to start in a few weeks so she was making arrangements to find a place to live and all that stuff."

"So, she was excited about it?"

Vanessa grinned and nodded. "Oh man, was she ever. This was what she worked for and she was so ready to go. I teased her, telling her that the little country mouse was going to the big city. She said she couldn't wait to blow out of here." She stopped for a moment and the grin faded. "I think she would have done well there. She had talent and getting in with a good company meant they were going to mentor her. I think she was going to go and never look back."

"What about her mom and her sister?"

She gave a light shrug to this. "They had each other, didn't they? I mean, Quinn had her kids and Kathleen was drinking herself into oblivion, and really, there was no saving her. I can't believe she's hung on as long as she has." She looked Tim over for a moment. "You're young, you seem bright. Haven't you ever wanted to get out of here? Go to some city and see what you can do?"

Tim shook his head. "I like it here. I don't think I'd do well in a city."

"Well, I sure as hell thought about it at your age. Still do sometimes. Anyway, to your question, you can't let family anchor you here and Kelly understood that. She knew the interstates go in both directions, that she could visit when she wanted. No, she needed to get away from this place, with all its baggage, and start over. That's what that last conversation was about, her getting out and starting a new life."

Tim nodded and scribbled notes, thinking about Amy suddenly, wondering if she wanted to go somewhere with more opportunity, where everything didn't remind her of her dead parents and her murdered brother. "When you heard that Kelly had vanished, did you think Barret Dedrick had something to do with it?"

She raised an eyebrow. "Who else would I have thought of? As far as I knew, Kelly had broken up with him for good years before, but remember what I said about some guys thinking they own you?"

Tim nodded.

"Well, there was a part of me that thought he might be involved. I could see it, you know?"

"How do you mean?"

She pointed in the direction of the salvage yard, her face letting him know there was some anger toward Barret rooted deep within her. "That knuckle-dragging motherfucker was a bully then and he's a bully now."

"What made you think he might have something to do with Kelly's disappearance? Anything solid that he said or did?"

She scratched at her chin where a red mosquito bite was beginning to well up. "He would call her from time to time, try to get back in touch with her, but she didn't want anything to do with him. That's one of the reasons she'd moved to Hogan, to leave all this shit behind and put some space between her and him." She looked tired then, as if she'd had to physically dredge up the memories. "We should go back now. I've got to check on the kids."

Tim nodded and drove her back to her place. As she was getting out of the Jeep, he said, "I have one more question for you."

"Okay, but just one. I have to get dinner going."

"Can you think of anyone else who would hurt Kelly?"

"I can't think of a single other person who would want to hurt Kelly. Her world wasn't all that big, Mr. Abernathy. Her family was just Quinn and her mom, Kathleen. I was her only real friend."

"Any serious boyfriends besides Barret?"

Vanessa shook her head. "No. After wasting so many years on him she kept things pretty simple. She'd go out, but there was no one serious. I think Kelly was keeping herself unencumbered so that she could get out of here without any attachments. I only wish she could have made it."

He thanked her and watched as she walked toward her house. The last thing he saw was her hugging her daughter, who was still drawing on the front porch.

15

Amber Prentice's rented cabin lay on the eastern shore of Lake Trumbull, about a fifteen-minute drive from the Beer & Bait. Larry Coogan and his partner, Darren Lewis, pulled off the main road that circled the lake into the gravel driveway that led to the small cabin.

The cabin was small, and it needed some maintenance for sure, but Coogan liked it. The little building was square, about twenty-five feet to a side, with weathered blue clapboard siding. A small deck with bowed railings faced the road. The white front door looked like it was newer than the rest of the cabin, but surface rust crept up from the bottom, like it had been installed but never painted. Wide white-trimmed windows were set on either side of the door. A propane tank was mounted on sturdy steel rails a few feet from the side of the house.

"How old is she?" Lewis asked.

"Eighteen," Coogan said.

"Huh. Well, that makes sense," Lewis said. "You'd have to be eighteen to enjoy living in this dump."

Coogan wasn't so sure. He pulled around to the rear of the cabin, which faced the lake. The water was about seventy-five feet from the screened-in back porch and Coogan had no problem imagining himself sitting out here with a cold beer in his hand and his feet up on the rail. An old couch sat on the porch and a pair of tree stumps served as end tables. There was a little beach down at the water's edge, but it looked a little mangy, with clumps of scraggly grass pushing up through the rough sand. A jet ski lay cocked at an angle near the water.

"You think we'll find anything out here?" Lewis asked as the got out of the car. He was squinting against the noon sun as he looked out over the water.

"Maybe, maybe not, but we might as well take a look," Coogan said as his eyes followed Lewis's.

They probably should have made it out here before now but between the crime scene at the store and their regular case load, they'd been working twelve-hour days and still falling behind. Besides, coming out here meant he wasn't at the Jackson residence. He'd limited how much contact he'd had with Fred Jackson because every time he spoke with the man he saw the loss of his wife and daughter in his eyes, and it was just too much to take. His stomach tightened with anxiety at just the thought of speaking with the man. He had nothing to report, and until he did he didn't want to talk to him.

They walked around the perimeter of the cabin to see if anything looked out of the ordinary, but the place was locked up tight and the windows were all in one piece. If anyone had been out here after the murders, they hadn't left any sign.

Coogan took out the key Amber had given him that morning when he'd stopped by her parents' house. She'd been glad to have someone check on her place because it was isolated and there were plenty of people boating and camping at the lake. Empty cabins were easy targets for kids looking for a place to hang out or meth heads looking for a place to rip off. She'd pulled him aside, out of earshot of her dad, and told him in a slightly embarrassed voice that he may find a few joints in her bedroom. He assured her he didn't care.

He turned the key in the front door's lock and they walked into a tiny galley kitchen, which butted up against a small dining room with a wooden table big enough for two people. From where they stood the two detectives could see a living room with a small bedroom off to one side and a door leading to a narrow bathroom. It would probably take about two minutes to search the tiny cabin.

They each checked the room's corners out of habit, making sure no one was lurking where they shouldn't be, then walked through the house. It was as empty as it appeared. Coogan saw Lewis's nose turn up at the clothes spread around the floor and the sink full of dishes, but he knew his partner was a neat freak who kept his home as fastidious as he kept his appearance. Coogan remembered being eighteen, though, and this was what it looked like. Nevertheless, he snapped on a pair of blue nitrile gloves before touching anything.

Nothing looked out of the ordinary, though. As he wandered through the cabin he saw only what he expected. Just the normal, ordinary stuff people kept in their houses when they weren't expecting company. A load of laundry was in a green plastic basket on the couch. Pink tennis shoes lay crookedly halfway underneath the sofa. There was a small bookcase along the wall with some romance paperbacks on it. A couple remotes for the TV and Blu-ray player sat on top of the coffee table.

As predicted, half a joint lay in an ashtray in the bedroom, but there was no evidence of anything stronger. He didn't care about pot anymore. People were dying in droves from opioids and heroin laced with fentanyl. It was almost quaint to see someone worried about being busted for smoking weed.

He walked back into the living room and sat down on the couch, feeling down between the cushions as he did so. There was nothing in the furniture and he sat there for a moment, zoned out. After a moment, a shiver went up the back of his neck.

He turned his head slowly until he was staring out the windows in the kitchen. There were no curtains on the windows, just vinyl blinds that were raised at the moment. Thick woods were visible across the lake road.

"Hey, partner," he said to Lewis, who was looking through papers on the kitchen table. "Why don't you take a walk with me?"

They strode up the driveway, checked both lanes for traffic, and crossed the two-lane road that circled the lake. All of the houses near this section of the lake were built near the water. From where Coogan and Lewis stood on the shoulder they could see just a little ways into the lush green overgrowth of the forest.

Lewis looked back at the house. "You think he was watching her?"

"I think it's a possibility. Remember what we found behind the Beer & Bait?" He nodded toward the trees that stood past the weeds. "I think he could stand in there and see right into Amber's little cabin if he wanted to."

"I knew I shouldn't have worn my good shoes today," Lewis said.

Coogan took a short hop over the drainage ditch next to the road's shoulder and marched through the tall weeds that had been growing all summer. He walked into the tree line past thin maple saplings until he reached thicker beech trees with smooth bark.

The only sounds were from traffic on the road and black flies buzzing around them. The canopy of leaves filtered the light so there were dark spots along the forest floor. It was a little cooler in the shade but Coogan could still feel the August heat beating down on him. He slipped his jacket off and laid it across his arm.

"He couldn't have been much deeper in than this," Lewis said. "He wouldn't have been able to see through the brush and leaves to the house."

"Yeah, you're right," Coogan said and he turned in a slow circle, studying the ground. The leaf litter was lighter now than it would be in a few months, but there was enough to hide the soil that would capture footprints. Then a fallen tree caught his attention.

He walked back toward the road a little way and came to a large black walnut tree that had fallen over. It was a big one, about two feet around and stretching out about sixty feet along the ground. The stump at the base stood about three feet high and he could see the hollowed-out middle where it had rotted from the inside out.

Coogan stopped short by about ten feet and stared at the ground. Lewis came up behind him and they stood there, looking. The dirt under the trunk was littered with footprints and garbage. Plastic bottles sat on the ground and an empty cigarette pack lay smashed in the soil.

Coogan moved to the right, away from the area with the footprints, and leaned on the downed trunk of the tree. To his annoyance, he was too short to see over it, but Lewis wasn't. Coogan looked at him. "Well, what can you see? Don't keep me in suspense."

Lewis took out his cell phone and held it at eye level, snapping several pictures. He held the device out for Coogan to see.

"You can see right into the kitchen window. I imagine at night, when it's dark and her lights are on, you can see right into the living room. Especially if the blinds are up like they are now."

"Sonofabitch," Coogan said. He looked down at the ground again as Lewis kept snapping photos. Farther down the trunk of the tree there was a second spot that caught his eye. He walked toward the top of the tree, where it was sunk lower into the earth.

Another little pile of garbage was mixed in among the lower branches that lay in a splintered mess where the tree had landed. There were footprints that looked the same as the ones Lewis was taking pictures of, and more sports drink bottles. This time there were also a couple wrappers from king-sized Hershey bars and another empty cigarette pack. It was the same generic brand they'd seen behind the Beer & Bait. Disturbingly, there were also wadded-up tissues mashed down in the dirt. He made a mental note to bag them for possible DNA analysis.

Coogan squatted his bulk down on his haunches to get a better look at the trash. The wrappers here were weathered and faded. He looked back to where Lewis was and could see the bright orange wrapper stretched around a Gatorade bottle. The ones in his pile were definitely older, because they were sun-faded. Even the chocolate wrappers looked like they had been wet and dried repeatedly, as if they'd been through a few spurts of rain.

He looked over the tree. From this angle he had no problem doing so because it was lower, and sure enough, he could see into Amber's cabin across the road. If he'd had even a cheap pair of binoculars from Walmart he'd probably have been able to read the titles off the books on her bookshelf in the living room.

"You've got that look you get whenever you've figured something out," Lewis said. "What's up?"

Coogan grabbed a branch and pulled himself up. Both knees let off loud cracks but Lewis had the good sense not to say anything to his older partner. "I think the pile up there," he said, pointing up near the stump, "is newer and smaller than the pile here. I'm guessing he spent some time down here watching her. Given how much trash there is, I'd say he did it multiple times."

"Like he was working himself up?" Lewis said.

Coogan nodded in agreement. "Yeah, I think so. See the Kleenex?"

"Ugh. So he's creeping around out here, watching her and getting his rocks off."

"Right, but that isn't enough for him after a while. The thrill of sitting out here in the woods and watching her fades over time and then he decides he's going to have to go for it and plans his attack on the store where she works."

"But why not do it out here at the house?" Lewis asked. "This is a hell of a lot more isolated than the store. Way less risk."

Coogan glanced back at the house. "Because she wasn't alone out here. Amber has a boyfriend, a guy named Jerry, and I'm guessing he was out here most nights. That's his jet ski we saw down near the water. The guy probably figured it was easier to attack her at the Beer & Bait at closing time when the store was empty except for her and Linda Jackson. After all, a high school senior who barely weighed a hundred pounds was less of a threat than a twenty-year-old guy who works in a warehouse."

"Plus," Lewis said, "if things go right, he gets two victims, Amber and Linda."

"Yep."

"So, what's with the newer pile?"

Coogan's face darkened and he looked from the pile to the house. "I think he's been back since he attacked the girls out at the store. I wouldn't be surprised to find out that since his first attempt was frustrated, he came out here to make another one. Remember, he killed two people at the Beer & Bait, so maybe he figured he'd do the same thing if Jerry was home. Just kill him and do whatever he wanted with her."

They stood in silence for a moment and looked out at the little cabin Amber had called home, but probably wouldn't ever again. Coogan shifted and looked around. He'd always liked the woods, and even though he wasn't much a camper, he did enjoy hiking sometimes. Now, though, the woods around the lake felt eerie, like they held a new danger.

Lewis was documenting the scene with photos and Coogan joined him, spending the next few minutes bagging the trash, grateful that he was still wearing his blue gloves. Then they headed back across the road and secured the cabin.

They were in the car and headed back to town when Coogan looked at Lewis. "You know, this probably isn't the first time this guy has done this."

"Yeah, I agree with you. Sneaking around the woods like that and peeping in windows isn't something he's only done once."

"Right, and the fact that he was organized enough to come up with a plan when his urges became too strong leads me to believe he has a fair amount of confidence."

"Yeah," Lewis said, "but he fucked up at the Beer & Bait. When Carol Jackson walked in and spoiled the deal, he panicked and killed her and her daughter. He could have just run away. Maybe he's not very experienced."

Coogan let out an exasperated sigh. "We need to start looking at registered sex offenders and parolees."

"Man, I hate dealing with those guys."

Coogan ignored the comment. It was a given that absolutely no one liked dealing with sex offenders. "You know what else we need to figure out?"

"What?"

"Where did she come to his attention? Did he see her out at the cabin and figure out where she worked or did he meet her at the store and track her out here? It could give us a clue to his identity."

"We'd better go talk to her again," Lewis said. "This is going to freak her out."

Coogan nodded. "No shit."

16

Charlie swiveled back to Tim. "How about the feature on Kelly?"

The full crew of the *Hogan Weekly Shopper* were in the small conference room at the paper's offices. Charlie sat at the head of the table while Tim, Alonzo, and Janey occupied the chairs down the sides of the table. Both of the young reporters looked at Tim. They were still pulling the local government beat, so his feature on Kelly kept their attention.

"That's going to require a little more work but I'm getting there."

Charlie's brow knitted. "Who else is there to speak with? You got the sister and friends, right?"

"One friend," Tim said. "There's an old boyfriend I'd like to talk with."

Charlie sat back in his blue chair and eyed Tim. "Barret Dedrick?"

"That's right."

The publisher pointed a finger at him. "I don't know if that's such a good idea."

"Why?"

"A couple reasons. First, the guy is a jerk. I remember him from the initial investigation where he was the prime suspect. His family has a little juice over in Berry Creek because their business is successful. Hogan cops made a lot of noise about him being a suspect and the authorities over there made things difficult on the investigators. As much as he claimed to be friendly with Kelly and still have feelings for her, he was uncooperative when they questioned him. Second, I don't know if he's a good source for the story. We want insight into Kelly's life. He's an abusive ex-boyfriend. What's he going to tell us? That she could take a punch?"

Tim sat up straight and looked at Charlie with shock. The publisher was usually the embodiment of mild-mannered, so to hear him speak like that was unusual. "Quinn said he never struck Kelly. If you don't want me to speak with him, I won't."

Charlie took in a deep breath. "He seems like a hitter. If you think he's got something to contribute, then fine, you can interview him. Just be careful. I know the family. Their garage is out there in the middle of nowhere and he's not shy about pushing people around. Like I said, he's got a little pull with the locals so if something goes cockeyed, they're likely to see you as the instigator."

Tim considered it and chewed his lower lip. Charlie had a point about Barret being a bad source for background on Kelly, but he believed people were the sum of their relationships, both good and bad.

Paulie didn't like Barret personally, but didn't think he was involved in Kelly's disappearance. Vanessa thought he was capable, while Quinn thought the guy hadn't been good enough for Kelly, but didn't consider him a suspect. Considering these differing opinions, he felt like he had to meet the man.

"I'll be careful. If he doesn't want to talk, that's fine. I won't push it."

Charlie nodded. "Okay. Call me if you need bail money."

●   ●   ●

Barret's place was at the top of a small hill. A large sign on the side of the road said "Dedrick Garage and Salvage." Below the logo, graffiti scrawled in red spray paint proclaimed them to be "Liars & Thieves." A red arrow running across the bottom of the sign directed Tim up a narrow road lined with scrub pine trees to a gravel driveway.

The check he'd run on the property showed that ownership had passed to Dedrick about eight years ago, after his father died. A quick Google search showed him the obituary of the man, dead from a heart attack before he was sixty. It was curious, though. The obit mentioned a wife but the property had gone to Barret.

As he pulled in, he saw a cinderblock garage painted red with five roll-up doors. The area outside the garage was littered with vehicles in various states of decay. Some were rusted-out hulks while others looked mostly intact, like roadkill that birds had been picking at. He pulled into a parking spot near a door with a sign over it that said "Office" in white letters.

When he got out of his Jeep he noticed the truck he was parked next to. It was a white Dodge Ram diesel with a single large chrome smokestack fitted into the bed. A bumper sticker on the driver's side rear window proclaimed "Trump that Bitch" and on the passenger's side a static cling cartoon Calvin pissed on Obama's name. He glanced down and saw rubber bull's balls hanging from the trailer hitch. If Tim had been playing redneck truck bingo he'd be collecting his prize.

Shaking his head, he walked around the truck toward the office. When he opened the door and walked in an electronic chime bleated.

The office was larger than he expected, fronted by a large wooden counter than ran the length of the room. Everything inside had the same coloration. The walls, ceiling, and floor were all a brownish-gray smear over light tan paint, the result of dirt and grease layering on each other for years. The air was cooler in the office than outside due to a window air conditioning unit mounted in the wall to the left of the door.

Behind the counter were two desks, and a dozen steel filing cabinets lined the walls. Above the file cabinets the walls were covered with car advertising: a large, metal orange-and-blue Gulf sign that had probably hung on the outside of a gas station back in the fifties now hung near the ceiling; next to it was a round Texaco sign emblazoned with the red star; and a red, white, and blue Sohio sign that was in better shape than the other two hung below them. Bikini calendars from years gone by were tacked up, presumably displaying favorite months with models who never aged.

The space on the walls not covered with signage or calendars was covered with copies of notices, each warning customers of obscure rules for doing business with Dedrick Garage and Salvage. Tim learned there were no refunds without the yellow slip, no returns at all on electrical parts, and they didn't accept checks from anyone.

Aerosmith's "Dream On" played from a set of reclaimed six-by-nine Pioneer car speakers sitting on one of the filing cabinets in the corner farthest from the door, adding a sound component to the visual mess of the office. Tim got the feeling someone had tuned in the local classic rock station about ten years ago and broken off the knob.

An overweight woman with dark hair going to gray and wearing a pink sweatshirt rocked herself out of a steel office chair and approached the counter. "Can I help you?"

Tim smiled and said, "I'm here to see Barret Dedrick. Is he around?"

She eyed him suspiciously and the smile disappeared. "What's it about?"

"Well, it's a personal matter. Is he here?"

Taking a deep breath, she turned her head toward the closed office door to her right. With a sharp voice, she hollered. "Barret! There's someone out here to see you!"

A chair squeaked and the door snapped open. A beast of a man walked out of the small office. He was as tall as Tim but had a good hundred pounds on him. His shoulders were wide and led to thick arms. A white shirt with the sleeves cut off stretched over an ample belly that had probably been built by draft beers at one of the bars in town. Blue jeans at least a size too small hid out under his gut.

"You don't have to scream like that, Ma. I can hear you just fine," he said as he approached the counter.

"I scream like that because you keep that door shut all the time. I don't know what you're doing in there that demands so much privacy."

"What I do ain't any of your business."

"Probably don't want to see it, anyway."

The large man let out an exasperated breath and turned to Tim. "What can I do for you?"

Tim smiled, trying to be friendly with an interview subject who could become hostile. A check of police records showed that Barret Dedrick had two assault arrests, one with the charges dropped, the other resulting in probation and anger management classes. The first had been here at the garage and the other had been a road rage incident. Tim had a feeling there were more witnesses on the road and that's why that charge had gone the distance. On a whim he'd checked with the Better Business Bureau and saw that there were several open customer complaints. Barret Dedrick wasn't universally liked.

He produced a business card and handed it across the counter. "I'm Tim Abernathy from the *Hogan Weekly Shopper*. Are you Barret Dedrick?"

"Yeah, that's me," Barret said as he studied Tim's card. "Look, we already advertise with the little paper here in town and the Warren and Youngstown papers. We don't draw too much business from Hogan." He held up the card. "We'll keep you in mind, though."

Barret turned back toward the office and Tim said, "Oh, I'm not here about advertising. I want to speak with you about Kelly Dolan."

The office was quiet for a moment, except for the music playing and the rattle of the air conditioner. Then Barret's mother came out of her chair again, this time with an angry look on her face. "Can't you people just leave him alone? He doesn't know anything about that girl or what happened to her. My poor boy has been bothered enough!"

Barret turned to her and put his hands on her shoulders. "Mom, it's okay, don't get worked up. Come on, now, I've got this."

"Don't say anything to them, Barret. They just want to put this on you and you've got nothing to do with it." She reached up and rubbed the side of his bald head with tenderness. "You don't have to talk to him."

He led her back to her desk and she lowered herself into the chair. She turned her attention to Tim. "You people should just leave him alone. The police said he was innocent. Isn't that enough?"

Barret glanced at him with gritted teeth and came back to the counter. He flipped up a large section of it mounted on hinges and pointed to the door. "Let's go outside."

Tim followed him out into the parking lot and squinted against the bright August sunlight. The office door slammed closed behind him. Barret leaned back against the big white Dodge truck and rested the heel of a black steel-toe boot on the bumper, settling Tim's curiosity about who owned it. He looked Tim up and down as he shook a Marlboro free from a hardpack and lit it with a silver Zippo. He didn't offer Tim one.

"Mom's not wrong, you know," Barret said. "I was cleared of all this bullshit years ago. You want to know who killed Kelly, go look somewhere else."

The guy was defensive already, Tim could see. He needed him calm, willing to open up and maybe give him a quote. Getting right down to asking him if he used to hit his girlfriend wasn't going to get the job done.

He held his arms out, trying to set the big man at ease. "Hey, I don't think you killed her and that's not what this about," Tim said. "Did you hear about the two women killed out at the Beer & Bait in Hogan?"

Barret shook his head. "I don't watch the news much."

Tim filled him in and he shook his head. "I don't see what any of that has to do with Kelly or me. I sure as hell didn't rob some store or kill those women."

"No one thinks you did," Tim said, trying to keep Barret docile. "In fact, there's no link between that case and Kelly's, except that those women being murdered kind of reminded everyone that Kelly's case still hasn't been solved and she's never been found. The fact that both incidents happened at isolated locations has people drawing conclusions where there may not be any."

"Well there you go," Barret said, blowing smoke up into the air. "Maybe it was the same guy."

"Well, the focus for my story is Kelly. We want to help bring a resolution to the case if we can, kind of give the community closure. I've been talking to her family and friends about her time here in Berry Creek, and that's why I'm here. You dated her, so I thought you might provide some insight."

Barret's eyes narrowed. "I'm sure her friends and family didn't have anything good to say about me. They never liked me much."

Tim smiled. "I'm more interested in what you have to say. Can you describe your relationship with Kelly Dolan?"

Barret glanced off into the woods, as if the answer to Tim's question could be found out among the pines and maple trees. "Christ, what can I tell you? We were just kids when we dated." He walked to the driver's side door of the truck, opened it, and reached in. He came out with a pair of sunglasses that wrapped around his big round head.

"I know you were young but you dated for a few years, right? You two must have had some fun. What did you do?"

Barret sucked on his cigarette and stared at him from behind the black lenses of his sunglasses. "Look, man, I busted my ass out here from the time I was a little kid." He waved his hand at the garage and the fence that stretched out around the salvage yard. "Everyone says I'm some kind of asshole but what I really am is successful. People don't get how much effort that takes. This is a business and there was a lot to learn."

That was certainly more than Tim was expecting from the man. He wanted to keep the conversation going. "You think people don't understand you?"

Barret grinned and shook his head. "I know they don't. My old man was a hardcase. He had me out here doing oil changes and tire rotations when I was still in middle school. By the time I was done with high school and seeing Kelly, I could tear engines down or swap them out. People don't see that as an accomplishment, though, you know? Not around here. All the doctors, lawyers, and business douchebags in Berry Creek see honest work as beneath them. Their kids were going off to college and shit, and they saw me as a goddamn grease monkey. Like keeping cars running wasn't as important as making some big sale."

Tim started to get it. Here was the insecurity Vanessa spoke about during their interview at Paradise. Barret was the poor, misunderstood guy who everyone looked down on. Even with his girlfriend dead, he was the victim. "So, when Kelly hooked up with you it made you happy?"

Barret grinned. "Ah, man, you should have known her. She was dynamite. You could see that she was going to do something cool. I mean, sure, her mom was a fucking drunk, but Kelly was awesome. She had talent."

"You mean her artwork?"

Barret nodded and stubbed out his cigarette. "Come here, let me show you something."

Tim followed the big man into the empty garage bay nearest the office. He reached up on to a shelf and slid a couple boxes out of the way. Then he pulled down a carton with the flaps folded over on one another. "J-23" was written on the side of it in black Sharpie. He pulled the flaps open and lifted out a motorcycle gas tank. It was polished and shined under the bright shop lights. The tank was painted metallic green with a dragon on it. The beast was several shades of red and breathed fire in several brilliant shades of orange. The whole thing was finished off with several layers of protective clear coat.

"You see this?" Barret said. "Kelly painted this for an old Harley I had. I sold the bike years ago but I kept the gas tank. I'll never get rid of this."

"That's amazing," Tim said, and pulled out his cell phone. He gestured toward the tank. "Can I take a picture of it? I think our readers would like to see an example of her artistry."

Barret set it down on a rolling cart. "Sure, go ahead."

Tim snapped several pictures, getting it from different angles. "When did she do this?"

"Her senior year of high school. See, this is what people don't get about me and Kelly. She understood me. No matter how stupid I was, no matter how I acted, she was cool. She was always there for me. That's love."

There was something there, in his voice. Barret had cared for Kelly, that much seemed true, but had he understood how to express that love the way she did? Had their relationship been a one-sided affair, with Kelly always giving and Barret always taking?

"Did you ever do anything like this for her?"

He shook his head, the sunglasses still hiding his eyes even inside the garage.

"I was never good at stuff like this. I mean, I kept her cars running. Her mom didn't have much money so Kelly and her sister always drove junk. I'd keep their cars on the road for them, fix stuff around their house, you know, that kind of stuff."

Again, Tim was surprised. He'd expected Barret to be more selfish. "She must have appreciated that."

"I guess," Barret said. "Is there anything else you need? I really do have some work to get back to."

It seemed like Barret wanted to be done but Tim still had questions, the unpleasant ones that really needed answers. He took a deep breath. "You two had bad times?"

Barret shrugged. "Everyone does."

"Not like this. There are rumors that you were physically abusive with Kelly. Is there any truth to them?"

Barret blew out a breath. "People have said that?"

"Yes, and it's going to be in the story. Do you have a response?" Tim knew this was the moment where things could go sideways. He couldn't print rumors, but prodding Barret seemed like the only way to get something out of the man. It would be easy for Barret to lash out, but instead he just answered.

"I was just a kid and guys that age, sometimes they lose their cool. You know what it's like with women."

Tim just stood still, unsure how to proceed. Barret was doing that thing all wife beaters, racists, and general scumbags did, assuming that because they felt a certain way about something, everyone else did, too. Tim recognized it for what it was, a deep-seated need to have their bullshit affirmed. He didn't want to give it to him, though. This guy's demons were his own to wrestle with, so he plowed ahead. "Did you ever hurt her badly enough she needed a doctor?"

Barret threw his hands up into the air but Tim saw something else cross his face: fear. For just a moment, he looked worried, then the anger reasserted itself. "Christ almighty, did Quinn say that? Tell me she didn't say that. I don't remember Kelly ever going to the doctor for something like that."

Tim froze for a second, unsure how he should proceed. Quinn hadn't told him anything like that. Hell, even Vanessa hadn't said anything like that. Still, if Barret assumed Quinn had told him that, maybe something had happened, something she hadn't mentioned during his interview with her. "Let's just say I have a source making those accusations. Someone knowledgeable about the situation. How hard did you hit her?"

Color crept into Barret's face, stretching up to the top of his head. "I think you should go now. I don't have anything else to say."

Tim swallowed, wanting nothing more than to get out of the garage, but he needed answers. "Mr. Dedrick, I heard about an incident with one of Kelly's boyfriends, a kid named Juan that you had an altercation with at Paradise. It's just beyond your fence back there, right?" He pointed out beyond the green fiberglass fence. "You struck him several times and threatened to drop him off the edge of the ravine. Do you have any comment about that?"

"That was a misunderstanding."

"How so?"

"She was, I don't want to speak ill of the dead here, but Kelly could be unfaithful. She was using that guy to make me jealous. We'd had a fight and she brought that guy around just to get me worked up. What happened with him wouldn't have if she'd just worked things out with me."

"Just so I'm clear, it's Kelly's fault you beat that kid up?"

Barret drew himself up to his full imposing height. Tim was suddenly aware of how much larger Barret was than him and how far off the beaten path he was. "Like I said, we're done here. You motherfuckers never know when to quit."

Tim held a hand up, trying to buy time. "Hey, this is your chance to give your side of the story, in your own words. You don't have to say anything, but the story is going to be written. You should take this opportunity to tell it the way you want."

The hair on the back of Tim's neck stood up and he turned his head. One of the mechanics from the other bays, wearing gray coveralls stained with grease, stood behind him. Tim stepped sideways and saw the man had a two-foot-long pry bar in his hand. The claw end hung in the air around his knee.

"Everything all right, boss?" the man said.

"It's all good, Eddie. I think this guy was just leaving."

Tim looked back to Barret and nodded. "I think I have all I need."

"Good."

Tim shuffled around the mechanic with the pry bar and walked back out into the afternoon sunlight, making a beeline for his Jeep. Barret followed him and leaned on the roll cage with one thick hand. Tim regretted not having the doors on. Nothing stood between him and Barret.

"Couple more things," Barret said.

Tim started the engine, anxious to go. "What's that?"

"Don't come out here again. I don't have anything else to say about Kelly. You fake news vultures don't understand anything and all you do is twist my words around."

Tim put his hand on the gearshift and put the Jeep in reverse, anxious to go if Barret decided to go for a third assault charge. He kept his foot on the brake. "You said you had a couple things. What's the other one?"

"If Quinn thinks I'm so dangerous and is so angry about how I treated her sister, why did she spend so many afternoons up here fucking me?"

Tim blinked. "Wait. She did what?"

Barret smiled, clearly happy to have Tim off balance. "After Kelly and I broke up, about a year before she disappeared, Quinn and her old man were having all kinds of problems. Let's just say she worked through them with me."

"But why?"

He rolled his head to one side and shrugged. "I guess getting her rocks off with me was cheaper than therapy. Hell of a lot more fun, too." He grinned, like it was a favorite memory. "That girl couldn't get enough that summer. She was a real freak, too. She liked it rough and dirty."

"Really? You're saying that you and Quinn had an affair?" Tim was flabbergasted and couldn't think of anything else to say. This was as unexpected as any revelation could have been. Barret took his surprise as a cue to keep bragging.

"The dirtier my hands were the more she liked it. She told me she liked going home and showering off my greasy handprints. She told me she wanted to leave a handprint on her ass for her husband to see, let him know that she was getting it somewhere else." The big man leaned back. "I guess she never did, though, 'cause they're still together."

"That really happened?" Tim said. Given what Quinn had said about Barret, he couldn't see the prim and proper housewife he'd interviewed coming down here to steal some time with him. It just didn't make sense.

"I've got no reason to lie." He leaned in again, close enough that Tim almost took his foot off the brake to drive away. "Quinn is full of secrets. You shouldn't believe too much of what she says."

They stared at each other for a moment, and Tim suddenly had more questions.

"What do you mean?"

"You should be careful what you print," he said. "I have a powerful, good attorney and he loves bringing suit against people who piss me off. If I think you're lying about me I'll sic him on you." He slapped the side of Tim's Jeep, leaving the air ringing with a hollow gong sound, and stepped back. "Now get out of here. And don't come back unless you want your ass kicked."

17

That night, Tim and Amy were enjoying an evening at home. The TV was off and they sat on opposite ends of the couch sharing a bottle of wine. He had one of her feet in his hands, massaging away the stress of her day.

"Mmm . . . that feels so good," she said as his thumbs worked the arch of her foot. She looked beautiful tonight, stretched out in a black t-shirt and cutoffs. He was dressed similarly except he wore orange basketball shorts.

"How was work today?" he asked.

"Ugh, we're so busy," she said. "This new client of ours has been having problems for years but they didn't know it because their in-house accountant wasn't any good."

"Oh yeah?" Tim said.

"Yeah, he didn't keep up on new regulations like he should have and now that he's retired, it's all coming out. We're going to have to refile the last three years."

Tim cringed at the thought of how many extra hours that would take but she didn't notice because her eyes were closed. "So, more long days?"

"Oh, I suppose there's going to be a few weeks of them," she said, "at least while we sort through the mess. Unfortunately, all their records have been stored in a warehouse so they're dirty and it looks like the roof leaked at some point. I don't mind the hard work but I dress too nice to end up gross at the end of the day. Once we're organized, though, we'll just start working them like any other tax returns. Don't worry, baby. I'll be around. How's your story going?"

"I think I'd rather be digging through boxes with you in a warehouse."

She opened an eye and looked at him. "Is it that bad?"

"Yeah, things are getting complicated. I told you about Paulie, the PI?"

"You did."

"And her serial killer theory?"

Amy nodded. "You don't agree with her?"

He dropped her foot and held his hands up. "I don't know. Paulie's convincing, that's for sure, but Coogan thinks she ought to be wearing a tinfoil hat."

She waved a foot in the air. "Hey, nobody said stop."

He smiled and started kneading again. "I mean, he has a point. If there was someone running around killing women, you'd think the cops would be looking for them."

She raised an eyebrow in disbelief and sipped her wine. "I know you think Coogan is a good detective, but you may want to keep an open mind."

"I am. Like I said, Paulie can be convincing, so I'm not discounting anything yet."

"But something else is bugging you, right?"

"Yeah. I met Kelly's ex-boyfriend today. He's a real piece of work." Tim related his interview with Barret. Amy's eyes grew wider as he spoke.

"Damn it, Tim, you need to be more careful. That guy could have hurt you."

"Nah, I don't think so," he said. "He's had enough run-ins with the cops that I don't think he'd do anything more than try to intimidate me, so I let him think he got to me. Something about him does bug me, though. He's got that whole caveman redneck thing going on. I have no problem thinking he could have killed Kelly."

She pulled her foot away and sat up with a concerned look on her face. "Then you need to stay away from him."

"Don't worry," he said. "I don't have any reason to talk to him again, at least right now. He did say a couple things that bugged me."

"Like what?"

"Kelly's friend Vanessa said he could be verbally and emotionally abusive, so I asked if he had ever hurt her badly enough she needed to see a doctor."

"Geez, that's coming on kind of strong, isn't it?"

"You don't get answers to questions you don't ask. Anyway, it worked. He asked if Quinn had told me that."

"What did you say?"

"I just let him think whatever he wanted. You should have seen the look on his face. There was fear there, like someone had said something they shouldn't."

"What do you think that means? Do you need to speak with Vanessa again?"

He considered it for a moment and then shook his head. "I think she would have told me if she had something concrete she could pin on him, like a police report or a trip to the emergency room. No, it seemed like Barret was worried that Quinn had said something."

"Are you going to speak with her again?"

He nodded. "Tomorrow, as a matter of fact. The thing is, she painted a picture of Barret being not good enough for her sister, and kind of an asshole, but she didn't make him out to be abusive. Now, though, I'm wondering if she's hiding something."

"You said she thinks Paulie is right about the serial killer?"

"Yeah."

"Maybe she's hiding something to keep the focus off Barret. If people think he hurt her once, they'll think he was capable of doing it again."

Tim nodded slowly. "She was awfully angry the police spent so much time investigating Barret and didn't come up with anything. Do you think it could have anything to do with them having an affair? Would she want the suspicion off him to hide that?"

Amy laughed, a short, sharp noise that made him feel like he'd missed something. "Are you really asking if a married woman would lie to keep her affair with the number one suspect in her sister's disappearance secret? I love you, baby, but sometimes you're kind of naïve."

He shook his head. "What is it with women and bad boys?"

She kicked at him playfully. "The same thing that is with boys and bad girls. You guys see a couple tattoos and piercings and you go all googly-eyed."

Tim thought about it for a hot second before smiling. "Yeah, you're right about that."

"In all serious, though, when you're talking with her tomorrow, be delicate about the affair. It's not going to be a topic she wants to discuss."

He nodded. "Yeah, good idea."

⊛   ⊛   ⊛

Tim pulled into Quinn's driveway at the time they'd agreed upon to finish their interview. With any luck it wouldn't take too long, but he couldn't get what Barret had said out of his mind. He wore khakis and a red polo today, which had made Amy joke that he looked like a character in an insurance commercial.

He knocked on the back gate and Quinn called for him to come in. There was no one in the pool this time, probably due to the day being a little overcast. He crossed the patio to the French doors and saw Quinn sitting at the table. She waved to him.

The house was quiet so the kids were probably out or in their rooms, Tim figured. Quinn gestured to a chair.

"Please have a seat," she said.

"Thanks," he said, and took a chair across the table from her. He unpacked his stuff, including his notebook and digital recorder, which he turned on and sat in the middle of the table.

"I want you to know how much I appreciate you taking the time to speak with me again," he said. "I think I'm getting a good picture of who your sister was from you and her friends." He almost faltered on the last word. It seemed like Vanessa had been Kelly's only friend. The words he would use to describe Barret weren't fit for polite conversation.

Quinn stood and walked into the kitchen. Today she wore a blue sweater with a gray pencil skirt and short black boots. "I'm grateful for this. After you left last time, I thought quite a bit about Kelly. I remembered just how much I miss her." She pulled down two glasses from a cabinet and removed a pitcher of lemonade from the fridge.

"Please, you don't have to do anything on my account," Tim said. "This may not even take very long."

She waved him off and returned to the table, setting one of the glasses down in front of him. He was struck by something Vanessa had said, about how Quinn liked to run the show, and how she liked to play the part of the dutiful mom. It seemed like she was still doing that.

"Don't worry about it," she said. "I was thirsty anyway." She sat down, taking the chair closest to him. "Anyway, I was thinking about Kelly and everything she's missed. I told you about Claire and how we're hoping she makes the swim team at OSU, but I realized that I'll never be able to share that with Kelly. Roger and I will relish our children's accomplishments and we'll comfort them when they fail, but I'm not going to be able to turn to her. I won't be able to call her to brag or even to complain. I've been robbed of that comfort."

She blinked rapidly and took a napkin from the holder in the center of the table. Tim remained quiet as she wiped her eyes. "I think I've become numb to the hole in my life where my sister should be. I know that people die. I'm not going to give you a speech about how life isn't fair. It's just that I feel robbed. Kelly wasn't sick, and she didn't have an accident. Someone just decided that she had to die, so they killed her."

She took a deep breath and composed herself. "I'm saying the word 'I' a lot, but you shouldn't think I'm selfish."

"I doubt anyone thinks that," Tim said.

She reached out and squeezed his hand. "Thank you. I know you're writing about Kelly, but what you need to understand is that she had people in her life who loved her and now that she's gone, we're what remains. Me, her friends, and even my mother, when she has good days."

"How does your mother feel about this?" Tim asked. "Do you think I could speak with her?"

Quinn shook her head slowly. "I don't think so. Her lucid days are few and far between. Most of the time she requires full care. You can try, but I think you'll be disappointed.

"You need to understand, my mother was an alcoholic before Kelly disappeared. After, it was the only way she could cope. I give her credit for trying to keep it together. I think she stayed sober for the first week of the search, but after that the police told us things didn't look good. My mother drank her way through every penny she had.

"It got to the point where I had to keep her away from the children because I couldn't trust her. I couldn't let her talk to the media because she wasn't sober enough for the interviews and I didn't want that to become the story. Eventually, my mother sat in her house and drank full time."

"Is that what caused her current affliction?" Tim asked.

"Not exactly," Quinn said, "but it exacerbated her existing problems. Something most people don't realize about alcoholics is that they don't eat very well, which makes them suffer from poor nutrition. My mother developed a vitamin B deficiency that permanently damaged her memory and sped up her dementia. Mom was already on this path before Kelly vanished but if I wasn't so busy coordinating the effort to find her, I would have spent more time with her. I would have noticed how bad she was and gotten her into rehab instead of shutting her away and ignoring her."

"Do you feel guilt about that?"

She wiped a tear away. "A little, but I consider my mother to be as much a victim of this killer as Kelly."

Tim checked his notes. Quinn had said her piece about how Kelly's death had affected her but he wanted more about Kelly the person. She was giving him what she thought he wanted. He had to assert some control over the situation to get what he needed.

"I'd like to hear some more about Kelly's time in school. I understand she showed an aptitude for art in high school. Is that when she started to decide her path in life?"

Quinn looked at him with a small smile. "Kelly always doodled and sketched. Her notebooks all through middle school were filled with drawings of Sailor Moon and video game characters like Mario and Pikachu. She would practice constantly, so much so that my mom would have to buy her extra notebooks. We didn't have a lot of money for hobbies, but drawing doesn't cost much."

She took a sip from her lemonade. "She took every art class that was available to her. Once she got to high school, the opportunities really opened up. We may have lived in Berry Creek's worst neighborhood, but we got the benefit of the great schools this town has. Most schools in this area barely have art classes, but here Kelly was introduced to different disciplines. She got instruction in drawing that helped her and also exposure to painting, sculpting, and computer editing software like Photoshop. I know it's kind of the norm now, but back then having access to that was a big deal. Kelly took to it like a fish to water."

Tim made a note to see if any of her teachers were still available. They might have some insight into Kelly's talent or examples of projects she worked on.

"I saw an example of her work when I spoke to Barret," Tim said, using her artwork as a way to breach that topic. "He showed me a gas tank she'd done for his motorcycle."

Quinn looked at him with a cool expression. He steeled himself. This was going to be unpleasant but it had to be done.

"I remember that well," Quinn said. "Kelly worked on it for over a month during her senior year. It was a birthday present." She smiled a bit. "The fact that he still has it makes me happy. There's very little of her artwork left in the world."

"Do you have any other pieces of hers?" Tim asked. "I could take photos to accompany the article."

Quinn got up from the table, walked into the living room, and came back with a frame about the size of a piece of copy paper. She set it down on the table and Tim saw it was a pencil drawing of a smiling older woman with long hair sitting at a picnic table.

"It's my mom," Quinn explained. "Kelly drew it at a picnic one Fourth of July when she was in college. We were all sitting around eating barbecue and drinking, just waiting for the sun to go down so we could set off the fireworks, and Kelly started drawing Mom. She said she liked the way the light was shining on her face, so Mom sat there and Kelly drew her." Quinn traced the light wooden frame with a finger. "I remember it because it was one of those times when everyone was happy. It was just a really nice day. We didn't have many, so it kind of stands out."

Tim stood up and positioned himself over it with his phone in his hands. He snapped a few photos and sat back down.

"I appreciate you showing me that," he said. "It will help our readers understand why Kelly was special."

"Thank you," Quinn said.

He took a deep breath. "When I was here last, you told me that you didn't think Barret had ever harmed Kelly physically. When I asked Barret that same question, his answer led me to believe that he had, and that you had knowledge of it."

Quinn sat back in her chair and crossed her arms over her chest. The look on her face told him that she wasn't happy.

"I don't know what you mean," she said. "What did Barret say?"

"When I asked him if he had ever hurt Kelly, he asked me if you were the one who told me he had." Quinn didn't say anything and Tim tapped his notebook. "Look, Quinn, clearly something happened between the two of them. What was it?"

"None of your business," she said. Her voice had a sharpness to it that told him she really didn't want to discuss it.

"If Barret hurt her," Tim said, "it could help people sympathize with her. We don't have to go into details, but if I can report that she was abused it helps accomplish our goal of getting people to come forward with information."

She shook her head and stared at him with eyes that were level and angry. "Barret is not the suspect here. The Buckeye Woodsman killed my sister. That's the story I want told. I want your readers to look at the people in their lives and give us the information we need to find and convict him. If you write a story about Kelly being abused by Barret then it all starts up again and we waste more time looking at the wrong person."

She reached out and gripped his hand with both of hers. "Please, I'm begging you, let go of this rumor about Barret. It doesn't mean anything and it will just set back our search."

Tim pulled his hand away. "Did you have an affair with Barret Dedrick?"

She flinched as if he'd raised a hand to her. "What?"

"Did you have an affair with Barret Dedrick?" Tim repeated.

She put a hand to her mouth and then her eyes grew hard. "I don't know what you're talking about."

"Prior to Kelly disappearing, did you and Barret have a relationship?"

Quinn crossed her legs. "I don't see how that could be relevant to the story or any of your business."

"If you had a personal relationship with the prime suspect in Kelly's disappearance and you worked to deflect scrutiny from him by withholding information about him abusing her, that makes it relevant."

She stood up and stalked away from him into the kitchen. Once there, she stood with her back to him, shoulders down, like she couldn't decide what to do. Tim sat still, calmly waiting for her to make up her mind. Finally, she turned and put her hands on the counter that separated the kitchen from the dining room.

"Roger and I were going through a difficult time," she said. "I'm not proud of what I did, but yes, I saw Barret a few times."

"He made it seem like it was more than that."

Her eyes flashed with anger. "That's wishful thinking on his part. It was over the course of a summer, maybe half a dozen times, and it happened before Kelly went missing. That's why I don't think it means anything to her case."

Tim stood up. "Quinn, you have to see that it looks bad. Kelly disappears and her ex-boyfriend hurt her? He's going to be a suspect. The fact that you had an affair with him and don't want him viewed as a suspect is relevant."

She slapped the counter with a hand, and the flat sound reminded Tim of a piece of meat being dropped. "Kelly left him for the final time two years before she disappeared. The two of them had an on again, off again relationship when she was in college because she was so far away. She came home one summer and they started seeing each other. One night they got into an argument and he gave her a black eye."

Tim was sitting back at the table, making notes. "That was the end of their relationship?"

Quinn nodded, a defeated look on her face. "He'd put his hands on her before, but he hadn't struck her. There was a lot of pushing and grabbing that she'd put up with, and I don't know how to explain why she stayed with him or kept going back to him. Their relationship had secrets, just like everyone's does."

Tim thought about the timeline. "What about after she graduated from college? When she came back here, why did she move to Hogan? Was it to put some distance between herself and Barret?"

Quinn nodded and her red curls hung in front of her face. She looked exhausted, like she'd been holding this in for so long the burden had been crushing her.

"She knew her career was going to take her away from Berry Creek. To make the money she wanted, she knew she would have to get in with a good firm and those are all in cities. Taking the house in Hogan meant there was less chance of seeing Barret. The one thing she understood from going away to school was that he would never leave here and she could. His roots were deep, so if she found a good job in Cleveland or Pittsburgh, she would have a fresh start."

"She wanted a job in one of those cities?"

Quinn pushed her hair back off her face with both hands. "It would let her get experience and still be close enough to help me take care of Mom. She wasn't as bad as she is now, you understand. Mom still lived on her own and wasn't in the hospital, but she needed us to check in on her, to make sure she was eating and that her house was clean. I didn't mind doing it all while Kelly was away at school, but with her back I needed help."

"So that's why she rented the house in Hogan." He sat back in the chair and thought about what Quinn had said. Something still puzzled him, though. "Hogan isn't that far from Berry Creek. Why did she think that would give her the distance she needed?"

"It was a compromise. Her first job, the one she had in Akron, was only a temporary position, but it would let her start building a resume. It kept her close enough to help take care of Mom but kept her away from Barret. By that point I don't think they'd spoken since he'd hit her, so it worked out. Her life was in a state of flux, but she was happy."

Tim stood up, prepared to leave. There didn't seem to be much more to speak with Quinn about and she looked emotionally drained.

"So, is this all going to be in your story?" she asked. "Roger doesn't know about me and Barret. We ended up working things out and I stopped seeing Barret that fall. I can't let him read about this in the paper, because it will humiliate him."

Tim didn't know what to say. It seemed too big of a decision to make on his own without speaking with Charlie. "I'll have to let you know," he said.

"This is a disaster," she said. "I can't believe Barret told you about us. He's so goddamn stupid. He probably doesn't even realize he's put a target on himself. Now the cops are going to be asking him questions again instead of looking for the person who really did this."

"Quinn, I'm sorry," Tim said. "I'll try to keep your relationship with Barret out of the story, if I can. No promises, though."

She looked up at him, defeated. "You know, I married young and made a good life when it could have been horrible. It takes hard work to hold a marriage together when it starts like ours did, but Roger and I have made it work. I wanted everything to be perfect, and that's just impossible. That summer with Barret was just me reacting to the fact that life isn't perfect, that it's difficult, and I made a bad decision. I went a little crazy and ended up letting off a lot of steam with him. That's all I'm going to say about it. It was a mistake and I wouldn't do it again. I don't know if that means anything to you, but it does to me."

Tim slung his bag over his shoulder. He really had nothing to say, not because he didn't care, but because her life was her business, and he wasn't her husband or her priest. If she wanted absolution, she would have to find it somewhere else. "Thanks for your time, Quinn. I'll see myself out."

18

Quinn was still livid two days later. Tim Abernathy had called three times since their last interview, but she ignored the calls. It seemed like the more she said, the more inaccurate conclusions he inferred. Whatever he had to say, she didn't want to hear it.

That morning she made breakfast for Roger and the kids before seeing him off for work, careful to keep her anger to herself. The kids both had morning activities; Claire walked to swim practice with one of her friends who lived close by and Patrick was hanging out at a friend's house for the day. She sat in her favorite deep-cushioned chair in the living room with a cup of tea cooling beside her on an end table.

It wasn't fair, really. What had gone on between her and Barret was no one's business except her own. The focus of the story should be Kelly and the Buckeye Woodsman. Paulie Carmichael had built up a substantial case over the years and not only couldn't they get the police to believe them, the one reporter still interested in Kelly's case was now making the same mistake the police had by focusing on Barret. It was just all wasted time.

Barret. That asshole had been the bane of her existence for as long as she could remember. She had never approved of him dating Kelly, but her little sister never listened to anything she said. No matter how many times Kelly came home crying because he said something cruel to her, she wouldn't take Quinn's advice and leave him.

It wasn't as if other guys hadn't been interested. Kelly had been pretty and smart, with a wicked sense of humor. No matter how many others asked her out, though, her heart seemed to belong to Barret alone.

As least, it had until that night when he'd finally hurt her. The details weren't important to the reporter's story, but Quinn remembered what Kelly had told her.

●   ●   ●

Summer 2007

"Is something bothering you, babe?"

Kelly rode in the passenger seat of Barret's pickup. One of his favorite things to do was take her out for long drives. Tonight, they'd gone over to Jupiter Joe's drive-in near Hogan for ice cream and then up to Lake Trumbull. They were driving along the lake road that ran all around it. Tonight, though, Barret was in one of his moods.

Sometimes he was so needy that it felt like loving him was a chore instead of something she enjoyed. She'd just finished up her sophomore year at Bowling Green and was home for the summer. At first, Barret had been ecstatic to have her back, but now, with August closing in, she could feel him closing off.

He sighed heavily behind the wheel, a passive aggressive noise that she had come to despise. It was clear he wanted her to work hard to discover what was bothering him. It was a path they'd gone down before and she was sick of it.

"It's nothing," he said. They were about halfway around the lake, which meant there would be at least another twenty minutes of him sulking before they got all the way around and started to head for home, unless she could change his mood.

"It's not nothing," she said, reaching over and putting a hand on one meaty thigh. "Come on, tell me what it is."

The sun was setting but he still had his shades on, making it difficult to see his face. "You're going back in a couple weeks and I'm going to be alone again."

And there it was. She was working her ass off at school trying to finish up her degree and he was making their separation all about him. It was selfish moments like this that made coming home difficult.

"Baby, you know I'm doing this for us," she said. "Why don't you come up and stay with me? We could get an apartment off campus." She squeezed his leg. "It would be fun. You'd like it. I've got a lot of friends."

"Sure, like I'd fit in with your college friends," he huffed. "Besides, I've got the garage. If I left, who would help Dad?"

"Barret, you're allowed to live your own life. You don't have to live and work with your parents forever."

He inhaled deeply, and she saw his fingers flex as they gripped the steering wheel. "They need me, Kelly. I can't just up and leave because I want to. I have responsibilities. It's different for you."

This was the kind of thing she'd had enough of. He frequently made little digs at her choices if he didn't agree with them. "I'm trying to better myself, Barret. It's not a crime to want to learn something new. I like art and there's nowhere around here I can learn what I need."

"I know that," he said. "And I know your art is important to you. I just don't know how it's going to help you make a living, especially around here."

She looked out the window and took a deep breath to calm herself. The two of them had been dancing around this topic ever since she'd started school. It was as close as he came to talking about their future. She turned back to him, sliding around in the seat so she could face him.

"Barret, we need to talk about what happens when I'm done with school." She used his name now, not an endearment, because she needed to know that he was hearing her. "You're right. There isn't a lot of demand for graphic artists around here, which means that I won't be staying. I have to go to where the work is."

He shook his head and turned away from her, staring out at the lake as he drove. "Do you think there could be jobs somewhere close by? I mean, Cleveland isn't that far, and you could work from home, right?"

There was desperation in his voice, she noticed. It wasn't something she could remember hearing before. It was unnerving, she realized, to know how much she meant to him.

"I'm going to have to intern for a firm to get experience. To do that I need to be in the office working with the staff. It's important for me to do that because it means making contacts that I'll need later to get hired. Getting in with a good firm is all about networking."

"It sounds like bullshit," he said. "You shouldn't have to suck up to people to get a job. They should want you for your talent."

She bit her lower lip and looked out her side of the truck. He was being obtuse and kind of sweet at the same time. How could she make him understand that working at an advertising firm or in-house for a corporation was different from what he did?

"I'm not sucking up," she said, keeping her voice level. "I'm working with people who will mentor me. They'll show me all the things I can't learn in school."

"All that time and money you've spent and you still won't know everything you need when you're done? Sounds like a rip-off."

"It's theory versus practice. You know how you go to your dad when there are things you don't understand? This is the same thing. I'll be working on real projects with someone looking over my shoulder who can steer me in the right direction. Do you understand?"

"I guess."

She ran a hand through her hair and gathered it up into a ponytail, getting it off her neck. He understood perfectly, she realized. He just didn't want to face any scenario that led to her leaving Berry Creek.

"Barret, moving away from here wouldn't be the worst thing. You're a good mechanic, which means you'd be able to find work anywhere. There's no reason for you to think you have to stay here."

He slapped a thick hand on the steering wheel, sending the truck over the double yellow line. Fortunately, no one was in the other lane. "How can you say that? My dad isn't doing well, so who is going to keep the garage going if I just run off? And what about your mom? You know she needs help. Are you just going to dump her on Quinn so you can go work in an office somewhere?"

His voice rose with his impatience. She realized that while he knew intellectually that change was coming, he may not have faced the possibility of it before now.

"I'm not selfish, Barret. My mother is. She's spent the better part of two decades drinking so hard that she blacks out. Do you understand that? My mom chose this with every bottle she poured into herself. Do you have any idea how many nights Quinn and I spent home alone because she was in some bar? Don't talk to me about responsibility. Taking care of myself is the most responsible thing I can do."

He slowed the truck and pulled into an empty parking lot that serviced one of the beaches on the lake. He parked across a couple of spaces and slipped the gear shift into park.

"I love you," he said.

Tears welled up in her eyes. She'd been meaning to have this conversation all summer but the timing had never been right and now it was happening anyway. Her throat got tight and pinpricks of heat rushed to her face. She finally found the courage to look at him.

"I know you do, and I love you, too, but I can't stay here. There's nothing wrong with this town. It just doesn't have what I need."

His eyes blinked rapidly behind the sunglasses. "It has me," he said, and his voice cracked a little. "I'm here."

She leaned her head back against the passenger side window. This was hard, much harder than she'd ever imagined. Were they breaking up? Was this it? "I know, but it's just not enough. Not this time."

Now the tears spilled over and ran down her cheeks. Her stomach knotted itself and she was having trouble catching her breath. She hadn't meant for this to happen, not this way. What she'd wanted was for the two of them to sit down somewhere and talk like adults. To figure out where they were headed and make a decision. Now it was all crashing down.

"I don't know what you want from me," he said. "You leave me alone while you're off doing who knows what and I wait here for you. Do you know how hard that is?"

Her eyes narrowed in confusion. "What do you mean? I haven't done anything with anyone. Is that what you think is going on? That I'm up at school partying?" She felt anger welling up inside her. "I'm busting my ass. You have no idea how hard it is. I'm completely alone up there. The only family I have worth talking to is my sister, and she's busy taking care of her kids and my mom. My mom, by the way, who is like a third kid for Quinn to take care of. I don't want to hear about how hard you have it. You have no idea how bad it could be."

He shook his head. "So you're going to play the mom card again, like you always do."

"You're home eating your mom's cooking every night while I'm living off ramen noodles. You have a real job that pays you while the only money I get is whatever Quinn and Roger send me. Yeah, I'm playing the mom card." She turned her head to look out her window. Even the sight of him was too much for her now. "Just take me home," she demanded. "I've had enough of this."

His hand reached for the key, but then he stopped and turned to look at her. "I can't believe this is how you treat me after everything I've done for you. I keep your cars running, did all that stuff around your mom's house, and I've put my life on hold while you go to school. I can see how much you appreciated that."

She barked a short laugh and leaned toward him. "You put your life on hold? Are you serious? Why don't you tell me exactly how your life would be different if I hadn't gone to school? I would really like to know how me not being around holds you back."

His jaw clenched as his teeth ground together and she saw him swallow. "You think I don't have plans? That there aren't things I want to do?"

"Well, considering you still live at home in your parents' basement, I can't imagine what big plans you have. I mean, you'd think finding an apartment would be first on that list."

She saw it in his eyes first. They changed, becoming flat and void of the usual spark that he got when he looked at her. Most people couldn't see what she did in Barret, but that look in his eyes was definitely part of it. He had a way of looking at her that made her feel like there were no other women in the world, at least not for him. Those eyes were vacant now, and she thought that maybe she'd gone too far.

"Hey, I'm sorry," she said. "I shouldn't have said—"

He reached out with one giant hand and slammed her against the passenger side window hard enough that she saw stars. The vision in her right eye went black as the shock of what happened jumbled her thoughts. Then his grip changed. He snatched up a handful of her red curls and jerked her head around so she faced him.

"I'm living at home to save money," he bellowed. "If we're going to get married, we're going to need a place to live and I wanted to buy you a house, you stupid bitch!"

She pawed at his arm to get him to release her but he slammed her face against the window again, sending fresh waves of pain through her skull.

Oh my God, she thought, *he's going to kill me*.

"You're ungrateful," he shouted, jerking her back and forth by her hair. "Everything I do for you and this is how you repay me, by breaking up with me."

He was too strong for her to break free, and if he banged her against the window again, she might pass out. She kept hold of him with her left hand while her right searched for her purse. It was a small one and her keychain was clipped to a loop on the outside. Her hand slid along the zipper until she found her keychain. In addition to her apartment and car keys, she had a small pepper spray canister on it. She jammed her thumb into the lever under the plastic guard on top of the cylinder and brought it up.

Barret saw it at the last second but wasn't fast enough to stop her. She roared at him, screaming unintelligibly with all the anger she could muster, and triggered the canister. The spray hit him directly in the face and he howled in pain. He released her and her hand felt along the door for the release. She found it and the door popped open, dumping her out onto the still-warm blacktop of the parking lot.

She raised herself up on all fours. Gravel bit into her knees and the palms of her hands as she tried to get control of herself. Everything had happened so fast that she was running on instinct, trying to remember all the lessons she'd learned freshman year when she'd attended a self-defense seminar sponsored by the college. Taking a deep breath, she stood up and faced the truck, holding the pepper spray out in front of her. It was still clipped to her purse, so the bag dangled and swung as she adjusted her aim.

"What did you do?" Barret screamed from the other side of the truck. "What the fuck was that?"

She backed away toward the edge of the lot and the road beyond it. If he came at her again he was getting another dose. She blinked and realized that some of the spray had gotten in her eyes as well in the tight confines of the truck cab. It didn't matter. She just kept up her slow retreat.

Her path gave her enough of an angle to see his side of the truck. Barret was on his knees, rubbing furiously at his eyes and vomiting on the ground. She saw him retch and try to hold it back, but he was unsuccessful and the chocolate shake he'd had at Jupiter Joe's erupted out of him and splattered across a white parking space line.

Satisfied that he was incapacitated at the moment, she unzipped her purse and pulled out her cell phone. She knew she should call 911, but something tugged at her even now. Through blurry eyes she called Quinn, the only person she could still count on.

⬤   ⬤   ⬤

Quinn had only been as angry as she had been that night a few times in her life. She had left Roger home to watch the kids and driven out to the lake herself to pick up Kelly. Barret was long gone, probably sitting at home waiting for the police to show up and arrest him, but no matter how hard she pressed Kelly, she wouldn't make the call and forbade Quinn from doing it.

Once Quinn got a look at her, though, her concern was for getting Kelly taken care of. Her little sister didn't want to go to the emergency room so they ended up back at her house. Quinn and Roger had done everything they could to treat her. After a shower, Kelly had finally fallen asleep in the guest room, where she was staying that summer.

Quinn took a sip of her tea and set the cup down. Her phone lay on the end table beside it and she picked it up, considering her options. She thumbed through her contacts list, settling on Jean Rodello at Channel 26. The reporter had interviewed her a couple times about Kelly and seemed sympathetic. Making up her mind, she thumbed the contact and listened for a ring.

● ● ●

Jean remembered Quinn and agreed to meet her for lunch. They were at a Panera Bread on the shopping strip. They sat at a table in one of the corners near a window, away from the other customers.

"Thanks for meeting with me," Quinn said. She had half of a bacon turkey bravo and a bowl of French onion soup in front of her with an iced tea. Jean was having a spicy Thai chicken salad and a bottle of water.

"Not a problem," Jean said. "I'm glad you reached out to me. I really should have been in touch with you since we're coming up on almost a decade since your sister vanished. I know the station will want to do a follow-up."

"I appreciate that," Quinn said. She reached out and took one of Jean's hands in her own. "You should know that of all the media outlets in town, your station has been the most thoughtful in following up with my family. We really do appreciate it."

Jean smiled and took a sip of water. "It's really the least we can do. So, what made you call me this morning? Is there an update in the case?"

Quinn pushed away her sandwich. "In a way. I was recently contacted by a reporter who was interested in following up on Kelly's story. Unfortunately, we ended up having a difference of opinion after a couple interviews."

"That's too bad," Jean said. "What did you disagree about?"

"I've been working with a private investigator to try and determine what happened to Kelly," Quinn said. "We have an idea that this reporter just sort of disregarded in favor of treading over some of the same ground we've covered. I don't know if it's because we're both women and he thinks we're not capable of figuring something like this out or if he has some other agenda."

Jean forked some chicken and lettuce into her mouth. "What's your theory?"

Quinn took a deep breath. "We think Kelly was murdered by a serial killer," she said.

Jean stopped, a bit of salad hovering in front of her mouth. "Really?"

"My investigator has identified four victims, all women, who have been murdered by this man." She paused and picked up her napkin, twisting it in her hands.

"Have you spoken to the police about this?" Jean asked. "I don't remember hearing anything about it."

"The police are aware of our suspicions but you're the first person I've spoken to about this, except for the other reporter this week. You're certainly the first television reporter."

"Who was the reporter?"

Quinn licked her lips. "I don't know if I should say. He may not appreciate it."

"It's all right," Jean said. "Reporters have thick skin. We know we're not going to make everyone happy all the time."

"Okay. It was Tim Abernathy over at the *Hogan Weekly Shopper*. Do you know him?"

Jean smiled. "I know Tim. He worked at our station for a few months."

"Oh," Quinn said. "Does this mean you have a conflict of interest?"

Jean shook her head and held up her hands. "Oh, no, not at all. I don't think you have anything to worry about with him not believing you because you're a woman. I've never gotten that impression from him and believe me, in this line of work you learn who the meatheads are very quickly. There's always some guy who treats you like an airhead because you're pretty or who wants to grab your ass because they gave you a job. Tim wasn't like that. I actually enjoyed working with him."

Quinn sniffed. "He seemed nice enough at first, but after a while I didn't like the conclusions he was drawing. Maybe I just read him wrong." She was quiet for a moment before continuing. "I also don't like how pushy he is. He seemed to be very interested in certain aspects of the story that had a more salacious bearing."

"Like what?" Jean asked.

"It's nothing I want to get into. Suffice it to say that they were of a sexual nature and, in my opinion, not relevant to the story. After our last interview I made it clear I didn't want to speak with him again, but he's been calling."

She dug her cell phone out of he purse and held it up for Jean to see. The call log under Tim's contact information showed all the calls he'd made to Quinn.

"I know he's supposed to be a respected reporter," Quinn said, "but honestly,

I don't think he's very good at his job. Quite frankly, I'm finished with him."

Jean set her fork down and made some notes. "What about the police? Are they taking you seriously?"

Quinn shook her head and looked down at the table. "No. I get the impression that they think I'm grasping at straws. The thing is, though, I am. They haven't been able to come up with anything new in my sister's case for almost ten years. What else am I suppose to do but grasp at straws?"

Jean sat back in her chair and considered Quinn for a few seconds. "Is your private investigator certain about this?"

"She is," Quinn said. "You should talk to her. I think she's absolutely brilliant and I think the police don't like her or her theory about the Buckeye Woodsman because she's made progress while they sat on their asses eating donuts." She gathered her arms around herself. "I'm sorry for that, but we've been waiting for so long that it's just been infuriating."

Jean's eyes narrowed. "Who is the Buckeye Woodsman?"

"That's what Paulie calls him. My investigator is Pauline Carmichael over in Hogan, and she has been an absolute blessing for us. She's incredibly smart, tough as nails, and she doesn't let anyone stand in her way."

"Will your investigator talk to me?"

"She will if I ask her to. It's up to her whether she wants to be on camera, of course, but I have no problem with it."

"This is very interesting."

Quinn leaned across the table. "I'll tell you something. It's long past time the public understood the danger they're in. There has been a man hunting women in Ohio for the last decade and no one is looking for him except Paulie. It's ridiculous."

Jean considered her for a moment before speaking. "Why don't you give me her contact info?"

●   ●   ●

Two days later Jean Rodello sat in a small conference room in the offices of Channel 26 ("Where coverage comes first!"). Her assignment editor, Annie Ito, leaned against one wall and looked at the whiteboard that took up most of another wall. The plump woman with straight dark hair had been around the station for almost ten years and was savvy enough to have outlasted three news directors, two general managers, and one station sale to a nationwide conglomerate. Now her eyes were focused on the notes Jean had written on the board.

"Are you trying to tell me that a serial killer has been running around since the late 2000s and the police aren't even looking for him?"

Jean nodded. "I spent almost four hours with Paulie Carmichael yesterday and she laid the whole thing out for me." She gestured to the file copies she'd gotten from Paulie that were spread out across the table. "She was very convincing. Her evidence is all circumstantial, but I think it's enough to start digging into. By the way, we have to get her on camera. Paulie is a real character. You'd love her."

Annie stepped back to look at the rough timeline Jean had drawn on the whiteboard with the names, locations, and dates of the four victims Paulie had identified. Jean watched the editor and crossed her fingers under the table. This was a good story and she wanted to run with it.

"What would you do first?" Annie asked, her concentration still on the board.

"The families," Jean said. "I'd talk to them first to get a human face on this, see what they think about it, and then talk to the police. Paulie told me she'd been over this with Detective Larry Coogan in Hogan and he pretty much laughed her out of the office."

"I know Coogan," Annie said. "He's a tough nut but he's smart. If Paulie couldn't convince him to look into this, we may not have the story you think we do."

"What do you suggest?"

Annie turned to her and pointed to the material. "There's definitely something here. If nothing else, it's disturbing to think this many unsolved murders are on the books. We can certainly do a series on them, but for now, contact Coogan. Let's chase down Paulie's theory from that end."

"Why?"

Annie sat down across the table form her. "First, I don't want you knocking on the doors of these families with a theory that their loved ones were murdered by a serial killer. If we do that, I want to say the police are looking into them in that regard, not just us. I'd hate to burn those bridges if it turns out your source is wrong. As long as we're seen as helping them, we can always go back to them later from the standpoint of investigating cold cases. For now, start with Coogan."

"What should my angle be?"

Annie shrugged. "Be cool with him, but tell him we have decent evidence that a serial killer may be on the loose and we'd like a comment. You're right about Paulie. She has a good theory and ample evidence of something going on, I'm just not sure of what it is yet."

"I can do that," Jean said.

Annie considered her for a moment. "You said Quinn Getty spoke to Tim Abernathy over at the *Weekly Shopper*?"

"That's right."

"I remember that guy from when he worked here. He seemed nice enough but had zero presence on camera. I almost fell asleep listening to him read the headlines."

Jean flipped her notebook open to review something she had written down. "Quinn Getty said Tim was harassing her. After their last meeting it looks like he called her a bunch of times. I imagine that he was trying to get her to comment further or to clarify something. Maybe she took it the wrong way."

Annie tapped a pen against her teeth, which was something she did habitually when she was thinking. After a few dozen clicks she pointed at Jean with the pen. "There might be something there as well. Maybe you should call Charlie Ingram over at the *Shopper*, ask him why his reporter is harassing the relative of a crime victim."

Jean leaned forward. "Are you sure about that? There can be a fine line between harassment and dogging down a story. We all make calls like that."

"When you do it, you're doing it for me. When someone else complains about it, it's harassment. Get a quote."

Jean nodded. "I'm on it."

●   ●   ●

Coogan's eyes were red from lack of sleep and every time he rubbed them it felt like he was grinding sand into them. He finally gave up, reached into his top desk drawer, and pulled out the bottle of Visine he kept there. He leaned back in his chair and squeezed a couple drops in each eye. The soothing coolness started immediately, so he just sat and enjoyed the silence. It lasted all of about a minute before his desk phone bleated for attention.

He blew out a deep breath and peeked at the caller ID readout and saw it was the media, specifically someone from Channel 26. If he had any sense, he thought, he would let the call go to voicemail. Lately, though, common sense seemed to be in short supply. He reached out and picked up the handset.

"Detective Coogan, Hogan Police. How can I help you?"

"Detective, it's Jean Rodello from Channel 26. I interviewed you last year about Hogan's opioid epidemic. Do you remember me?"

He kicked back in his chair and put his feet up on the corner of his desk and sighed. Normally media requests went to the department's information officer but right now, he was the only one in the office. Plenty of reporters had come through Hogan wanting to talk about addiction problems, but he remembered Jean. She had been more insightful than most. Hopefully she wanted to talk about that again, because he was tired of discussing the Beer & Bait.

"Sure, I remember you, Jean. What can I do for you?"

"I got a call from Quinn Getty. She's Kelly Dolan's sister. Do you remember her?"

"Sure, I know Quinn." Little alarm bells started ringing in his head.

"Well, I had a very interesting conversation with her and another one with her private investigator, Paulie Carmichael, regarding Kelly's disappearance. Quinn thinks some of her concerns are not being taken seriously by law enforcement."

Coogan's feet dropped off the desk. He rubbed his forehead with his free hand because the alarm bells were getting louder, causing a headache to form.

"Jean, I'm not sure what you're talking about," he said. "I don't know of any recent updates Quinn or her investigator have brought to our attention."

"It's strange that you would say that, detective. Paulie told me that she had quite a conversation with you about her theory regarding Kelly's disappearance. Tell me, do you have a comment about the Buckeye Woodsman?"

This was too much. The last thing he needed was Kelly Dolan's ghost coming back to haunt him. He knew without a doubt that somehow this all led back to Tim Abernathy and the questions he had been asking. There was no way two media outlets were simultaneously interested in the same nine-year-old case. He just didn't need this conspiracy theory crap today.

"Jean, the Kelly Dolan investigation is active and being worked diligently by the City of Hogan Police Department and our law enforcement partners in Humboldt County and the State of Ohio. We have no updates to provide at this time."

"Detective, I appreciate that, but I need to know your thoughts on Paulie Carmichael's Buckeye Woodsman theory. Are the women of northeast Ohio being targeted by a serial killer?"

He knew he had to be cautious here. This was the sort of story that could get legs in social media if he wasn't careful. If word got out that a serial killer was at large and the police weren't even considering the possibility, they would look inept and foolish. The stack of casefiles on his desk and the Beer & Bait murders demanded his attention. He didn't have any spare time to devote to debunking Paulie Carmichael's theory.

"Jean, I did speak with Paulie about her ideas, but I wasn't convinced. From what I understand, Paulie is a professional who has an excellent reputation as an investigator. I have nothing but respect for her. In this case, however, I don't agree with her assessment of Kelly's case."

What he really thought was that Paulie Carmichael had too much goddamn time on her hands and Quinn Getty had too much money to spend. Kelly had most likely been kidnapped and killed by someone she knew. Murders by strangers were rare. He knew this to be true not only from the data provided by annual FBI reporting, but from his own experience. Nothing Paulie told him was convincing enough to change his mind.

Right now, though, he wanted to present Paulie in as good a light as possible so the media didn't have any reason to disbelieve him. It would be too easy to dismiss her as a crank and have that misconstrued as not believing her because she was a woman or for some other reason. The truth was, if Paulie was any kind of decent investigator, she'd be a cop and not someone who earned a living performing background checks for landlords or following cheating husbands.

"Detective, I spent hours with Paulie going over her casefiles and I have to tell you she was very convincing. We plan on running an interview with her."

Coogan felt like throwing the phone at the wall. Trying to control the media was like trying to herd cats. They both did whatever they wanted and were likely to go in a different direction than you wanted purely out of spite.

"Jean, I understand completely. As I recall, Paulie can be very persuasive. I'm afraid I can't comment on this Buckeye Woodsman person because I simply don't believe that he exists. The thing you have to remember is that over a large enough geographic area and a long enough timeline, there will be unsolved homicides. If someone were so inclined, they could look at those cases and begin to draw connections between them. I can't do that, though. As a police officer I have to form theories around evidence."

"And you don't see that in Paulie's theory?"

"I afraid I don't," he said. Eager to change the subject, he decided to throw a question back at her. "Can I ask if Tim Abernathy is working with you on this story? I've had recent conversations with him regarding Kelly Dolan."

"You'd have to speak with Quinn Getty about that," Jean said. "I can tell you that one aspect of our story is that the police and other media outlets may be disregarding Paulie Carmichael's Buckeye Woodsman theory in favor of focusing on Barret Dedrick."

"I never mentioned Barret's name," Coogan said.

"No, but haven't you been chasing him without success since Kelly vanished?"

Coogan seethed inside. The department had never released Barret's name as a suspect because he had never been charged. Doing so would have been irresponsible. That didn't change the fact that everyone knew he was the prime suspect.

He remembered digging into Barret's past and knew the guy had a couple minor busts related to his temper. The police in Berry Creek were protective of him. On the few occasions Coogan had gone over to talk with him, the local police usually showed up shortly after his arrival. They hadn't interfered with him, but their presence had emboldened the mechanic to be less forthcoming than Coogan liked.

"I'm afraid I'm not at liberty to discuss suspects in the case," Coogan said. "I can tell you that we've followed every lead that has been generated."

"But none of those leads have led you to a suspect or solved the case, is that correct?"

What he wanted to tell her was that this wasn't some police procedural where the murderer was careless enough to drop a clue so some detective could look brilliant around the third commercial break and slam dunk the case.

The truth of the matter was that Kelly's disappearance haunted him. He wasn't about to tell some reporter that, though, and it would probably take about three Crown Royals before he even admitted it to Darren Lewis. There weren't very many open cases on the books in Hogan, but Kelly's just hung there, year after year. It was unthinkable that someone was able to kidnap her and then disappear without answering for it. No matter how many cases he solved, he wasn't going to have peace of mind until he knew what happened to Kelly.

Now, though, he had Tim Abernathy and Jean Rodello digging around in the midst of a double homicide. There weren't enough hours in the day or manpower available to solve all the crimes that came across his desk.

"You're correct, Jean. Kelly's case remains open. I just want you to understand, though, that no one in this department has stopped looking."

"I certainly didn't mean to imply that," she said.

The hell you didn't, he thought.

"I'd like to come out and conduct an interview on camera," she said, skipping right past any response he might have. "What would be a good time?"

"I'm afraid I have to let you go now," he said. "The Beer & Bait case has us pretty busy."

"Can you give me an update on that?" she asked.

"No comment," he said, and hung up the phone.

❂   ❂   ❂

It was late afternoon in the *Weekly Shopper* bullpen when the phone rang. Charlie was the only one in the office because Tim was at the library doing research on Kelly Dolan, Janey was chasing a city council story, and Alonzo had the day off. He picked up the receiver.

"*Hogan Weekly Shopper,*" he said. "Charlie Ingram speaking. How can I help you?"

"You can tell Abernathy to quit making my life hell," said a gruff voice on the other end of the line.

Charlie looked at the phone and considered hanging up. It was too late in the day for an episode of Cranky Coogan. If the detective was worked up, though, maybe he could calm him down.

"Detective," he said. "It's so very lovely to hear from you. What can I help you with today?"

"Ingram, I'm serious. Your reporter is getting people riled up and I just don't need it. I've got a double homicide and a stack of case folders on my desk that have me busy enough for two people. Now I've got him digging around in cold cases."

Charlie took a deep breath before answering. He thought Coogan was a fine detective, but he had a personality like sandpaper. Tim must be doing his job right if he was this angry.

"I assume you're talking about Kelly Dolan's unsolved murder?"

"I am," Coogan said.

"Well, I assigned Tim to that story, Detective Coogan. What has you so upset?"

"He came here asking questions about Kelly and I gave him background. You understand? I cooperated with him and tried to help."

"And we appreciate that."

"It sure as hell doesn't seem like it," Coogan said. "I warned him not to give any attention to Paulie Carmichael and her serial killer theory and now I've got the TV news calling me up to tell me they're going to put the story on the air."

Charlie was confused. Why on earth would Tim be speaking with TV outlets about his story? "Whatever Tim's done, I'm sure he had a good reason," Charlie said.

"Oh really? What reason could he have for this? Thanks to him I'm going to be inundated with calls asking me if Bigfoot is running around Ohio killing people. I specifically told him I didn't want this kind of attention. What the hell kind of journalism are you practicing over there?"

Charlie thought for a moment. He knew Tim had spoken with Quinn Getty, but he didn't know anything about TV outlets being involved. It also sounded like Coogan was rattled. He wondered if it was possible the detective was making a mistake.

"Detective," he said, "I'm not sure why any other media outlets are involved in this story. I can tell you I certainly didn't authorize any such contact. In fact, I can't see any reason for Tim to speak with another journalist about this. Are you certain he did?"

Now it was Coogan's turn to be silent. Charlie worked a pen back and forth across his fingers while he waited patiently for an answer.

"No, I'm not certain," Coogan finally said. "But don't you think it's more than a coincidence that a few days after I speak to him about Kelly Dolan I've got another reporter in here? That woman's been missing for nine years and no one ever asks about her. Now I've got two reporters doing so inside of a week."

"It could be a coincidence," Charlie said, not missing a beat. "Stranger things have happened. I'll talk to Tim and see what's happening, but I have to tell you, it sounds like he's been doing his job."

"Really?" Coogan said, and Charlie could almost see the snarl that must be on his face from the tone of his voice. "Well, tell him to lose my number. I'm done talking to him."

The line went dead and Charlie was thankful that cell phones couldn't be slammed down, although he was quite sure Coogan had wanted the satisfaction of doing so. Charlie hung up his own phone and thought about calling Tim. Then the phone rang again.

He picked it up, bracing himself for another tirade from Coogan, but was surprised when no one hollered at him. He gave his usual greeting and was surprised again by a female voice.

"Hello, this is Jean Rodello calling from Channel 26. Is this Charlie Ingram?"

"It is. I've seen your work, Ms. Rodello. You did a very good job on the hospital closing last year. What can I do for you?"

Charlie liked to start every conversation that might be adversarial with a compliment. It usually put the other person off kilter. He wasn't sure that was the case here, but since Coogan was just on his line complaining about Tim stirring things up with TV reporters and he now had one on his line, it was a good bet.

"Thank you very much, Mr. Ingram. I appreciate that."

"Please, call me Charlie."

She cleared her throat a little before starting. "Charlie, one of your reporters, Tim Abernathy, spoke with Quinn Getty about her sister Kelly Dolan."

"That's right," Charlie said. "We're doing a story on Kelly Dolan's disappearance."

"Well, I've known Quinn Getty for a few years, also from covering her sister's story. She contacted me and said that Tim has been harassing her."

Charlie gripped the phone a little tighter. "I find that hard to believe."

"I'm sure," Jean said. "But she described her interviews with him and showed me phone logs proving how often he called her. Do you have a comment?"

"You're running this as a story?"

"We're thinking about it. Quinn claims that Tim is concentrating on tabloid aspects of the story rather than giving credence to her theory that a serial killer is responsible."

Charlie sat upright in his chair. "You're aware of the Buckeye Woodsman theory?"

"We are."

"And you're running it as a story?"

"We plan to."

"Do you have a source besides Paulie Carmichael?"

"I really can't get into the specifics with you, Charlie, but we're comfortable with what we have."

"I'll take that as a 'no.' Don't you think that's irresponsible? You could be getting people upset over nothing."

"Can I quote you on that? That warning the public about a serial killer is irresponsible?"

Charlie's normal reserve was wearing thin with this conversation. He took a moment to consider the situation and realized that right now, the best thing to do was probably get out of it.

"Jean, Tim Abernathy is a professional journalist who has never had a complaint lodged against him. That's my only comment."

"Thank you, Charlie. Just to let you know, I'll be contacting Tim next."

"Well," he said, "I'm glad you're doing at least that much of your job correctly." He hung up the phone and sighed. That last little dig probably wasn't a good idea, but even he had limits.

"Tim," he said aloud to the empty office, "what have you gotten us into?"

19

It was about six in the evening but Tim was headed back into the office at Charlie's request. Amy still wasn't home from work but he'd sent her a text letting her know where he was. Charlie had been cryptic on the phone, only saying that he wanted to discuss the Kelly Dolan story. Tim had written it up and checked it in on the server around lunchtime.

The weather was beautiful as he parked and walked toward the front of the building. The heat of the day had blown off to the east when the sun started to drop and now a pleasant breeze was doing a bang-up job of keeping things just right. Hogan's Main Street was quieter now because the majority of shops were closed as the sun headed lower in the western sky. He saw people down the street milling around in front of the Peppermill for dinner. Up the street the opposite way was a small neighborhood bar called the Nightingale, where a few patrons were standing out front enjoying a smoke on the sidewalk.

He knew that if he took a drive around town he'd see people sitting on their front porches enjoying the cooler night air. They'd be talking to their neighbors and keeping an eye on the kids playing in their yards.

Tim entered the office through the front door. Charlie was sitting at his desk, engrossed in reading a document. He had his reading glasses on and glanced up as Tim sat down at his desk. The look his face was dour.

"What's wrong?" Tim asked without greeting him. He figured they might as well get to whatever was bothering him.

Charlie waved the stapled papers at him. "This is your Kelly Dolan story. I'm not printing it."

Tim shrugged. "If it needs a rewrite just tell me what changes you need."

"Tim, I wanted a profile on Kelly Dolan," Charlie said.

Tim pointed to the document. "And that's what you got."

"Well, I also got your half-baked theory about one of her old boyfriends being the prime suspect in her disappearance."

"I don't name Barret Dedrick in the story."

Charlie shook his head. "Well, you do name her sister and state that she had an affair with the suspect." He tossed the story on Tim's desk. "Did you really think I would allow that to see the light of day?"

Tim glanced at the story. Writing it, he'd known he was stretching the assignment, but every word of it was attributed and valid. He didn't see the problem.

"Charlie, everything I wrote is true. Barret and Quinn are both on record regarding their affair and he is a suspect in Kelly's disappearance. This story is the truth and it's newsworthy."

Charlie shook his head and stood up. "It's salacious and outside the bounds of your assignment. I wanted you to speak to her family and friends so readers were reminded of who she was. We talked about this. I just wanted a profile of her and an update on the investigation. What you've written is a half-assed allegation that the police aren't moving forward because they don't have enough evidence to prosecute their prime suspect, and you want to tell the whole world that her sister slept with the guy."

Tim crossed his arms over his chest defiantly. "It's true."

"Is it? Where is the quote from Coogan telling me that Barret Dedrick is a suspect?"

Tim took a deep breath. "He didn't give me one, which is why I don't name him in the article."

Charlie narrowed his gaze. "What do you mean he didn't give you one? You went and spoke with him." He picked up the article and held it out. "The part of this that deals with him discovering she was missing is brilliant. Didn't you discuss suspects?"

Tim sighed. "After he related the details of her disappearance to me, I asked him about Paulie's Buckeye Woodsman theory, which just seemed to piss him off. He walked away, and with the Beer & Bait investigation keeping him busy, I haven't been able to get back in touch with him."

Charlie turned on his heel and walked toward the back of the office, fuming. Tim was pretty sure that his publisher was as angry as he ever got. He opened his mouth to apologize, but Charlie spun around.

"You were expressly forbidden to talk to anyone about this serial killer idea," Charlie said, his voice so loud that Tim was surprised. "I told you that. Why would you do this?"

Tim stood, tired of defending himself for digging up a good story. His own voice rose like it had that day in the parking lot with Coogan. "I didn't have a choice, Charlie. I needed Quinn to speak with me and she wanted to push the Buckeye Woodsman theory. It's all she wanted to talk about, that and how Kelly's disappearance affected her. It was like pulling teeth to get her to talk about her sister, so I listened to her and got what I could."

"And that included getting her to talk about her affair with Barret?" Charlie said. "How did that even come up?"

Tim took a deep breath. "Barret brought it up when I asked him if he ever hurt Kelly. He wigged out and asked where I'd heard it and went off on this tangent about how he'd had an affair with Quinn one summer. So, I asked her about it and she confirmed it."

Charlie walked back over to his desk. "Well, you've stepped in it this time. All this extracurricular sleuthing you've done has knocked over a hornet's nest."

"What do you mean?"

"I got two calls. The first was from Coogan complaining about you giving credence to Paulie's unsubstantiated theory, so now other media outlets are calling him."

"Whoa," Tim said. "I haven't spoken to any other media about this. Just him."

"Don't interrupt. He got a call from Jean Rodello at Channel 26 about Paulie's theory, and she's running a story about the Buckeye Woodsman. That story is out in the wild and Coogan blames you."

Tim was flabbergasted. "I don't understand. I spoke with him about it but I didn't write it up in the story or talk to anyone else about it except Quinn. How is this my fault?"

Charlie pointed at him. "Well, my second call was from Jean, asking about you harassing Quinn Getty."

Tim felt his jaw drop. "I don't understand that at all. What are you talking about?"

"Quinn felt like you were harassing her and called Jean, so now in addition to her Buckeye Woodsman story, she has a story about you bothering the sister of a crime victim."

Tim shook his head. "This is not my fault."

"Oh, yes it is," Charlie said. "You did what I told you not to do and now it's blowing up all over us."

Tim opened his mouth to object but Charlie shook a finger at him like a teacher scolding a student. "Don't," Charlie said. "I'm not interested in hearing it. You may think you can just do whatever you want because this is a small-town paper, but we have to follow the same code of ethics everyone else does. That's why we talk about your stories and how you're going to approach them. You don't get to just do whatever you want because if you do, it puts this all at risk."

Tim had never seen Charlie this angry. He held his hands up to try and tried to think of something that would calm him down. "Charlie, I just didn't think—"

"I know you didn't, Tim," the publisher snapped. "And now we're all paying for it." He paused for a moment. "I need you to make changes to that story."

"Like what?"

"I want all references to Quinn and Barret's affair removed and I don't want anything in that story except for a profile of Kelly and Coogan's recollection of the day of her disappearance. Do you understand?"

"Yes."

"Good. Get it done and take a week off."

Tim looked at him. "You're suspending me?"

"I am."

"Just for this?"

Charlie came around the side of their desks and nodded. "Yeah, you need to understand what you did wrong. I also don't need the distraction of having you underfoot while I deal with the mess you've made."

"What do you mean?"

"When these two stories hit the air, we're going to be inundated with calls. Everyone in the media likes a serial killer so this story is going to get picked up." He took a deep breath. "I don't want you speaking to anyone about this. If you get calls from reporters just say that all comments regarding both stories will come from this office. I'll talk to them."

"You don't trust me to talk with reporters?"

"It's about managing this mess so people still trust us when it's all over. Now, get your changes made. We still have an issue to print this week."

20

Tim let himself into the trailer and dropped his laptop bag on the small kitchen table that served as his home desk. After setting up his laptop, he grabbed a beer and opened his story to work on the changes Charlie wanted. The story was still good, even with the changes, but it pained him to make the cuts. He didn't know if Barret had killed Kelly, but the guy certainly seemed like the kind of person who could. On the other hand, Paulie had some good points. Tim just wanted to give the public as much information as he had to see what shook loose in their collective memories. Someone somewhere had to know something.

The shadows were growing long in the yard outside the trailer by the time he finished the story, two empty beer bottles sitting next to his laptop. He checked it onto the *Shopper*'s server for Charlie's review and officially started his week-long suspension.

The clock on the microwave said it was nearly eight thirty. He stretched and his joints popped. A sour look crossed his face as he realized tonight was going to be an extremely late one for Amy.

Her new job was kind of a pain in the ass, especially on a night like this when he needed to talk to her. He opened the refrigerator to grab another beer and noticed pickings were a little slim for dinner, which meant they'd need to order out again. He was hungry because lunch had been light and a good eight hours ago. He drained half the beer in one swallow and made a mental note that if they went anywhere, it would probably be best to let Amy drive.

This definitely wasn't what he thought domestic life would be like. Not that he was blaming her for them being out of groceries, but they were going to have to get on some kind of shopping schedule. It seemed like they were always running in two different directions.

A car pulled into the driveway and he pushed the thoughts from his head and went outside to greet her. Shopping and other domestic chores were nothing they couldn't deal with.

His thoughts of a happy reunion crashed a moment later. Instead of Amy's old Chevy, a polished, glossy black Mercedes E-class coupe sat at the end of the gravel driveway. The car easily cost more than their trailer. In fact, it might be the nicest car to ever pull into the West Wind.

The engine shut off and the doors opened. A tall, thin man with dark hair who looked about ten years older than Tim exited from the driver's side. He raised a hand in greeting and Tim returned it.

The guy was dressed in a charcoal-gray lightweight suit that definitely didn't come from Macy's. Underneath the suit jacket he sported a white shirt opened at the throat with no tie. Tim saw Amy get out from the passenger side, smoothing her skirt as she did so. His eyes flicked back to the driver and he noticed him looking at Amy, and not in a way Tim appreciated.

What the hell is this? Tim thought. He hopped down from the small set of aluminum steps that served as a back porch for the mobile home and approached the couple.

"Hey honey," Tim said. "Something wrong with your car?"

She nodded and closed the door to the car. Tim couldn't help but notice it sounded like a muffled whisper compared to the metallic clang of his Jeep.

Amy brushed away a strand of hair that had fallen in front of her eyes. "Yeah, it wouldn't start. Aaron was nice enough to give me a ride home." She pointed to the man in the suit. "Tim, this is my boss, Aaron. Aaron, this is my boyfriend, Tim."

Aaron smiled and put his hand out. Tim awkwardly switched the beer to his left hand to shake with his right. The guy had a firm grip and strong, smooth hands. Tim noticed that his teeth were blindingly white, even in the gathering darkness.

"Good to meet you, Tim," her boss said.

"You too, Aaron," Tim said. "Nice to put a face with the name that's been making her put in all those extra hours."

Amy's head snapped around and her eyes were wide. "Aaron, I'm sorry. He shouldn't have said that."

"Come on, Amy," Tim said, still shaking his hand. "I'm sure it's nothing Aaron hasn't heard from his own wife," Tim looked back to Aaron. "Am I right?"

Aaron dropped Tim's hand but his smile didn't falter. "Actually, I'm divorced," he said, and then he turned away from Tim. "Don't worry about it, Ames. We have been pulling some long days. Some of the other guys have told me how hard that can be on their families."

Tim became self-conscious immediately. It dawned on him how this looked, him coming out of a trailer with a beer in his hand wearing jeans and a t-shirt while this guy looked like an ad straight out of *GQ*. He could feel a beer buzz creeping up the back of his skull. Even worse was the way Amy was looking at him for what he'd said. The expression on her face told him he'd crossed a line. "Hey, I didn't mean anything. Bad joke. I pull some pretty long hours myself."

Aaron reached out and patted Tim on the shoulder. He tried to ignore how condescending it felt. "No harm, no foul. Don't worry about it." He turned to Amy, who was standing in front of the car. "Will you need a ride to work tomorrow, Ames? I can pick you up on the way in."

Tim shook his head. "Thanks, but I can give her a ride." Between the car, the suit, the teeth, and a haircut that probably cost more than dinner on their last date, this guy checked every box on his mental list of men he'd rather didn't give Amy a ride.

She was quiet for a moment, letting his suggestion hang in the humid air before answering. "That's really very nice of you, Aaron, but Tim can give me a ride."

He opened the door to his car and leaned on it. "It's not a problem. Just shoot me a text if you change your mind."

She smiled and nodded. "I will. Thanks again."

"Is your car still in the parking lot at work?" Tim said. "I can go over and take a look at it tonight."

"No need," Aaron said. "I called my guy and he's picking it up. I'm sure he'll have it done by tomorrow afternoon."

"You didn't have to go to all that bother," Tim said. "I'm pretty good with cars."

Aaron dismissed his protests with a wave of his hand. "Don't trouble yourself. Mario is a master mechanic. The best in the area. Why struggle when a professional can do it?"

Tim could feel heat rising in his face and he had the overwhelming urge to kick a hole in the grill of Aaron's German pecker enhancer. However, he could see Amy was already upset so he just nodded. "You're absolutely right, Aaron." He took two steps forward and shook his hand again. "Thanks again for bailing her out. It was very nice of you."

Aaron's gaze slid from Tim to Amy. "Like I said. No problem." He held up a hand. "See you tomorrow, Ames." He slipped behind the wheel and closed the door. The motor started with a soft purr and he backed out of the driveway.

Tim steeled himself as the car pulled out of sight. He thought his best bet would be to head off trouble by concentrating on her car. "Why didn't you call?" he said. "I could have picked you up."

She gave him a cold look that he recognized as trouble. "I did call. Texted you, too. I tried to get ahold of you for half an hour. Luckily, Aaron hadn't left yet, so I wasn't stranded."

"That's weird. I didn't hear anything." He reached into his back pocket for his phone and found it was empty. Then he remembered going to the office. "Oh geez, I think I left my phone in the car."

He walked to the Jeep and opened the door. Sure enough, his phone was in the cup holder where he'd left it. He reached in and pulled it out, holding it up for Amy to see.

"Sorry, babe. That was my fault."

She stood there, sweaty, her heels sinking in the gravel of the driveway, and just looked at him. He noticed her hair, which had been put up perfectly this morning, was now hanging loose and her makeup looked smeared from the heat.

"Do you even know what a phone is for?" she said. "If the battery isn't dead, you leave it in your car."

He shrugged. "You're right. I haven't been there for you. I apologize."

She turned and started for the back door, mounting the steps with purpose. They made their way inside and she walked into the kitchen, opening the fridge. "Do you have one of those for me?" she said, pointing at his beer.

"There's no more? Sorry. I didn't realize it was the last one."

She closed the door and walked past him toward the bedroom. "Don't worry about it."

"Amy, come on."

She held up a hand as she walked away from him. "Don't worry about it. It's just the perfect end to a lousy day."

"So, now you're mad at me? I didn't do anything."

He could feel the fight coming now, like a thunderstorm on the horizon, rolling in with a rumble. It seemed inevitable but he held out hope that if he could just say the right thing he might get it to pass them by.

She turned in the door of the bedroom, jacket in her hand, silhouetted against the bedroom light. She looked beautiful.

"I'm not mad at you, Tim. I'm exhausted and hungry and I feel dirty. I just want a shower and some dinner. Do you think you could handle it?"

Did he think he could handle dinner? Was that a shot at him? Like grabbing some take-out was too difficult for the guy who couldn't even remember where his phone was? "Sure thing, Ames," he said, the nickname he'd heard Aaron use slipping out of his mouth before he even knew it was going to happen.

She just looked at him. "What does that mean?"

"Nothing. Are burgers okay?"

The jacket she'd been holding dropped to the carpet and she took a few steps down the narrow hallway and stopped with arms crossed and a hip cocked toward him. "Do you think something is going on with me and Aaron?"

The thunderstorm was here, he realized, and it was going to be a hard rain. "No, I don't think that at all."

"That's good," she said, "because it's just a nickname I got tagged with at work. It doesn't mean anything."

"I didn't say it did."

Her eyes narrowed and her head tilted in a way that hinted at the anger swirling beneath the surface. "I'd like to think you understand I would never cheat on you. I mean, you know that, right? It's not something that needs to be said out loud, is it?"

He paused, her words hanging there in the empty space between them. "I do know that," he said, "but I saw him and the way he looked at you. You're spending all these hours together and he's got his own cute little name for you. I know guys and how they think. I'm saying he wouldn't mind if there were something between you."

In the harsh light of the hallway fixtures he could see tears roll down her cheeks. "I can't deal with this right now. I'm exhausted, so I'm going to take a shower and go to bed."

"Amy—"

She held up a hand. "Just leave me alone, Tim. I thought you were more mature than this. Maybe you should sleep on the couch tonight."

His mouth was dry and his mind was blank. He wanted to say more but nothing seemed right and the last thing he wanted was to make the situation worse. "That's fine. Whatever."

She walked into the bathroom and closed the door with more force than usual. Tim moved into the living room and the "Excellence in Journalism" award on the bookshelf caught his eye again. He picked it up, blew the dust off the frame, and stared at it.

Everything had gone downhill since he'd received it. Work at the paper was crazy with Charlie's reorganization. Amy moving in with him had brought its own challenges. He thought it was all that he wanted, but rather than the orderly life he thought he would have, it was just chaos. If this was what life was going to be like, maybe it was time to change things.

Of course, as bad as things were going for him, they were going great for Amy. The firm she worked at was small but they were growing. The thing was, it was just the kind of place a smart accountant could grow and she wasn't just smart, she was amazing. Would he be acting selfishly if he asked her to give that up so he could chase a better career somewhere else?

The sound of the shower kicking on grabbed his attention and he considered that if he had acted like a grown-up, he could be in there with her instead of out here, alone, nursing a grudge Amy didn't deserve. He set the award facedown on the shelf to escape its gaze and picked up his phone to order a pizza. He was probably okay to drive, but with the luck he'd had so far today he'd probably get a DUI and end up spending the night in jail.

21

Things were grim the next morning. When dinner arrived, Amy had eaten in the bedroom while Tim sat at the
opposite end of the trailer in the living room. That also ended up
being their sleeping arrangements.

Amy hadn't wanted to talk much and to tell the truth, he wasn't sure he
wanted to hear what she had to say. He'd been wrong, no doubt about it, and
when they finally talked about what had happened the previous night, he was
going to come off like a horse's ass. So, when they woke up on this Friday
morning he'd driven her to work and dropped her off without more than half
a dozen words spoken between them.

He drove back home and sat on the couch with the TV providing background noise. For the last couple years his life had been so busy he had grown
used to not having any downtime. In college he'd studied all the time and
after that he'd worked two jobs until getting hired on full time at the *Shopper*.
Now he was stuck with nothing to do.

Daytime TV didn't hold his attention. He had no interest in watching
fake judges hand down rulings between arguing roommates or finding out

which guy was a baby daddy. He made himself an omelet, checked Twitter, and saw the usual political nonsense dominating the headlines. He shook his head. People put so much emphasis on what the president and Congress were up to that they failed to understand how local government impacted their lives more. That's why local journalists were so important.

Amy texted him around 11 a.m. saying that her car was finished and that she would be on time that evening. She said they could talk then. His heart sank. Clearly they needed to get through this, but he wasn't looking forward to a long discussion. He knew he was wrong, she knew he was wrong, why couldn't he just apologize so they could move on?

Just before noon his phone chimed with a text message as he was dozing on the couch. He looked at his phone and saw the message was from Paulie Carmichael. She wanted to know if he would meet her for lunch. Having nothing better to do, he accepted her invitation.

At ten after twelve, he walked into the Italian Social Club situated near the tracks leading into downtown Hogan. The joint was a member's only club started almost a hundred years ago by Italian immigrants who came to the area to work in the nearby steel mills. He didn't know if the clientele was still strictly Italian or if they had opened up their membership. Over the years he'd heard rumors of gambling being run out of the place, but he'd never been inside before.

The lights were dim inside the club and it took Tim's eyes a moment to adjust. When they did, he saw Paulie gesturing to him from a stool at the end of the bar. He walked over and took the one next to her. The bar looked like well-kept mahogany, polished to a deep shine. It wasn't difficult to imagine decades of bartenders rubbing it clean.

"Good afternoon, Paulie," he said.

"What's happening, Tim?" she said. "You want a drink?" She had a glass on the table already. It looked like some kind of whiskey on the rocks. Thinking of last night, he shook his head.

"Just a Diet Coke. It's still a little early."

"Suit yourself. I thought you writers were all hard-drinking types?"

"Not since the 1940s, I think." He grabbed a menu from a chrome holder on the bar. "What's good here?"

"You can't go wrong with a burger."

He closed the menu and put it back. "That sounds good."

Paulie signaled the bartender with a raised hand and he looked over at her. "Can we get two number ones, Donnie? Well done? And a Diet Coke." The man nodded and got Tim his pop before slipping the order through the back window into the kitchen. Tim looked at Paulie.

"You should know that I'm probably done with Kelly's story, because I've been suspended."

"What happened?"

He explained what went down with Charlie and the phone calls from Coogan and the TV station.

"I'm really sorry," she said. "Coogan is still an asshole. He just can't deal with someone having an original idea."

Tim shrugged. "It's my fault. I blew the assignment. Charlie was very clear he didn't want me to chase your Buckeye Woodsman theory."

Paulie eyed him for a minute. "Quinn called me. She's pretty upset about the situation."

Tim sipped his drink. "Imagine how I feel."

"She's feeling frustrated again," Paulie said. "When she first came to me, it was because she'd lost faith in the police. When I told her that in my opinion, Kelly was killed by a serial offender, she felt vindicated. It was exactly what she needed to hear."

"I would imagine any kind of progress made her happy after years of nothing happening," Tim said.

"She was excited, for sure," Paulie said. "It wasn't enough, though. I went to Coogan with everything I had and he said he couldn't make a case or even start investigating. He'd already made up his mind that Barret was his guy."

Tim sighed. "And when Quinn saw me going down the same path it set her off?"

Paulie nodded. "I got a call from that chick over at the TV station and gave her a briefing yesterday. They're going to run with the serial killer angle and castigate Coogan and the police for ignoring the evidence I found."

"They'll do it Monday," Tim said. "Today is Friday and no one watches the news on the weekend except for the Sunday morning political shows. But it will be all you hear about next week."

"Doesn't your paper go out on Saturday?"

"Yeah, but that's because people are out shopping on the weekend. You've got to know your audience."

Their lunch order came out of the kitchen and the bartender set the plates down in front of them. Paulie ordered another drink and when she saw Tim eye it, she said, "Drinks for lunch are one of the perks of being your own boss."

"You know what else is going to happen?"

She shook her head around a mouthful of cheeseburger.

"I'm going to be cast in the role of villain because I focused on Barret, just like Coogan did. The story will need a narrative, and it's going to be one of men not believing women when a woman has been killed."

Paulie stopped in mid-bite and then she nodded. "Yeah, you're screwed."

"Thanks for trying so hard to make me feel better."

She shrugged. "It is what it is, kid. I'm not here to stroke your ego."

"Why are we here, Paulie?"

She set her burger down and eyed him, which made him suspicious. He dragged a French fry through some ketchup and let her take her time. He had nowhere to be for a week.

"Normally I don't care much about the press," she said. "I use them when it's convenient and ignore them when it isn't. Don't be angry about that, okay?"

"What are you saying?"

"I like you, Tim. You're smart and you do a good job, so I wanted to be straight with you." She glanced around the club before continuing. "Quinn used you to get the Buckeye Woodsman out into the public. I just thought you should know."

"But you called me after you read my story about the Beer & Bait, not Quinn."

"And I still believe the prick that murdered these other women killed Linda and Carol Jackson out at the lake. That's why I called you. Quinn, though, I think saw an opportunity to push her agenda. She's tired of the police not believing us and she saw this as her chance to get the public on her side."

"When I interviewed her, she wasn't interested in speaking about the information that I'd found out from Barret. No matter what I said, she either wanted to talk about how Kelly's death affected her or the Buckeye Woodsman."

"You have to understand, Quinn is driven to find Kelly's killer and you were just a means to that end," Paulie said. "That's why she agreed to an interview with you. She's learned to be very media savvy over the years."

"Then why do you work for her?" Tim said, his voice louder than he meant it to be. "If you don't like her and knows she uses people, why would you be her investigator?"

Paulie smiled and shook her head. "Why? Because her checks clear, Tim. I have a mortgage and car payment just like everyone else. You think I have to like my clients to work with them? Shit, I wouldn't have a business if I did that."

"I guess money makes it all good." It sounded bitter, and even as he said it, he knew he was being childish.

"I'd like to retire someday," she said. "That means I follow cheating husbands around, do background checks on thieving employees, and take on clients I'm not especially fond of. And yeah, I do it for the money. It's not greed, it's just economics in an area where making a living is tough." She paused for a moment, taking a breath before continuing. "You should know, if things had gone according to plan, it would be you breaking the Buckeye Woodsman story, not that reporter over at Channel 26. You wouldn't play ball, though, so now you're just collateral damage."

Tim didn't know what to do. Being used by someone pushing their own agenda was something every journalist had to be wary of. He thought he had been in this case. Now, though, it was clear that he'd been too interested in chasing the story. He'd let himself be used. Disgusted with himself, Quinn, and Paulie, he stood up from his stool.

"Thanks for nothing."

She reached out and grabbed his arm. "Hey, this kind of bullshit is going to happen. You think I've never been used by some client?"

He shook his arm loose. "I thought you cared about all those women you told me about. Now I can see that was just fake drama to lure me in."

Now it was her turn to slide off her stool. She stood a good foot shorter than Tim but that didn't stop her from blocking his path. "I didn't lie about anything. Every detail I told you is true and I couldn't get anyone to listen to me."

Tim turned and saw the other people eating lunch looking at them. He didn't care. "So, you used me?"

"You let yourself be used."

He opened his mouth to clap back at her, but she was right. The rush he'd felt at getting such a good story handed to him with a bow wrapped around it had blinded him. There was no one to blame but himself. He'd forgotten that the first rule of journalism is to be skeptical of everyone. It had been his own eagerness that dug the hole he was in. He dropped ten bucks on the counter for his lunch and left without saying another word.

●   ●   ●

After arriving home, Tim moved like a whirlwind through their trailer, cleaning and making plans for dinner. His life was in the dumps personally and professionally, and it was too difficult to deal with. He felt like he could handle one, but not both.

After cleaning, he took a break and tried to forget his meeting with Paulie. He was still pissed, but he needed to put it away where it wouldn't interfere with his plans for tonight. Amy was his main concern. He'd been an incredible dumbass last night and he had to make up for it. What he understood now was that he was incredibly lucky to have her.

A bouquet of roses sat on the small kitchen table and Amy's favorite dish, chicken marsala from Barussa's, was warming in the oven. A bottle of wine chilled in the fridge. A nervous shudder moved up his spine as he surveyed his preparations.

His relationship with Amy was the most serious he had ever been in. There had been other women, in college, but no one he had lived with. No one he had felt this way about. He sat down on the couch to collect himself.

She'd been so angry last night that he wouldn't be surprised if she came home and started packing.

Things had moved quickly over the last year, including their relationship. He'd developed feelings for her long before she reciprocated and when she had, they'd been neck deep in the excitement of catching a madman. The life they led now was mundane by comparison.

Was he being selfish? Lately, his thoughts had been about himself; what was good for him, how he felt. It didn't seem fair to her. He stood and rolled the vacuum cleaner into the kitchen closet and closed the door just as a car pulled into the driveway.

He took a deep breath and opened the door for her. A smile painted itself on his face and she stepped up into the narrow hallway that ran between the kitchen and the bedrooms.

There was no matching smile on Amy's face.

She threw him a look full of sand and squeezed by him on the way to the kitchen. He took a deep breath and followed her. Her purse and laptop bag dropped onto the small table and threatened to knock over the vase full of flowers. She turned to look at him.

"Is everything okay?" he said. Then, he thought, *Stupidest question ever.*

"No," she said. "Everything is not okay. In fact, things are pretty goddamned far from okay, Tim. I got taken off the account today."

"The one with all the hours?"

Her eyes grew huge with anger. "Not the point right now, do you get that? I wanted to work with that customer. It was what I wanted and now it's gone."

"What, just because of what I said yesterday? That can't be it."

She ran a hand through her hair and pulled the bun down, shaking it out. "Of course it was what you said."

"What? It was just a crack about your hours. I didn't mean anything."

She stepped toward him and put a finger in his face. "Yes, you did. You've made it clear you hate the hours I'm working and you've been a real pain in the ass about it. I've put up with it because I love you and want to be with you but you have to learn some boundaries. These people I work for aren't like Charlie and the firm isn't like a small-town newspaper with a handful of employees. They're old-school conservative."

"What does that mean?"

"It means they believe in family and it's a tough place to be a woman but the opportunity is worth it."

Silence widened the gap between them and Tim reached out to put a hand on her shoulder but she pulled away.

"What happened?"

She wiped a tear from her eye but he got the feeling it was anger, not sadness, that produced it. She pulled out one of the chairs at the table and collapsed into it. Tim did likewise with the other one. "Aaron called me into his office and asked me about your comment, if the hours we've been putting in were causing problems in our relationship. I told him they weren't, that I was happy with the work. Then he said that I looked a little tired and that it might be a good idea if I took a break for a while. So, for the next two weeks, I've been reassigned to cover one of the other accountants who is on vacation. It's less stressful and I'll be home every night on time, just like you want."

Tim rested his head in his hand. This wasn't what he wanted and he certainly didn't want her angry. He reached for her again and this time she let him take her hand. "I'm sorry. I shouldn't have said anything to him. I was just joking and he took it way too seriously."

She looked up at him with anger in her eyes. "But you weren't joking. He knew it and I knew it. This is your problem, Tim, not mine. I worked my ass off to get that opportunity."

He was quiet for a moment. "It's just two weeks?"

She shook her head. "You're still not getting it."

"No, I know, I just meant it's only two weeks, not a permanent reassignment."

Her hand slipped from his and she sat back in her chair, pulling away from him. Her eyes narrowed to slits. "You know, when you were working two jobs I was nothing but supportive and you were putting in way more hours than me. Do you think I was crazy about that? You were gone every weekend morning for months when you were on TV until you got fired, and even when that happened, I supported you. Do you remember that?"

Tim looked at her and then let his gaze fall away. "Yeah," he said quietly, ashamed of what he'd done to her. "I remember. Babe, I'm so sorry. I really do love you. This is just tough for me because it's so new. I really am trying."

She came up out of her chair and stepped around the table before bending in close. "I know you love me, Tim, but I need your respect, too. If we stay together, we're going to have hard times. We have to get through them without fighting with each other."

He nodded. "What are you going to do?"

"Take my punishment and hope I get back the job I want." Now that things had calmed down, she took a look around. "Did you clean? It looks really great in here."

He smiled. "I know it doesn't make up for what happened, but I'm trying. I also have dinner ready. Chicken marsala."

"You cooked?"

He feigned horror. "Oh, God no. I ordered in. I figured things were bad enough already without trying to poison you."

She hugged him. "Good call."

●   ●   ●

After dinner they were relaxing on the couch when Tim told Amy about being suspended and why. Her eyes were as big as saucers when he was done.

"You aren't fired, though, right?" she asked. "Because we still need to make rent and my pay is still pretty awful."

"It's just a suspension," he said. "No work for a week."

"And no pay?"

"And no pay," he said. "I looked at the numbers earlier today. We should be okay. Are you mad?"

She reached out and took his hand in hers. "No, I'm not. I mean, I'd prefer you didn't get in trouble at work because paying the bills is a habit I'd like to maintain, but it sounds like Charlie overreacted. Besides, Quinn took advantage of you. I know you try to be careful about it, but it's going to happen. We'll be fine. Just don't complain about eating baloney for a few days."

Tim scratched the back of his head. "Yeah, I guess tonight's dinner was as good as it's going to get for a while."

She leaned in and kissed him. "Well, I appreciated it."

He felt like things were moving in the desired direction when his phone rang. He looked at the number and saw that it was the local area code but he didn't recognize it. He almost let it go to voicemail but thought better of it and answered. If it was a scammy robocall he could always hang up.

"Hello?"

"Is this Tim Abernathy?" The voice was that of a young girl.

"It is."

"This is Claire Getty. We met when you interviewed my mom the other day about my Aunt Kelly."

He sat up and Amy shifted away from him. He gestured for her come closer, though, and put his phone on speaker. "I remember you, Claire. What can I do for you?"

"I need to talk to you about my mom. Can we do that?"

Tim took a moment before answering. The story wasn't his any longer, and besides, just talking to this girl might piss off Charlie even more. He was about to blow her off when he saw Amy nodding her head in the affirmative. He silently mouthed "really?" to her and she nodded again.

"Sure, Claire," he said. "That would be fine. What would you like to talk about?"

"I can't do it over the phone. My mom is going to be home any minute. Can we meet somewhere tomorrow morning?"

"Anywhere you like," Tim said.

"Do you know where Paradise is?"

"Yeah, I've been there, but I think someplace a little more public might be better. There's a coffee shop on the strip near that yoga studio. How about there?"

"No, that won't work," Claire said. Her voice sounded nervous now, like she was shaking. "I don't want anyone to see us. Paradise is out of the way. Please? About nine o'clock tomorrow?"

He muted the phone so he could talk to Amy. "This sounds janky as hell. No way am I meeting a teenage girl alone at the local makeout spot."

"Tomorrow is Saturday. I'll go with you."

He grinned. "Yeah?"

She smiled back. "Yeah. It will be like old times."

He unmuted the phone. "Okay, I'll see you at nine. What's this about?"

"Sorry, I have to go," Claire said. "Mom just pulled in." The line went dead.

Tim looked at Amy. "Well, that was weird."

*   *   *

At 8:45 the next morning, Tim swung open the white gate that blocked the trail leading around the cornfield to Paradise. His Jeep bounced over the ruts and a few minutes later he and Amy pulled through the knee-high grass and parked near the burn barrel.

They stepped down onto the ground and Tim pointed to the makeshift seating. "Did you have a place like this growing up? Someplace all your boyfriends took you to?"

She looked around. "Sort of. We all used to meet at Holly Shannon's house and hide out in her basement. Her mom was divorced and worked the afternoon shift, so we kind of had it to ourselves." She looked up at him. "Not all that many boyfriends, though. How about you?"

"Not really. PlayStation online took up most of my time."

"Geez, no wonder you didn't have any girlfriends."

"I couldn't figure out how to beat *Final Fantasy*, so girls were a total mystery."

He took a look around. They were alone out here, which concerned him a little, but he figured that he and Amy were pretty resourceful. They'd been in tougher situations than meeting a sixteen-year-old high school student.

He peered through the trees. "That's Barret's salvage yard over there," he said, pointing at the green fencing. "We won't be going over there today."

After a few minutes they heard someone moving through the brush and turned to see Claire jogging toward them on a path from the tree line. She was wearing long shorts and a t-shirt. Her hair was pulled back in a ponytail and her forehead glistened with sweat. Tim raised a hand to wave and she raised one in return.

Claire was breathing hard when she reached Tim, so she bent at the waist to get catch her breath. After a moment she pulled a small water bottle from the pack at her waist and took a long pull. Then she looked up.

"Sorry, it's a two-mile run over here from my house," she said. "I normally don't have a problem with it but the humidity eats into my time."

"How long did it take you to get here?" Tim asked.

Claire looked at her Apple watch. "Almost twenty minutes, if you can believe that."

"That sounds pretty good to me," he said. To cover the same distance through the woods he'd probably need twice the time and an ambulance at the destination. He really should get in better shape. "This is my girlfriend, Amy. Amy, this is Claire Getty."

Claire walked over to where they stood in front of the Jeep and they shook hands. "Nice to meet you," Claire said.

"So, what did you want to talk about?" Tim asked. "And why are we doing it out here?"

"Things have been kind of crazy around my house since you interviewed my mom."

"What's been happening?"

She took a deep breath and shook her head. "Mom and Dad have been fighting about her calling the news. He thinks she should just let Aunt Kelly go, and Mom says she can't do that. I think Dad is just tired of dealing with it." She sounded sad. "It's been almost ten years and he said he feels like their lives are on hold. Every time they talk about it, Mom gets madder and madder."

Tim nodded, not knowing what to say. How did someone live with a loss like that for so long, without answers or closure? He had no idea. "I think it's probably normal for them to have disagreements like that. It's a stressful situation."

She rubbed her nose and swatted at a bug on her shoulder. "I know, I just wish they'd figure out what they want to do. It's hard on me and my brother to hear them fighting all the time. Patrick has been spending all his time with his friends."

"Claire, I can't do anything about that. Your mom is pissed at me."

"Yeah," she said, "I know. The thing is, I heard you guys talking during your interview and I don't think she was telling the truth about the last time she spoke with Aunt Kelly."

Now Tim was interested. "What do you mean?"

She got a puzzled look on her face. "Well, Mom said that the last time they spoke was on the phone on the Friday before Labor Day, but I don't think that's right."

"That's what she told me," Tim said. "Your aunt's phone log had two calls, one to a friend and one to your mom."

"I know, but I think Aunt Kelly was at our house that night after I went to bed. I heard their voices and they were arguing."

"Are you sure about that, Claire? You'd have been, what, seven years old?"

"I've heard my mom and dad fight enough times that I know my mom's tone when she's angry. They were definitely fighting."

"About what?"

"Taking care of Grandma."

"They were fighting about Kathleen? About her drinking?" Tim remembered that Quinn and Kelly's mom was currently hospitalized, but he couldn't remember how long she'd been like that. What he did remember was that she'd been at Kelly's house the day Kelly vanished, because Coogan had mentioned her in his report.

"That's right," Claire said. "I don't remember the specifics but Mom wanted Aunt Kelly to help take care of Grandma. She was drinking really badly and I remember Mom wouldn't leave me and Patrick alone with her. I didn't realize why at the time, but Grandma's breath always smelled funny. Now I know why."

"How did she want Kelly to help?"

"Well, like I say, I don't remember all the details, but Mom thought Grandma couldn't live alone anymore. She said it was time for her to live with us or Aunt Kelly."

A light clicked on for Tim. "But Kelly was moving away. All the way to Boston. Did your mom think she was getting stuck taking care of your grandmother?"

Claire nodded. "I think so."

Tim glanced at Amy. "I could see Quinn being angry about that. She'd just helped Kelly get through school and now she was going to have to take care of her alcoholic mom. That would make anyone angry."

Amy turned to Claire. "Have you ever spoken to your mother about what you heard that night?"

She nodded. "I did, but she said I'm confused. She said they actually had that fight a couple weeks before Aunt Kelly disappeared, not that night. She says I was just a mixed-up little kid."

"Have you told anyone else about this?" Tim asked.

"No. I mean, who would listen to me? Like you said, I was seven. Anyway, that night wasn't the first time they'd fought about Grandma, so for all I know, Mom is right."

"Was your dad home? Was he involved in the argument?"

Claire shook her head. "I don't think so, but I'm not sure."

"What do you mean?"

Her brow furrowed as she struggled to recall details. "I remember my dad was out of town on a business trip. Sometimes he has to go out to sites and we would stay with Mom. Anyway, I fell asleep while Mom and Aunt Kelly were fighting. I remember it was late because it was dark outside and I was tired from going to a water park that day with Mom and Grandma. I woke up later because I heard more voices. I think it was my mom and dad talking about Grandma and what to do. Dad must have come home and Mom was still pissed. She can talk for hours when she's mad."

"Is that why we're out here, Claire? Are you afraid she'll be angry if she sees you talking to me?"

The teen took another pull on her water. "Oh, you have no idea. She's out running errands this morning and if she saw us together, she'd probably call the cops on you."

Tim grinned.

"Oh, I'm not even joking," she said. "I heard her tell Dad that you're a real asshole. Sorry, but that's what she said."

"No problem," Tim said. "I've been called worse by people I actually like. What made you call me? If your mom says you were mixed up, what makes you think you're not?"

Claire looked a little worried now, like she wasn't sure about what she was doing. "Okay, my mom insists to everyone that Aunt Kelly called her on that Friday and that's the last time she heard from her, right?"

"Sure."

"Well, my mom takes pictures all the time. Like, thousands of them. I don't know if you noticed, but the walls in our house are covered with pictures of our family. It's really important to her."

"Okay."

"Well, after you were at our house I started thinking about that night again because I couldn't figure out why my mom would be lying to you. Then I figured she wouldn't. I mean, what would be the point of lying to you about that night?"

"Right."

She dug into her little pack and pulled something out. "I went into one of the old photo albums she keeps on the bookshelf in the living room and found this."

Tim took the photo and he and Amy looked at it. A very-much-younger Claire and Patrick were on an inflatable tube coming out of the end of an enclosed yellow slide at a water park. In the photo, they wore swimsuits and were laughing as the tube skipped into a pool of water. The date in the lower right corner of the photo was 09/03/2010. Tim looked up at Claire.

"This was taken the day you were at the park?" he asked.

She nodded slowly. "It was. I don't remember much about it, but I think we were at Maui Surf up near Erie."

"Can I keep this?"

She nodded again. "Just don't tell Mom I gave it to you. I'd never hear the end of it."

"Okay," Tim said. "If you think of anything else, please call me. I don't know exactly what this means, but it was really brave of you to call me."

"Being brave has nothing to do with it," Claire said, and her voice picked up a hint of anger. "I'm just sick of her shit. She drives us so hard, like it would be some sin if we were average. Everything I do has to be centered around swimming and poor Patrick can't bring home any grades less than an A." She paused and took a deep breath. "I'm sorry, I shouldn't have said any of that."

Amy smiled at her. "Don't worry about it. Parents can be tough. Do you need a ride back? We won't take you all the way, just far enough so you don't have to run through the woods."

Claire smiled and shook her head. "No way. I have a few more miles to go to get my training in for today. Saturday is cardio day. I'll see you guys later."

Tim raised a hand in a wave. "Thanks."

Claire turned and headed off the way she came. Tim turned to Amy.

"What do you think it means?" Amy asked.

Tim sighed and shrugged. "I don't know. The only thing it proves is that they went to a water park. For all I know the date on the camera was wrong." He pointed into the woods where Claire had run off. "She was seven and heard sisters arguing about what to do with their drunk mother. It's just one more piece in a story I'm not even reporting on anymore."

"So, what are you going to do?"

He looked at her and smiled. "I'm going to check it out. What else have I got to do for a week?"

22

Larry Coogan looked over an analysis of Toyota FJ Cruisers registered to owners in Ohio provided by the Bureau of Motor Vehicles. The BCI investigators had taken wheelbase measurements and tire impressions from the vehicle evidence found on the access road behind the Beer & Bait and in their estimation, the offender had driven that style of sport utility vehicle.

He was convinced that identifying the offender would be done by examining the evidence left behind at the crime scene and, in his experience, vehicle information could be useful for drawing a connection between the crimes and the offenders. When he'd received the report from the BCI, he'd pulled up everything he could find about the vehicle on the internet. Now he knew more about this model of SUV than he'd ever wanted.

The FJ Cruiser was a sporty off-road vehicle, perfect for running around trails or camping. It had been popular when it was introduced in 2006 and production had run until 2014. That meant the newest one was five years old, which worked in their favor. Hogan was in the middle of the Mahoning Valley, which was General Motors country. If he were looking for a Chevy

Blazer or a GMC pickup he might throw in the towel and quit his job. There were literally thousands of those running around.

He checked the production data and found Toyota had built just over two hundred thousand units for sale in the United States. About five hundred of those were registered in Ohio, which made sense to him. The FJ Cruiser was approaching collector status because Toyota wasn't making any more and they had a strong fanbase. Anything made of metal started to rust out in Ohio after a few years, so he had no problem believing many of the SUVs had migrated south and west. He selected the "county" column on the BMV spreadsheet and filtered it to exclude any counties not in northeast Ohio. Unfortunately, Ohio had eighty-eight counties, so about two dozen remained in his search results, and the many FJ Cruiser owners appeared to live in those counties. There were still almost two hundred of the SUVs on his list.

He sighed. His hope had been that he'd be able to knock that number down further. It took him another hour to prepare ownership lists for individual counties and send them out to police departments with requests to question owners. The problem was, those departments had their own crimes to investigate, so it would be hit or miss whether they would get on the job any time soon. The Humboldt County list he kept for himself and his partner, Darren Lewis. If this guy was a local boy, they'd be the one to collar him.

●   ●   ●

Two hours later, he swung their silver Dodge Charger north on State Route 9, aiming it at one of the little townships in the northern part of the county. Darren Lewis cracked a window in the passenger seat to blow out the smoke from his cigarette.

Lewis held a printed copy of the list in one hand. There were a dozen vehicles on it. One of them had a line drawn through it, the only one registered to someone who actually lived in Hogan. It had been a twenty-year-old kid who'd bought the SUV at the beginning of summer from a used car lot in the center of town. He'd had a good alibi for the night Linda and Carol Jackson had been killed, so they were headed out toward the next one on the list.

"I think we're looking for a vehicle with damage on the passenger side," Lewis said.

Coogan eyed him suspiciously. "What makes you say that?"

The other detective tucked the printout under his leg and pulled out his phone. He tapped the screen and opened an app. "The night of the attack at the Beer & Bait, a pickup truck was sideswiped at a campground out at Lake Trumbull."

"I didn't know that," Coogan said.

"It was only reported last night," Lewis said. "The pickup truck owner came into the admin building and reported it in person at the desk."

Coogan's mind raced. An accident meant they could have physical evidence. "Is he sure about the date and time?"

Lewis nodded. "Just after ten o'clock. He said he and a buddy parked on the side of the road near their campground, driver's side out, after they'd been at a bar. They got back to their campsite at nine forty-five. They heard something but didn't see the damage until the next morning, around eight.

"I'm guessing they'd had a few too many over at the Pony Bar on the south end of the lake and parked their pickup crooked when they got back. They probably thought they hit something driving back drunk so they didn't report it. These old boys love their trucks, though, and he couldn't take looking at the damage, so he called it in to his insurance company. They demanded a police report before they would move ahead with the claim."

Coogan reached for his cell phone. "We need to get someone from the county's crime scene investigative division out to look at that truck." Hogan didn't have CSIs of their own and relied on the county or state to provide such services.

Lewis put a hand on his arm. "Concentrate on driving before you kill us, man. I already have them rolling."

"Really?"

The other detective smiled. "Yeah, as soon as I saw the report this morning. If they find paint transfer on the pickup they'll run an analysis and call me."

"Hell yeah," Coogan said. His spirits were buoyed by the good news.

Fifteen minutes later they pulled into the driveway of a small ranch house. A bright orange Toyota was parked off the driveway in a muddy section of the yard. Coogan walked up to the house and knocked on the door. Lewis took a walk around the SUV, looking for damage.

A short, wide woman in a floral housecoat and curlers in her hair answered the door. Coogan flashed his badge. "Good afternoon, ma'am. I'm looking for Scott Davidson."

She let out an exasperated sigh and turned her head to her left. "Scotty! What the fuck did you do now? The cops are here again!"

Coogan took a step back when he heard footsteps tromping across the floor. A skinny little guy with no shirt on and wearing jeans and boots walked up to the door. He had stringy, unwashed hair and a couple days' beard growth on his face. His chest was concave enough that he looked like he might belong in a tuberculosis ward.

"I didn't do nothin', Mom." He looked at Coogan. "Who are you?"

Coogan introduced himself and pointed at the vehicle in the driveway. "Is that yours?"

Scotty opened the wooden screen door and stepped out. He lit a cigarette and took in the FJ Cruiser like it had sprouted from the ground overnight and he was seeing it for the first time. After a moment of silence, he looked at Coogan.

"Yeah, that's mine. What about it?"

"Did you steal that damn thing?" his mother said. "I knew you didn't save up for it like you said."

He turned and waved her away. "Mom, I didn't steal it. I bought it off Randy, like I said." He took a drag on his cig and looked at Coogan. "Don't listen to her. She always thinks the worst."

Coogan nodded and ran through his list of questions. Where had he been the night of the attack? A party. Could anyone corroborate that? Sure, everyone at the party. Scotty was even able to provide some names and numbers. Did he ever camp out at the lake? Sometimes, depending on if he could get someone to go with him. Did he know anything about the attack on the Beer & Bait? Just what his mom heard on the news, he didn't really keep up on current events. Where had he gotten his car? From the aforementioned Randy two weeks prior. It still had the temporary tags on it.

Satisfied they'd gotten everything they could, Coogan left his card and they got back in their car.

"I think we're going to run into some problems with this," Lewis said.

"What do you mean?"

"That kid and the first one? Those are the guys who own twelve-year-old off-road vehicles. They aren't using them as their daily drivers to get to work. Instead, they modify them with lift kits and skid plates so they can run them all over the woods and trails. From what Amber described, we're looking for a guy in his late thirties to early fifties."

Coogan blew out a deep breath. "Yeah, probably. We'll just work our way down the list, though. Keep eliminating them. You never know when you're going to ask the right person the right question."

Lewis nodded in agreement and looked at the list. "Did you examine this before you volunteered us to run all over the county?"

"Not really."

"So, you don't know who is next?"

Coogan looked at him. "No, why?"

Lewis broke into a smile. "You're going to be lucky to get through the day without a complaint filed against you."

＊　＊　＊

Coogan made the turn to go up the hill to Dedrick Garage and Salvage and felt something squirm in the pit of his stomach. It wasn't fear; he certainly wasn't scared of the big man or his family connections here in Berry Creek. It was that when Kelly Dolan vanished, Coogan had been sure Barret was responsible. The guy checked off every box the police had for a suspect.

He had a relationship with the victim, he was abusive, he had the opportunity, and she had rejected his attempts to reconcile their relationship, so he had a motive. All those years ago, his gut had screamed, "This is the guy!" but they couldn't make the case. That sense of not being able to trust his gut had him twisted up.

Now they were out here asking him about another case. Lewis was right. At the very least, Coogan would probably get a complaint filed against him.

He parked the car in the middle of the gravel drive and they got out, each scoping out the garage, the parking lot around it, and the open gate leading back to the salvage yard. It was just something they did, watching each other's backs, ingrained from working together for years.

Coogan walked toward the office door, but turned and wandered past it, to the gate leading into the salvage yard. There were acres of junk cars, trucks, and even a couple school buses neatly arranged into rows. People walked around the yard, picking at the auto carcasses like vultures.

"You're not supposed to talk to me without my lawyer around, remember?" said a loud voice from behind him.

Coogan turned and saw Barret Dedrick standing behind him. He wore a blue Rogers Racetrack t-shirt with the sleeves cut off, jeans ingrained with dirt, and black steel-toe boots. Black sunglasses wrapped around his bowling ball–sized head.

"Actually, you're not supposed to talk to me without a lawyer," Coogan said, "and that's really only in regards to Kelly Dolan. I'm here about something different."

"I don't give a fuck what you're here about," the big man said, and he jerked a thumb over his shoulder. "Take a walk."

Coogan took a deep breath and bit back his first response. He didn't need trouble, and he wasn't in Hogan now. This was Berry Creek, and a lot of money lived here. The kind of money that kept Barret and his family insulated from problems like cops asking questions. What he needed were answers.

"We'll be out of your hair in no time, Barret. What can you tell us about a Toyota FJ Cruiser registered to your business?"

Barret raised an eyebrow, clearly not expecting that question. He pointed into the salvage yard. "It's in there. Why?"

Darren Lewis walked up behind him so silently that the big man actually moved sideways to give him some room when he noticed him. The detective walked through the gate and Coogan followed him. Barret grunted and quick-stepped to catch up to them.

"What the hell do you want with my parts truck?"

Coogan spotted the SUV parked near the fence just inside the gate. It was yellow and had the model's signature white roof. There were a few dents in the body, including some on the passenger side. It looked pretty well used.

"You've had this for a long time?"

Barret huffed but nodded. "Yeah, I bought it new."

"And it's a 2007?"

"Last time I checked. What's all this about?"

Coogan held up the folded list and made his way over to the driver's side. "We're checking on FJ Cruisers in relation to a crime."

He cupped a hand over the windshield to block out the sunlight and bent over the VIN tag. It matched the vehicle ID number on his list, and he put a checkmark next to it.

Looking at Lewis, he said, "It checks out." He turned his attention back to Barret. "You drive this?"

Barret rolled his eyes so hard Coogan was afraid he might have to pick them up off the ground. "We all drive it."

"Who's 'we'?"

"Everyone who works here. Like I said, it's a parts truck. We use it to deliver parts to customers."

"Is that why it's all beat to shit?"

Barret crossed his arms and huffed. "I need it to run. I don't care what it looks like."

Coogan ran a hand over the passenger side door. There were dents and scrapes all along it, some with rust in them, some newer. Maybe it was the vehicle they were looking for, maybe not.

"Can you provide us with a list of everyone who has access to this vehicle?"

"I'm sure my attorney can do that for you as soon as we see a warrant."

His voice was shot through with defiance, which was about what Coogan expected. Barret and clan Dedrick had been on the receiving end of an investigation once before and had learned from it. Treating him like a brain-dead asshole would be a mistake.

"Look, Barret, we're investigating a crime that probably doesn't have anything to do with you, but we have to be thorough."

"What's this all about?" Barret said. "What crime?"

"The attack at the Beer & Bait," Coogan said.

"Oh, hell no," Barret said. "You think I killed those women? Now I am calling my lawyer."

Coogan stepped up and jabbed an index finger in his face. "Go ahead and call him. See if I care." It was the exact wrong tact to take and he cursed himself for losing his cool. He gave Barret credit, though, the big man didn't back down.

"You think I won't? You can't come out here and harass me every time someone is murdered. I didn't have anything to do with that."

Coogan stood solid. Things were on the edge of going bad, but they didn't have to. He could still control this. All he had to do was cool things down, de-escalate the situation so it didn't turn into a gasoline fire involving lawyers and his chief. He threw Barret a small grin.

"Hey, Barret, we don't think you had anything to do with that. Looking around here, I can see you don't need to stick up convenience stores for register money. I get that. Why don't you just give us your alibi and we'll be on our way."

Barret eyed him with suspicion. Coogan could almost see the gears inside the lunk's brain starting to turn with the realization that maybe this wasn't as bad as he thought. All he had to do was answer a couple questions and he'd get rid of the cops.

"When was this?"

Coogan gave him the date.

Barret nodded and stared off for a second. Whether he was getting his thoughts together or coming up with some half-assed story, Coogan didn't know.

"I was home watching TV with my girlfriend, Karen."

"You're sure about that?"

"Pretty sure. I think I had a few beers and watched the Pirates game."

Coogan took out his notebook and made a note. "Can you give us her contact info so we can verify your alibi?"

Barret eyeballed him with contempt. "I could but I'm not sure I want you digging into my life."

Coogan looked at him. "I wish you could just give me a straight answer. It would make things so much easier."

Barret shrugged. "Wish in one hand and shit in the other, see which fills up faster."

Lewis's face scrunched up behind him in disgust but Coogan didn't give Barret the satisfaction. He'd heard worse in his time. "I think we have all we need."

"Good," Barret said. "I've got work to do and I'm getting tired of answering questions about shit I didn't do."

The two detectives walked back toward their car and had just reached it when Coogan turned back to Barret. "What do you mean by that? We've only been here ten minutes. That's hardly taking up too much time."

"You, sure, but that reporter was out here pissing all over the place asking about Kelly. I don't need all this crap dug up again, you understand? I didn't hurt her."

"What reporter?"

"From that paper over in Hogan. Abernathy, I think."

Coogan leaned back on the hood of the car, ignoring how hot it was from the afternoon sun. "What kind of questions was he asking you?"

Barret was irritated now, Coogan could see, and he almost let a smile slip across his face at the man's predicament. Talking to Tim Abernathy frequently made him feel the same way.

"The same shit you guys asked me when you thought I killed her. Accusing me of hitting her, asking if I had something to do with her disappearing." Barret pointed at Coogan and Lewis. "I told him if anyone was to blame it was you guys."

"What's that supposed to mean?"

"It means that if you guys would do your jobs, we'd know where she was."

Lewis walked over and put a hand on Coogan's shoulder. "Hey, come on, partner. Let's go. We got what we came for."

Coogan shook off his hand. His first instinct was to swing on Barret and lay him out. Let all his boys in the garage see him lying in the gravel, spitting blood onto the ground from a punch Coogan knew he could throw.

Barret had been getting by his whole life bullying people with his size and attitude but even the newest rookie wouldn't be intimidated by him. He'd been in enough scrapes that knocking down an asshole like this would be something he could do and not even think about tonight before bed. He looked Barret in the eye.

"Thanks for your help," he said and handed him a card. "If you think of anything, give me a call and let me know. Anything at all. You never know where the clue is going to come from to break a case wide open."

Barret dropped the card into the dust. "Whatever."

Coogan got back behind the wheel and Lewis took the passenger seat. They watched Barret stomp off, obviously pissed. He looked over his shoulder a couple times but they didn't stop observing him until he was back in the garage. Coogan dropped the Dodge into gear and rolled down the driveway as slowly as possible.

"I'm proud of you," Lewis said. "I thought for sure you might give in and put a lump on that guy's skull."

"No, as much as I hate that guy and I still think he's dirty for something, we have to be able to prove a charge. Right now, we don't have anything."

Lewis looked back up the driveway. "You think that mope was out at the Beer & Bait?"

"Who the fuck knows, but probably not. I mean, he's a little bigger than the description, but he's got the right car, he lives in the geographic area."

"Well," Darren said, "that's a bit of a reach. I can't see him pulling a job like that."

Coogan sighed. "Yeah, I know. I'd just like to put him in jail for something. Anyway, who's next?"

●   ●   ●

It was around five in the afternoon when they crossed off the last FJ Cruiser from their list. None of the owners were good suspects. All of them either had bulletproof alibis or, in the case of two of them, vehicles that were inoperable because they were being restored.

They were at the north end of Lake Trumbull and heading back toward Hogan. Their last visit had been with a guy and his wife who liked to run the trails in the woods near the lake. Their red SUV had scratches in the paint but no obvious signs of damage that would account for the damage to the camper's pickup truck.

Coogan pulled the Dodge in to a parking lot near a public beach for the lake. "Hey, didn't we want to speak with someone out here?"

"I think what we wanted to do was head home," Lewis said. "It's quitting time."

"Yeah, I know, but we're all the way out here and we're going to be busy tomorrow." He rubbed his eyes. Lewis was right; it had been a long day and heading back to the station sounded good.

"Who is it?" Lewis said.

"What?"

"Who do you want to speak with? Man, you're falling asleep over there. We'll be lucky to make it home without you nodding off behind the wheel and killing us."

Coogan picked up a tall cup of coffee in a paper cup with a lid. "I'm good. I've got my go juice right here." He took a sip. "I wanted to talk with a caretaker for the campgrounds. His name is Dennis Linchin and he lives out here somewhere."

Lewis frowned and flipped through his notebook. "I don't have anyone like that on my list."

"He was quoted in Abernathy's story," Coogan said. "I reread it last night and checked my notes. We never spoke with him." He was quiet for a moment and looked out at the late afternoon sun hitting the water with golden light. "Those kind of guys know everyone, so if someone has been sneaking around these woods, maybe he's seen them."

Lewis blew out a breath. "All right. Do you have an address?"

"Yeah," he said, and gave it to him.

Lewis punched it into his phone and got directions. "Okay, Google says we're only twelve minutes away. Let's get this done so we can knock off for the day."

It took fifteen minutes to locate because the farm house at the address was set back off the road almost half a mile. Coogan followed the dirt driveway between flat fields that lay fallow. They looked like nothing had been planted in them for years. Thick clods of light brown dirt full of weeds lay in rows as far as he could see in both directions.

The house itself was old and run down. Coogan figured it had been built at the turn of the last century. Like similar homes in the northern part of the county, it was two stories tall and had a wide wraparound porch. As they drove closer, he could see that it had a slate roof.

While the bones of the house seemed straight and good, it was clear that someone was neglecting it. Coogan couldn't tell what color the paint on the house had started life as, but now it was a faded, weathered gray that was peeling off to expose the wood below.

The driveway ended in a little parking area that had been cleared near the front yard. Coogan pulled the Dodge in and parked at an angle. There weren't any other vehicles visible.

"Maybe no one is home," Lewis said.

"Maybe we should have called first," Coogan said.

"It's a creepy enough place," Lewis said as he got out. "I'll knock on the door."

Coogan watched him mount the steps to the front porch and he walked around the side of the house. There was a small garage tucked in there. It looked as old as the home and had carriage doors rather than a more modern roll-up door.

A small gap in the doors let him see inside. The sun was casting shadows from behind the garage so he couldn't make out the model of the car inside, but he could see it was as high as a truck. He saw a license plate in plain sight but he couldn't open the doors farther to get a look at the vehicle without a warrant, so he took his radio out and called in the plate number.

Lewis came down off the porch and walked over. "Doesn't look like anyone is home, partner. Want to hang around?"

Coogan thought about it for a minute and shook his head. "Nah, let's head home. We can catch him at work tomorrow morning. Let's go."

They got back in their ride and had turned around to face the road when they saw a pickup truck coming down the driveway toward them. At the same time, Coogan heard his radio squawk with a response to his license plate inquiry. The plate number belonged to a ten-year-old Chevy Silverado pickup truck, owner Jaqueline Llewelyn, Barber Street in Hogan. Coogan tapped the brakes and pulled onto the stubby grass at the side of the driveway. He looked at Lewis. "That's pretty damn peculiar."

"Maybe she's a girlfriend?" Lewis said.

"Yeah."

The pickup pulled up and stopped beside them. The driver leaned out. "Can I help you fellas?"

Coogan flashed his badge and introduced himself. "We just wanted to ask you a few questions about what happened at the Beer & Bait if you have a few minutes."

The guy nodded forward. "Sure, no problem. Would you mind if we do it up at the house? I need to take a piss."

"No problem," Coogan said.

The blue pickup rolled up to the parking area and Coogan swung the Dodge around in the wide driveway. He saw Dennis walk into the house with a case of Pabst Blue Ribbon under his arm. The guy wore a black Ozzy Osbourne t-shirt, camo cargo shorts, and beat-up low-top hiking boots.

"You think that case of beer is a nightly thing for him?" Lewis asked.

Coogan chuckled. "I think that's a safe bet."

After a few minutes Dennis Linchin came back out onto the porch. The guy was taller than Coogan and a little wider in the shoulders, with dark wavy hair. He had one of the PBRs cracked open already and carried the case in his other hand. "You guys want a beer?"

Coogan shook his head. "No, we're good." He decided to get down to it. He and Lewis fell into their usual routine: he asked the questions while Lewis observed the subject from behind him. "We don't want to take up too much of your time, but we figured that somebody who works the campground and lake all day might be able to help us."

"Well, I'll certainly try," he said, "but I really don't know anything more than what I heard on the news."

Coogan noticed the guy's eyes were red and watery with slightly dilated pupils. He was pretty sure that if he gave the guy a breathalyzer test right now, it would be even money as to whether he was legal to drive or not. "I read your interview in the *Hogan Weekly Shopper*," Coogan said. "You're a caretaker for the campgrounds near the lake?"

"That's right."

"Over the last six months or so, have you noticed anyone creeping around in the woods near the Beer & Bait or out at any of the cabins on the eastern side of the lake?"

Dennis took another sip of beer and sat down on the porch, stretching his boots out onto the steps. "I can't say that I have. The lake is full of people from May to September. After that the water gets too cold and folks stay away or go back to their office jobs."

Coogan put a foot up on the second step, leaning toward him. "Well, we're looking for someone who is a little more along the lines of a Peeping Tom. You know, some dude creeping around checking out the girls. I know there's no shortage of guys like that down by the beach, but the guy we're interested in is doing it from the woods where it's hard to see him."

The caretaker ran a hand over his stubbly beard. "I'm sorry, guys, but I can't think of anyone like that. I mean, sure, some guys do a little rubbernecking when the girls are lying on the sand but as far as hiding out in the woods? No, I haven't heard anything like that. Why, you find something out there?"

Coogan ignored his question. "How about the access road behind the Beer & Bait?"

Dennis looked at him with one eye closed against the dipping sun. "You mean the one leading back to the gas well?"

"That's right."

"Well, sometimes there are kids back there when they want some alone time. You know, drinkin' or screwin' and what have you."

"You ever see anybody watching them?"

"No, sir, can't say as I have."

Coogan leaned a little closer. "How about you? You ever scope them out when they're back there?"

Dennis looked at him kind of cockeyed. "Come on now, boss. I ain't like that."

"You sure?"

The caretaker laughed and put a hand on his case of Pabst. "Shit, man, this is how I spend my nights. I have a couple drinks and watch some baseball on TV."

"That's how it is, huh?"

He raised the can and took a pull. "That's how it is."

Coogan leaned back and the license plate call from dispatch tickled his brain a little. "You do any other work out here?"

"Like what?" He raised the beer can up and waved it at the yard. "This place ain't had any crops grown since my ma passed away. She used to grow corn, but I'm no farmer."

"You good with cars? Like working on them?"

Dennis focused harder now, like he was unsure of where this was all going. "I can keep that pickup running, but that's about it. Why?" He finished off his beer and tossed the can back toward a pile of empties on the porch near the small table and chair. Then he reached into the case for another.

Coogan kept his eyes focused on Dennis as he asked his next question. "Because I'm wondering why you have a Chevy in your garage that doesn't belong to you."

Dennis froze for a second and his eyes hardened. "Well, fuck a duck."

There was a split second where Coogan recognized that the situation had gone from friendly to fatal. The caretaker's hand started to come out of the case of Pabst and instead of a beer, Coogan saw a small revolver. He jumped forward, throwing all his body weight against Dennis Linchin.

"Gun!" he screamed to Lewis. "He's got a gun!"

Standing as he was, he had a height and weight advantage on the caretaker, so he pushed him back against the porch steps. Then the guy grabbed him by the throat with his left hand and squeezed, choking off his air. Coogan forced his considerable bulk against the guy's right arm in an attempt to get the gun. It swiveled toward him and he saw the short barrel worked to the asshole's advantage. As small as it was, it looked like the black eye of death staring at him.

Then he heard a roar of anger and something with the force of a small truck hit him, crushing him into Linchin. It was Lewis piling on. The caretaker was bent backward under their combined assault and Coogan was able to twist the revolver out of his grip. He managed to untangle his arm enough to toss the revolver off the steps into the dirt of the front yard.

The weight on his back finally lifted and he sucked air back into his starved lungs. Linchin pushed away from him, trying to scramble up onto the porch. Coogan brought his knee up as hard as he could and drove it into the man's crotch. He felt it connect solidly and Linchin howled in pain. His hands moved to protect himself from another kick but Lewis pinned them above his head.

"Stay still, damnit!" Coogan said. "You're under arrest!"

Coogan reached for his handcuffs and the guy squirmed again, trying to climb up the steps toward the house. This time he punched Linchin in the face with the hand holding the cuffs and the caretaker's mouth exploded with a spray of blood. He screamed again and Coogan put his knee on the guy's chest, pinning him against the edge of the top step.

Lewis held one hand out to him. "Here, cuff him."

Coogan slipped one handcuff on and they rolled him over to complete the task. He gulped down deep breaths and looked at Linchin. The caretaker was banging his head against the porch and making a high-pitched keening noise somewhere between a shout and a whine. Coogan glanced at Lewis.

"What the fuck was that all about?" Lewis said. "Why did he do that?"

Coogan spit into the dirt, still trying to catch his breath. "I don't know." He pulled his radio out and called in to dispatch.

◉   ◉   ◉

Coogan and Lewis made their way over to the garage where Coogan had seen the license plate from the gap between the doors. Dennis Linchin was handcuffed and secured in their unmarked unit. It didn't have the cage a cruiser would, but the kiddie locks were on and Coogan had warned him he'd shoot him if he ran.

"Hey," Coogan said, "thanks for helping me back there. I think he was about half a second away from shooting me."

Lewis clapped him on the shoulder. "No problem, partner. I'm just glad you saw the gun. That was pretty ingenious on his part."

Coogan felt a shiver run up his spine. He definitely hadn't expected this guy to have a revolver shoved down in a case of beer. "Yeah, if I hadn't been looking right then . . ." His voice trailed off.

Lewis gave his shoulder a squeeze. "Don't think about it, man. That's not how it went down."

Coogan blinked back the adrenaline that was still rushing through him. "Let's see what we have here. I think we have probable cause now."

They each took a garage door and pulled them in opposite directions. Coogan let out a low whistle when he got a look at what was in the garage. He pointed at the vehicle. "That's not a Chevy pickup truck."

Lewis shook his head. "No, it isn't."

A blue Toyota FJ Cruiser sat in the garage. It was backed in with the distinctive grill facing them. Coogan double-checked the license plate with a call to dispatch and the results were the same.

Lewis homed in on the passenger side. He'd removed his suit jacket and left it on the hood of their car with Coogan's, and his tie was loosened. "Check this out," he said.

Coogan took a look back at their car to make sure Linchin wasn't up to any shenanigans, then stepped around the front of the SUV. The passenger side mirror was crushed against the door and fresh scratches decorated the paint.

"That's exactly what we're looking for, isn't it?"

Lewis nodded. "It sure is."

He moved back around to the driver's side of the car and pulled out his cell phone. He took a picture of the VIN tag and stepped back into the fading evening light. Flashing red lights from approaching cruisers were moving up the road toward them.

Lewis handled the arriving officers, telling them where to set their perimeter, and transferred custody of Dennis Linchin to one of them. Before long their chief arrived and Coogan moved to brief him.

Raymond Brussard had been chief for about five years. Ray was in his late fifties, six feet tall, and had a build that said he'd once worked out but was slowly going soft. He'd come from Youngstown PD and once told Coogan he was running out the clock on his retirement in a nice, quiet small town after two decades spent chasing gang members. He was sorely disappointed tonight. "You guys okay?"

Coogan nodded. "Yeah. We might be a little sore in the morning, but we're doing a damn sight better than him."

Ray looked at the suspect and saw him being treated by an EMT on the back of an ambulance. "Why don't you fill me in?"

Coogan gave him the story and finished up with what he'd found out about the Toyota in the garage. "It hasn't been registered for ten years. That's why it didn't come up on our list of vehicles to check."

Ray looked at the SUV. "Maybe he's been stealing plates and driving on those when he takes it out."

Coogan shrugged. "Could be. Why would he go to that much trouble?"

Lewis walked back over to them. "Chief, do we have clearance to enter the house? We want to take a look around."

Ray pulled his phone out and Coogan saw him open his email. He thumbed the first one and nodded. "You're good to go. I've got the search warrant here from Judge Rodinger." He looked up at them. "Let's go see what this asshole has been up to."

23

This is just going to piss Coogan off," Tim said as he got out of Paulie's car. It was Monday morning and she'd rolled by his trailer to pick him up about ten minutes prior.

"I don't care," she said. "He called me down here and I didn't want to come alone." She stopped in the parking lot of the City of Hogan's administration building and looked at him. "Thanks for coming with me. I know you weren't happy after our last conversation."

He shrugged. "Don't worry about it. Water under the bridge. Besides, Jean's stories went live this morning and my phone is ringing nonstop. I'd rather talk with you and Coogan than all the reporters calling me."

Jean's reporting on Paulie's Buckeye Woodsman theory had led the morning news broadcast on Channel 26. Now other outlets were picking it up and running with it.

"Isn't this something you should be reporting?"

"Probably," he said, "but Charlie still has me suspended, so let him deal with it."

They walked into the building and signed in. Tim was prepared to wait in the lobby like he normally did when he visited Coogan but this time the detective opened the door to the bullpen right away.

He held out a hand to shake Paulie's. "I'm glad you could make it."

"What's this all about?" she asked.

He ignored the question. "Why is Abernathy here?"

"Told you," Tim said.

"He's here because I want him here," Paulie said. "Now, why did you want my material on the Buckeye Woodsman?"

Coogan swung the door wide and pointed back toward his cubicle. "Come on back and we'll talk."

Tim and Paulie gave each other a glance and followed him. Coogan went past his cube and led them to a conference room. File folders covered the surface of a conference table. Two whiteboards, one mounted to a wall with a movie screen down in front of it and one on an easel, had notes and pictures covering them. Coogan closed the door.

"Please, have a seat," he said.

Tim was so stunned to hear pleasantries from Coogan that he took the offered seat. Paulie sat down beside him and put her voluminous bag on the table. Tim looked around the room at the notes and spotted photos of the Beer & Bait. "Did you catch someone?"

Coogan looked at him and Paulie. "We haven't announced it yet, but yes. We've made an arrest in the Beer & Bait murders."

"Who is it?" Tim asked. He pulled a notebook from his back pocket. He might be suspended but he couldn't stop chasing the story.

Coogan looked extremely uncomfortable but he answered. "A man named Dennis Linchin. He's a caretaker out at the Lake Trumbull campgrounds."

Tim blinked hard. "Are you serious? I interviewed that guy."

"I know," Coogan said. "That's what made me want to talk to him as a possible witness. While we were doing that, we had cause to effect an arrest."

Tim opened his mouth to ask another question but Coogan held up a hand. "Hold on, I'm getting there." He turned to Paulie. "After we arrested him, we searched his house and found evidence of other crimes."

Paulie put her hands on the bag she was carrying. "That's why you want-ed me to bring my research? He's the Buckeye Woodsman?"

Coogan cringed at the mention of the nickname, but he nodded. "It looks like he has committed multiple murders, including some that intersect with the victims you've identified."

Paulie's face hardened. "Show me."

Coogan walked over to the whiteboard mounted on the wall and raised the projector screen out of the way. A timeline was written on the board in blue dry erase marker. There were multiple names on it, some that Tim rec-ognized.

Paulie erupted. "I told you! I told you and you didn't listen to me!"

Tim looked to Coogan, who just stood there. "Yeah," he said. "You did tell me."

Paulie slammed a fist down on the table and the water bottles on it shook a little. "If you'd just listened to me, Linda and Carol Jackson might still be alive."

"I don't think so," Coogan said. "I mean, yeah, you were right about him existing, but it's not like you told me who he was or where he lived."

Paulie just stared at him. "You could have been looking for him all along."

Coogan leaned into the table. "Paulie, what you have to understand is that the four cases you brought me were all open. There are investigators in each of those jurisdictions who are looking into those cases. No one ever stopped or called them closed. We just didn't know we were looking for one offender."

She shook her head. "The cases were all cold and they were treated like cold cases. You know what that means as well as I do. Unless someone came forward with new information, no one was actively investigating them."

Coogan shrugged. "We do the best we can with the resources we have. You want us to do more? Help raise taxes, because paying officers is the only way that will happen."

Sensing things were going off the rails, Tim spoke up. "What did you find in Linchin's house?"

"After we arrested him," Coogan said, "we obtained a search warrant. The inside of his house was like something from those hoarders TV shows.

Just a mess everywhere. We spent all weekend digging through that shit and there are still guys from the BCI out there. Anyway, he had a box in his bedroom closet with souvenirs. That's how we've tied him to those particular crimes."

"What kind of souvenirs?"

"Driver's licenses or other personal items. I'm not prepared to release all that right now, but the evidence definitely ties him to the crimes."

"Have you questioned him?" Tim asked. "What does he have to say?"

Coogan groaned. "Oh, yeah, we questioned him. It got to the point where we had to tag team him because he wouldn't shut up. He admitted everything, including his involvement at the Beer & Bait. It was like he was just waiting for someone to talk to about what he's been doing."

Tim pointed at the names on the whiteboard. "He admitted to all those killings?"

"He did."

"Did he say why he committed them?"

Coogan got a look of dismay on his face. He closed his eyes and then opened them. "He was raised by his mother after his father took off, and he really, really didn't like her. There were disfigured photos of her all over the house. It's an old tale, but there's a reason it gets told so often."

"So, he killed all these women because he hated his mother?" Paulie said.

"I guess, but he's only been in custody for two days. I'm sure his court-appointed attorney and psychiatrist will have more to say about it. We're checking to see if he had a juvenile record for Peeping Tom arrests or arson. We've seen this sort of thing so often that we know what to look for now that we have a suspect."

Paulie got up and walked to the board. Her finger traced the names and Tim counted along with her from his chair. She reached for a red marker in the aluminum tray that ran along the bottom of the whiteboard and circled four of the names. "These are the ones I knew about."

There were eight of them in total, Tim saw. The four that Paulie had circled, Linda and Carol Jackson from the Beer & Bait, and two others that predated all of them.

"Why isn't Kelly's name up on the board?" she asked.

Coogan shook his head. "Because we don't think he did it."

The private investigator turned toward Coogan. "That's bullshit." She jabbed a finger on the timeline in the gap between Alissa Moldanado in 2007 and Debbie Jo Riggle in 2012. "This is where Kelly's name should be, in 2010."

"I can't put her name on there, Paulie."

"Why not?" she said. Tim noticed she was breathing hard.

"He was doing time in Lucasville for grand theft auto between 2008 and 2011. It wasn't him. I'm sorry."

Tim knew that Lucasville was the Southern Ohio Correctional Facility. Not only had Dennis Linchin been incarcerated, he'd been more than a four hours' drive away from Hogan. There was no way he'd killed Kelly.

Paulie found her chair and sat down with a look of defeat on her face. "I was so sure it was him."

Coogan sat down across the table from her. "Look, I understand how you feel. I've been on Kelly's disappearance from day one and nothing would make me happier than to make a case against him for it, but I can't.

"However, I didn't call you down here to tell you that. I want you to consult with us as a contractor on the murders we think he did commit. I'd like you to walk me through your research. It will help us make a case against him for everyone up on that board."

Paulie considered Coogan for a moment and then Tim saw her look at the board. He couldn't imagine what she was going through, to be right about so much but wrong about Linchin's involvement with Kelly. It was a rough break, but at least some good was coming from it.

She turned back to Coogan. "I charge fifty bucks an hour and you're on the clock."

Coogan nodded. "Then we should get started."

⚙   ⚙   ⚙

Three hours later, Paulie and Tim left the administration building and walked into the warm afternoon air. She immediately lit up a smoke and leaned against the fender of her Saturn.

"I can't believe he was able to kill eight women," Tim said.

Paulie shrugged and tapped ash on the blacktop. "I can. He had time and distance on his side. He was out there sneaking around in the woods in that truck of his, spying on people from the trees. Even if someone got his plate, it wouldn't have led back to him."

One of the surprising things Coogan had discovered at Linchin's house was that the Toyota FJ Cruiser hadn't been registered with the state for more than a decade. Whenever the killer used it, he would steal license plates from another car in a store parking lot. That way he looked legal but nothing tied back to him. It was risky if he got pulled over, but as long as he avoided that it worked for him.

"I think I only missed those first two women because they were outside the time parameter of my search," she said.

Tim nodded in agreement. Coogan had gone over all the murders with them. Dennis Linchin's first two victims had been sex workers at truck stops, one near Akron and another near Lorain. Coogan emphasized that most serial killers work in areas they are comfortable in, and Linchin was no different. He dealt with his mother's disapproval and tirades by driving around late at night and had become familiar with truck stops. That was where he had first hunted.

Linchin later worked in the gas industry when he wasn't stealing cars and was an avid hunter. After his first two victims he'd adjusted his methods to incorporate his love of the woods. He'd discovered that he could roam the backwoods and access roads like a phantom because no one expected to see him there.

"I wish it was him," she said. "I know that's a bullshit thing to say, but I really want this thing with Kelly to be over. I just want to call Quinn and tell her, 'Hey, I know who killed your sister and I can prove it,' but the call I'm going to make will be very different."

"You helped catch a guy who killed eight women, Paulie. That's a win in anyone's book. Hell, you were the only one looking for him."

She inhaled on her cigarette and looked up at the sky. "I'm going to call Quinn when I get back to the office, before this story breaks in the press. I don't know what her reaction will be."

Tim laughed. "She'll probably find some way to blame me."

The look on Paulie's face stayed serious. "You should be careful. It's been on the news all day that a serial killer has been at large for a decade and that TV reporter has been linking Kelly's case to him. Now we have proof that the killer exists, but has nothing to do with Kelly's case. I imagine there are going to be hurt feelings all around. You and I could bear the brunt of that."

"The facts are what they are," Tim said. "I didn't report any of that. Jean and Channel 26 did. If they aren't careful and end up looking stupid, that's their problem. I'm going to write up the facts."

"Well, after everything you heard today, your story should be a hit."

Tim looked back toward the admin building. "Do you think he let me sit in because he saw me taking hits in the press about investigating Kelly's case?"

Paulie stubbed out her smoke. "Could be. Who knows? Maybe Coogan isn't quite the butthead I think he is. Come on, I'll give you a ride home so you can get to work and I can go make my call to Quinn."

24

Tim took a break from writing his story when Amy got home from work. She kissed him on the forehead and went to change out of her work clothes. Since he was working on a story he hadn't really been assigned, he decided he could stop whenever he felt like it. He got up from the table and moved to the couch. When Amy emerged from the back of the trailer he had a glass of lemonade waiting for her. He'd decided to give up beer since the incident with Aaron and Amy hadn't asked him to buy any.

She walked into the living room looking much more comfortable in jeans and a pink t-shirt. He moved his legs out of the way and she sat down on the opposite end of the couch with an audible sigh of relief.

"Hard day?" he said.

She sipped her drink. "Not so much hard as mind-numbing. No one gets into accounting for the excitement. It was everything I could do to keep my eyes open around three o'clock. How was your day?"

He told her about the meeting with Coogan and Paulie. She shook her head and he saw a look of amazement on her face. "Geez, you're suspended and still managed to have a more exciting day than me."

"It wasn't the news I wanted," he said, grimacing. "I mean, if Linchin isn't the guy, so be it. Nothing we can do about it. Now it leaves the question of who did take Kelly."

"What about the ex-boyfriend?"

"Barret? Could be. Quinn didn't seem to think it was him. I mean, hell, she had a relationship with the guy."

Amy looked at him, her lovely blue eyes watching him as she calculated something in her head. "What is it?" he said.

"From what you've told me about him, Barret is the guy I would suspect."

"Why's that?"

She gave him that little grin she had that told him he was missing something. "Look, I mean this in the nicest way, but sometimes you're a little naïve about people and it can lead you to overlook things."

Tim felt a little heat rise up in his face. He got like that when she had to explain something to him that was perfectly clear to her. "What do you mean?"

She took a moment and slid a little closer. "When I was in high school, there was a guy who had a thing for me. His name was Bennie and his mom knew my mom, so we were kind of familiar with each other. Over time, he developed a crush on me. At first it was kind of sweet, but after a couple dates I knew I didn't feel the same way about him. I hate to say it, but he was a real straight arrow and I could tell we weren't going to click. I just wasn't into him because I didn't want a Boy Scout. I called him and let him know, which I thought would be the end of it."

Tim started to feel uncomfortable. "But it wasn't?"

She shook her head. "No. I didn't hear from him for a few weeks and didn't give it much thought. I had other stuff going on. Then I noticed he kind of crept back into my life. I'd see him when his mom visited and we'd say hi or talk about school. After a while he would like my posts on Instagram and leave comments. That kind of stuff.

"Then he got a little closer. He'd leave notes in my locker or on my car. I finally met him down at Jupiter Joe's, you know, a public place, which is what you're supposed to do when someone makes you uncomfortable."

He reached out and took her hand, squeezing it for support. She squeezed back, so he kept on holding it.

"Anyway, I told him again that I wasn't interested. I tried to explain it to him, which means I overexplained. I just kind of rattled on and I guess he was tired of listening to me because he leaned over and kissed me."

Tim's eyebrows shot up. "Whoa, really?"

"Yeah," she said. "That was one of the single most uncomfortable things I've ever had happen to me. I was so surprised that I pushed him away, hard, and he ended up on the ground. There were all kinds of people at the drive-in, so he was really embarrassed."

"Wow, that's tough," Tim said. "Did he ever do anything else?"

She gave him a little shake of her head. "No, I didn't see him too much after that. I felt kind of bad, though, because his mom stopped talking to my mom."

"That's sounds like her problem."

"I know," she said, "but I can't help the way I feel."

He blew out a breath and squeezed her hand again. "How does that relate to Barret?"

"Bennie was just some high school kid I went out with a couple times. I thought he was a really nice, plain vanilla guy, and all it took was a little attention from me and he turned into the kind of guy I finally had to shove down in public to get him to leave me alone."

"And Barret isn't a plain vanilla guy," Tim said.

She shook her head. "Uh-uh. From the way you've described him, he's a bully who likes to get his own way. If Kelly got stuck in his head the way I got stuck in Bennie's, imagine what he'd do."

"Yeah," Tim said. "Barret is definitely the kind of guy who would be determined to get what he wanted. If he wanted to get back together with Kelly and she didn't want to, that may have made him angry enough to kill her."

Amy nodded. "I could see that. I mean, we watch these true crime shows and people kill for way dumber reasons than that." She drew little circles in the palm of her hand. "You know, guys get a bad rap sometimes."

"How's that?"

"I'm not excusing anyone, but we do expect you guys to pursue us. That's just the way things are, and that's got to be confusing."

"You have no idea."

"Right? I mean, sometimes we welcome the attention and other times we don't. That's why I don't think a kid like Bennie is going to go on and abuse the women in his life. It took a hard shove but he got the message and he learned from it. From the way you described him, Barret seems like the kind of guy who would have gotten up off the ground and punched me in the mouth."

"Yeah," Tim said. "I could tell he definitely wanted a piece of me and all I did was ask him some questions. It's easy to imagine what he'd do to someone who broke his heart or humiliated him."

"He sounds dangerous," she said. "If you're going to be looking into him as a suspect in Kelly's disappearance, you'll have to be careful. No story is worth getting hurt."

"I wish you hadn't said that."

"Why?" she said.

"I've just had a terrible idea," he said. "You feel like taking a ride?"

●   ●   ●

Tim pulled up to the gate in Quinn's old neighborhood around ten o'clock. It was a warm night and the top was off the Jeep. He looked over at Amy and smiled when he put the gear shift in park. "Let me grab the gate."

She put a hand on his arm. "Are you sure about this? What if someone calls the cops or something?"

He shrugged. "Then we'll leave. The worst thing they can do is write me a summons for trespassing. If I don't get at least a few of those in my career I'm probably not a very good reporter."

The wooden gate was weathered with chipped white paint and didn't have a lock on it, so he swung it open and let it hang on the big spring hinge. It bounced slightly in the Jeep's headlights and he moved up the trail. There was nothing visible except ruts in the dirt, corn stalks to the left, and waist-high grass to the right.

The Jeep moved slowly down the trail, the big tires easily handling the dry, hardpacked dirt even without the four-wheel drive. After a few minutes they saw the circle of cobbled-together furniture around the burn barrel. No one was in attendance tonight and it was dark except for their lights. He killed the engine and they looked up at the stars. "I can see why someone would call this Paradise."

"It's really beautiful back here," Amy said. "No wonder the kids like it."

He leaned over and found her face in the dark. Their kiss lasted long enough that his eyes adjusted to the inky blackness. "Thanks for coming with me."

"Well, it beats sitting at home," she said. "I've been kind of bored lately. Getting out sounded like a good idea."

Tim rummaged in the center console and came up with a small LED flashlight. They got out and stood in the grass. "Vanessa said the kids dragged all this crap from the salvage yard, so I figure there must be some holes in the fence."

"That's how you want to break in?"

"I prefer to think of it as sneaking around," he said, but she was right. Driving back here was simple trespassing. Going into the salvage yard and the office was quite a bit more serious. He stood still a moment and made sure he wanted to take the risk.

The cops had Linchin for the Beer & Bait, as well as six other murders. His mind went to Amber Prentice, who'd found the courage to run into the dark woods on a night very much like this one. He wondered if Kelly Dolan had faced a similar choice. Had she fled her house into the thick trees behind it, hoping to escape whoever had come for her? If the two of them had been that brave, could he be any less?

He reached down and found Amy's hand. "Let's see if we can find anything on Barret."

The moon wasn't full but it still gave off enough light for them to navigate through the trees. They moved slowly, trying not to make noise in case Barret had a junkyard dog patrolling inside.

Tim hadn't seen one during their interview, but you never knew.

They came to the green fiberglass panels that made up the fence and Tim looked them over as best he could in the darkness, which was to say he couldn't see anything. He broke down and turned on the flashlight.

The light played against the green fiberglass, turning it opaque at some angles and translucent in others. They walked along the fence, dodging small trees and bushes that had grown up against it. Mindful that the ravine ran along somewhere nearby, he studied the way the panels were wired to a heavy metal pipe frame. Eventually he found what he was looking for, a loose panel where the wire had been stripped away.

He reached out and pulled on the lightweight panel, dragging it aside so it made a wobbling noise in the evening air. Amy went stiff beside him as the sound reverberated. He paused for a moment to see if anyone reacted, holding a deep breath, but when he heard nothing he let it out. His heart was beating hard in his chest and he wondered again if this was the right thing to do. Amy slipped inside the yard and put his musings to an end.

The area they stepped into had pyramids of exhaust pipes and mufflers stacked like offerings to some god of scrap. He shined the light around the ground and found a way through the rusty pipes to a larger path.

Tim had spent plenty of time in boneyards like this. When you needed to keep a used car on the road because you depended on it and couldn't afford to buy new from a parts store, places like this were where you shopped. Heck, even if you could afford it and just didn't want to spend the money it made sense to come in here and peel off what you needed from some junker whose life on the road had ended.

He knew there was organization here, even if the untrained eye didn't see it. No one would ever buy these old mufflers or pipes for use on other cars, which meant they were in a section full of scrap to be recycled. The wide path they stood on had ruts full of tire tracks leading to it and beyond.

He shined the light low on the dirt. "We should be able to follow this up to the front of the yard. I think I saw a back door in the office that led directly out here, so maybe we can use that to get in. Be careful in here. All these edges are sharp and I have a feeling every inch is covered in tetanus."

The path ran parallel to the garage and office building at first, but quickly curved toward it as they approached the edge of the yard. They walked past piles of steel rims, old tires, and hundreds of wrecked and rusty automobile carcasses. These cars were arranged by make and model so pickers could be directed to vehicles with the parts they needed.

They were silent as they walked through the rusting hulks and Tim's mind went back to Kelly. On that dark Friday night nine years ago, had she taken a similar walk? Had she hoped and prayed that someone would come to her aid as she was taken from her home? No one had. That much he knew for sure.

As their journey took them around a far bend near the edge of the property, Tim began to smell used motor oil and grease. He flashed the light up on a collection of barrels set up on wooden pallets. This was probably where Barret stored all the used fluids from the garage until they could be hauled away. Some looked almost brand new, while a few looked so old and dilapidated he couldn't believe they weren't rusted through. Yellow paint marker on their sides noted what was in each.

Amy slapped at something on her arm. "Man, what is up with the mosquitos in here?"

"It's all this junk. There are a million little places for standing water to collect so they breed like crazy." He kept his mouth shut about the prevalence of snakes in junkyards like this. As tough as Amy was, she probably didn't want to have to watch out for snakes hunting mice and bugs.

A few minutes later the path finally wrapped around to the back of the garage and Tim could feel his sweat-soaked t-shirt sticking to his back. There was a back door but there were no windows for him to look through. The flashlight was aimed at the ground and he could see Amy's face in the reflected light. "I'm going to try the door." She nodded her agreement.

He put his hand on the knob and rotated it slowly, trying to make as little noise as possible, and pulled. The door opened silently on a darkened garage bay. He let out a deep breath and they stepped inside.

"I wasn't sure if we were going to walk into a dark garage or someone's weekly poker game," he said.

"Do you think they have alarms?" she asked.

"I don't hear any if they do," he said. "Maybe just on the doors facing the driveway." He shined the light around the garage. To their left, three bays had cars in them, with two up on lifts, but the rest were empty. He looked right and saw the door leading into the office. "That's where we want to go."

The office was dark except for one small lamp on the desk where Barret's mother had been sitting. There was one camera in the corner but there were no wires coming from it. If he had to bet, and he was just by being here, he guessed it was a phony.

"His office is over there," he said, pointing to the doorway just past the counter. "If there's anything to find here, I think it will be there."

"Let's take a look," Amy said.

The door was open so they walked right in. The first thing that struck Tim was that Barret was every inch the slob he thought he would be. As organized as Barret's salvage yard was, his office was a disaster.

A desk that seemed too big for the space squatted in the middle of the room with an office chair behind it. The brown material of the chair was smudged black with grease in places and the arms were wound with duct tape. Tim sat down.

"Do you think the computer is worth looking at?" Amy asked.

"Probably," he said. "I wonder if it's password protected." He moved the mouse and the square monitor lit up. The ancient Gateway was logged into a parts supplier website. Tim looked down at the top of the desk.

The top of it had a blotter calendar laying under stacks of paper and what looked like an ignition module. The papers were mostly invoices for sales to customers and bills from vendors. Between the car parts and paperwork, Tim didn't see anything that caught his attention.

"What does 'J-23' mean?" Amy said from a corner opposite the desk. Tim looked up and saw her holding a calendar. This one had photos of hot rods rather than bikini models.

"I don't know," he said. "Why?"

She held the cover of the calendar up. "This is from 2010. That's the year Kelly disappeared, right?"

Tim stood up and looked at the calendar. "Is that written somewhere?"

"Right here," she said, pointing at a page. "Friday, September third, 2010. Wasn't that the day she vanished?"

Tim looked at the notation. It was written right where Amy said. "That can't be a coincidence. Where did you find the calendar?"

"It was on a magnetic clip stuck to this side of the file cabinet." She pointed to the side of the cabinet that faced the wall. He saw that it was a narrow space that could be used to hide things from view, but also keep them easily accessible. "What do you think it means?"

"I'm not sure, but it seems familiar," he said. "I think I've seen it before." He pulled out his cell phone and snapped a few photos of the calendar.

He sat back down at the desk and looked it over again, this time with something specific in mind. The desk was littered with Post-it notes of varying colors, receipts, invoices, and the desktop calendar. Looking at that last item, he moved some of the papers out of the way to see if it would pay off, but it was six months out of date.

The computer monitor winked off as the machine went to sleep and the action drew his attention. Sticky notes were stuck all over it and one caught his eye. It was yellow, wrinkled, and worn, but Tim saw "J-23" written on it. He pointed to it. "I've got another one over here."

Amy was at the file cabinet digging through the drawers. She looked up at him and nodded. "It must mean something," she said. "Why else would he keep that calendar?"

"I don't know," Tim said. He dug into the three drawers running down the right side of the desk. The first one was a small drawer that seemed to be a catchall. It held pens, notepads, and paperclips. The second one was full of more paperwork that seemed to be car titles. He closed it and slid the third one open. It was a deep drawer where hanging files would normally be stored. Instead, he saw stacks of college-ruled notebooks.

Tim selected one from the top of the list and opened it. His eyes opened wide as he looked at the first page. "J-23" was written top to bottom in six columns across the page. The handwriting was neat but cramped, as if the author had labored over the work.

He flipped through the notebook, and each page was the same. Two hundred pages of the same thing written over and over. He laid the notebook on the desktop and dug into the others stacked in the drawer. Some of them looked older, not quite yellowed with age, but their pages weren't the crisp whiteness he'd expected. All of them had "J-23" written over and over in them. Some were neat, while others were quite sloppy.

His mind flashed back to the day he'd come to interview Barret and met his mother. She'd complained about him sitting in his office with the door closed. Tim had thought he'd been shutting her out or watching porn, but maybe he'd been sitting here filling up notebooks with this odd notation.

Amy closed the bottom drawer of the file cabinet and the noise woke him out of his reverie. "Well, I don't see anything else. How about you?"

Tim looked at her and held up a notebook. "Oh, yeah. Check this out."

Amy flipped through the pages and her eyes widened. "What the hell? Why is he doing this? What does it mean?"

Tim shook his head. "I don't know. This must mean something. That calendar you found proves it has something to do with Kelly, but what?"

Amy crouched down beside the chair and put a hand on his knee. "You said you've seen this written somewhere before. Was it here? It must have been, right?"

Tim thought back to that day. He certainly hadn't been in this office because he hadn't made it past the confines of the outer office with the long wooden counter. Barret had walked him outside to his truck, but he didn't remember seeing anything there. Then it hit him.

"I remember," he said. "Holy shit, I know where I've seen this."

"Where?" Amy said.

"Help me clean this up and shut off the lights. I'll show you."

They closed up the drawers and Tim took a picture of the notebooks and a few pages inside. They shut off the lights and he led Amy back into the garage. He snapped on the flashlight and the light fell against the shelves set against the back wall.

"What did you see?" Amy asked.

"When Barret talked to me, he was rude and cranky, except when he talked about Kelly and her artwork." He put the flashlight between his teeth and reached up on the shelf. His fingers closed on the same box Barret had pulled down the day he was here. He set it on the floor and shined the light on the box. "J-23" was written there in black Sharpie.

"Holy cow," Amy said. "What's in the box?"

Tim handed her the light to free up his hands and pulled open the flaps. "It's a motorcycle gas tank Kelly made for him. Check it out." He held it up in the air for her to see.

The metallic green paint glittered in the bright flashlight beam and he watched as Amy took in the painted dragon with fire shooting from its mouth. "She made this for him?"

"She did," he said.

Amy ran a hand over the tank. "Maybe this is the only thing she ever created for him that he still has."

"Maybe," he said. "But what's up with that repetitive writing in the note-books?"

She shook her head. "I don't know, but it must relate to her somehow."

Tim looked around. There wasn't much else to search so he shined the light up the shelves. Nothing else caught his attention.

"We should go," he said. "I think we've pushed our luck far enough."

Amy nodded and glanced nervously toward the big roll-up doors. "I think you're right. Let's go."

They made their way out the back door to the salvage yard. Leaving was easier than coming in because they knew the way. Tim kept a quick pace but was careful not to trip over anything or lose his footing in the ruts. He stopped when they came to the area where Barret stored his recyclable fluids.

"What is it?" Amy asked.

Tim shined the light over the barrels. Most of them were regular fif-ty-five-gallon metal drums you'd expect to see around shops. They'd be full of oil and grease, transmission fluid, and coolant. "These all have writing on them."

He'd noticed it on their way in. All the barrels had notes written on them in yellow paint marker. Now that he took a good look at them, he could see that there was a date and then some kind of code. Tim tapped it. "This is probably a note so they know what's in the barrel."

He shined the light around the area. There were probably a hundred of the damn things sitting up off the ground on wooden pallets. Most of them were stacked four to a pallet and banded together so they could be moved with a forklift. Tim had worked one summer on a loading dock and had seen similar setups.

They stepped off the dirt path and made their way among the barrels. To-ward the back of the pile, near the fence, Tim spotted one sitting all by itself on the ground. Grass grew up around it and branches from a maple sapling hung over it. The light fell on the paint marker notation and his hand started to shake.

It said "J-23."

"Tim," Amy said. "We should go."

He stood staring at the rusty barrel and then reached out a hand to touch it. He pushed against it and it felt full. Liquid sloshed around inside. He turned to Amy and saw the fear on her face. "Are you okay?"

She straightened up. "I think so. Do you think we should come back with the police?"

"And tell them what?" he said. "That Barret is writing goofy shit in a notebook? That a barrel has a peculiar note on it? No, we need more than that."

He leaned in close and examined the barrel. The top was closed with a clamp that ran around the circumference of the lid. A large bolt closed the clamp and Tim sighed. He had a pocket tool but the pliers were too small to get a grip on the nut locking it closed. "Damn it, I need a wrench," he said. "Maybe they keep one out here."

He played the light over the other drums but didn't see anything he could use. Just as he was about to suggest walking back to the garage to steal one out of a toolbox, he spotted something hanging from a pole pounded in the ground. Drum clamps lay in a pile at the bottom of the pole and a large adjustable wrench hung from a bungee cord. He grabbed it. "This should work."

He walked back to the drum and fit the wrench over the bolt holding the clamp closed. It was rusted and resisted his first attempt to turn it. Sweat from the humid night air ran into his eyes and he brushed it away with the back of his hand. He reset the wrench and tried again. The whole drum shifted from the effort but the nut broke loose. He worked quickly, until the nut spun with his fingers. The clamp loosened enough that he could lift it off the drum. He dropped it in the grass.

He looked at Amy. "You ready?"

She nodded and gripped his shoulder. "Okay, go ahead."

A sense of dread fell over him as he pulled the flat lid from the drum. A horrific smell rose up when the inner gasket of the lid pulled away from the rim. Tim dropped it and it clanged off the clamp.

Amy shined the light on the top of the barrel and he could see it was full of used oil. The inky fluid reflected the light and then something moved within. The oil shimmered silently as a face rose up and broke the surface.

Tim jumped back away from the drum and Amy screamed. It was a high-pitched sound but she cut it off by putting her hand over her mouth. Tim pulled her tight and hugged her to his body.

"That's her," she said, her voice muffled by his chest. "Oh my God, Tim. He's been keeping her out here in a barrel all these years. How could he do that? How could he say he loved her but do this to her and her family?"

He shook his head and hugged her tight. "I don't know, but we need help. This is bigger than a story now. We need to let someone know."

He took the light from Amy's shaking hands and put the beam back on the figure entombed in oil. He couldn't tell if it was Kelly or not, but the face was frozen in a silent scream, its mouth open and full of oil. He put the light between his teeth and snapped a photo, documenting the scene. Then he sent a quick text.

"We need to get out of here," Tim said. "This isn't safe. If Barret comes back here and finds us, he'll kill us."

Amy nodded in the light. "Yeah, let's go."

They turned and fled the scene, moving at a fast jog along the wide dirt path toward the hole in the fence. They ducked through the missing panel and started making their way through the trees as fast as they could.

They were almost back to the Jeep when a gunshot split the warm night air.

25

Tim reached behind him for Amy's hand and dragged her down to the dirt with him. He could hear voices ahead of them near where the Jeep was parked. There were lights on now, bright ones, like floodlamps biting through the darkness. They sat still in the brush and heard an angry voice.

"Why the fuck did you shoot me?" a male voice said. "What are you doing?"

Tim strained to see across the distance. It was about twenty yards and as his eyes adjusted to the light he was able to make out two figures. They stood just outside the circle of seats set up around the burn barrel. He blinked once and realized he knew them both.

"You think I'm going to let you kill me like you did Kelly?" he heard Quinn say. "No way. You're going to pay for what you did."

Tim could hear anger in her voice. He rose up on his knees just enough to see through the trees. The scene was as bad as he imagined. The light was coming from Barret's Dodge Ram pickup. It was parked behind and to the right of Tim's Jeep. Barret was on his knees with one hand holding his shoulder while Quinn stood over him with a handgun. She looked every bit an avenging angel. He turned back to Amy. "She's going to kill him. What should we do?"

Amy looked at him with wide blue eyes. "If you say something, will she listen to you?"

He looked back toward the scene unfolding before him. For all his earlier bluster, Barret looked small now, pitiful in the harsh lights of the truck.

"I didn't kill anyone, you crazy bitch!" the big man said. "Why are you doing this after everything I did for you?"

"Shut up!" Quinn screamed into the night air. "You haven't done anything for me! All you've ever done is take! I fucking hate you!" She kicked him viciously in the shoulder where he'd been shot and Barret howled in pain. Tim watched as he curled up on the ground to protect himself.

"Now tell me where Kelly is," Quinn said. "Tell me or I'll shoot you again, and I'll keep shooting you until you tell me or die. I'm done fucking around with you."

Taking a deep breath, Tim made a decision. "Stay down," he said to Amy. Before she could say anything, he stood in the cover of the trees and shouted. "Quinn, stop!"

She turned and pointed the gun in his direction, eyes blazing with anger. "Who's there?"

"It's me, Tim Abernathy. Please put the gun down."

"Not until he tells me where my sister is!" she raged. "What are you even doing here?" Quinn said, holding the gun steady as she squinted into the trees.

"I found Kelly," Tim said, moving forward through the brush until he was in the clearing. "I can show you where she is."

She moved toward him in halting, stumbling steps. "You found Kelly?"

"I did," he said and pointed back toward the salvage yard. "She's in there. I can show you but we have to get Barret some help. He's bleeding, Quinn. You shot him. I'm just going to call the police and get them out here. Let them take care of it." He pulled out his phone and thumbed the fingerprint ID so the screen came to life.

She turned back toward Barret with that dazed look on her face. Tim saw her raise the gun again. "He doesn't deserve any help."

Barret held up a bloody hand. "He's bluffing. You'll never find her without me."

"Shut up!" Quinn said, and pulled the trigger. The sound of the shot washed over Tim and he jumped, dropping his phone. He bent to pick it up but Quinn shouted at him.

"Stop! Before we call anyone, I want to see my sister." Her voice was hard now and the dazed look had been replaced with one of determination.

Barret lay on the ground staring up at Quinn. Tim could still hear him breathing and moaning, so Quinn's second shot hadn't been fatal. At least, not yet. "Jesus Christ, she's not going anywhere!" Tim said. "Let's get him help so you don't get into trouble for killing him."

She gestured at him with the gun. "Show me."

"Quinn, I found her," Tim said. "Are you really going to shoot me?"

The gun came up and she seemed to center it directly between his eyes. "Show me where my sister is. It's been nine years and I want to know."

The barrel of the gun looked as big and dark as a coal mine, even in the light from the truck. Tim nodded. "Okay, come with me. I'll show you."

She waved him back toward the fence with the gun. "Lead the way."

Tim turned and started back toward the salvage yard. He thought of Amy then and veered to his right, trying to lead Quinn away from where she was hiding. They were almost past her when Quinn stopped and spun to her left.

"Who's that?" she cried and pointed the gun where Amy was crouched down among the trees.

Tim turned back toward her. "Stop! She's with me. Don't hurt her."

Quinn stepped back and waved her free hand at Amy. "Get over there with him." She turned back toward Tim. "Is there anyone else out here?"

Tim shook his head. "No."

She gestured with the gun again. "Then get moving and show me where my sister is."

They walked back through the trees and found the gap in the fence. Tim used his flashlight out in the open now, no longer afraid of drawing attention. He let Amy go in first and worked to keep himself between her and Quinn's gun. Quinn had trouble moving the panel aside to slip in and Tim grabbed Amy by the arm. "If you get the chance, run. I'll keep her busy so you can get help."

She shook her head but then Quinn was behind him. "Let's go."

"What were you doing out here with Barret?" Tim said. "It's awfully coincidental the two of you would be out here the same night as Amy and I."

Quinn took a step back, putting a little room between them. "I wanted to know why he told you about the affair." She balled her free hand in frustration and struck her leg. "I just couldn't understand why he brought that up."

"Why would you meet out here?"

"We didn't," she said. "I invited him to my house. Roger is away on business and I made arrangements for the kids to stay over with friends. I just wanted to confront him."

"What did he say?"

She laughed him off, a snide little sound. "He was angry that you asked him if he'd ever hurt Kelly. He thought you got that from me." She was silent for a moment. "It doesn't matter anymore."

"So why did you come out here?"

The gun stayed steady on them. "He has cameras and motion sensors in the garage. You tripped them and he got an alert on his phone. He could see you weren't parked out front so he figured you snuck in the back. I went with him and we found your car."

Tim shook his head. "Do you really think this story is going to hold up?"

Quinn's eyes narrowed. "What do you mean?"

"I mean this bullshit you're slinging about Barret killing your sister. We both know it isn't true."

"You don't know what you're talking about."

He walked in a slow circle, away from Amy and back toward the gap in the fence. "Really? I know Kelly was never at her house that Friday night. She never made it home from work. You had the cops fooled from the beginning."

"Shut up," Quinn said. Her attention, and the gun, stayed on him and he made sure to keep it that way. Amy took a tentative step backward and he encouraged her with his mind to run. She looked at him with a pained look on her face and then vanished silently into the dark.

"Kelly called Vanessa," Tim said, keeping Quinn's focus on him, "and told her about the job in Boston and then she called you. Vanessa told me how excited she was, how she couldn't wait to get out of this town and finally start her life free of Barret, and you, and your mother."

The gun shook in her hand. "Just stop. You think you're so smart and you don't understand a damn thing."

"No," Tim said. "I'm right and you know it."

Quinn took a deep breath and Tim could see her chest rising and falling with the effort. There was no doubt she was angry, that she was fighting a battle within herself. "You know what? I don't even need you to show me where she is. I'll just have your girlfriend do it."

"Will you?" Tim said.

Quinn turned to point the gun at Amy and found only empty space. She'd successfully slipped away into the darkness of the rusting hulks. Quinn screamed and turned back. "All you had to do was write the story that I wanted you to write. Was that so difficult?"

"You wanted me to write that story to help you put the blame on someone else. You never believed in Paulie's Buckeye Woodsman theory. You figured that the cops would look for him and never suspect you. You were just using those murdered women as a smokescreen."

He took a deep breath and paused, trying to give Amy as much time as he could to get away and maybe find help. "You should know, Claire told me how Kelly came to your house that night, how you argued about your mother and what you expected from her now that she was done with school. That was it, wasn't it? You didn't want to be stuck with your mom."

Quinn put both hands to her head and howled in frustration. Tim thought about jumping her but she was too far away. If he tried to cross the ground between them, she could still get the gun back on him, maybe even shoot him the way she had Barret.

"It's over, Quinn," he said. "Just stop. Enough people have died."

She brought the gun down and pointed it at him. "Just show me where she is. I want to see her."

"You really don't know where she is?"

Her head slowly shook. "I want to see her."

"Okay. Follow me."

he's over here," Tim said, pointing toward the section of the yard where the drums were stored. "Why don't you let me go now and put the gun down? No one here is your enemy."

The gun came back up and her eyes searched the darkness. "Where?"

"You should prepare yourself," Tim said. "It's pretty rough."

"Just show me."

They walked up the wide path to the stack of drums and Tim shined the light on the one holding Kelly. "She's over there."

Quinn put a hand to her mouth. "Oh my God. What did he do to her?" She walked around him, careful to keep her distance, and stared at the figure in the drum. Kelly's body had settled a little bit in the inky blackness of the used motor oil but her face was still visible. Now that he was seeing it a second time, he was struck by how eerie the dead woman was. The slick oil formed a shiny liquid death mask over her features. Tim looked away.

"I wondered what happened to her," Quinn said. "All these years she was just a couple miles from me."

"Quinn, we have to get Barret help," Tim said. "He's going to bleed out."

Her gaze didn't move from the figure in the barrel. "Let him. I don't care what happens to him."

"How is he mixed up in this?" Tim said. "I'm right, aren't I? Kelly came to your house that night and you argued. That's when you killed her, right? So, how does Barret fit into all this?" Then it came to him. "He helped you, didn't he? Barret helped you move the body."

Quinn leaned back against another drum but continued holding the pistol in his direction. "Kelly called me as she came home that night and she was so excited about her new job in Boston that she couldn't stop talking about it. I didn't want to hear it, though. I lost it and just screamed at her to shut up. Then I just slammed the phone down. I didn't want to talk to her anymore."

"Why? What had you so worked up?"

"When was I going to get my time?" Quinn said. "How much was I supposed to put up with before I was too old to enjoy my life?"

"You didn't want to be stuck taking care of your mother?"

"Kelly drove straight to my house," Quinn said. "She was worried that I was angry and felt bad about getting me worked up. She came in and sat down at the same table where you interviewed me."

Tim felt a chill climb up his spine.

"We talked, and she told me . . .

⊛   ⊛   ⊛

". . . I'm sorry, Quinn. I know this is a lot to dump on you but I can't turn this opportunity down," Kelly said. "It could be years before an offer like this comes around again."

Quinn sat in her preferred chair at the table right off the kitchen where her family ate the majority of their meals. It was the same chair she sat in to eat breakfast and dinner, where she sat to write out the monthly bills, and where she sat to help her children with their homework. This chair was where she could feel her ass spreading wider as the years ticked by.

She was calmer now—the tea they shared helped with that—but she could still feel the simmering anger that Kelly's announcement had ignited within her. She took another sip of the chamomile before answering her sister. "Kelly, I understand what you're saying, but I'd like you to see things from my perspective with regard to Mom. She's not getting any better. If anything, she's drinking more than ever now that she's on disability."

Kathleen had stopped working months ago because she was having headaches and was slurring her speech even when she wasn't drunk. Her doctor had implored her to stop drinking because she was causing brain damage but she either wouldn't or couldn't. Now she spent her days sitting in front of the TV, drinking Boone's Farm flavored wines from the bottom shelf of the grocery store.

"Kelly, you're my sister and I love you. I'm proud of you for doing so well at school and getting a job, but I kind of thought you'd hang around here and help out once you graduated."

Kelly reached out and took her hands in her own. "Quinn, I know she's a lot, but I need this. You have Roger and he makes great money, but I've got no one. I have to take care of myself."

"Honey, you don't have to be alone," Quinn said. "You're smart and pretty, and now you've got your paper. You could find someone."

Kelly eyed her and tilted her head, letting her hands slip away. "Quinn, I don't want to be with anyone right now. I want to concentrate on my career."

"Because of Barret?"

Kelly bit her lower lip and held it before answering. "I want to make sure I'm in a good place before I find someone. What happened with Barret was a mistake because I let him have too much control over me. If I get a good job and some money behind me I don't have to worry about being dependent on anyone."

"Kelly, I understand, but I just can't do all this on my own anymore. Roger is always working, the kids need constant attention, and I have to run over to check on Mom almost every day just to see if she's eating. You owe me."

Kelly sat back and crossed her arms over her chest. "I owe you? How do you figure?"

Quinn sat back in her own chair and matched her posture. "I put you through school, both high school and college—"

"Oh, here we go," Kelly said.

"You're damn right," Quinn said, and suddenly the embers of her anger flared to a roaring bonfire. "We helped pay for everything: tuition, books, and your rent. We gave you food money. So, yeah, you owe me, and I expect you to help me take care of Mom."

Kelly shook her head in anger. "I'll do what I can, Quinn. Maybe we can get her a nurse to come by. I've been looking into it and there are agencies that we can call. I'll be making enough to send some money home."

Quinn was incredulous. Her little sister was as jacked in the head as ever. "Oh really? Your starting salary in an entry-level position is enough to let you live in Boston, save up a nice nest egg to keep you independent, and send money back home to help pay for home health aides? Even you can't believe that."

"Quinn, come on, it won't be that bad."

"That's because you'll be gone and I'll be left behind to pick up the pieces, again, like always. You'll move away and I'll never see you again, let alone get a check from you. There will always be something more pressing. You'll have rent or student loan payments or some other damn thing and I'll be here by myself, like always."

"Calm down," Kelly said. "We can figure this out."

"Oh, go fuck yourself," Quinn said. "You're getting what you've always wanted."

"And what's that?"

"Your ticket out of here," Quinn said. "You used me and my family to get through school and now you don't need us anymore."

Kelly got up and stalked around the kitchen. "That's not true, Quinn, but I need this. It took everything I had to get through this last year of school. Between my coursework and getting away from that abusive asshole Barret, I barely made it. I cried myself to sleep every night." Her voice hitched and she swallowed hard. "I finally figured out I was with him not because I wanted to be, but because it felt like no one else wanted me."

She walked over and knelt down in front of Quinn, putting her hands around her sister's. "I love you and Roger and appreciate everything you did for me. Don't ever think I don't love you for what you did. But there's no way I'm putting my life on hold to help take care of a woman who never gave me a second thought."

"Kelly, that's not true," Quinn said. "You know it's not."

"You know it is," Kelly shot back. "How many nights did you have to make dinner because she was in some bar? How many times did we have the lights shut off because she couldn't pay the bill?"

"She has a problem," Quinn said. "You don't cut family off because they're going through bad times."

Kelly leaned her head against Quinn's knees. "We went to school on the free lunch program because she drank the grocery money."

Quinn leaned down and stroked her hair. Tears formed in her eyes. "I know, but those days are past us. She's an old woman who can't take care of herself and she has no one else. What are we supposed to do? Just let her die? Is that what you want?"

Kelly looked up and Quinn saw her eyes were also full of tears. "Yes. Whatever, Quinn. I just don't care about her anymore."

"I know you don't mean that, honey. You're just angry, and I understand."

Kelly shook her head with determination in her eye. "I'm dead serious. I can't maintain a relationship with her, Quinn. She'll be like an anchor around my neck, constantly pulling me down. How much money and time do you devote to her? And what do you get for it? The glory of cleaning up her puke and the pain of watching her destroy herself?"

"What else am I supposed to do?" Quinn said. She was sobbing now, and put her hands on Kelly's shoulders. "She's our mother. We have to take care of her."

"That's bullshit, big sister. We're adults now. We don't have to do a damn thing. Fuck her. I'm going to go live my own life. If you want to take care of her, go ahead, but I'm gone."

Quinn nodded forward, resting her head against Kelly's. "Don't you understand? I've never had that choice. All you two have ever done is take from me, and I'm sick of it."

Kelly pulled away and looked up at her. "You've always had a choice. You just usually make the wrong one. Put Mom in a home or let her rot, I don't care, because I'm leaving."

The rage inside Quinn boiled up and exploded with a grunt. She lurched forward from the chair and pushed Kelly down, pinning her against the floor.

Her hands found her throat and she squeezed. Kelly looked up at her with wide eyes.

It seemed to take forever. She throttled her sister's neck until she felt a bone break and then she squeezed harder. Kelly clawed at her but Quinn dodged her hands, moving her knees up over her sister's shoulders to help pin her down. Kelly's face turned red and her mouth opened and closed as she struggled for air. Her legs kicked crazily at the kitchen tiles. Quinn, mindful that her children were asleep just down the hall, ground her teeth to keep from screaming. Just when she thought she wouldn't have the strength to go on, Kelly went limp and her eyes rolled back.

Quinn leaned forward, physically exhausted. Kelly didn't move beneath her. After a moment she rolled off her sister and felt the sides of her neck for a pulse, just like she'd been taught down at the community pool when she'd taken a first aid course. There was nothing.

Horror ripped through her and her hands started to shake. Kelly was lying dead on her kitchen floor. Her little sister. She backed away and thought, *What have I done? That's my sister.*

Then she snapped to and her instincts kicked in. There were the kids to think of. She snuck down the hall and looked in on them, trying to be as quiet as possible. Claire was snuggled under her *Little Mermaid* comforter and Patrick had a case of kid sleep, the kind where nothing short of cold water would wake him up.

She crept back down the hall to the kitchen and looked at Kelly. Her body was contorted, showcasing the violence of her death. Her arms were spread wide and her legs were splayed where she'd kicked in an attempt to gain leverage over Quinn.

It occurred to her that she had to do something with her, and quickly. Roger would be home in the morning and the kids could wake up at any time. It suddenly hit her that there was no one to call. Her husband wasn't home, and even if he was, he would go to the police. Roger wasn't built for making tough decisions.

She slumped into her chair and looked at the cell phone in her hand. The contacts scrolled by and she saw that there was no one who would help. All the names belonged to parents in the PTA, moms whose kids played with her kids, or women she had lunch with occasionally. There were no friends, no one she could trust.

Then she came across Barret's name. She hadn't seen him in over a year, not since the last time she'd used him to cheat on Roger. The last time she'd used him to make her feel something. After a moment's hesitation she clicked on the small green phone icon.

The phone rang and as hopeful as she was that he would answer, she was almost as hopeful that it would go to voicemail. After four rings, though, he picked up.

"Hello?" a deep voice said. "Quinn, is that you?"

She almost couldn't speak. It actually took two tries for her to find her voice, but then she did. "Barret?" she sobbed. "I need help."

Half an hour later the source of Kelly's misery and Quinn's salvation stood in the kitchen looking down at the woman he had once purported to love. He was dressed like he always was, in a black racing t-shirt stretched over his massive chest, worn blue jeans, and steel-toe work boots. Insanely, Quinn thought of the time he'd bent her over a car in his garage, taking her roughly one night last summer when she was desperate to lash out at Roger. She shook her head to clear it.

Beneath the t-shirt his chest rose and fell in quick breaths. "Quinn, what the fuck did you do?"

Barret knelt down beside Kelly and put two fingers to her throat, as if her bluish skin wasn't enough of an indicator that she was dead. He pulled his hand back. "She's really dead."

She sat in her chair, a red dish towel balled up in her hands. "Keep your voice down. The kids are asleep."

He glanced toward the back of the house and lowered his voice to a harsh whisper. "You killed Kelly, Quinn." He advanced on her, his face a mask of twisted anger. "What do you expect me to do here?"

"Help me."

"Quinn, you need to call the police."

She snapped to and stood up. "We can't call the police," she said in her own whisper. "I have kids, Barret. How am I supposed to raise them from prison? Who will take care of my mom? We just need to hide her until I can figure something out."

He ran a hand through Kelly's hair. "Quinn, you can't just hide something like this."

"You have no idea what you can do until you have to," she said. "Right now, we're the only two people in the world who know about this. All we have to do is hide her and then live our lives. We can do this."

"You're insane," he said. "People are going to wonder about where she is. You can't just make someone vanish."

Quinn knelt beside him. "The only people who really care about her are right here in this room. It's just you and me. There will be questions, sure, but I can deal with that."

Barret looked up at her and she noticed his eyes were red and swollen. She could tell her words were getting to him. "What about your mom?"

"My mom can't remember to eat most days," Quinn said. "The only thing she remembers is to get a fresh bottle when the one she's working on is empty. I can deal with her."

He dipped his head. "What do you expect me to do?"

"We need to hide her and make it look like she went home. No one knows she was here."

He turned his head and looked into her eyes with tenderness. "I love her, Quinn. I'm not going to do this."

Quinn reached out and put her arms around his shoulders, drawing his massive bulk against her body. "That's why you have to do this. You loved her so much that you once tried to put her head through the window of your pickup truck. I'm the one Kelly called that night and I kept her from calling the police. If it wasn't for me, you'd probably be in jail right now."

She reached up and wiped his tears away with the dish towel. "I get it now, I do. She was easy to love but she had a way of driving you crazy, and that's what happened here tonight. I couldn't get her to understand and I just lost it for a moment. You can understand that, can't you?"

He blinked and rubbed at his eyes. Then he nodded.

"We have to make sure she's well taken care of," Quinn said. "No one else can do it the way we can." She paused and he squeezed her, holding her tight. She tipped her mouth toward his ear. "Will you do this for me?"

She felt a small tremble through his large arms and he pulled away. "I'll take care of it."

They stood up and Quinn glanced nervously down the hall. "We have to move fast."

Barret bent down and scooped Kelly into his arms. "Just get the door. I'll take care of the rest."

●   ●   ●

"And he did," Quinn said to Tim. She came up off the drum she'd been leaning against. "He drove off with her and I never saw her again until to-night."

"But the police found her car, phone, and purse at her house," Tim said. "How did you two swing that?"

"That was the easiest part," Quinn said. "I just drove her car over to her house with all that stuff and left it there. Barret picked me up when he'd finished hiding her."

"And no one saw you?"

"You saw where she lived," she said. "There's hardly anyone out there to see anything. The bigger risk was leaving my kids alone, but they never woke up."

"Barret didn't trust you, did he?" Tim said. "That's why you didn't know where Kelly's body was."

Quinn pointed a finger at him. "You're right. As sentimental as he was kneeling beside her in my kitchen, when he picked me up at her house he explained that he wasn't going to tell me where she was. It was his insurance that I could never blame him for her disappearance. He figured out pretty quickly that with Kelly missing he'd be the first person the police suspected. So, we made a deal. I would divert attention away from him and he would keep her body hidden."

Tim rubbed his forehead in frustration. Amy had escaped, and Quinn knew it, so what was her plan? Why was she still here telling him all this? "Quinn, why don't you put the gun down? It's over."

The gun came up again, like Tim mentioning it had reminded her of what was going on. "I might be going to jail, I might not."

"Barret is probably lying dead in the grass. How will you explain that?"

She shrugged. "You mean the man who killed my sister? The man I shot when he tried to do the same to me because we figured out what he'd done?"

"Oh, come on."

She moved closer and for second time that night he looked straight down the barrel of her gun. "You're the hero here, Tim. The reporter who figured out what Barret had done and where he'd hidden Kelly. It's just a shame he killed you before I shot him." She set her feet and brought up her empty hand to steady her gun hand. "It's just a shame I couldn't save you."

There was a crunching noise behind Tim and he turned to see someone come around the side of a stack of flattened car chassis. "I can't fucking believe you," Paulie said, stepping into the oversplash from the flashlight. "How many people have to die for you?"

He stepped back and saw that Paulie had a gun of her own in her hand and it was pointed at Quinn. "Put it down," she said, "or I'll shoot you where you stand."

Tim shined the light in Quinn's eyes and saw the desperation in them. She blinked rapidly and held a hand up to block the beam. She was clearly surprised by the appearance of the private detective. The gun remained in her hand, though, and aimed at Tim.

"What are you doing here?" Quinn said. "You shouldn't be here."

"Put the goddamn gun down," Paulie said.

It was clear that Paulie wasn't playing games. One way or the other, things were going to end in the next few seconds. Tense silence filled the air and then Quinn chose self-preservation. The gun dropped onto the dirt with a dull thud. Amy came out from where Paulie had been hiding and ran to Tim, hugging him.

"How did you know to come here?" Quinn said. "There's no way she called you and got you out here that fast."

Paulie gestured with the gun again. "Get on your knees."

She was all business, Tim noticed, ignoring Quinn's words as she moved around behind her and cuffed her former client's hands.

"Texting me that picture was a good idea," Paulie said, looking at Tim. "But you really should have called the police. That's what I did."

Tim could hear sirens echoing through the air now, growing louder as they closed in on the salvage yard. Amy looked up at him. "I made it out of the front gate and saw Paulie coming in. I didn't know who she was but I knew you needed help."

"Thanks, honey," Tim said. "Good call." He looked at Paulie. "I was going to call the police from the car when we were leaving. After we found Kelly we were afraid someone would come across us out here so we just wanted to get away. We didn't plan on running into Barret and Quinn out at Paradise."

"You should always call for help first," Paulie said. "Remember that." She moved toward Quinn, who was still kneeling on the ground. "As for you, I can't believe you used me for all these years to help cover this up."

"It was easy," Quinn said. "You believed everything I told you. Everyone did."

Paulie stooped down until she was inches from Quinn's face. "You know what? Fuck you."

27

The sun came up in the east to greet Tim and Amy as they sat on the tailgate of a Berry Creek Fire Department pickup truck. The little brush fire truck sat in the parking lot of Dedrick Garage and Salvage surrounded by police cruisers from the town, county, and the state patrol. There was even one familiar unmarked silver Dodge Charger from the Hogan PD.

They'd provided statements to the Berry Creek detectives investigating Barret Dedrick's murder while the county coroner visited Paradise to collect his body. The salvage yard gate was open and a second coroner's van had entered a couple hours before to see what they could do with Kelly Dolan's remains. Tim had no idea how they would move her to the county seat for an autopsy and he really had no interest in learning. Both he and Amy were exhausted. She leaned against his shoulder, wrapped in a scratchy wool blanket provided by the fire department.

The detective who took their statement asked them to hang around for a while, but Tim figured it was more of an order. Besides, he felt too tired to hike to his Jeep and it was probably blocked in by the team investigating

Barret's death. He closed his eyes and leaned his head on Amy's. Then he heard a voice calling his name.

"Hey, Abernathy," Coogan said. "Are you sleeping over there?"

Tim cracked an eye open and found the detective and Paulie Carmichael staring at him. He was grinning like a madman and both were drinking from large cups of coffee. "Good morning, detective, what can I do for you?"

"I'm sure the Berry Creek EMTs already asked this, but are the two of you all right? Are either of you injured?"

Tim was honestly surprised by this concern for his well-being. "I'm okay. Amy?"

"I'm fine," she said.

"Good. Now, Paulie has filled me in on what she knows and my colleagues over here in Berry Creek gave me a rundown of what you told them. Come by the station later and I'll have you both make a proper statement for me. Closing a nine-year-old homicide involves a mountain of paperwork."

"Are you certain it's her?" Tim said. "I mean, I imagine it is, but even Quinn didn't know for sure what Barret did with her."

"The coroner will do his thing to confirm it, which will take a while, but for now I'm satisfied. Of course, we're still going to search the rest of the yard." He stole a glance back at the gate to the junkyard. "Darren Lewis is in there right now making sure the Berry Creek guys don't overlook anything."

"What's going on with Quinn?"

Coogan sighed and it was the sound an exasperated man makes when he's reached the end of his rope. "She's in a county holding cell and her husband already got her a lawyer. From the way she's already refusing to cooperate, I'd guess the prosecutor is in for a fight."

Tim thought back to the stack of folders on the detective's desk and realized the guy's job was never complete. Even a victory like today's didn't stop the flow. He glanced at Paulie and held out his hand. "Thank you for saving me back there," he said. "I don't think she'd have gotten away with that plan she was cooking up, but I have no doubt she would have killed me to try."

Paulie took his offered hand and shook it. "No problem. I appreciate you contacting me as soon as you found her. I've been looking a long time."

"Me too," Coogan said. "I can't tell you three how much it means to close this one. We conducted countless searches in those woods behind her house and collected hundreds of witness statements. There were times when I thought we were never going to close it, that she was going to stay lost forever. Now, we're here with the sun coming up and we know where she is. I can finally mark her case closed."

Coogan reached out and put a hand on Tim's neck where it met his shoulder. "This is a hell of a thing you did. Since her sister killed her, and her mom is off in la-la land, no one else is going to care, but I appreciate it. If Charlie gives you a hard time about going back to work, just let me know. I'll have a few choice words for him."

Tim was genuinely touched and swallowed hard. "Thank you."

Then Coogan looked at Amy. "And thank you, too. Don't think for a minute that I don't know how much you helped him. And for God's sake, make him take you out to places other than crime scenes. You deserve better."

She smiled at the detective and Tim's heart fluttered a bit, just like it always did. "I will."

"Do you need a ride home?" Coogan asked. "I think we're done with you guys so I can arrange something."

"My Jeep is back at Paradise near Barret's truck," Tim said. "Can I have it?"

"I don't see why not. It wasn't involved in the crime." He looked over at his Dodge. "I don't know if my ride will get you back there, though."

"Mine will," Paulie said. "If you're okay with that."

"I leave them in your capable hands," Coogan said. "I have a junkyard to search."

       ●   ●   ●

Paulie gave them a ride to Paradise and waited to make sure his Jeep started, in case Barret had done anything to it. Twenty-five minutes later, Tim and Amy made it home.

"I need a shower," Amy said, and started stripping off her clothes. "I can feel the crud from that place all over me." Tim raised an eyebrow and followed her into the bathroom.

Later on, they lay in bed, luxuriating in the air conditioning after a night spent running through humid air. She made satisfied noises as he rubbed aloe vera on her mosquito bites. "That feels heavenly," she said. "I'm not going to tell you to stop."

He gave it another five minutes or so and then he did stop as the exhaustion finally caught up to him. "Thank you for coming with me last night. You didn't have to do that."

"I was bored," she said. Her voice sounded soft and very far away. She curled into him and pulled a comforter over them. "Your life is different from mine. It's fun to visit there sometimes."

"I love you," he said, and she was silent except for her deep breaths. As he lay in bed, drifting off to sleep, his mind raced. There was so much to do, and he couldn't keep up with it all. Then his eyes closed.

It was early afternoon before they woke up, both of them opening their eyes as a delivery truck rumbled by. Bleary-eyed, Amy turned to him. "Are we getting up?"

"I am," he said. "I have some stuff to take care of. You can stay in bed if you'd like."

She answered him by pulling the comforter up over her shoulders.

He went out to the kitchen and made himself a cup of coffee. Then he took a notebook out and started writing. He made notes on everything that happened the previous night. Then he made notes on everything leading up to it.

What Amy had said about his life was true. It was boring most of the time but the stories he covered intrigued him. Even when it was nothing more than sitting in a meeting listening to politicians, it was better than most of his friends' jobs.

He checked his phone and saw that the discovery of Kelly's body was the top headline on all the local news stations. Given how much people loved it when a cold case was solved, he had no doubt the story had the legs to go regional or even national. He'd had enough sleep. Now it was time to work. Taking a deep breath, he picked up his phone. Charlie answered on the second ring.

"Hey, boss," Tim said. "I think we need to talk."

"So do I," Charlie said. "Can you come in?"

"I'll be there in ten."

* * *

Tim walked into the offices of the *Hogan Weekly Shopper* and dropped into his desk chair with a groan. The few hours of sleep he'd gotten was enough to get him started but his body ached for more. There was nothing for it, though. Stories didn't write themselves.

Charlie glanced over his reading glasses from the desk facing Tim's. "You look pretty rough," he said. "You okay?"

"I am," Tim said. "I assume you've seen the news."

"Uh-huh. All the TV stations seem to have the story while I have nothing."

Tim smiled. "I think I'll have a scoop for you, provided I'm off suspension."

"Fill me in on what happened out there."

Tim laid it down for him and Charlie shook his head when he finished. "So, Quinn killed her own sister."

"And used Paulie and me to cover it up," Tim said. He was quiet for a moment and swallowed. "Charlie, I want you to know I understand why you suspended me. In fact, I'm very happy that first story about Kelly never saw print. That would have been catastrophic to my career."

Charlie nodded and looked him over. "I know you think I was being tough on you, but people depend on us. In an age where everyone is cynical about journalism and eager to call any story they don't like 'fake news,' we have to do our jobs right every time. We can't ever give them reason to doubt us."

"I understand."

"I hope so, Mulder."

Tim glanced up, confused. "What?"

"Look around this office," Charlie said. "You'll notice I don't have posters of UFOs hanging on the walls saying 'I want to believe.' That's because I only believe what you can prove. There's no give on that. You find reputable sources for everything you want to write. You do the job with integrity. Understand?"

Tim nodded. "I do."

"Okay. Now let's talk about how you're going to write this story."

●   ●   ●

The story was published in Saturday's edition and copies vanished from their usual spots around town, which made Charlie and his advertisers happy. Tim got a call from Coogan and met him at the Peppermill downtown for lunch the following Monday.

He walked into the restaurant and was immediately grateful for the air conditioning. It was another scorcher outside. He saw the detective already sitting at a corner booth with Paulie Carmichael. Coogan spotted him and waved him over.

The police detective had a cup of coffee in front of him and Paulie had a beer. Tim greeted them both and a waitress came over to take his drink order. He asked for a Diet Coke and glanced at Coogan, wary of the detective. "So, what's up?"

"I thought we should all get together and compare notes," Coogan said. "It's been a complicated time and I want to make sure nothing gets overlooked."

"That makes sense," Tim said. "It's not every day you close ten murders by two different killers." The waitress came over with his drink and they ordered lunch. Tim almost felt like skipping the meal, but Paulie and Coogan ordered, so he did too. "What's going on with Dennis Linchin?" Tim asked as the waitress walked away. "It's still weird to think I spoke with him the morning after the murders. I mean, he was just standing there cool as ice watching all you police going in and out of the Beer & Bait."

"Some of these guys like the attention," Coogan said. "They'll come back to the scene of the crime to get a thrill from all the chaos they've caused. Now, with Linchin, I think there may have been more to it. He may have wanted to see how much we knew and scope out whether we were looking for him. I agree with you, though. He was one cool customer."

Paulie spoke up. "You told me he had a problem with his mother; that's why he was killing these women?"

"That's right," Coogan said. "We've spoken to him quite a bit because he loves to talk, but I have to tell you, I wish he'd shut the hell up."

"He likes to brag?" Paulie said.

Coogan nodded. "He sure does. Everything he says is geared toward two things: justifying his actions and driving home the point that he's brilliant. I get the feeling he's been waiting to talk to someone about this for a long time. The sad thing is, he doesn't realize how pathetic he is."

"What do you mean?" Tim said.

"He's a textbook offender," Coogan said. "His mother was a single mom and it sounds like she was overbearing. Dennis reacted to that by turning inward and becoming an introvert who took refuge out in the woods. He was raised on that farm where we found him and he says he spent all his time hunting and fishing because his mother couldn't follow him. Bertha Linchin was overweight, so she spent most of her time in the house overseeing the farm hands she hired."

"Did she abuse him?" Tim asked.

"Physically?" Coogan said. "I don't know. If she did, he's not admitting it. It seems like she was verbally abusive and neglectful. I pulled his school records and he had learning disabilities but she didn't seem to follow up on the guidance counselor's advice."

"How did he do with girls?" Paulie said. "A lot of times these guys can't interact with women normally, so their desire turns into something dark."

Coogan pointed at her. "Give the lady a prize. Berry Creek had a Peeping Tom problem for a while right around the time Linchin was in his mid-to-late teens. Remember that I told you we'd be looking at his juvenile record? Well, we found two arrests in his teens for sneaking around the woods at night and peeking in cabin windows during the summer."

"When I interviewed you about him, you told me you found evidence of that in the woods near the Beer & Bait and Amber's cabin," Tim said.

"Yeah, it's possible he's done this everywhere he's worked," Coogan said. "I have no problem believing he'd creep around the woods in the dark watching people in their houses. To do the things he's been accused of, he'd have to."

A shiver moved up Tim's spine and once again he thought of how rural Hogan was, how the trailer park he and Amy lived in butted right up to woods. The whole area was like that. Anywhere a house hadn't been built or a building erected was covered with trees. He'd always enjoyed that, but now the thought of some maladjusted creeper using them to watch people gave him pause. He thought back to the camping trips he and Amy had enjoyed, how they'd laid out on a blanket looking up at the stars on warm, clear nights. The thought that someone like Dennis Linchin could have been watching them at such an intimate moment terrified him. At those moments he was totally focused on her, so anyone with anger in their heart could easily sneak up on them.

Coogan took a sip of his coffee and continued talking. "I spoke to a school counselor who tried to help him in high school. Linchin didn't have many friends and was essentially a loner. The counselor recommended that Bertha Linchin get him additional help, but I can't find any evidence she ever did.

"We located a farm hand who worked for Mrs. Linchin. He told Lewis that the workers didn't trust the kid. There were a series of small fires on the farm, one of which almost burned down the barn. I don't have any way of knowing if he wet the bed but I'd bet on it."

"What about cruelty to animals?" Paulie said.

"No reports of that," Coogan said, "but who knows? He checks all the serial killer items on my list."

"What about later in life?" Tim asked.

"After school he had trouble finding work until the shale boom," Coogan said. "When they started opening natural gas wells around here he worked as a roughneck with a couple different outfits. We're still talking to people, but it seems like he would get on a slow burn about some imagined slight or when guys would rib him a little and then he'd explode. We're starting to match up events like him being disciplined or fired with the crimes we know he committed."

"Let me get this right," Tim said. "He'd have a bad day at work and attack someone?"

"It's called a triggering event," Paulie said. "These killers can't deal with stress the way other people can. They have a need to prove their superiority, so when something happened like his mother abusing him or someone at work giving him a hard time, he couldn't deal with it. What he could do was find some woman when she was vulnerable and attack her. Taking out his suppressed rage on them made him feel better."

"Paulie, you're good at this," Coogan said. "I should have listened to you. One of the reasons I invited you here today was to tell you that." His voice was calm, Tim noticed. "I'll tell you something else, and I don't even care if Abernathy hears me. I was wrong to ignore you when you came to me with this. I should have looked into it more closely. If I had, maybe Linda and Carol Jackson would still be alive."

Tim turned to see Paulie blinking rapidly, then she dabbed her eyes with a napkin. "I appreciate you saying that, Larry. It means a lot." She reached out and squeezed his hand. "What's going to happen to him?"

"Prison," Coogan said, "probably forever. The arrest was solid and we found a ton of evidence in his house. Ohio has the death penalty, so his court-appointed lawyer will make a deal to keep him alive and the prosecutor will take it to spare the families a lengthy trial. He'll live in concrete and steel for the rest of his life."

Paulie raised her beer. "Here's to hoping it's a short life."

"I'll drink to that," Coogan said with a raised coffee cup.

"I read your story," Paulie said, turning her attention to Tim. "You said some very nice things about me. Thank you."

"You deserved every one of them," Tim said. "Thanks again for saving me and Amy. If you hadn't come along, we'd have been in a world of trouble."

She took another sip of her beer and wiped her mouth with the back of her hand. "I've got news for you, kiddo, you were already in a world of trouble. I think Quinn was going to kill you. You did good getting her talking and buying time but I think she was working her way up to it."

Tim thought back to the way she had rambled, telling him the whole sordid tale. It did seem like she had been building up to something. "Maybe she was unburdening herself. Confessing her sins before she committed one more murder."

"Could be," Paulie said. "She didn't have any problem filling Barret full of holes. Of course, I think she hated his ass."

"Yeah, she did," Coogan said. His voice had less anxiety now than out at the salvage yard. In fact, now that Tim got a good look at him, he decided the detective looked more relaxed overall. Maybe finding Kelly's killer had relieved him. "She resented him a great deal for hiding Kelly's body. It was his insurance against her implicating him in the murder."

"Quinn likes being in control," Paulie said. "Is she talking to you?"

"She's made a statement, yeah," Coogan said, "but it wasn't worth anything. She's lawyered up now, so all future conversations will be taking place with the prosecutor. I'm out of it."

"Our statements should be enough, though, right?" Tim said. "Paulie and Amy overheard her ranting to me."

"It certainly gives us a place to start. An investigator for the county prosecutor will take over from here and start to find evidence backing up what she said, but I think we all know what happened."

"So, Quinn strangled her?" Tim said.

"Looks like it," Coogan said. "The coroner gave me the preliminary report on Kelly this morning. Cause of death is homicide due to manual strangulation, which confirms what she told you."

"That was fast work," Tim said.

"Not if you ask him," Coogan said. A disgusted look crossed his face. "It took him hours to strip the oil off her and her skin is permanently stained. He couldn't stop complaining the whole time I was there. The only good thing about putting her in that drum was that it preserved the evidence. Without any air getting to the body, we had more soft tissue to work with than if he'd buried her somewhere."

Tim thought back to what he'd seen, a beautiful young woman entombed in used motor oil. It didn't seem like a good thing in any respect. "Has she been charged yet?"

"No, not officially, but that will happen this week. She's a suspect in two homicides, so she probably won't get bail. She'll stay in county lockup until the trial. I can't wait to see what defense her lawyer springs on us."

"Probably insanity," Paulie said. "You'd have to be crazy to do what she did."

They sat in silence for a moment. "Have you spoken with her mother?" Tim said.

Coogan sighed before he answered. "I tried, but she wasn't conscious. I have no idea if she understood what I was trying to tell her or not. I feel kind of bad for her. She's essentially lost everyone at this point."

"She did it to herself," Paulie said with a hint of anger in her voice. "I know it's easy to hate Quinn for what she's done, and believe me, I have more right to do that than either of you for the way she used me. The thing is, she started out with too much pressure on her when she was just a kid.

"Quinn told me how she started taking on responsibilities when she was just a little thing, younger than ten. Their dad took off, leaving Kathleen alone, and she drank her pain away. Quinn was cooking, cleaning, and paying bills by the time she was a teenager. She even accomplished some good things."

"Well, she did a few wrong, too," Coogan said. Tim thought the sarcasm was a little much.

"She snapped," Paulie said. "No doubt about that, but she also kept Kelly on the straight and narrow and got her through high school and college, all while being a young mother herself and helping her husband get through college. If she'd just kept her shit together, we'd be lauding her for her efforts instead of demonizing her for her actions."

"Life is just a series of choices," Coogan said. "People make bad ones every day and those are the ones I care about. You choose to live your life well and Tim writes stories about you. You screw up and kill people? I arrest you."

"And I still write stories about you," Tim said.

⊕　　⊕　　⊕

That night, Tim sat outside their trailer on an aluminum glider with Amy curled into him. They had the outside lights off and the sun was going down as dusk settled in. He was enjoying the silence while he thought about his day. His fingers intertwined with Amy's and he smiled looking at her. "How was your day, baby?"

She shifted around so she could face him and smiled, that same smile that made his heart skip a beat whenever he saw it. "I got some good news today."

"Yeah?"

"I got my account back and an apology," she said.

Tim sat up. "From Aaron?"

She nodded and grinned in the dim light. "You bet."

"What did you say to him?"

"I went into his office this morning and told him how unfair he'd been removing me from the account and that I wanted to be reassigned. I also told him I was doing good work so I expected to be treated better in the future."

"That's fantastic," Tim said. "How did he take it?"

"You know, better than I thought. He sat back in his chair, looked me over, and asked me out to dinner."

"What?"

She shook her head and gave him a skeptical glance. "You really need to be less naïve, man-o-mine. You'll believe anything. Anyway, he heard me out and I got what I wanted." She was quiet for a moment. "After what happened in the junkyard, I just wasn't going to let anyone treat me with anything less than the respect I deserve. Does that make sense to you?"

He leaned forward and hugged her, pulling her close. "It sure does." He held onto her for another moment and let her go.

She leaned back against him and they watched the sun dip below the trees that surrounded the trailer park. After a while the stars came out, dotting the sky with pinpricks of light. His gaze dropped to the dark woods and he thought about Dennis Linchin and what they'd talked about at lunch. He expected another shiver to climb up his spine but nothing happened. He put his arms around Amy and hugged her. Whatever bad juju he'd been feeling was gone with her in his arms.

That's what love is, though, isn't it? Drawing strength from the person you're with and giving it to them in return. He hugged Amy tight and settled in to enjoy a beautiful evening.